Mx3

ART WIEDERHOLD

ISBN: 978-1-4907-4521-3 (sc)
ISBN: 978-1-4907-4520-6 (e)

Trafford rev.   09/04/2014

North America & international
toll-free: 1 888 232 4444 (USA & Canada)
fax: 812 355 4082

I dedicate this book to the women and events that have shaped my life and enabled me to become who I am today.

Ue o muite arukou

The driver stopped the cab on the road overlooking the old house. His passenger, an elderly American gentleman with short silver hair and glasses whom he'd picked up at the Shimizu Ryokan, opened the door and stepped out. The man studied the old house with, so the driver thought, a sense of fondness.

"Please wait here. I won't be long," the man said.

The driver nodded and watched as the man made his way carefully down the snow-covered road to the flat ground in front of the house. He noted that the man was older but not bent and he walked without the aid of a cane. In fact, his gait was strong and sure.

Athletic.

And he wore a black leather jacket, blue jeans and short boots.

He thought the man was the type who was comfortable in his own skin and who was accustomed to living life on his terms. He wondered where he'd come from and what events made him who he is?

This was the first time the driver had been out this way. He never would have known about the house had it not been for the gaijin.

"How did he know it was here?" he wondered as he watched the man look around. "What possible connection could he have with such a place?"

A light snow had fallen two days earlier and covered the house and grounds with a thin white shroud. The snow made the old house look forlorn, almost like it had been weeping. He wondered why this gaijin wanted to come here. Why would he have such an interest in this house?

The house was a two-story, thick-walled house built sometime during the Edo Period. It stood three feet above the ground on a raised platform.

Its exterior was peeling and the upper window was partially open. It had obviously been abandoned many years before.

He watched as the gaijin climbed up onto the porch with some difficulty. He slid the door open and went inside.

The driver pulled his cap down over his eyes and decided to take a short nap.

He woke an hour later and checked his watch. He stretched, looked around and saw no one. He hit the horn to let the gaijin know he was still waiting.

Nothing.

Curious, he stepped out of the cab and walked down to the house. That's when he noticed something strange.

Something that was impossible.

He'd watched the man walk across the snow covered ground to the house. Yet, when he looked down, the only footprints he saw were his own. He stopped and looked around, thinking that he must have missed them somehow.

He found nothing.

"How did he walk across snow without leaving footprints?" he asked himself as he walked up to the house.

That's when he saw that the thin layer of snow on the porch was also undisturbed.

"How can this be?" he thought.

He called out several times, only to hear his own words echo through the empty house. He slid the door open and stepped inside. The floor was littered with debris or all sorts. It, too, had not been disturbed.

For years.

He walked through the house. In the rear room of the first floor he saw an old, dust-covered Buddhist shrine on a raised platform. On the wall above it was an old, dust-covered framed black and white photo depicting a typical Japanese family from the 1960s.

He walked up the single flight of stairs to the second floor. All he saw was a small, very old, dust-covered wooden desk and chair in the front room. Above that hung a framed drawing of a large-eyed waif standing beneath a European style street lamp. It looked as if it had been there forever.

He called out again.

Nothing.

An uneasy feeling struck him.

He knew he saw the gaijin enter the house. Yet there was absolutely no sign of him anywhere. He decided to drive back to the ryokan to see if his passenger had somehow made it back…

Asakusa Shrine was a one-story wooden structure with a high pitched roof. The entire building, save for the roof, was painted bright red and the paved path leading up to the shrine was flanked by traditional lion dogs, put there to keep evil spirits away. One reached the shrine by walking through a tall wooden "gate" that flanked the path.

It was part of the Asakusa Kannon Temple complex in the northeastern part of Edo and had been constructed around 645 A.D. That made it nearly 900 years old when a young samurai and his pretty companion arrived.

The complex consisted of several gates, the Goju-no-to (Five Story Pagoda), and the famed temple itself. The streets around the temple were filled with shops and stalls hawking all sorts of goods. Everything from fine porcelains, lacquered ware and silks to grilled meats and fish or bowls of steaming noodles.

They stopped at a vendor and he purchased two skewers of grilled meat. He gave her one and they ate while they walked.

When they came to the temple gate she stopped.

"This is it," she said.

"Asakusa Temple? Why did you bring me here?" he asked.

"You'll see," she replied.

He followed her through the gate, making sure not to step on the path that led directly to the temple. She warned him not to step on the path.

"You must walk along side of it," she instructed.

"Why is that?" he asked.

"That path is the one the god uses to go to the temple. Only he can step on it. Everyone else, even the bokushis, must walk beside it," she explained.

They stopped at a small well outside the temple. He watched as she used the long-handled wooden ladle to scoop water from the well. She then poured it over her hands and feet to clean and purify herself before entering the temple. She then handed him the ladle and stepped back.

He shrugged but followed her example.

He didn't believe in gods, but he felt it was best to humor her.

"Now we can go inside," she smiled.

As they approached the steps, the bokushi came out to greet them. He had a wide grin on his face—one that told the young samurai that he was in trouble.

She was dressed in a neat, clean but plain cotton kimono and sandals of woven bamboo. Her hair was long, beautiful and tied in back by a bright, red silk ribbon. She was just five feet one inch tall and very pretty. She had a soft, sweet voice and a smile that lit up the world.

He was slightly younger, tall, broad shouldered and handsome. His hair was cut short save for the traditional top knot. He wore a black yukata, reed sandals and a sheathed katana tucked into his sash.

He had come to Edo in search of employment.

Being skilled with both the katana and yumi, he hoped to get hired by one of the powerful daimyo who frequented the Hojo stronghold in Hachioji, which was to the west of Edo. He'd heard that several important daimyo would be visiting the castle at the end of the month and decided to try his luck.

He'd met the girl along the way only three days earlier in Chiba. He was seated under a shade tree eating a rice cake and minding his own business. She walked over and sat beside him and struck up a conversation. The next thing he knew, she was accompanying him to Edo.

She had insisted on it.

Being somewhat shy and awkward with women, he couldn't figure out a polite way to tell her no. Anyway, she was very pretty and he kind of like her.

A lot.

And she said she knew the quickest, easiest road to Edo. And she'd made the journey fun. She talked a lot and made him laugh. She had a bold, almost daring way about her that he found attractive. She was honest and totally unafraid to speak her mind. These things set her far apart from any woman he'd ever met. And this made her even more appealing to him.

All in all, it was an amusing situation. He had a feeling he was about to discover just how amusing it was.

The bokushi looked at them then smiled at her.

"Ohayo gozaimasu, M.-san," he said with a bow. "Is this the young man you spoke of yesterday?"

"Hai. He is the one," she said.

The bokushi looked at him and grinned.

"Please come inside so I can perform the ceremony," he instructed.

"Ceremony? What ceremony are you talking about?" the samurai asked.

"Our wedding ceremony of course!" she said.

"Wedding ceremony? Are you crazy?" he asked, obviously shocked by her announcement.

"I thought that since we decided to visit the temple, we should get married," she explained.

"We? You brought me here! I didn't decide anything," he protested.

The bokushi looked at him then at her.

"You didn't tell him?" he queried.

"No, she did not!" the samurai said as he squinted at her. "When did she speak with you about this?"

"She came here last evening and asked me to perform the ceremony," the bokushi replied.

The samurai looked at her with a raised eyebrow.

"I see. And just when did you decide we should marry?" he asked.

"The day I first saw you, of course," she replied.

"Why didn't you let me in on this?" he asked.

"I didn't want to trouble you with the details. Besides, I didn't think you would have any objections. After all, I'm a very good catch," she said.

"Oh really?" he queried as he smiled at her.

"I did discuss it with you on the way here. I didn't hear you object," she pointed out.

"I just listened to humor you. I don't even recall you asking me about this," he said. "I never said I agreed to this, did I?"

"You never said that you disagreed, either. So, since you didn't, I went ahead and made the arrangements," she explained.

He looked at the bokushi.

"What do you have to say about this?" he asked.

The bokushi laughed.

"I think you lost all hope of escaping the moment you entered my temple. The decision has already been made for you. You might as well get used to it, my boy. I'm certain that this won't be the last time she makes up your mind for you," he said.

"So, I'm doomed?" he asked.

"I'm afraid so," the bokushi replied.

"I thought the husband is supposed to make all of the important decisions in the family," the samurai said as he looked at her.

The bokushi laughed.

"You'll quickly learn, as I have, that such notions are merely myths. Consider this to be the first day in your learning process," he said.

She smiled at him and his knees nearly buckled.

"You do want to marry me, don't you?" she asked.

"Do I have a choice?" he asked.

"No," she and the bokushi said at once.

He laughed.

"I just wish that you had consulted me first," he said.

"Why? There was no need to anyway. The outcome would still have been the same," she said as they followed the bokushi...

It was an exceptionally warm day for Tokyo. J. left his office in the Ginza and took the subway to his home in Meguro. Unfortunately, there were no available seats and he was forced to stand the entire way home. As he stood holding onto the support, he glanced up at one of the small ads above him.

The ad depicted a samurai in full battle armor atop a dark brown horse looking out over an oncoming army.

He smiled.

He knew exactly what it advertised. In fact, it was a book his mother was reading at this very moment. He also knew why she was reading it. It was the same reason she had read each one of the author's novels. All but the last two were in English. That didn't stop his mother from purchasing them online and reading them from cover to cover.

This one was different.

While his earlier novels had gone unnoticed, this one had become the most widely-read novel in Japan. He looked around.

He saw two young women nearby. Each was reading a copy of the novel.

Several women at his office were also reading it. He found this unusual. He'd read his earlier novels. They were high-adventure, sword and sorcery and science fiction novels that mostly appealed to males. But his latest novel had become a huge favorite with the woman in Japan.

He knew it was a novel closely based on Japanese history. That also amused him. Imagine a gaijin writing a historical novel about Japan that was a best seller in Japan!

M. had purchased the book two days earlier. She was surprised to see it on display at a bookstore in the Ginza. Most of his novels never made it to bookstores. If they did, those stores were not in Japan.

Yet here it was. In the window, no less.

She went inside and saw that several young women were standing in the checkout line with copies of the book in their hands. M. took the last book from the table and joined them. As she looked at the cover, she was amazed to find out that the entire story was set in early 17th century Japan.

And the entire book had been translated into Japanese.

She purchased the novel and hurried home on the train. As she rode, she started to read the book—and nearly missed her stop because of it.

As she walked home from the station, she let her thoughts drift back to that long-ago winter's day when she received his first letter. She was just 17 then. A high school girl in a small rural area far off the beaten path. A friend of hers had encouraged her to add her name to the list of a well-known pen pal club called Japan International Social that specialized in helping Japanese women find American penpals and, hopefully, husbands. When she joined, she never expected anything to come from it.

Then she got his letter.

The idea that he had taken the trouble to join the club and write to her, excited her. She wrote back and their friendship began.

His second letter included his photo. He was young and handsome and had mischievous eyes and a nice smile. She sent him her photo which her friend had taken of her. She was standing in an open area with her hands clasped. She had on a white turtleneck sweater and dark slacks.

To her surprise, his next letter arrived with 24 Japanese postage stamps for her to use when writing. He had taken great pains to acquire the stamps and had sent them to her. She knew he was serious now.

And generous.

During their correspondence, she learned that he worked for a bank during the late fall and winter months and played semi-pro baseball. He wanted to become a professional player—in Japan! He wrote that he was a huge fan of the Yomiuri Giants and was able to name all of the key players. Unlike most Americans his age, his goal was to play baseball in Japan instead of America.

Her parents were also surprised by this. They said she had found a most unusual American friend, too.

She smiled at the memories and continued reading...

Their wedding night was a mixture of humor, awkwardness and experimentation. He had never experienced a woman. She had never experienced a man. In the end, they got it right and their first official night together as man and wife was filled with passion.

As was the next morning

And afternoon.

And night.

They left the ryokan near Asakusa and took the road west through Edo.

At the time, Edo was just beginning to find itself as a center of commerce, religion and power. Several important daimyo had begun erecting castles in and near the town and more and more people were migrating to it.

But the real center of power was Hachioji. It was there they were headed. And the young samurai and his bride were about to embark on a life they had never imagined.

He was upstairs in the shower when he heard the phone ring. He turned off the water and reached for the towel when he heard his wife run up the stairs. She opened the door and handed him the phone.

"It's your publishing agent," she said. "She says it's very important."

He took the phone.

"Hello Liz," he said.

"I have great news for you. It's about your latest novel," she said excitedly.

"Bushi?" he asked as he dried himself off.

"That's right. You must have been psychic when you told us to translate it into Japanese and market it there. Your book is the best-selling novel in the country right now. In fact, it's become the best-selling foreign novel in Japanese history," she said.

"I can tell that from the royalties," he said.

"That's not why I've called," she said. "We want to send you to Japan for an entire month on a multi-city book tour. We even have several newspapers and magazines eager to interview you and an appearance on Tokyo Tonight. We'll pay all of your expenses and you can even bring you wife with you."

"Fantastic! When do we leave?" he asked.

"In three weeks. I'll email you all the details and your plane tickets," Liz replied. "I'm so excited for you! I'm so excited for our company, too. This is so big!"

"No problem. We already have our passports so there won't be any delays," he said. "You're right. This is wonderful news."

He handed the phone back to R. and grinned.

"We're going to Japan," he said.

Namida ga koborenai youni

Hachioji was a mountainous area several miles west of Edo. It was nestled at the foot of Takao Yama amid beautiful forests and green, open fields. The town itself was picturesque and crowded with ryokans, ryorya, shops, pleasure houses and gambling dens. It was a typical castle town and dominated by the massive and newly constructed Hachioji Castle.

The castle, along with an even more formidable keep at Odawara, was the stronghold of the powerful Hojo clan. Hachioji was still a work in progress. When completed, it would be the largest, strongest, most impregnable fortress in the country.

Lord Hojo Ujitero had ambitions.

Large ones.

The castle was a monument to his overly inflated ego.

And he was about to butt heads with two of the most powerful daimyo in Japan.

It was into this situation that the young samurai and his new bride walked. He'd heard of Lord Hojo.

Everyone had.

And everyone knew he was increasing the size of his army—much to the displeasure of Toyotomi Hideyoshi who viewed Hojo's military buildup as "ambitious and threatening.

Toyotomi was the Emperor's Chief Imperial Minister. He had served as one of Oda Nobunaga's lieutenants and had continued Oda's plans to unify all of Japan after the Shogun's death. After defeating several rivals, the Emperor had elevated him to the rank of Chief Imperial Minister in 1585. Toyotomi spent the next few years conquering large areas of

Shikoku and Kyushu, thus earning the nickname Hachiman or God of War.

But his ambitions bred enemies.

And Hojo Ujitero was one of them.

The young samurai decided to try to get an audition with him first, so after securing a room at a nearby ryokan, they walked over to the castle. They followed the main road to the wooden bridge and walked across it. On the other side, was a flight of stone steps that had been cut into the mountain. They followed those up to the main gate.

They saw an older samurai standing guard and walked up to him. The older man was dressed in finely-made yoroi and wore a katana at his side while he stood guard with a spear. The man was thick bodied with strong legs and a graying beard and mustache.

"I'd like to have an audition with Lord Hojo," the young samurai said.

The old samurai squinted at them as he leaned on his spear.

"And just why do you wish to see Lord Hojo?" he asked.

"I am in need of a position. I have heard that Lord Hojo is seeking retainers," he said.

"So he is. And you think you're good enough to be hired?" the samurai asked.

"I hope so. I'm very skilled with a katana and a yumi and I can ride a horse," the young samurai replied.

The old man eyed M.

"What about you?" he asked.

"I am his wife," she said. "We were married one week ago."

"And you need to support her, is that it?" he asked the young man.

"Hai," he said.

"Why do you want to be a samurai? Why not work as carpenter or even a farmer?" the old man asked.

"I have no skills other than those I've mentioned. My father was a samurai and I learned what I know from him," the young man said.

"I see. Where is your father now?" the old man asked.

"Dead," the young man replied.

"Since you've taken the trouble to come here, I guess I should at least allow you to try and see Lord Hojo. Just follow that path up to the great house and tell the guard why you've come. But Lord Hojo is a very busy man. You may not get to see him," the old man said.

"Arigato. May I ask your name?" M. asked.

He looked at her and smile. It was a pleasant, playful smile she thought.

"I am called Hachiman," he replied.

"Hachiman? Isn't that what they call Toyotomi?" the young man asked.

Hachiman was the Japanese god of war. Toyotomi earned that nickname through his many victories. He'd managed to defeat everyone but the Hojo clan, and that still bothered the Hell out of him. He also had designs on the Shogunate along with Tokugawa Ieyesu.

"I'm the real Hachiman," the samurai smiled.

"What makes you say that?" the young man asked.

"I've been in more battles than he has," Hachiman said with a wink at M. "How many have you been in?"

"None yet," the young man said.

"Why you're nothing but a koinu (puppy)! As a matter of fact, that's what I'll call you. From now on, your name is Koinu-san," Hachiman said with a grin.

M. laughed and looked at her husband.

"I think I'll call you that, too," she smiled.

They all laughed.

"How old are you, Hachiman-san?" he asked.

"I am 65 years old," Hachiman said.

"Shouldn't you be retired?" Koinu asked.

"Retired to do what? Most bushi never reach my age. This is all I know and I like it. So there is no sense in retiring," Hachiman said.

"I've noticed that you walk with a limp," M. said.

"That's a reminder from my last battle. I used to be a commander then. I rode a horse, too. During the battle, an arrow found its way through my leg and actually pinned me to the horse. We both went down quite hard. My horse bled to death in minutes. I might have, too, if my men hadn't found me and pulled me out from under him.

That was seven years ago. I have not been able to ride a horse since," Hachiman explained. "I have been guarding this gate ever since I was able to walk again. You might say that Lord Hojo has put me out to pasture—like an old warhorse."

They laughed.

"Daimyo like him don't care about men like us. To them, there is more where we came from. But I have seen many samurai pass through this gate. Most are like you. They come seeking employment. The word is out that Lord Hojo is adding to the size of his army. Usually, when a powerful man like him does that, he is preparing for war," Hachiman said. "Be careful in there, Koinu-san. I would hate for your new bride to become a widow before the two of you have tasted life together."

"I'll be careful," Koinu replied. "I have more than just myself to think about now."

"Make sure you keep that in mind, too," M. said with a smile. "I want to have children with you. Many children. I can't do that if you're dead."

Hachiman laughed.

"I like you," he said to her. "You have good sense and spirit."

Koinu bowed to Hachiman and followed the path to the manor house. M. stayed at the gate to chat with Hachiman.

"Who else is visiting the castle today?" she asked as she eyed a row of banners that were placed against a stone wall.

"Lord Toshii Maeda and Lord Date Masamune are here today. More will come tomorrow. Lord Hojo has asked them to visit. I think he's trying to forge alliances with them," Hachiman said. "But both Toshii and Date are allied with Toyotomi and I doubt either will switch alliances. I know for a fact that neither man likes nor trusts Lord Hojo."

"Isn't Lord Tokugawa Ieyesu allied with Toyotomi?" she asked.

Hachiman nodded.

"Then perhaps it might be best if my husband fails to be hired by Lord Hojo?" she asked.

"Especially if he wants to stay alive," Hachiman said with a grin. "From what I've seen and heard the last few months, I fear that the final days of the Hojo clan are approaching. Lord Toyotomi wishes to rule all of Nihon. Lord Hojo stands in his way."

"What will you do if war comes?" she asked.

"I have served the Hojos since I was your husband's age. I will do what they charge me to do. I will stand my ground and fight until the life leaves my body. It's what a samurai is expected to do," he answered stoically. "If war comes, I hope your husband is on the winning side."

"So do I," M. said.

Hachiman smiled at her.

"My life is nearly at its end. Yours is just beginning. I want you both to live long and enjoy it," he said.

"Do you have family?" she asked.

"I had four sons," he said. "Smallpox took three before they were ten years of age. The other died in a battle that proved to be for nothing. But at least he died with a katana in his hands and with honor. Although I'd much prefer if he'd lived—and so would he."

He looked down at the ground.

"I have done the unthinkable. I have outlived all of my children," he said.

"I am sorry," she said as she touched his shoulder.

"Don't be," he smiled.

M. sighed.

She put the book aside to rest her eyes. The marriage scene had been amusing, but she had a difficult time imagining a Japanese woman of that era being so forward and bold. The young samurai had been caught off guard but went along with her plans.

She looked up at the poster.

"Would he have reacted the same way had I been that bold? Or would I have frightened him away?" she wondered.

Since his female character had her name, she wondered if he was trying to send her a subtle message in the hope that she read the book. Is that why this had been marketed in Japan?

She thought about the fact that all of the main female characters in his novels bore her name. She knew that wasn't a coincidence. Her son was right. A. had never stopped thinking about her and she had never stopped thinking about him.

"This is silly! We haven't seen each other for decades. Even if we met again, what would we even talk about? What would we have in common after all this time? Life experiences?" she thought.

She decided to stop reading for a little while and start preparing dinner. J. would be home soon and he'd be hungry. And she, too, was getting hungry.

R. watched while A. worked out in the home gym. He worked out five times a week. Each night, he did something different to keep his body challenged. She liked the way he looked, too. He looked better than most men half his age and showed no signs of slowing down.

"What should I bring to Japan?" she asked.

"I'd say a week's worth of clothes and nothing else. We can have our laundry done at the hotels and anything else we need, you can buy there.

You'll have to rent a cell phone when we get to Tokyo. Your phone won't work there," he said as he finished a set of back presses.

"Are you sure?" she asked.

"Positive," he replied. "You'll see. And save room for souvenirs. I know how you get when you shop. Hell, we might have to mail everything you buy back home to avoid buying another suitcase to put it all in."

"I'm not that bad!" she protested.

He laughed.

"I'm not the one who has 230 pairs of shoes all over house," he said. "And don't you dare buy another pair until all those are worn out!"

"You'll be busy with book signings. When will I be able to shop?" she queried.

"You'll have time. I'm sure M. and her friends will be able to show you some really nice places. Just don't buy a damned thing that's stamped made in China. We can get that crap here," he said.

She nodded.

He despised Chinese made things and refused to buy anything from there. He thought the Chinese only made cheap junk that broke easily. Each time she had brought anything home with that label on it, he forced her to return it.

"We'll leave in a few days. We'll fly American to San Francisco then JAL straight to Tokyo," he said.

"What about Manila?" she asked.

"I've booked a flight for you from Osaka to Manila. I have another stop to make so I'll join you there a few days later," he said. "We can spend a week in the Phils then fly back home."

"Okay," she smiled. "Why aren't you flying with me?"

"I have one more place I want to see again before I leave Japan," he said.

Lord Hojo's gosyuden (palace) was a magnificent multi-storied, many roomed structure with upswept roofs, several gates, narrow shuttered windows and stone and wood walls. It was painted white with gold trim and the roof tiles were of terra cotta. A waterfall cascaded down the mountain just beyond the southeast wall and the surrounding gardens were well laid out and maintained.

Koinu looked it over with interest.

The gosyuden was obviously built to impress. It was a monument to Hojo's egotism and inflated self-worth. Koinu knew that such displays would eventually lead to Hojo's downfall.

He also realized another thing.

Although the castle sat high atop Fukusawyama and was larger than most such castles in Japan, it was far from being completed. Obvious flaws in its defense works were everywhere. If it should be attacked before those flaws were corrected, Hachioji would fall quickly—and hard.

He also saw sat that castle, unlike others of its kind, had no main keep. It consisted of the manor house and a system of baileys or small defensive towers and walls. Koinu wondered if this was because Hojo hadn't gotten around to constructing a main keep or he figured that no one would dare attack Hachioji?

He had learned about such things from his late father. He'd taught Koinu what to look for while inside a castle or military camp. He knew how to spot weak points and points that were too strong to attack. Based on what he'd been taught, Hachioji looked alike a disaster just waiting to happen.

"But why?" he wondered.

When Koinu reached the manor house, a guard directed him to the end of a very long line of samurai hopefuls. There were hundreds of men. Most were the same age as him. A few looked like seasoned warriors. He sighed and got in line.

It had been early morning when he got on line. It was late afternoon when he finally got in to audition with Lord Hojo. By that time, the daimyo was very tired and he almost dismissed Koinu off –hand. Koinu's "audition" was abrupt and fruitless.

M. was waiting for him when he left the building.

"How did your interview with Hojo go?" she asked as they walked down the path toward the gate.

"It did not go well at all," he replied. "He said my skills were good but he disliked my demeanor. He said I wasn't respectful enough. Hojo isn't looking for good samurai. He's looking for ass-kissers."

"There will be other chances. Perhaps with a lesser daimyo? It does not matter who employs you, does it?" she asked.

"Not really. Do we still have money?" he asked.

"A little. We can last a while longer if we are careful," she said.

"Then I can wait," he said.

"But not too long, eh?" she smiled.

When they reached the gate, Hachiman smiled.

"How did it go, Koinu-san?" he asked.

"He sent me away. He told me to return in another month when I learned to be more respectful of someone in his station," Koinu said.

"He likes ass kissers. I didn't think you were one of them. I'm glad you're not. I'll be off duty in another hour. I'd like you to come to my house and eat with us tonight," Hachiman offered.

When Koinu hesitated, M. gripped his arm and said they'd be happy to accept his invitation. Hachiman laughed. Her gesture told him who made the decisions in their family. She was much like his wife when they first married.

"Excellent. Please wait under those trees for me. Once I've finished here, we can walk to my house. I'm sure my wife will enjoy meeting you both—especially you, M.-san," he said with a wink.

Although caught by surprise, Hachiman's wife, Yoko, welcomed her dinner guests warmly. She was short and matronly with a quick smiled and good humor. As she set out extra bowls and utensils for their guests, she good-naturedly exchanged insults with her husband. She then left for a few moments and returned with large bowls of noodles and steamed vegetables and some fresh fried fish.

"Go jiyu ni," she said cheerfully as she and Hachiman dug in. Koinu and M. looked at each other, and then joined them.

"Where are you from?" Yoko asked them.

"I am from Nagoya," Koinu replied.

"I was born in Yufuin," M. said.

"I never knew that. What else don't I know about you?" Koinu asked her.

She smiled.

"Oh, there are many things yet to learn about me," she said. "But there is no rush as we have our entire lives ahead of us to learn about each other."

Hachiman laughed.

"How did you meet?" Yoko asked.

Koinu related how they'd met and gotten married. When he was finished, both Hachiman and Yoko laughed heartily.

"So, you are on your shinkon ryoko (honeymoon)?" Yoko queried as she poured the sake into four cups.

"Hai," M. smiled.

"So, how good is he?" Yoko teased.

Koinu blushed.

"He is very good," M. beamed. "And we will both get much better with practice."

Hachiman laughed and slapped Koinu on the back with enough force to cause him to spill his drink.

"Don't feel embarrassed, Koinu-san," he said. "All women talk this way about their husbands. You'll get used to it in time."

"What are you doing for money?' Yoko queried.

"We have some," M. said shyly.

"Will you be able to get by?" Yoko asked.

"To be honest, we have only enough money for a day or two," M. said.

Koinu squinted at her.

"I thought you said we could last a few more days?" he queried.

"I said we could if we were careful," she replied. "We will have to be very careful, too."

Hachiman looked at his wife and nodded. She got up and left the room. She returned a few seconds later with a small wooden chest. She handed it to Hachiman. He opened it, reached inside and took out a handful of coins, and gave them to M.

She stared at him in surprise.

"We couldn't," she said.

"We insist. There are other daimyo visiting the castle this week. When you get a job with one of them, you can pay us back," Hachiman said.

"Arigato gozaimasu! You are too generous and we have only just met!" M. said as she bowed her head.

"Take it and don't worry about it," Hachiman said. "I like you two. Koinu-san, you remind me of myself when I was your age. I went through the same thing you're going through. But I wasn't married then, either. You two need the money more than we do right now."

He smiled at Koinu.

"You married well, Koinu-san. M.-san is a real treasure. You will go far with her at your side. Make sure you take good care of her," he said.

"Getting married was her idea," Koinu said.

Hachiman laughed.

"In that case, consider yourself fortunate that she chose you," he said. "Come to think of it, that is exactly how Yoko and I married over 40 years ago."

Omoidasu haru no hi

M. put the book down when she heard her son enter the house.

"I am up in my room," she called out.

He walked up the stairs and greeted her. He saw the book lying face-down on the table and noticed she had nearly finished it.

"You're going through it quickly," he observed.

"It is a very good and fast read," she said. "It's one of his very best."

"Several people in my office are also reading it. They said that your old friend is a best seller here in Nihon. His book is a big success," he said as he sat down.

He smiled at her.

"Did you know that he's coming to Nihon?" he asked.

"A. is coming here? Where did you hear that?" she asked in surprise.

"I read it in the book section of the Asahi Shimbun today. He is coming to Nihon for two months on an extensive book tour. He will arrive in Tokyo in two weeks and is scheduled to make several book signings and news paper interviews. He is also scheduled to appear on three television talk shows," he said as he showed her the article.

He watched the expression on her face and smiled knowingly. Her feelings for him were obvious, even after so many years.

"What enduring love," he thought. "It's like the love one only reads about or dreams of."

She'd done her best to go on with her life. She married and tried to make the best of things. But his father always cheated on her. Sometimes, he'd get drunk and strike her. He'd even disappear for days at a time. She endured it all stoically, like someone who deserved to be punished for something she did wrong.

She deserved better, he thought.

She deserved to be happy.

"I see that he is planning to visit Yunohira. It says here that he has booked a room at the Shimizu Ryokan for seven nights. That is where he spent three weeks on his first visit to Nihon," she said.

"Didn't you make that reservation for him?" J. asked.

"Hai. He wrote me that he wanted to stay in a ryokan instead of a hotel. He wanted to experience something that was uniquely Nihon-jin. So I put him in the very best ryokan I could find. I wanted so much to please him," she smiled.

"Apparently you did. He's never forgotten the ryokan or you," J. said.

"What do you mean?" she asked.

"He has used you as the model for all of his main female characters. And they all bear your name," he pointed out. "I think you still hold a very special place in his heart and you always will."

She smiled at the idea.

"And I doubt that a single day has passed without him thinking of you—and you of him," J. said.

"Am I so obvious?" she asked.

J. nodded.

"You must think I'm so foolish," she said.

"No. You are never that, Mother," he assured her.

R. watched A. as he went over his itinerary online. She stood behind him and put her arms around his neck as she kissed his cheek.

"Now that we're really going to Japan, I'd like to meet M.," she said.

"So would I. We've been internet friends for such a long time, I'm anxious to meet her in person. Why do you want to meet her?" he said.

"I want to see what my competition is really like," she teased.

He laughed and pulled her onto his lap.

"You have no competition," he assured her. "Besides, M. is married and has a grandchild. Surely you're not jealous of her!"

"I'm jealous of all your women friends—especially her," R. replied.

"I'm glad you still care after all these years," he said.

"I have to care. You're all I've got," she smiled. "And I don't want to lose you."

"Don't worry about that. You'll never lose me. You're stuck with me forever—just like that fortune teller in New Orleans said.

"What if your first girlfriend shows up?" R. asked.

"In that case, I may have to think about it," he joked. "Especially if she's still pretty. By the way, M. knows that you're jealous of her."

"You told her that?" R. asked.

"Yes. She thinks that's very flattering and cute," A. replied. "She said she can't imagine anyone as young and pretty as you being jealous of a harmless little old Japanese lady like her."

"She may be little and older than me, but she is Japanese and she's far from harmless," R. joked. "Are we going to meet her entire family?"

"Probably," A. said. "That's usually how it goes there. It's like the Phils in that respect."

"Oh. That's good. That means you won't be alone with her," R. teased as she hugged him tighter.

"Not if you're going to be clinging to me like this the entire trip!" he said.

"I might do just that. There are a lot of beautiful women in Japan and I know how much you like them. So, I'll have to keep my eyes on you all of the time," she said as they kissed.

As Koinu and M. walked back to the ryokan, they happened to pass a tavern just as three somewhat inebriated samurai stepped out. The one in the middle saw M.

"And how much do you charge?" he queried.

They stopped and turned around to confront him. He looked them over and repeated his question, then offered to pay her twice what her "escort" was paying her.

"That is my wife you're speaking to," Koinu said sternly. "And you have just insulted her. I demand you apologize at once!"

The samurai squinted at him.

"Go away, boy, before you get hurt," he said. "Do you know who I am?"

"You're nothing but some old, drunk with a sword and bad haircut to me," Koinu said sarcastically. "Again, I insist you apologize to my wife."

"Bah. Who do you serve?" the samurai demanded.

"No one but me," Koinu answered.

"Go away—but leave the woman here so she can experience a real man," the samurai replied scornfully.

"Apologize or draw—if you're man enough!" Koinu challenged

"If you insist," the samurai sad as they squared off. "After I kill you, I'll take the woman as a prize."

They circled each other warily. The samurai drew his katana and held it overhead with both hands. To his puzzlement, Koinu's katana remained in its sheath. The samurai shouted and moved in. Koinu dropped to one knee and drew in the same motion. Before the older man could react, the blade sliced his right hand off at the wrist. He stared in disbelief as it fell to the ground, still clutching his katana. Then he, too, fell to his knees.

The other two men gaped at Koinu, who stood his ground.

Without a word, they picked their friend and his severed hand off the ground and hurried away.

Koinu sheathed his katana.

"That will teach him some manners," M. said with a smile.

"I think I may have just started something," he said as they walked on to the ryokan.

The recruiting sergeant squinted at him.

"Are you sure you want to do this?" he asked.

"Yeah. I want to do my part," A. said. His tone was somewhere between humble and Brooklyn-cocky.

"Your number is really high. That means you don't have a prayer in Hell of being drafted. You could just sit this one out and avoid all that shit over there," the sergeant pointed out.

"I know," A. said. "But I still want to do this."

"Why are you so adamant about going to Nam?" the sergeant asked.

"Patriotism. Family tradition. Call it whatever you want. But this is something I feel that I have to do," A. replied.

"Okay. I'll sign you up. What MOS?" the sergeant said.

"Infantry," A. answered.

"I used to feel that this country needed more good men like you. After two tours in Nam, I'm not so sure anymore. You can still change your mind about the infantry. Look, kid, you qualified for every damned MOS the Army has. You can pick whatever career field you like. Whatever suits you. I see that you worked as a reporter. We do have journalists in the Army. Why not shoot for that?" the sergeant urged.

"If I pick that, can I still go to Nam?" A. asked.

"Hell, son. You can go anywhere you want with that MOS," the sergeant said.

"You've got yourself a soldier," A. said as he signed the paperwork. They shook hands.

"Welcome to the Army, son. You report to Ft. Hamilton at six a.m. sharp on the fifth. Here's a list telling you what you need to bring. We'll supply everything else," the sergeant said.

"Thanks, sarge," A. said as he left the office.

The sergeant leaned back and shook his head. The sergeant at the desk next to his asked how high A. had scored. He showed him the test results.

"Holy shit!" he exclaimed.

"Hell, Jack. That kid got the highest scores I've ever seen. He'll be our boss in a couple of years is he decides to stay in," the sergeant said.

"If he survives Nam," the second sergeant said.

"Yeah. There is that!" he nodded.

M. stood a little over five feet tall and had a slender, almost delicate-looking figure. Her hair was shoulder length, jet black and mixed with red/brown highlights and some strands of silver that had crept into the mix recently. She usually wore eyeglasses and had pretty, deep dark eyes and a pleasant smile.

She had been married to her husband K. over 40 years and they had produced three children. Her life had been ho-hum at best for several years. She was the typical Japanese housewife and she was bored.

Her husband purchased a computer for her. Her friend talked her into joining Facebook so she could connect with people in other countries and develop new friendships. When she did, she never expected to make contact with anyone like A.

She found him interesting and even exciting.

What surprised her most is he found her to be interesting and exciting. And even beautiful and sexy. This amazed her. She had stopped thinking of herself in those terms a long time ago. Even her husband didn't seem interested in her anymore.

Just when she was about to resign herself to living the rest of her life out as a typical bored elderly woman, here was this younger gaijin who had breathed new life into her. He was funny, charming, handsome and romantic. He was adventurous and had lived the kind of life she'd only seen in movies or read about in novels.

And he was attracted to her!

As time went on, she found herself getting more and more attracted to him, too.

M. was a little surprised when the package came. Normally, he always emailed her to tell her one was on its way. This one arrived unexpectedly and it was larger than usual.

When she opened it, she saw it contained two copies of his latest novel. One was in English. The other in Nihon-go.

She smiled.

"Bushi" was a story about a young samurai and his wife at the start of the Tokugawa Shogunate. He had told her it was based on a series of very vivid dreams that he began having after they started corresponding with each other on Facebook. Although the characters in his dream were nameless, he was positive that the samurai was him in a past life and his wife was her. He was also convinced it was the reason they had met.

He had a very Buddhist-like philosophy, which she found strange and appealing. When "Bushi" was finished, A. had insisted it be translated into Nihon-go and marketed in Nihon. To his surprise, the book became an almost-overnight hit. At the moment, A. was better known in Japan than he was in his native United States.

She smiled when she read the dedication.

"To my beautiful lady. I will be your samurai forever."

"How romantic of him," she thought as she sat down to read it.

As she did so, she wondered if a certain other woman who happened to have the same first and last name she did was also reading it.

His grandmother sat and listened while A. explained his decision to enlist. She'd heard this before. All five of her sons had enlisted. Three had fought in World War II. Her youngest had fought in Korea and the early years in Vietnam.

All had survived.

His father hadn't. He had been sent to Korea before he had a chance to marry A.s mother. She was just 16 when he was born and not ready by any means to be a mother. So she gave A. to her mother to raise. His father was killed in action less than a month after arriving in Korea. They never found his body.

Just a few scattered pieces of it.

Now, here he was, about to follow in the family tradition. Another in a long, long line of W. family soldiers.

"What about M.?" she asked. "Did you tell her?"

"No. She hasn't answered any of my letters. She's too busy with school to bother with me now. There's no need to tell her anything. This is my decision. It's something I feel that I need to do," he said.

"And you're going to Vietnam?" she asked.

"I volunteered," he said.

She nodded.

"When do you leave?" she asked.

"Next week. I go to Fort Knox for training, then to Indianapolis for school. That should take about four months. After that, I head for Nam," she explained. "I'm not coming home for leave after school. I'm heading straight to Nam."

She nodded and hugged him.

"Please come back to us," she whispered as she kissed his cheek.

"I will," he promised.

M. didn't know about A.s military background until his first novel was published many years later. She learned from reading his biography on the inside cover. This revelation shocked her. She realized then why he attempted to bring up the subject of soldiers. Her rather curt response had caused him to remain silent about his own involvement.

She had inadvertently offended him and he never mentioned it again. But she'd given him her honest opinion. She had no way of knowing he'd been a soldier or had fought in the war. She often wondered how she would have reacted had he told her. She was so young and naïve then. She knew the war was wrong because that's all she heard on the news. She'd never met a soldier and wasn't curious at all about what they did. She just knew that soldiers fought other soldiers and they killed each other.

And she found that to be deplorable.

That had been her second mistake.

Now, she wished she could speak with him, to learn more about him and what he did and why he did it. Back then, she had no concept of "patriotism" or "serving one's country". War was terrible and soldiers were killers. That's all she knew or felt she needed to know.

Now, here she was, decades later, eagerly reading his latest novel as she had all of his previous ones. Ever since she'd discovered his books online, she just felt compelled to read them. The novels had given her insight into his personality.

"Bushi" did that even more so.

Other parts of his biography, which was now online on the publisher's website, also surprised her. He was on his second wife, a gorgeous Filipina named R. and they had a son, C. who was autistic. He lived in a very old house in St. Louis and had traveled all over the Earth. But he never forgot who he was or where he came from. Brooklyn was still very much a part of him and he was more than a little proud of it.

He also loved cats.

He always had cats around him while growing up. She knew he always would.

Something new had also been added. A. had become a paranormal investigator. A ghost hunter, if you will. This really fascinated her—and scared her.

Hachiman and Yoko were out for an evening walk when they saw the three samurai shuffle past. He immediately recognized them from their visits to the castle. He also saw that the man in the middle was being supported by the other two—and his hand was missing. All he had left was a badly bleeding stump.

"What happened to Kenshin-san?" he asked.

"He got his hand lopped off by a young samurai after he insulted his wife," the man on the right said. "I never saw anything like it. He used the drop and draw on him."

"He's the fastest I've ever seen," Kenshin groaned. "I should have apologized instead of challenging him."

Hachiman watched as they continued to the castle. He and Yoko looked at each other.

"Koinu?" she asked. "Is he that good?"

"He never said, but he is not the type to boast," Hachiman smiled. "Kenshin is one of the best swordsmen around and it looks like he's more than met his match. If Koinu used the drop and draw, then he is like lightning with a blade."

He walked over to the wall mount and slowly drew the katana from its sheath. It was a fine sword. One of the very best.

During his stay at the Shimizu Ryokan, he'd met a very old man. The man said he had been a teacher before and after the war. During the war, he'd been a captain in the Imperial Army and he had fought in China. He said he had two sons but both had been killed during the war when the American planes firebombed Tokyo in retaliation for the attack on Pearl Harbor.

He and A. talked for hours.

When the old man checked out of the ryokan, he presented A. with the katana. A. was dumbstruck by the gift.

"This katana has been in my family for 300 years. It has been passed down from father to son for generations. Since I have no one left to pass it down to, I am giving it to you. I know you will appreciate and treasure it as I have. Maybe one day, you will also have a son and you can pass it down to him," the old man explained.

Because of Japanese laws, A. had to have the blade dulled before he could send it home. When he finally received it weeks later, he mounted it on the wall of the apartment. Every once in a while, he drew the blade to lightly oil it and practice a few moves he'd learned from watching samurai movies.

And the katana felt very comfortable—almost natural—in his hands.

Now, there he was in the living room, going through a series of movements he'd read about in a book. His grandmother stood several feet away and watched as he practiced. When he finally slid the katana back into its lacquered sheath, he smiled at her.

"You look so natural doing that. It looks like you've been using that sword for your entire life," she remarked. "Where did you learn that?"

"You know, Ma, I'm not sure. It just comes to me from somewhere deep inside of me. Maybe when I come back, I'll have an edge put back on it," he said as he sat down.

She smiled.

He always said "when" not "if". He knew he would be back. The alternative never entered his mind.

Hitoribotchi no yoru

Tan Son Nhut was the busiest airport on Earth. Not only did it serve all of the international flights going into and out of Saigon, but it also was the home of several U.S. military flights and air wing units.

A.'s World Airways flight landed on the runway at 5:45 a.m. He was with a dozen other newbies, most of which were draftees. When the 747 rolled to a stop on the tarmac outside the terminal, A. and the rest of the passengers grabbed their carry-ons from the overhead bins and shuffled toward the door.

As soon as the airtight hatch hissed open, the cool air inside was nearly instantly replaced by a wave of warm, humid air. When he deplaned and climbed down the steps to the tarmac, he saw rippling waves of heat rising from the ground all around him. Seconds later, he began to sweat.

A lot.

A sergeant came out and told them to wait right where they were. A few minutes later, a cart drove up with several duffel bags. The driver stood up and shouted for them to pick up their bags NOW!

They did as they were told. Once all of the bags were unloaded, the cart left. A. looked around. The airport was indeed hectic. He watched as several more civilian airlines circled and came in for landings while several others took off. People and workers were everywhere. He checked his watch.

7:12.

A small yellow bus drove up. It stopped right next to them. A corporal stepped out and called out names from a clipboard he carried. Seven of the men who were with A. got on and the bus left.

8:04.

A second bus rolled up. The driver opened the door. He looked at them.

"Which one of you is A.?" he asked.

"I am," A. replied.

"You wait here. The rest of you guys, get on the bus. Move it!" the driver barked.

He watched the bus drive off. Seconds later, another bus rolled up. The door hissed open and he got on. The driver smiled.

"Welcome to Vietnam," he said.

The driver took him to another terminal. This was decidedly military. There were MAC SOG emblems everywhere and everyone was in fatigues. When he got off the bus, a Staff Sergeant looked him over.

"You A.?" he asked.

"Yes I am, sergeant," A. answered.

"Your connecting flight to Da Nang leaves in one hour. It will be on the runway behind the terminal," the sergeant said as he looked over his file. "It says here that you asked for this slot. That true?"

"Yes, sergeant," A. said.

The sergeant smiled and extended his hand. A. shook it.

"I hope you know what you've gotten yourself into, son," he said. "That's in bandit country. You'll see all kinds of action up there."

"That's why I'm here," A. said.

"God bless you, son—and good luck," the sergeant said.

Early the next morning, three samurai arrived at the ryokan as he and M. sat eating. Koinu immediately recognized two of them from the run-in the night before. He leaned over.

"Here comes trouble," he said.

One of the samurai spotted him and nodded. They walked up to where they were seated. The third man, a stern-looking older samurai of obviously higher rank, scowled at Koinu.

"Lord Date Masamune requests your presence—at once," the samurai said. "Please come peacefully."

Koinu looked at him, and then back at M.

The samurai looked at M.

"You must wait here," he instructed.

"Will I be allowed to return?" Koinu asked.

"That depends on Lord Date's mood," the samurai said.

Koinu nodded and smiled at M.

"Wait for me. If I am not back tomorrow morning, please inquire about my fate at the castle," he said.

She watched as he followed the three samurai out.

They led Koinu along the main street and up the path toward the castle.

"What's your name?" he asked the head samurai.

"Buntaro Goji," the samurai said.

"I am Watanabe Akira," said the one next to him.

"That man you maimed was Kenshin Saito. He is—or rather was—Lord Date's best swordsman," Buntaro said. "No one had ever defeated him until you came along."

"That move you did was quite impressive," Watanabe said. "Quite impressive indeed."

"Do you know of Lord Date?" Buntaro asked.

"Everyone knows of Lord Date," Koinu said.

M. put the book down and smiled.

She was always amazed at A.s knowledge of Japanese history. He knew places, dates, names, events and Japanese culture better, she thought, than most Japanese. He seemed especially knowledgeable of Date Masamune. She often wondered why he had become so fascinated with that particular daimyo.

Then one day, he told her about a dream he'd had of being on a battlefield—in ancient Japan—fighting side-by-side with a samurai that had a very distinctive crescent shaped crest on his helmet. Each time he'd had such a dream, he saw that crest. So one day, he decided to scour books about the samurai and daimyo.

Then he saw a painting of Date Masamune and knew that samurai was him. After that, he studied everything he could about Date. The more he learned, the more impressed by the man he became and the fonder he grew.

She smiled.

"Could he have served under Date Masamune in a past life? Are his dreams really past-life memories that are returning to him?" she wondered. "Almost no gaijin know who Date was and what he'd done. Only A. knows or cares about that particular daimyo. Why?"

She'd told her husband about A.s dreams and his actual love for ancient Japan. Even K. thought that A. had been a samurai in a past life, especially since he knew about Hachioji Castle, which isn't exactly on a "must see" list of Japan's tourist sites. He even knew the differences between the real Hojo clan and the Late Hojo clan.

Very few Americans would know or even care about such things.

"I have tried to test his knowledge by throwing out names of very obscure daimyo and events. When he writes back, his answers have so much historical detail that he leaves me speechless at times," she said.

"I must ask him to teach me how he does that," K. smiled.

"Does what?" she asked.

"Leave you speechless," he said with a grin.

When Koinu and his escort walked through the gate, he winked at Hachiman. The old samurai smiled and laughed.

"So it was Koinu!" he thought. "I wish I could be there for this interview!"

Da Nang.

It was 9:47 a.m. when A. and several other soldiers stepped off the connecting flight from Saigon. They stood on the tarmac and watched as several VNAF fighters took off on another run into the Central Highlands. In the distance, he saw several Hueys lift off and a local civilian airliner come in for landing.

At the time, Da Nang was almost as busy as Tan Son Nhut. Only in this case, most of the traffic was military. Da Nang was the home to the VNAF and three Tactical Fighter Squadrons (TFS), a permanent USMC battalion, and companies of Army, Navy and Air Force personnel and an equal number of South Vietnamese soldiers and airmen. The TFS flew F-4Es armed with missiles, and machine guns. The VNAF guys had inherited a squadron of Douglas AC-77D armed with "Spooky" cannon, also called "Puff the Magic Dragons". When they swooped down and opened up on the enemy below, nothing was left standing.

Twenty-minutes later, a 2.5 ton covered truck pulled up. The driver leaned out and called out a unit number. Ten of the newbies climbed aboard and away they went. A. was conspicuously the last man left.

It was another hour before two soldiers in a jeep drove up. Each was dressed in jungle fatigues, a helmet and a bullet proof vest. They were both armed with M-16s. The guy riding shotgun looked at A.

"Get in," he said.

"Don't you want to see my orders?" A. asked as he tossed his bag in the back.

"You A.?" the soldier asked.

"Yep," he replied.

"Then I don't need to see your orders," he smiled. "Put on that steel pot and vest. This ain't no Sunday drive in the park."

After a two hour drive, they reached their destination. The drive took them along a meandering dirt road and past trees, rice paddies, and several varieties of huts and across two rivers. The road was bumpy and pitted.

Not the best conditions for a jeep ride, especially if one was in the back seat.

The camp, which the driver called Fort Nowhere, was set up just outside a small, neatly arranged village. The village had a Catholic church, a school that looked like it was built by the French decades earlier, a small hospital, a large Buddhist temple, a good sized open air market and several cafes.

On the northern end were a series of rice paddies with several small houses. Beyond that stood a line of trees that marked the beginning of the jungle. The village was between the paddies and the base camp.

They drove through the village and over a small wooden bridge to reach the camp. An alert-looking guard waved them through and shook his head. A. knew why, too. He'd seen other soldiers, just like him, come through that gate. A, wondered how many were still alive inside?

The base camp was located 22 miles west and south of the Chu Lai and 20 miles to the north of nowhere. The provincial capital, Pleiku was to the south. Dak Toy was almost 12 miles directly west.

The camp was surrounded by a barbed wire perimeter and a sandbag wall. There were two watch towers looming above an open central area and a dozen metal Quonset huts. The sign over one read: Mess Hall— Enter at Own Risk. Right next to that, appropriately enough, was a hut labeled DISPENSARY.

He laughed.

They stopped in front of a hut with a sign bearing the words: ASYLUM.

"This is our HQ. This is where you get out. See ya around, A.," the driver said.

He grabbed his gear and jumped out. He smiled at the sign and opened the door. There were three men inside seated behind desks. The one closest to the door grinned when he saw him.

"You must be A.," he said as he got up to shake hands. "My name's Simmons. I'll be teaching you the ropes so you don't get yourself killed while you're here."

"Nice meeting you," A. said.

The second man got up and shook his hand.

"Welcome to our happy little home, soldier. I'm Lt. Barrows. Until things change around here, I'm your company commander," he said as he took the file from A.'s hand.

"It says here that you're a journalist," the LT said. "What the fuck are you doing out here with that kind of MOS? You should be at HQ in Saigon."

"That's not where I wanted to go," A. said as he explained it all to them.

Simmons and the LT looked at each other. Simmons shrugged.

"I hope you realize what you've gotten yourself into," the LT said. "This is a forward base. That means we see all kinds of action. You've got to be alert and observant at all times. Charlie's out in that jungle and he likes to pull all sorts of shit on us. Think you're up to this?"

"I'll give it my best shot, Sir," A. replied.

"Don't bother with that "sir' shit. Out here, rank means nothing. We're in this together—all the way. We eat, sleep and fight together. And we watch each others' backs. Got that?" the LT said.

"Got it!" A. said.

The LT smiled.

"Me and Simmons will try to keep you from getting killed. It's not that I like you. I hate doing all that fuckin' paperwork," he said.

The third man laughed and walked toward A. with his right hand extended. A. shook it.

"I'm Major Drum—go ahead, say it. I've already heard all the jokes," he smiled. "For lack of anyone else, I'm the CO of this Hellhole. We have four platoons here and enjoy very good relations with the local villagers. I intend to maintain those relations. How about you?" he said.

"I've studied Vietnamese culture and history. I'm eager to meet the people here so they can teach me their customs and language. I'm also very interested in learning about the Montagnards," A. said.

The LT beamed.

The CO laughed.

"That's right up the LT's alley," he said. "He's our expert on local customs and works regularly with the Montagnards. The closest tribe is the Sedang. If you want to meet the Montagnards—

"---I'll take you to them," the LT said.

"Are you going to write dispatches for the newspapers?" the CO asked.

"That's the plan," A. answered.

"What are you gonna write?" asked the LT.

"The truth," A. said.

"That'll be refreshing," the CO said. "And different."

"I'll say," the LT agreed.

He knew what they meant.

American soldiers had taken a beating in the press. The liberal anti-war machine had done its best to convince the public that the war couldn't be won and our men were little more than armed criminals who raped and murdered their way across the country. They had conveniently omitted the atrocities the VC committed against their own people or the fact that the Vietnamese hated and feared them. Even the NVA detested them. Their brutalities had only served to turn the Vietnamese people against them. The NVA considered the VC to be nothing more than highly dangerous fanatics. They didn't like or trust them.

But the American press never mentioned any of that, nor the scores of mass graves left behind after the VC swept through villages. The press was too busy fomenting unrest by fanning the flames of the anti-war fever.

And A, blamed one man for the mess.

Walter Cronkite.

That so-called "journalist" had stood on the ground of the US Embassy in Saigon and proclaimed that the Viet Cong had taken the Embassy. They were inside the compound, he'd said. And all was lost.

And he said this while the US Embassy guards and ARVN troops were slaughtering the VC right behind him. They had, in fact, NOT taken the Embassy nor anything else during their great Tet Offensive. In fact, the NVA and VC had lost almost 80,000 men during the offensive. It had been their worst failure of the entire war.

But good old Walter stood there and proclaimed that the war "unwinnable". When A. watched the report on TV, he got sick to his stomach. He knew it was a bald faced lie and from then on, he'd considered Cronkite and all television "journalists" traitors. And he completely lost any and all trust he'd had in the media.

This distrust led him to become a journalist. He was determined to bring dignity, truth and public trust back into the profession. He had no idea just how really difficult that would prove to be.

Simmons led him to Barracks Four which was about 200 yards from the Asylum. It contained 24 bunks and an equal number of lockers and foot lockers. Two large fans, one at each end of the hut, circulated the semi-humid air. About a half dozen men were lying around, listening to Radio Saigon, writing letters home or just napping.

One short, burly-looking guy smiled and walked over to shake A.s hand.

"Sammy Gonzalez," he said.

"A," he replied. "Nice meeting you."

"I know that accent! You're from Brooklyn," Gonzalez said.

"You know it," A. smiled.

"What part?" Gonzalez asked.

"Bushwick," A. said.

"I'm from East New York—I grew up on Atlantic Avenue. I think we're gonna get along real good, A," Gonzalez smiled.

The next man sat up and stopped writing when they approached. He and A. shook hands.

"I'm Henry George. I'm from Pittsburgh," he said. "Good to have you aboard."

The other men also shook hands with A. Simmons showed him to the bunk next to George's.

"This one's yours, A. I hope you have better luck than the last guy who slept in it," Simmons said.

"What happened?" A. asked as he put his gear on the bunk.

"He got bit by a two-step," George said.

"The viper?" A. asked.

"Yeah. He was dead before he hit the ground," Gonzalez said. "Poor bastard was gonna go home the next day. He went home, but not the way he expected. That damned snake was in the latrine and he didn't bother to check before he went in."

"It bit him in the dick," Simmons said. "Even he'd lived long enough, nobody here was gonna suck the poison of that wound!"

They all laughed.

The samurai escorted Koinu along the main road and up the side of the mountain to the section known as the Ashida bailey. The bailey contained several smaller guest houses, stables and well-kept grounds. It was one of the stronger points of the castle.

As they escorted him to the central guest house, Koinu noticed there were several samurai moving about. Most stopped to watch them pass by. One pointed at koinu and whispered something to the man standing next to him. Both nodded.

Koinu wondered what they were talking about.

He also began to wonder if he should start worrying...

Fort Nowhere had begun its miserable existence as a firebase three years earlier. A few weeks before A.'s arrival, the boys at Regiment in Da Nang decided to move the artillery pieces to a new firebase closer to Pleiku. The artillery company was moved with the guns and they were replaced with four platoons of infantry.

The CO said the base was the Army's "red-headed stepchild". Something they really had no idea what to do with. But they were the only troops in the area.

"Every once in a while, we get a few replacements. We get supplied every six weeks with crap for the mess hall. We get other necessities from the locals and the Montagnards bring us fresh game during holidays. Other than that, we're pretty much on our own out here. We are a tightly-knit bunch. We have to be.

You can go into the village after duty hours. They have a camera shop in the market. You can get film from them and even have it developed there. Any dispatches you send have to go through me first—just to make sure you get things right," he said as they walked around the camp.

Simmons had outfitted A. with all the necessities. He had an M-16, helmet, bullet proof vest, and even a .45 sidearm. He was to keep his rifle loaded and on hand at all times—especially at night.

"Charlie likes to play games at night. He's been real quiet lately, but don't get too comfortable. He's out there watching everything we do," the CO explained. "The locals are friendly and they actually like us. And the women are damned pretty."

"So I've noticed," A. smiled.

"It's hard not to. If you decide to get involved with one, make sure you understand the customs about that. They have certain traditions and her parents will have to meet you and approve of you. It's a very ancient culture with a long, colorful history. The LT will fill you in on most of that. So will the chaplain. Flynn mingles with them all the time. He speaks fluent Vietnamese, too. Between those two, you should be able to get answers to any questions you might have," the CO said.

They stopped and watch a group of Vietnamese women carry heavy containers from the latrines to an open area on the other side of the camp. The women had kerchiefs covering their mouths and noses.

"They burn our shit for us. They cart those cans from the latrines to a pit about a hundred feet away and dump the shit into the pit. They throw kerosene on it and light it. When the shit is burned away, they hose off the cans and put them back into the latrines," the CO explained. "That way, our guys don't have to mess with it. We take up a collection each payday and hire the women to do that and most of the housekeeping around here. They repair our uniforms, wash our clothes, sweep up and clean the mess hall. They need the cash for their families and we don't have to do any mundane shit but survive," he said.

The camp was kind of open to the locals most of the time. The men knew most of them and they knew the men. Most of the time, it felt like there was no war going on.

The CO stopped in front of the Asylum.

"That's all I've got, A.," he said. "After chow, the LT will show you around the village. I think you'll enjoy that. See you later."

Ue o muite arukou

J. came home after an evening out with his friends. It was past midnight. As he approached the house, he looked up and saw that the light in his mother's room was still on. It was unusual for her to be up at this hour.

He entered the house and called out.

She responded as always and he walked up the steps to her room. She smiled at him.

"I'm surprised you are still up, Mother," he said.

"What time is it?" she asked.

"It's 1:45," he replied.

"Oh my! I didn't realize it was so late. I was so busy reading that the time just flew by," he said as she put the book face-down on the table.

He noticed that she was half finished.

"It must be a very good book," he commented.

"Oh, it is! I just can't stop reading it," she said with a yawn. "I guess I will stop for now."

"Two of my friends told me they were reading it," J. said. "They urged me to read it as well."

"You normally read his books after I am finished. I'm sure you'll like this one. It's sort of different," she said.

He nodded and said good-night.

As he undressed for bed, he smiled. He wondered if A. knew that his mother had read every one of his novels and how he'd react if he found out.

The villagers smiled warmly at them. At first glance, A. thought they each lacked several teeth. He quickly realized their teeth were covered by a dark orange, almost brown stain.

"What's with their teeth?" he asked.

The LT smiled.

"They get that from chewing the betel nuts," he said.

"What's that?" A. asked.

"Betel nuts are about the size of quail eggs and are dark orange inside. The locals pick them, boil them then dry them in the sun. Then they slice them and wrap them in pepper leaves and chew them. Sometimes, they add curry powder, which makes them spicy. The juice from the nut stains their teeth.

The stain isn't permanent, but some of the older people do permanently stain their teeth as a sign of status. These are ancient customs. Most of the city people don't chew the nuts because they think it's too low class," the LT explained.

"Why do they chew them?" A. asked.

"It's a natural stimulant. The nuts are packed with caffeine, like Kola nuts. They chew them to keep themselves going during long working days. I chew them when I'm on night watches and long patrols," the LT said.

"What do they taste like?" A. asked.

The LT stopped at a stall and bought one. He handed it to A.

"You chew the leaves, too," he said. "Go on. They taste pretty good."

He sniffed it. It had a smoky kind of aroma that wasn't bad. A. decided it was harmless and bit into it. As he chewed, he felt a sudden surge of energy.

"Not bad. I guess I'll take them along when I'm on night patrol," he said. "They might come in handy."

"You'll do okay here," the LT said. "Just stay aware of your surroundings at all times and avoid doing anything stupid and you'll get out of this alive."

"Going home in a body bag isn't anywhere on my 'to-do' list," A. said.

"Keep it that way," the LT. said. "And that's an order!"

Date Masamune was an almost legendary figure. In battle, he wore a distinctive crescent shaped crest on his helmet and had a reputation for audacity that was second to none. Date liked to do things his way. He had a keen eye for battlefield tactics and easily adapted his strategy to fit a given situation. Usually, he won.

This earned him many admirers.

And enemies.

As a child, he'd contracted smallpox. This cost him sight in one eye. It was said that he plucked the useless organ out himself when a member of his clan pointed out that an enemy might be able to grab it during a fight.

This added to his legendary status and earned him the nickname of "Dokuganryu" (One-eyed Dragon).

At this time, Date served under the powerful daimyo Toyotomi Hideyoshi. He knew that Toyotomi was in cahoots with Tokugawa to seize control of the entire country. He wasn't sure what they had in mind. Nor was he sure he wanted any part of it.

He did know that the powerful Hojo clan, with their double fortresses at Odawara and Hachioji, stood in their way. Hachioji was a massive castle situated on high ground. It was still under construction. If the Hojos were allowed to complete it, no army on Earth would be able to take it from them.

Odawara was even more formidable.

It was on even higher ground and although it had been under siege several times, it had never fallen. It had plenty of fresh water and thick walls. Hojo Ujiteru could hold out indefinitely there.

Date Masamune had just taken control of the Aizu region after a series of bloody campaigns against the powerful Ashina clan and their allies. An ally of the clan, the Hatekayamas, invited Date's father, Terumune to dinner in an effort to have him rein in Masamune.

When Terumune said he had no control over his son, they kidnapped him. Date was out hunting at the time. When he heard about the kidnapping, he fell upon the Hatekayamas just as they attempted to cross a river. In the ensuing melee, his father was killed along with all of the kidnappers.

Date accused the Ashina's of being behind it and launched a brutal and ruthless campaign against them. They were no match for his tactical genius. After several years of fighting, the Ashina's were crushed and Date became the Lord of Aizu.

Even then, things didn't go smoothly for him.

His mother, Yoshihime, insisted he step down and allow his younger brother, Kojiro, to take over. When he refused, she attempted to poison him. In retaliation, he killed his brother to clear his own path to power. His mother then fled back to her brother's home among Mogami clan.

But he was more than a warrior.

Date was a patron of the arts and highly learned and cultured. He was open to foreign ideas, products and even allowed Christian priests to preach in his provinces and win converts. His ports were open to foreign trade ships and this once nothing backwater began to grow in wealth and power under his guidance like no other place in Japan.

If one could apply the term to a daimyo in the early 178th century, then Date Masamune would have to be considered a true Renaissance man.

Koinu had heard these stories long before he'd come to Hachioji. And the more he learned about Date, the more fascinated and impressed he became.

They entered the guest house and found Date and his second in command, Rozo, waiting for them in an inner room that opened into a beautiful Zen garden. The daimyo looked him over carefully as he walked around. Koinu stood straight and remained expressionless.

Date eyed Koinu with interest.

He liked the way he carried himself. He sensed that he was unafraid, even though he had no idea why he'd been summoned.

"Kenshin told me that you used the drop and draw technique on him. He said you were so quick, he never had a chance," Date began. "Who taught you?"

"My father," Koinu said.

"Your father? Was he a samurai?" Date asked.

"Yes," Koinu said.

"Whom did he serve?" Date asked as his interest in the young man grew.

"No one in particular," Koinu replied.

"Was he ronin?" Date asked.

"He was a survivor," Koinu answered with a smile.

Date laughed.

"And what about you? Are you a survivor? He asked.

"So far," Koinu said.

Again, date laughed. He was beginning to like this young man.

"How many duels have you fought?" he asked.

"To be honest, I have never bothered to count," Koinu replied. "Six. Perhaps eight. Does that matter?"

"Not to the men you've killed," Date smiled.

"I didn't kill all of them. I fight to win. If I can do that without killing an opponent, that suits me well."

"On a battlefield, you must kill to survive. There is no quarter given nor expected. Have you ever fought in a battle?" Date asked.

"Not yet," Koinu said.

"I have fought many. I'm sure I will fight many more. How many battles are you willing to fight?" Date asked.

"As many as necessary," Koinu replied.

Date smiled.

"I like your answers. You are very direct and honest. I can tell that you are a man who can be trusted. Someone who will tell me the truth instead of what you feel I want to hear. What is your name?" he asked.

"Monoto Tetsuya," he answered. "But everyone here calls me Koinu."

Date laughed. So did his officers.

"And how did you come by such a name?" Date asked.

Koinu told him. Date smiled and nodded.

"Then that is what I shall call you," he said. "Kenshin is one of my best samurai—or was until you rendered him useless. I understand why you did it and he has already told me it was his fault. He will apologize to you and your wife later, when he is able.

Since you have ruined him, I need someone just as good to replace him. Kenshin has recommended you."

Koinu looked at Date in bewilderment.

Date smiled.

"I'm offering you a position in my army. Is that not why you came to Hachioji?" he asked.

"Hai," Koinu replied.

"Then I am offering you what you seek. Do you want the job or not?" Date asked.

"Hai. Of course I do. I want that very much. Arigato gozaimasu, Lord Date. Arigato!" Koinu said as he accepted the offer.

He had expected to be punished.

Instead, he was hired to replace the man he'd maimed. And it was because of his recommendation.

"From what Kenshin has told me, I see no need to have your skills assessed by my weapons master. Your father trained you very well. Does he still live?" date asked.

"No, Lord Date. My father died of smallpox when I was 12 years old, as did my mother and two brothers. I was the sole survivor as I never contracted the disease," Koinu explained.

"I see. I regret that I did not get a chance to meet them. We leave for Sendai in two days. I expect you and your wife to accompany me. Do you have any idea what you've gotten yourself into?" Date smiled.

"What do you mean?" he asked.

Date sat him down and told him of the current political situations and how some scenarios might play out. He also told him that there was a possibility that he might find himself on the losing side in all of it and how that might go for him and his wife.

"Now that you know all this, do you still want the job?" he asked.

Koinu smiled.

"Since I know of your reputation, I trust that you will place us on the winning side. Hai. I still want the job," he said. "But I must tell you that although I will serve with you with honor and loyalty you to best of my abilities, my first and foremost loyalty is to my wife."

Date looked him in the eye.

He noticed that Koinu didn't flinch or blink. In fact, he had remained calm throughout the entire interview. He knew of Date's reputation but wasn't awed by it. Date decided he was exactly the kind of man he needed.

He smiled.

It was a warm, disarming kind of smile.

"Excellent. Come back here in two days. We leave at midday. Don't be late," Date said.

Koinu bowed and left.

Date grinned.

One of his captains, an older samurai named Rozo, looked at him.

"Why do you like him so much? He seems cocky and too blunt in his replies. Lord Hojo turned him away because he did not like his demeanor," Rozo said.

"Hojo turned him away because Koinu wouldn't kiss his ass," Date said. "That's another reason I like him. He speaks his mind. He is who he appears to be. There is no deceit in him. He's the kind of man I know I can trust.

Most daimyo see those as flaws. I see them as strengths. So does Kenshin."

"I still don't understand what you see in him," Rozo said.

"I see myself," Date smiled.

On the way out, Watanabe told him that Kenshin wished to see him. Koinu nodded and followed him to a room in the back of the guest house. He found the samurai seated upright on a low-backed cushion and sipping sake from a cup. There was another cup on the floor in front of him. He looked at Koinu and smiled.

"Please join me," he offered.

Koinu thanked him and sat down. Kenshin poured sake into the cup and handed it to him. Then he raised his cup and bowed his head.

"I wish to humbly apologize for insulting you and your lovely wife. That was the sake talking last night. I am much more reasonable and mannerly when sober. Please convey my apologies to your wife," he said.

Koinu raised his cup and bowed his head slightly to show that all was well between them now. They drank.

Kenshin smiled.

"That was quite a move you made on me. I have never seen anyone so quick. I didn't even see you draw your katana," he said. "Who taught you?"

"My father," Koinu replied.

"Your father? What is his name?" Kenshin inquired.

"Minoto Kyu," Koinu replied.

"Minoto Kyu? Did he serve Oda Nobunaga?" Kenshin asked.

"Hai. He served Lord Oda for over 25 years," Koinu replied. "Did you know him?"

"Know him? He and I fought together on many occasions. How is he now?" Kenshin asked.

Koinu told him.

Kenshin shook his head sadly.

"Your father was a good, loyal friend. I am sorry for your loss. I wish I had known his whereabouts years ago so I could have visited him. Let's drink to him!" he said as he refilled the cups.

Kenshin laughed and wiped his lips afterward.

"I guess I shall have to learn how to fight left handed now," he joked. "Perhaps you can teach me your drop and draw move? I only need one arm for that!"

"I would be honored to teach you," Koinu replied.

"I like you, Koinu-san. I think you and I will become good friends, even if we did get off on the wrong arm—I mean foot," Kenshin laughed. "I am regretful that our chance meeting wasn't under better circumstances."

"So am I, Kenshin-san," Koinu smiled as they had another cup.

Nijinda hoshi o kazoete

The next morning, A. was walking the perimeter with Simmons. They were making sure the Claymores were still pointed away from the base camp. They had to do this each day because Charlie liked to sneak up to the mines and turn them around.

"Be careful out here. You don't want to run into that two-step viper in the dense brush," Simmons warned.

"Is it as deadly as they say?" A. asked.

"That's the deadliest snake in Nam, A. It's the local cobra. It gets its name because the venom is so strong, it'll kill you before you can take two steps," Simmons said. "We had a guy killed by one of those things a week before you got here. He never had a chance. You have to be careful out here. This ain't Brooklyn."

He was right.

Vietnam was the home to several species of snakes and insects that were deadly to humans. It even had tigers prowling the deep rainforests. But the viper was the most feared of them all. Nobody survived a bite from that snake.

The Central Highlands were also the home of one of nature's more hilarious species. The men called it the "fuck you lizard" because it's mating call sounded like someone hollering "fuck you" in a high-pitched voice. This led to many a nervous newcomer loosing a barrage of bullets in the general direction of the sound, thinking they were being taunted by a VC hidden in jungle.

The older guys, who knew about the lizard, often urged the new guys to open fire on the hidden VC. Then they laughed when the OIC chewed them out for wasting ammo and firing without being ordered to do so. It had become a sort of initiation joke.

The "fuck you lizard" or Tokay gecko, was about 20 inches long. Its high-pitched cry was one of the eeriest things a guy could hear in the jungle at night. They were normally colored a pale blue-green and had very large, round eyes. Up close, they looked kind of comical and they were completely harmless.

The LT had told A. and the rest of the new guys about this. And he threatened to put anyone who fired at the lizard on permanent shit burning detail. Since that was the worst job in camp, A. made certain to ignore the lizard's call when he heard it two nights later.

And the cry made him laugh.

The next day, they walked to the castle and told Hachiman what happened. The old samurai smiled and congratulated Koinu.

"You'll do well. Lord Date is very shrewd and skillful when it comes to avoiding major conflicts. Right now, he is allied to Lord Toyotomi, so he is well-connected. He's a good, honorable man and a very bold and brilliant field commander. But most important, you will stay alive," he said. "Please come back to visit us whenever you like. You are always welcome at our house."

When they reached the guest manor, Date smiled.

"Koinu-san. You are early. I like that. Is this your wife?" he asked.

Koinu made the introductions. Date greeted her warmly.

"I want you to ride next to me. I want to get to know you better. Both of you. Do you ride a horse, M.-san?" he asked.

"Hai. I can ride very well," she answered much to Koinu's surprise.

"I didn't know you rode horses. Why didn't you tell me this?" he asked. She smiled.

"You never asked me," she said.

Date laughed.

"I like you, M.-san!" he beamed. "Koinu-san will go far with you at his side!"

He turned to Watanabe and told him to find them horses. Watanabe bowed and ran off.

"These horses will be yours to keep," Date said. "They are part of your retainer. Buntaro and Watanabe will help you find suitable quarters when we reach Sendai. I think you'll like it there. I'm very proud of what I've accomplished in Sendai."

The DMZ, or Demilitarized Zone, was established as a dividing line between North and South Vietnam after the First Indochina War. It ran along the Ben Hai River about 100 kilometers north of the provincial capital city of Huy. When A. got there, the DMZ was around six miles wide.

It was anything but a "demilitarized" zone.

Some of the dirtiest, bloodiest and nastiest fighting took place in that strip. Over the years, it had been heavily mined by both sides and just about every rock, tree and blade of grass had been scorched by napalm and other ordnance.

"We call it the grinder," Simmons explained. "because it eats up men and materials. It's a real no man's land."

"What units fight there?" A. asked.

"Only the best. Special Forces, Airborne, Rangers…the best. And we always run up against their best," Simmons said. "And nobody backs down. Not even an inch."

Before A. arrived, the old strongholds at Khe Sanh and the Rockpile had been abandoned. Both had been the sites of some particularly bloody battles. Hundreds of good men gave their lives to keep those places out of enemy hands.

The NVA now controlled both. In fact, they had even rebuilt the old airstrip at Khe Sanh for their courier flights into the south.

That was just another paradox of this war.

"We fight hard to keep or take a place then abandon it later. Then the enemy comes back in and takes over and we have to do it all over again," Simmons said. "This is madness, A. Madness of the worst sort. Nothing ever makes sense here and you never get used to it, either."

A. thought back to what he'd read about Hamburger Hill. It had taken U.S. forces ten days to drive NVA forces from the summit. They made 11 assaults up that muddy slope and lost 119 men doing it. Then, a day after we took it, we were ordered to abandon it.

And the NVA re-occupied it one week later.

Simmons was right.

Nothing in Nam made any sense.

U. saw J. seated at a table in the cafeteria and walked over to join him. J. noticed she was carrying a copy of "Bushi". He smiled and greeted her. She was one of the office managers at his firm and eight years his senior, but they had become fairly good friends.

"My mother is reading that same book," he said.

"Oh?" U. queried.

"She has all of his novels. She ordered them online when they first came out. They are all in English, so she always keeps a dictionary near her," J. said.

"Have you read any of his novels?" U. asked.

"I've read most of them. He's quite good at writing adventure novels and science fiction. But I prefer his erotica. How many have you read?" J. asked.

"This is only my second. His previous book was translated into Nihon-go, so I read that first. He seems to know our culture and history very well," she said.

"That's because he's spent a lot of time here," J. said. "My mother said that he really loves our country, but only the older parts. He's not too crazy about Tokyo and other large cities."

"And how would she know that?" U. asked.

"Oh, she and A, were friends decades ago, In fact, he originally came to Nihon to visit her twice. They would have been married if it weren't for a series of silly misunderstandings," he answered.

"Please tell me more," she urged.

J. told her all he'd been told by his mother over the years. He even told her about the poster hanging on her bedroom wall. When he was finished, she had tears in her eyes.

"How wonderfully romantic—and tragic," U. said as she wiped her tears with a napkin. "Is that why he uses your mother's name for his main female characters?"

"I think so. She is in almost all of his novels. I think he still loves her, too," J. said thoughtfully. "I feel so sad for them both."

"Perhaps you can get them back together? I've read that he is coming here for a big book tour next month. You should try to get your mother to go to one of his signings," U. suggested.

"I showed Mom his itinerary in the paper and suggested that she go to see him. That's all I can do right now. I'll suggest it again after he arrives in Tokyo."

"Don't suggest, J.-san. Urge her to see him. They both need to see each other again," U. said.

He nodded.

Omoidasu haru no hi

The afternoon rains came each day like clockwork. These mini-monsoons lasted less than 20 minutes and inundated everything and everyone. When they stopped, the hot afternoon sun boiled the sitting pools of water and sent up curtains of wavy heat and the humidity soared to levels that A. never imagined possible.

If you got caught in the downpour, your uniform remained clammy and damp for hours afterward. Your clothes clung to you like a shroud which left you with heat rashes and fungus infections, like crotch rot and athlete's foot.

It infested all of the warm, moist areas of your body like your armpits, the crack of your ass, your crotch and the spaces between your toes. There was no way to avoid it. Everyone had it to one degree or another.

Even A. was no exception.

Despite going through enough talc and baby powder to cover a football field, the fungus still made a home in his armpits and crotch. Cortisone and anti-fungal creams provided some relief. But this was temporary at best. This was one thing A. really hated about Nam.

It was especially bad when you were on a long range recon patrol.

When you're out in the jungle for days on end, there's no place to wash up. There were no tents. No sleeping bags. Hell, that shit only got in your way and slowed you down. You slept where and when you could.

But you never really slept.

If you stayed too long in one spot, you ended up getting covered by insects of every shape and size and variety you could think of. The older guys told A. that he'd get used to it after a few days.

They were wrong.

This patrol was a cakewalk.

Five days out and five days back with no encounters.

The CO met them when they staggered back to base camp.

"How'd it go?" he asked.

"Too easy, Sir," the LT said. "We didn't see sign one of anything and we went all the way to the river."

"I don't like this," the CO said. "When it's this quiet, it means hat Charlie's up to something. It could be something big, too. He's watching us and waiting for the right time to make his move. You and your men get some chow and stand down. But stay alert tonight."

"Will do, Sir," the LT said.

K. came back from his walk and saw his wife seated in the living room. She was still reading "Bushi" and hadn't even heard him come in. He walked over and squatted in front of her, then took the book from her hand. She just about jumped out of her skin.

He laughed.

"Konnichiwa," he smiled. "Is your mind back in our time now?"

She blushed.

"Gomen nasai. I was so involved in the story that I didn't hear you. When did you return?" she asked.

"Just a moment ago," he said as he sat down. "So, this book is that good?"

"It is very good," she said.

"Your friend is very popular. I see people carrying and reading this book everywhere I go now. I even hear young women and some men discussing it. You must feel very pleased for him," K. said.

"I am pleased. He has worked so hard for this. He emailed me and wrote that this was a huge surprise for him. I think you should read it," she said.

"I'm too busy to read a book," he grumped.

"Oh? Doing what? I have not noticed," she said. "Did you do something? If so, I must have missed it."

"I'm too busy keeping you happy," he said.

She laughed.

It was a laugh filled with sarcasm.

"If you are, then I really have not noticed," she said. "I still think you should read 'Bushi'. All of our children are reading it. You will be the only one who has not so if we discuss it, you will have no idea what we are talking about."

"Has your friend told you when he will arrive?" he asked.

"Not yet. He said he will tell me once everything is finalized. Then we can plan to meet," she said.

"Just don't elope with him. I would miss you and his wife would not like that," K. teased.

"Why would he want me when he has such a beautiful young wife?" she asked.

"You have a point. If he chooses you over her, I'd fear for his sanity—and taste in woman and his judgment," K. said.

"Oh? So you were crazy when you chose me?" she asked.

"Maybe—but you chose me. I didn't chase after you. You chased after me. I should have run faster!" he joked.

"You can run now, if you wish," she offered.

"I would but my legs are older now and my knees give me pain," he said.

"Well, then walk. I promise I won't come after you," she shot back.

"Whatever happened to that sweet, quiet young woman I married? The one who never talked back or argued with me?" he asked.

"She grew up," M. replied.

"Well, bring her back. I miss her," he said.

"She's gone forever. You will have to get used to me the way I am now," M. said.

"I'm not sure I can deal with you anymore," he said.

"Then I humbly suggest that you try to learn," she said politely.

That night and several ones after it, passed quietly. The men passed the time with writing letters home, playing the radio, drinking, playing cards and wandering through the village. Each night, the sky became lit by thousands upon thousands of stars, their light made that much brighter because it wasn't filtered through street lights like they were in New York.

The night sky almost awed A. He spent a few minutes each night just gazing up into it and eventually learned to identify the various clusters and constellations.

There was a strange serenity to Vietnam.

An almost eeriness.

But there were other ways to relieve the boredom. One of the favorites was playing practical jokes on each other. A. had become the victim of a couple and he'd played a few of his own. Their favorite targets were the LT or CO.

In fact, it was A. who came up with the latest one.

They snuck over to the officer's quarters and used their entrenching tools to dig the pit. When they were through, it measured some four feet long, two feet wide and about two feet deep. They then used their helmets to convey water from the tap on the side of rec hut to the pit. Within an hour, the pit was completely filled with water.

They knew the CO would make his nightly run to the rec hall for a cold beer. So they grabbed a case of 33 and sat against the side of a hut across the way to watch the fun.

Sure enough, the CO came out 20 minutes later. The pit was at the bottom a flight of steps and it was dark. The CO walked down the steps and suddenly found himself face-down in a pit filled with muddy water.

They laughed so hard they couldn't stop. The CO crawled out of the pit and walked over to them. A. handed him a beer. The Co looked at them and laughed. Then he sat down and drank with them.

"You guys got me good tonight. I'll give you this one. You know I'll retaliate, right?" the CO said.

"Sure thing, Sir," Simmons said. "Just make it a good one."

He did exactly that—the very next night.

They were in their hut getting ready for chow when the lights suddenly died. Before anyone could ask what happened, someone lobbed a smoke grenade into the hut. It went off with a dull 'bang' and flooded the entire hut with thick, red smoke.

As the men fumbled their way out of the hut, they heard someone laughing.

It was the CO.

"Gotcha!" he yelled.

The men shook their heads and laughed.

"It's on now, brother!" Simmons shouted.

"Bring it, Simmons! Let's see what you've got!" the CO said as he passed out cold beers.

The jokes were all in good fun and nobody ever got mad. And everyone was a target. There were booby-trapped lockers and bunks that fell apart when anyone laid down on them, boot laces tied to bed posts or to each other, helmets filled with water and other liquids and even booby-trapped latrines and coffee urns "flavored" with laxatives.

Through it all, A. snapped his photos and wrote dispatches which the CO approved and sent to the civilian press at Saigon HQ.

Kenshin's wife, Mariko, stood by and watched as her husband and son Kenji, practiced the drop and draw technique with Koinu. They had started these lessons as soon as her husband was strong enough and they worked diligently to get it right.

Koinu's quickness amazed her. She had seen other samurai use the technique but none had ever done it with such lightning speed. Her son, Kenji was 19 and had been well-trained by his father. But even he was having difficulty mastering Koinu's technique.

Watanabe and Buntaro sat nearby and watched with several other samurai. When the session ended an hour later, three very perspiring men bowed to each other and walked into Kenshin's house where Mariko had some cold water waiting. They drank heartily. They heard the door slide open.

Kenshin smiled as Watanabe and Buntaro entered.

"I don't see how you do it, Koinu-san," Buntaro said. "I have never seen such speed on the draw."

"I give all the credit to my father," Koinu said modestly. "He began training me when I was old enough to hold a half-sized wooden katana. We worked hours at a time. He was very patient with me, too. After he taught me how to use a blade, he handed me my first yumi (bow) and added that to my training. He taught me how to ride and handle a horse in between that."

"I knew your father. He was one of the best—but you are much faster. I doubt that any man alive can defeat you in a fencing match," Kenshin smiled.

"M.-san can," Buntaro said. "I've seen her defeat Koinu-san in many fencing matches."

"Only she does it with words," Watanabe added with a smile. "You may be fast with a katana, Koinu-san, but your blade is no match for her tongue."

They all laughed.

M. laughed when she read this.

"This is probably how K. thinks of me now," she thought.

Her friendship with A. had fortified her. He'd always told her she was smarter than she thought she was and had a good, sharp wit. He encouraged her to let that side of her come out and allow the real M. to blossom.

Little by little, she did just that.

Much to K. surprise and bewilderment. His "meek" little wife had begun to assert herself and much of that assertion came out as sarcasm.

What's more was the fact that she was surprisingly good at it. Some of her comments even made him laugh. She also had an almost poetic way of insulting at times, too. He also discovered that she still had many dreams of her own she wished to make real—with or without him.

"When we married, you promised me that we'd travel. I am still waiting for you to fulfill that promise," she said one morning.

"What are you talking about? We travel every day!" he said.

"To where?" she asked.

"We go to the stores, you take me to the gym and my karaoke pub, and we go to doctors' appointments. We travel much each and every day," he said.

"That's not the kind of traveling I meant. You promised me we'd travel all over the world after our children were grown. Our children have been grown for many years and we haven't even left Tokyo!" she said.

"Oh, that!" he said.

"Hai. So when are we going to take a trip?" she asked.

"I'll let you know when the time is right," he smiled.

"Don't wait too long. If you do, I may already be gone by the time you decide to take me somewhere," she said.

"I have to take my other woman someplace first. Any suggestions where I should take her?" he teased.

"You can both go where it is very hot," she said.

"Australia?" he asked.

"I was thinking of someplace further down," she replied. "And you can visit your parents once you get there."

He muttered something and got up to leave.

"Where are you off to?" she asked.

"Someplace cooler. It's much too hot in here now," he smiled.

The LT and the CO were always making bets with each other. Most of the time, the loser had to buy beer or do something highly embarrassing. Most of the time, the LT was the loser and he was getting a little tired of this.

So he came up with something he was positive he'd win. In fact, he was so sure of this, he pressured the CO into a most unusual bet.

Whoever lost had to get one of those slinky Vietnamese dresses with the slit sides and a coolie hat, put it on and walk down the main street of the village at high noon. The CO was just as sure he'd win this bet, so he agreed to it.

Simmons, A., George and few other men witnessed the bet and it was on. The bet involved climbing one of the trees inside the camp. Whoever reached the top fastest, won the bet and the loser had to wear the dress.

On Sunday morning, the entire company gathered around the tree to watch. The CO went first. As he climbed, Simmons timed him with a stop watch. It took him 43 seconds to reach the top. He shinnied down and grinned at the LT.

"Beat that!" he challenged.

The LT took a deep breath, let it out, and climbed up the tree. When he reached the top, Simmons called out the time.

"Forty seconds flat!" he said.

The LT climbed down and grinned at the CO.

The CO frowned.

"When?" he asked.

"Today—at noon," the LT said.

The CO nodded and headed back to his quarters. To everyone's surprise, he came out at exactly noon wearing a bright yellow dress with gold edging and a coolie hat. The men clapped and whistled and called him "honey" and "sweetie". The Co took it all good naturedly and walked through the gate with most of the men following after him.

As soon as he hit the main street, all traffic of every sort came to sudden stop. The people lined up on both sides and smiled and laughed as the CO paraded up and down the street for the next 20 minutes. Even the kids laughed. A few people snapped photos. One elderly villager ran up and handed him a bunch of flowers he'd snatched from a market stall. The CO took them and smiled graciously as he played along with the joke.

When he walked back to the camp, he smiled at the LT and batted his eyelashes.

"You got me good this time. Just wait until you see what I have in mind for you next!" he warned as he handed him the flowers while the rest of the men laughed and applauded.

Koinu had lost his wager with Kenshin and the penalty was most embarrassing. When Date saw him walking through the castle decked out in full geisha regalia, he stopped in his tracks and called him over.

Koinu shuffled over as best as he could, as it was difficult to walk in the tight kimono. He bowed to Date.

"Turn around. I wish to see all of this," the daimyo instructed.

Koinu did as he was asked. Date smiled then totally lost it. He laughed so hard and long that he began to sweat and tears rolled down his cheeks.

"Very nice, Koinu-san! After seeing you like this, I feel you have found your future profession once your days as a samurai have ended," he joked.

The rest of the samurai and their wives laughed heartily. Koinu smiled and bowed politely, then shuffled off.

"How long are you supposed to dress like that?" Date asked.

"Until the sun sets," Koinu replied. "Wearing this gives me a new respect for what women go through to look pretty."

"And you do look pretty!" Watanabe said as everyone laughed.

"Did M.-san help you dress?" Date queried.

"Hai. It took us two hours to get it right, too," Koinu said. "It's so tight! I can barely walk in this."

This elicited more laughter from the other men.

Date shook his head.

"Of course, you are planning to get even with Kenshin now," he said.

"Of course!" Koinu admitted.

"Please keep me informed and enjoy the rest of this fine day," Date smiled.

Koinu bowed and shuffled away.

Date laughed and went back inside.

M. stopped reading and laughed. The scene was improbable but almost logical. Bushi and samurai here know to have rather risqué and odd senses of humor. She could actually imagine them making such a bet, too.

She wondered what prompted A. to write such a scene.

As she sat giggling, K. entered the room. She told him about the bet. Even he had to laugh as he allowed the image to float into his mind. That's when he noticed M. looking at him strangely and smiling.

"Why are you looking at me like that?" he asked.

"I was just trying to imagine you dressed as a geisha," she said. "Can you picture yourself in the entire costume, with a wig and makeup? Think of it!"

He tried not to, but the image found its way into his mind. Once it settled there, he simply couldn't dislodge it. And the longer it remained, the more vivid it became. Then he began to laugh.

And laugh.

She did, too.

Then he looked at her and smiled.

"Now, imagine yourself dressed as a samurai. Picture yourself in full yoroi, seated on a horse," he said.

They both laughed again.

She laughed harder because she envisioned herself trying to keep the heavy helmet and face protector from sliding down and pushing her head into the chest piece. She thought she'd look like a turtle and this made her laugh harder still. When she explained it to K., he laughed so hard he cried and hugged her.

The RPG round struck the front of the Quonset. It blew a hole in the metal skin and sent pieces of shrapnel and other debris sailing through the length of the structure.

Just about everyone rolled off their cots and hit the floor. Five more rounds followed in quick succession. A. watched as several lockers fell to the floor and spilled their contents as they blew apart. The place quickly filled with dust and smoke and he couldn't see a thing.

Dead quiet followed.

They grabbed their guns and helmets rushed outside to man the perimeter. The expected attack didn't come.

"Charlie!" A. said. "Just another night attack to wear us down."

Simmons who was in his boxers and nothing else, nodded. Most of the guys were in their underwear. Even A. All he had on was his briefs, dog tags and helmet. A couple of the guys were naked. All in all, they were a comical looking lot.

Charlie often used tactics like this to wear down soldiers prior to an all-out attack. After several sleepless nights, the idea was to make the enemy too tired to fight back. It was a page right out of the "Art of War".

"Stand down!" the LT hollered.

The men relaxed their guard and looked around. Several of the huts had been hit this time. A. looked at their hut and cursed. It would take all night to repair it just so Charlie could blow it apart again tomorrow. The war was becoming an exercise in futility.

"That was close!" Simmons said. "My locker's toast and most of my shit is gone. How'd you do?"

"I'm afraid to look," A. said.

To his relief, his locker was still intact. The floor was littered with all sorts of gear and debris and the lights didn't work.

"Anybody get hit?" asked the LT.

"Don't look like it," George said.

"We're alright, LT," Simmons said. "Pissed off but otherwise okay."

"Charlie wasn't trying to kill anyone tonight," the LT said as he sat down on a cot and lit a smoke. "They hit hut number two and the dispensary."

"Too bad they didn't take out the chow hall. That would have saved a lot of us," one man joked.

"I think they're setting us up for the big one, so stay on your toes," the LT said.

"Why don't we see about heading this off, LT?" Simmons asked. "Instead of waiting around for Charlie to make his move, let's take the fight to him."

"I'm up for it," A. agreed. "Maybe it's time to let those bastards know they're fuckin' with the wrong people."

The other guys voiced their approval. The LT looked them over as he finished his cigarette. He tossed the butt on the floor and ground it out with his foot.

"Saddle up. We leave in 20," he said.

Ten men left the camp that night. They went over the rear wall and crept along the edge of the rice field until they reached the jungle. They stopped and looked around. Outside of the usual insect sounds, all was quiet.

"Those bastards are out there somewhere," the LT whispered. "Somewhere close."

He pointed at A., Simmons and Gonzalez.

"You go to the left and head into the brush," he said. "Kill anybody you see."

He pointed to three other men and told them to go right while he led the rest of the men straight ahead. They knew they had to be quiet and watch out for vipers. You always had to watch out for the vipers.

Simmons, A. and Gonzalez made their way through the dense brush as quietly as possible and kept their eyes on the deep shadows the entire time. Charlie could be anywhere. The last thing they needed was to walk into an ambush.

Gonzalez, who was in the lead, raised his right fist. A. and Simmons waited while he went on ahead. He returned five minutes later.

"There's six Dinks seated in front of those trees just ahead," he whispered as he pointed. "Do your thing."

Simmons nodded. He loaded a grenade into the M79 and aimed it at the base of the trees. He took a deep breath and fired. The grenade went off with a loud roar and sent up a shower of bright sparks. They heard yowls of pain and waited. Seconds later, three dark clothed VC limped by. Gonzalez opened up on them.

Two fell.

The third turned and ran as A. fired after him. It was so dark, he couldn't tell if he'd hit him.

They heard two more grenades go off to their right. The explosions were followed by rifle fire and yelps of pain and screams. They made their way toward the sounds. When they reached a small opening, they saw three VC running toward them.

Simmons, A. and Gonzalez stood up and fired straight at them. All went down hard and didn't move. They waited. A few minutes later, the LT and the other guys walked out of the jungle.

"Hold your fire, Simmons! It's just us," he shouted.

Simmons smiled and lowered his weapon.

"How many you get?" the LT asked.

"I counted eight kills and one possible," Simmons answered.

"We nailed three back there," the LT said. "That's 11. Not a bad' night's work if I do say so myself."

Just then rest of the men came out of the brush.

"We spotted a narrow footpath leading east," Cruz said.

"Show me," said the LT.

Gonzalez looked at the dead VC and smiled.

"At least these assholes won't be bothering anyone again," he said.

"Amen to that, man!" Simmons said.

The path wound deeper into the jungle and ended at a small clearing. The LT looked around.

"Fan out. Look for spider holes—and watch out for traps," he said.

The men spread out and slowly walked through the clearing, keeping their eyes on the ground. Both the NVA and the VC liked to hide underground. The NVA dud entire complexes of several rooms and even had communication lines and hospitals down there. They were well-manned and had more than one way into and out of the complexes. The VC dug "spider holes" of one or two rooms, usually in clearings or villages. They used them to hide from The U.S. and ARVN soldiers or to stash weapons and ammo. They hid in them during the day and came out at night to harass bases. They were called spider holes because they resembled the lairs made by the trap door spiders.

The ones in the villages were hidden almost anywhere. Sometimes the locals helped them hide because they were VC sympathizers. Most of the time they didn't tell because they feared VC reprisals, which could be incredibly brutal.

They searched for almost 20 minutes. Then George's foot hit a soft spot. He stopped and motioned for the others to come over.

They gathered around as George uncovered the wicker door.

"Spider hole," he said.

"Look around, men. If there's one, there had to more. They always have another way out. Be careful. This area might be booby trapped," the LT said.

They spread to cover more ground. Ten minutes later, the LT found the exit. He motioned for them to cover both doors.

"Now we know where they are," he said. "Any of you guys tunnel rats?"

"I've done some rat work," a short Latino said. "Want me to check it out?"

"You sure you want to do this, Cruz? "the LT asked.

"Why not? I've got nothin' else to do right now," Cruz said as he stripped down to his shirt.

The LT handed him a flashlight and his .45.

"Go slow and make sure you have a quick way out. Don't get yourself killed on me. You know how much I hate doing paperwork," the LT said.

Cruz smiled.

"I'll try not to. How far in you want me to go?" he asked.

"As far in as you feel good about," the LT. "I leave that part up to you."

Cruz nodded.

The LT lifted the trap door and watched as Cruz entered the spider hole. Twenty minutes later, he walked up to them from behind and tapped the LT on the helmet.

"How'd you get here?" the LT asked.

"I came out the back way. There's nobody down there, LT. The place looks like it's been deserted for a while, too. All I found was some old bottles and cigarette butts," Cruz said as he dressed.

"Good work, Cruz. Let's blow this place so Charlie can't come back and use it," the LT said.

Simmons set the timers on two satchel charges. He handed one to George then took off toward the back door of the spider hole. George tossed the charge into the hole.

"Fire in the hole!" he shouted as everyone took cover.

"Fire in the hole!" they heard Simmons yell.

The charges went off at almost the exact same instant. The explosions kicked up columns of dust and dirt as the tunnels collapsed.

"That's that. Let's head back to base," the LT said.

Hitoribotchi no yoru

M. was reading the book when K. stepped out of the shower. He was totally naked and just chatted with her as he walked around the house. After a few minutes of this, M. decided to have some fun.

"As long as you like being naked, why don't you walk around our neighborhood like that for the next hour or two?" she suggested.

"You want me to embarrass myself as I don't have an object now to be proud of?" he teased back.

"Now?" she queried with a sly smile on her lips. "You mean you were proud of it before?"

"Of course I was!" he said as he puffed up his chest.

"Then I guess it does not take very much to make you proud," she said.

"How can you say such a thing? You never thought that way before! It was always good enough," he said defensively.

"That is because I never had another object to compare it with," she said.

"Oh? And you do now?" he asked.

"Not yet," she teased.

"Does that mean you're planning to?" he asked.

"Perhaps," she smiled.

"Oh? And who do you plan on comparing me to?" he asked.

"I think I may start with the ten year old boy down the street," she joked. "And work up from there."

"Humph! Why not start with a cat instead?" he asked.

"I do not want to shame you that much," she said. "Perhaps comparing you with a small bird may be fairer."

He muttered something unintelligible and walked out. She laughed.

A moment later, he came out wearing nothing but a baseball cap. She looked at him and smiled.

"Are you taking my suggestion?" she asked as she tried to keep a straight face.

"Hai. I won't stay out very long," he replied.

"It isn't very long, is it?" she teased.

"I meant time—not length," he corrected.

"You do not have the length and you never take very much time," she said.

"My, but aren't we sarcastic today!" he remarked.

"I can't help it," she smiled.

"Maybe I should stay inside. I don't want to get anything sunburned," he said as he looked at the sky.

"How can you get anything sunburned when it's always in the shade?" she teased. "Even if you did, no one would notice."

"Not even you?" he asked.

"Especially not me," she smiled.

"Just for that, I will go out!" he said as he headed for the door.

She watched in amusement as he opened the door, stepped outside, and shut it behind him. She quickly ran and locked it. Just as he turned around, two elderly ladies happened to pass the house. They looked at him and bowed.

"Konbanwa, K-san!" the both said as they laughed.

He turned beet red and tried to go back inside. To his horror, the door wouldn't open. He knocked and told her to let him back in. She decided to let him stand outside for another minute or so and laughed as he kept knocking and pleading with her to let him in. When she finally let him back in, he stomped past her and sat down on the couch.

"Back so soon?" she queried with a grin.

"I didn't want to get arrested," he replied as he crossed his arms.

"For what?" she asked.

"Indecent exposure," he said.

"Oh. I doubt that would have happened," she said calmly.

"Why do you say that?" he asked.

"In order to get arrested for such a crime, you would need to have something indecent to expose," she said.

He looked at her and broke into laughter. So did she.

The entire company was loaded onto copters and taken to the edge of a long, narrow valley flanked by thick jungle and uneven hills. A sluggish stream meandered through it, making it a perfect breeding farm for mosquitoes.

When the last man's feet hit the ground, the LT led them into the valley. The M.I. boys at Da Nang had told them that a battalion of NVA troops were going to cross into the valley later that evening. They wanted them ambushed and driven out.

The closest infantry were the guys at Fort Nowhere. They were tough and experienced at ambushing the enemy. There were 160 soldiers on the mission that day and everyone expected a quick and easy ambush-like their last three had been.

This was A.'s first combat mission. He hung with Simmons in the front of the pack, about 30 yards from the LT and the radio man. The day started out hot and humid. It was downright steamy as they walked slowly through the valley.

No one talked.

Or laughed.

All you could hear were the muffled footsteps and heavy breathing of the men as they moved through the waist-high grass. Three men were walking point.

Everyone was watching for vipers.

"Did you hear?" Watanabe asked as he hurried into the room.

"What?" Date asked.

"Toyotomi is attacking Odawara," Watanabe replied. "He marched his army there yesterday."

"That's insane. No one can take that castle," Date said. "No doubt, he'll summon me to come help him. I want no part in this war. I don't wish to waste good men and resources trying to take Odawara and I have no personal grudge against the Hojos."

"What will you do? You know he will order you to join him," Koinu said.

"I'll drag my feet as long as possible. With any luck, Toyotomi will be defeated before we get there. I don't think he's acting alone. I'm sure Tokugawa is behind this," Date said.

He put his hand on Koinu's shoulder.

"It is just as I feared. If Hojo falls, this war will spread quickly. We'll have no choice but to get caught up in it. I want to bide my time. I want to see what transpires in order to choose which side to fight on," he explained. "If Hojo wins, we'll fight under his banner. If he loses, we'll decide between Tokugawa and Toyotomi.

My loyalties are flexible. The main thing is to survive," he said.

Koinu nodded.

Date grinned at him.

"Your loyalties are to your wife," he said. "That is what you told me when I hired you. I will hold you to that for M.-san's sake. If everything suddenly goes badly for us, I want you to take her and flee to safety. Above all, you must survive. That has always been the way I've lived my life. I have suffered more than one defeat, but I always came back stronger for it. You serve no purpose by dying. Remember that, Koinu-san," he said.

M. set the book down and sipped her tea as she thought about the scene.

To the samurai, M. was the ideal woman. He loved her deeply and was fiercely loyal to her. So much so, that he would never dream of touching another woman. He had eyes and love only for her and she for him.

"Does A. feel that way about me?" she wondered. "Is that the way he would have been with me?"

She loved the samurai's courage and honor and the fact that he was afraid to show his love for M. Or to be human. He had even had the audacity to inform Date Masamune, his daimyo, that even though he would always serve him with honor and courage, his foremost loyalty was to his wife.

"How unconventional!" she thought. "It's Bushido with touches of Chivalry. Does A. live his own life by such codes? Is the samurai him?"

Shiawase wa kumo no ue ni

He heard the crack of the rifle and saw the point man go down. He hit the dust just as all Hell broke loose. Bullets hissed overhead and clipped off the tops of tall blades of grass. Other hit the ground in front of him and kicked up clumps f dirt, which splattered on his face and nearly blinded him. He heard shouts and more shots.

Curses.

An RPG round whistled past and blew a nearby tree in half. He watched as it groaned pitifully and toppled to the left. More RPG rounds exploded around him and sent up clouds of dirt, dust and grass. He heard a couple of men scream in pain and realized they'd been hit.

Then he remembered the point man.

He'd fallen less than twenty yards from him. Although his hands were wet from sweat and his heart was beating like snare drum, he had to find out if the guy was still alive. He took several breaths and exhaled each, then decided to go for it.

As bullets hissed overhead, A. low crawled through the dense grass to the stricken point man. When he reached after what seemed like an eternity, he heard rasping sounds as his chest heaved up and down. He sidled up next to him and looked in his eyes. The kid stared at him and grabbed his shirt.

"Do you hear them?" he gurgled as blood trickled from the side of his mouth.

"Hear what, Josh?" A. asked as he looked for the wound.

"Angels. I hear angels," the kid said as he stopped breathing and looked up at the sky.

Not knowing what else to do, A. knelt and cradled the kid's head as the light slowly left his open eyes. He reached down and shut them. A bullet struck the earth directly in front of him and snapped him back into the reality of the moment. He grabbed his M-16 and low-crawled away, leaving poor Josh behind.

It was his first look at death.

Up close and personal. He had no time to think about it then. He was too busy trying to keep from joining him. He wasn't interested in hearing any angels.

But he'd never forget that soldier's face. Never forget the way he looked as the life left his body and the light faded from his eyes.

His heart was in his throat now and cold sweat covered his body. His brain fought hard to make sense of the chaos around him. He heard and saw explosions. Watched as some of his platoon mates rose to fire above the grass. He saw another man go down as blood exploded from his chest. Then another. He knew it was impossible to run in the grass.

Impossible to see.

If anyone was in charge, he had no way of knowing. If the LT was shouting orders, he had no way to hear them. All he heard were the hisses and ricochets of bullets, the dull whistles of RPG rounds and the intermittent pop-pop-pop of return fire as the battle's intensity increased with each passing second.

For the first time in his life, he knew fear.

If time passed, he didn't realize it.

He felt as if the entire world was in suspended animation. Everything moved in slow motion and the battle began to take on a very surreal aspect. He couldn't see where the enemy was. He didn't know where his own men were.

He made his way slowly through the grass.

Inch by sweat-soaked inch.

He heard something moving just ahead of him and stopped. His heart almost froze as he saw the business end of an Ak-47 emerge from the blades of grass right in front of him. Nervous, he reached out with his left hand and parted the grass. The young NVA soldier stared back at him, but didn't pull the trigger.

Seconds crawled by like years as both men hesitated. A. decided to gamble. He raised his right hand and waved and shook his head to indicate he didn't want to shoot. The NVA, who could not have been older than 20, nodded and lowered his rifle.

They both smiled.

He watched as the NVA slowly backed away and vanished into the grass. He breathed a sigh of relief and did the same.

He realized that the NVA soldier didn't want to be there any more than he did. He was probably a conscript who really didn't give a rat's ass who won the battle. The kid just wanted to get home in one piece.

"Good luck, soldier," A. said.

A bullet hissed through the grass and struck the ground not six inches in front of him. A. rolled to the side and looked around. More shots struck the dirt next to him. He rolled onto his back, held the rifle above the grass and fired a few rounds.

The battle was now in full metal mode. As the firing and explosions grew louder, he thought he heard the LT shouting behind him. If he was, A. had no idea what he was saying. He low crawled over to a nearby fallen tree and saw several NVA soldiers scrambling through the brush. He pointed his rifle in their direction and emptied his magazine. The NVAs hit the dirt and fired back. A. took a grenade from his web gear, pulled the pin and counted to four before lobbing it at the enemy.

It exploded and the firing stopped.

He scrambled to his immediate rear. He saw men running while firing all around him. He grabbed the second magazine from his helmet band and reloaded his rifle. He was about to leap up and run for the rear when he saw and RPG round strike Sergeant Geary in the middle of his back and blow him to bloody bits. The horror of that moment froze him in place.

The he felt a hand on his shoulder.

It was the LT.

"Fall back! Do you hear me, A. ? Fall back now!" he yelled.

Three NVA charged out of the brush, yelling and firing. A. turned and fired every last round he had at them. Then he turned and ran after the rest of his platoon. He didn't know if he'd hit any of them.

He didn't want to know.

He reached the spot where the LT had told everyone to gather. The LT was already on the horn calling for a napalm strike and extraction. He tossed the mike back to the radio man.

"Everybody get into those trees! On the double!" he yelled as he pointed to a tree line about sixty yards away.

They ran as hard as they could with enemy fire lending wings to their feet. They reached the trees in seconds and took cover.

That's when they heard the jets.

He watched as two aircraft came in fast and low. He saw them eject two large canisters. A split second later, twin fireballs mushroomed above the trees on the other end of the valley and engulfed the entire battlefield in a rolling wall of gasoline-powered flames.

As the napalm did its terrifying work, A. covered himself and quivered. For the first time in his life, he actually prayed.

The flames blackened everything for hundreds of yards. It seared through the heavy vegetation with a vengeance. About 20 minutes later, the flames had all but died out, leaving cindered tree trunks, blackened earth and grass and death behind. The air was now choked with the distinct odors of charred vegetation and human flesh and traces of gasoline. A. had never smelled anything like it. It was a smell that would stay burned into his memory forever and even cause flashbacks whenever he barbecued. It was the single most sickening thing he'd ever smelled.

Or seen.

But the enemy fire had stopped.

"On your feet!" the LT shouted. "Let's get out there and find our men. We leave nobody behind!"

As A. staggered into upright position and shouldered his rifle as he looked around. Black smoke and bright red-orange pockets of flame were everywhere.

He felt suddenly dizzy. He fell to his knees and puked his guts out. When he was through, he thought that he wasn't the first G.I. ever to do that. He wouldn't be the last, either.

He saw a couple of the others doing the same and didn't feel so bad after that.

"You okay, A.?" Simmons asked.

"I think so, man. Is it always like this?" he asked.

"Beats me, dude. This was my first action, too. Shit, my knees are still shaking," Simmons replied with a smile.

They laughed.

"I wonder if you ever get used to this?" A. asked as they walked across the smoking ground.

"I hope not," the LT said as he came up behind them. "This sucks a big one. Better get a move on. Those choppers will be here in a few minutes to take us home. Let's find our dead and wounded so we can get them out first."

M. was having lunch with her friend Y. As they ate, the subject of A.s book came up. Y. remarked how quickly it had become popular in Japan and wondered if she should read it.

"Oh, I highly recommend you read it," M. said. "It's an excellent book. I think you'll be amazed at his portrayals and historical accuracy."

Y. smiled.

M. had told her about her friendship with A. in great detail. They had grown very intimate indeed. Most of the time, he was all she talked about.

"You know that A. is coming to Japan soon?" M. asked.

"Really?" Y. asked.

"Hai. His publisher is sending him here to promote the book. He will be here for five weeks. He's bringing his wife with him," M. explained.

"Are you going to meet him?" Y. asked.

"Of course I am! I am very anxious to finally meet him in person after all this time. I am also very worried," M. said.

"About what?" Y. asked.

"What if he doesn't like me?" M. asked.

"After some of the emails you showed me from him, I don't think you need to worry about that at all. He already likes you and very much. In fact, I think he may even love you," Y. pointed out.

"You think so?" M. asked.

"Hai. And I think you love him, too," Y. said. "And I know why. He is exactly the kind of man you've always wished for. He is the type of man you never knew existed outside of movies or books. The two of you were drawn to each other from the moment you made contact. It's as if the gods put you together."

"The gods have bad timing as we are both married to other people," M. said.

Shiwase wa sora no ue ni

Hachioji was a disaster.

When Hojo Ujitero learned that Odawara was under attack, he marched most of his army out to try and lift the siege. He erroneously believed that Toyotomi had thrown his entire army at Odawara and left on 1,300 samurai behind to defend Hachioji.

It was exactly what Toyotomi had been waiting for.

He sent 50,000 men under the command of Maeda Toshii and Uesugi Kagekatsu to take the massive fortress. It fell in less than five hours and everyone inside was slain.

The news reached Date at Sendai the next day.

When Koinu heard the news, he immediately wondered if his friend, Hachiman, had somehow survived. He decided he would go there as soon as possible. Date saw the look of concern on his face and asked what was troubling him. When Koinu explained, Date nodded.

"I have no choice but to join Tokugawa at Odawara now. Your presence won't affect the outcome of the battle one way or another. Go and seek out your friend, Make sure of his fate and see that his family is cared for. Then return to Sendai as quickly as possible. Upon your return, if you learn that I am still at Odawara, join me there," Date said.

He reached Hachioji late the following afternoon. Smoke still rose above the great manor's smoldering timbers and, outside of the cries of the carrion birds circling overhead, the place was quiet.

Eerily quiet.

Hachioji was now a mass grave.

The grounds inside and out, were littered with pieces of broken yoroi, shattered weapons and pools of blood. Maeda and Uesugi had made sure that the bodies of their own dead were carried away. The Hojo dead were left in place for surviving relatives to tend to.

He paid no mind to any of this.

Instead, he hurried straight to the main gate. That was Hachiman's post. He knew the old samurai would be there and nowhere else. He knew he would not back down. As he approached the broken gate, he saw several pieces of mangled armor and discarded weapons. All looked like they belonged to samurai in Maeda's clan. Against the wall, in a seated position, with his naginata in hand, was the lifeless body of his friend.

He walked over and knelt beside him.

The old samurai had a smile on his face and his lifeless eyes stared straight ahead. There were five arrows in his chest.

Koinu smiled.

"They couldn't get past you man-to-man. It took archers to bring you down. I wish I could have seen you in action, my friend. I wish I could have fought by your side," he said as he reached out and closed his eyes.

"Sayonara," he said.

At that point, a group of samurai from Maeda's clan walked up to the gate. They watched Koinu pray next to Hachiman's body. After a while, they knelt with him…

After ensuring that Hachiman's body was placed in the shade of a large tree, Koinu raced down the path and into the town. He hurried straight to Hachiman's house. He wanted to be sure his wife was safe. When he arrived, the house was deathly quiet.

He called out her name several times.

When she didn't come to the door, he walked up and slid it open. He found her on her knees in the middle of the room in a doubled over position. There was a large pool of blood beneath her. He sat down in front of her and wept.

Rather than be taken prisoner, she had committed seppuku. She had to have known that the castle had fallen and knew that meant her beloved Hachiman was dead. Koinu resolved to give them both decent burials somewhere on the castle grounds—even if he had to dig their graves himself.

He recaptured his composure and enlisted the aid of several locals. They carried the bodies up the path and into the castle to a grove of small trees.

"Bury them here," he instructed. "And please make a good job of it."

He watched as they dug a large, deep, rectangular grave and gently placed Hachiman and his wife into it side-by-side. Koinu jumped in and placed Hachiman's right hand in his wife's left. After he climbed out, he told the others to cover them grave.

While they worked, he took a piece of timber from the ruins of the manor and made a simple marker. He placed this at the head of their grave and then bowed respectfully. The other men watched and also bowed.

Koinu turned to the workers and gave them each some money as he thanked them for their service. Then he walked down the path toward the main gate. The other men shrugged, picked up their shovels, and followed.

M. put the book down and leaned back in her seat. She could easily picture the scene as A. had written it. The other samurai had knelt out of respect for Hachiman. Koinu's actions were heartfelt and sincere. It had been his way of repaying their kindness to him and his wife. And he did it because they were friends.

The young samurai did what he believed was right.

She smiled.

"Is that the way A. lives his life?" she wondered. "Is the samurai in the story really him?"

She stretched, got up and walked to the window. It was raining now. She stood and watched the drops make ripples in the puddles in the yard below and thought back to her days with him. She wondered if he had shown such signs of his personality back then? If so, had she misread them? At the time, A. was a puzzle to her. She had much difficulty with his language and wasn't sure what to say or how to react. The uncertainty had caused her to remain silent at times—which she knew also confused him.

She smiled at their awkwardness.

"We were so innocent then. So naive," she thought.

Ue o muite arukou

When the Hojo clan surrendered Odawara Castle, the victorious Toyotomi ordered Hojo Ujitero and his eldest son to commit seppuku while he watched. With their deaths, the power of the Hojo clan was forever broken. The survivors were forced to submit to Toyotomi's authority. Those who didn't were either forced to commit seppuku or sent into exile.

He then ordered that the entire castle at Hachioji be destroyed and had his men circulate rumors that the ruins were haunted in order to make certain that no one would ever attempt to rebuild it.

He then turned his attention to Date Masamune. He was still furious that the daimyo had arrived too late to participate in the siege of Odawara and was about to exile him to a remote region of Hokkaido. But Tokugawa intervened and Date was spared this indignity.

Realizing he had narrowly escaped a fate worse than death, Date returned to Sendai and began to rebuild his army.

As A. walked across the clearing, he saw several smoldering bodies. There were dozens of them. Although each was badly charred, most appeared to be NVA. A handful were American soldiers. Most were already dead before the strike.

At least A. hoped they were as he stopped to retrieve their dog tags. He placed them on their chests so they could be identified and moved on. About fifty yards later, he spotted a partially singed NVA soldier leaning against a burnt tree trunk. He walked over and saw it was the soldier he'd met in the grass.

The soldier looked up at him as A. let him drink from his canteen.

"Thank you," he said in English. "Please tell my family that I died well."

He reached into his chest pocket, took out his wallet and handed it to A. It contained his photo, ID card and about 1000 piastas.

"Promise me," he gasped.

"I promise," A. vowed.

"You are a good friend," the soldier said as the breath left his body.

He continued his walk across the field with the rest of his platoon. He found a wounded G.I. and helped him stand. His left leg was shot up and he could barely walk. A. helped him hop back to the LZ and got there just as the first chopper arrived. The rotors kicked up dust and dirt as it touched down.

"He looks like Hell," the door gunner said as A. helped the wounded man onto the chopper.

"I feel a lot worse than I look," the soldier joked. "If you think I'm bad, you shoulda seen the other guy!"

Battlefield humor.

If you didn't have it, you'd go insane. It was sort of a defense mechanism. Every soldier had it, from ancient Egypt to Nam. Soldiers laughed at death in an effort to cope with their fear of it. He stepped back as three more wounded men got loaded onto the shopper. One had to be carried on in a blanket. He looked barely alive.

He stepped back and watched as the chopper took off and another circled the field and came in for a landing. More men got loaded onto this one. All of them dead. There were eight of them. Eight young soldiers who paid the ultimate price in the service of their country. A. that chopper left, A. wondered how many more will go home in body bags before this was over?

Four more choppers came in to take the rest of the platoon out. They had started out with 48. Thirty one were going back alive. Half were wounded. Two were critical. A third of them would only see home in coffins.

He had no idea how many NVA had been killed. They didn't bother with a body count. They left the enemy soldiers right where they fell. They would never get home. Their families would never know where and how they had died.

Then he remembered the wallet.

He took it from his pocket and looked at the photos. One was of an elderly couple. The other was of a young woman with two small children.

His wife and kids?

"Whatcha got there, A.?" Simmons asked as he looked over his shoulder.

"Something I got from a dying NVA soldier," A. replied. "I promised him I'd tell his family what happened."

"You gonna keep that promise?" Simmons asked.

"Yes," A. replied. "I have to. He didn't want to be here anymore than we did. I'll explain it to you later. War sucks."

"Tell me about it. This ain't nothin' like those movies!" Simmons joked.

When Koinu told M. about Hachiman and his wife, she fell into his arms and wept. He held her close and stroked her hair to comfort her as he, too, choked back tears of his own. He'd been told that a samurai isn't supposed to weep. That was a sign of weakness. But to him, shedding tears over the loss of a good friend was a sign of his own humanity, an acknowledgment of a great loss. Besides, his father told him that is was alright for a samurai to weep at such times.

"We are warriors, true," he'd said. "But more than that, we are human. If the occasion calls for tears, shed them and let others think what they want."

"My father was always right!" he thought as he hugged her tightly.

M. got a surprise visit from her daughter, A. They went into the living room to chat. M. served some light sugary cakes and cold tea. A. noticed the copy of "Bushi" on the table. She opened it and smiled when she read the dedication.

"So he is the samurai and you are his lady?" she teased.

"In truth, I like to believe so," M. replied. "He told me that I am his muse. That I inspired him to write the novel and have it translated into Nihon-go and marketed here. If I am responsible in any small way for his success, I am very happy for him."

"I'm very excited that we all get to meet him soon. You have told me so much about him and I like the way he looks in his photos," A. said. "Will you try to steal some private moments with him?"

M. blushed.

"Whatever do you mean?" she asked.

"You know what I mean, Mom. You told me about your dreams!" A. smiled. "I know he will want to spend some private time with you, too. Perhaps you and he can have an affair while he's here?"

"Now you're being silly! His wife will be with him. Even if I wished to do that, how would I ever be able to arrange such a thing?" M. asked.

"Oh, you'll find a way—if you truly wish to," A. said with a grin. "I remember that one email he sent you about what he would love to do with you if you ever had a chance to spend time alone with each other. It was so erotic! It made me wish he had written that to me! He is very much attracted to you. How does that make you feel?"

"It makes me feel young and happy inside," M. answered. "And confident."

"Is that why you have been crossing swords with Father?" she asked. "I was here during one of your exchanges. I've never heard to answer back before and I was really surprised at how quick and sarcastic you were. So was Dad!"

M. smiled.

"There have been many other such exchanges between us," she admitted. "And I am enjoying each one."

"Do A.'s emails have anything to do with this?" A. asked.

M. nodded.

"He encourages me to be myself. To be stronger. So, little by little, I began to do so. Now, I don't hold back," she said.

"What has A. said about this?" A. asked.

"He said he was proud of me," M. beamed. "He said if we were married, that's the way he'd expect me to be and he would expect me to voice my opinions on things that were important. He said that a silent wife is an unhappy wife."

"Wow! No wonder you love him!" A. said thoughtfully.

M. blushed at her use of the word "love".

"Did he ever tell you why he chose to include Date Masamune in his novel?" A. asked. "That was an unusual choice."

M. explained A.'s dreams to her. A. listened quietly then shook her head as it sank in.

"Then he is Koinu! He is a reincarnated samurai and 'Bushi' is his autobiography. And if it's his autobiography, then you are the M. in his book! No wonder you are so drawn to each other," A. said excitedly as if she'd had an epiphany.

"Or she is the M. he met many years ago," M. guessed.

"I don't think so. Have you read her description? She sounds exactly like you. So, M. is you and no one else," A. argued. "So, would you give yourself to him if he asked you to?"

M. smiled and nodded.

"Then make sure you find time to make that happen," A. advised. 'Then you can tell me all about it later!"

They looked at each other and laughed.

Namida ga kaborenai youni

Because of his victories at Odawara and Hachioji, Toyotomi Hideyoshi was named the "great unifier" by the Emperor. He was now second only to the Emperor in power and quickly moved to institute several changes in Japanese laws. These laws, such as the one where only samurai could carry swords in public, had a lasting effect on Japanese culture.

It was then the "god of war" set his sights on Korea. He assembled a huge army and ordered several of his loyal allies to accompany him on the campaign. Among them was Date. When he wanted to bring Koinu with him, his wife Megohime, intervened.

She reasoned that Koinu should not be separated from M. when she might be pregnant as that would put a strain on their marriage. She also pointed out that Date needed to keep someone at Sendai he could trust and that Koinu was that man.

Koinu was both disappointed and relieved when Date told him he would remain at Sendai. Although he felt that his place was at Date's side, he really didn't want to be separated from M. for a long period of time. Date had read his thoughts.

"I will have more than enough bushi for this campaign. Toyotomi has only requested that I bring half of our men. You, Buntaro and Watanabe will remain here as my eyes and ears. Understand?" he said.

Koinu nodded.

"Then we will speak no more of this," Date smiled. "I have my orders. Now you have yours. We must both do as we are told, neh?"

Koinu laughed.

Date pounded his back and laughed with him.

"If anything happened to you, M. and my wife would make my life miserable. It would be a true living Hell. It is bad enough to face one angry woman. But two is impossible!" he said.

When Koinu returned to his home, M. greeted him with a big, warm hug.

"What did Masamune-san say?" she asked.

"He ordered me to remain here and be his eyes and ears while he's away. He also said his wife would make his life miserable if he separated us while you are expecting," he replied.

"Oh?" she queried.

He squinted at her.

"Are you pregnant?" he asked.

"Not yet," she smiled sexily as she motioned for him to follow her to the futon...

Date and his wife, Megohime, walked through the garden of his castle.

"I am happy that you decided to keep Koinu-san here," she said.

"You decided that. I just carried out your suggestion," he grinned. "As I always do."

She giggled.

"M.-san will be so pleased! She cannot bear to be separated from him for very long. So you have made all three of us happy," she said.

"One more samurai will make little difference in Korea," he said. "By the way, when is M.-san going to give birth?"

"Nine months after he makes her pregnant," she smiled.

Date laughed heartily. He knew then that he'd been had.

"But why must you go?" she asked.

"Lord Toyotomi has ordered me to. He still doesn't trust me after I arrived late at Odawara. He would have exiled me to Hokkaido if Lord Tokugawa hadn't interceded. I owe Ieyesu-san much," Date said.

"So does Lord Toyotomi want you to accompany him because he needs a good general for the campaign? Or does he wish to keep an eye on you?" she asked.

"Both of course," Date said.

"Do you trust him?" she asked.

"I trust no one who has such power," he replied. "But Lord Toyotomi effectively rules Nihon now. So I will obey his commands and serve him to the best of my abilities until someone comes along to depose him."

"Is anyone strong enough to do this?" she asked.

"Not now—but in a few years?" he said.

When they reached base, A. peeled off his dirt and sweat stained uniform and threw himself under the shower. When he felt he was clean enough (one never truly felt clean in Nam), he went to the mess hut and forced down some unidentifiable gray thing the cook claimed was meat. He just wasn't sure what kind.

After eating, he walked over to the chapel to talk to Father John Flynn. He showed him the wallet and told him of his promise.

Flynn shook his head.

"War makes too many widows and orphans and it serves no purpose that I know of," he said.

"How can I get this to his family?" A. asked.

"I suggest you take it to the Buddhist temple in the village. One of the monks there might be able to help you," Flynn said.

"Thanks, Padre," A. said. "I'll head over there right now. It's too damned bad I can't deliver this in person. I'd like to personally tell his family what happened and how I probably wouldn't be here now had he pulled that trigger. I owe that kid. I'll always owe him. If I could, I'd help out his family."

Flynn nodded.

"Good luck, son," he said.

The temple stood less than 500 feet from the Catholic Church and school. It was a large, very old, wooden structure with a high-pitched roof and thick timber supports. It was at least 30 feet tall at its center.

He had seen the monk around many times and had even spoken to him a few of those times. The man was about 50 or so, with a neatly shaved head and he wore deep orange and maroon robes. He was a very open and jovial man, too.

When A. entered the temple, the large bronze Buddha seated serenely in front of him caught his attention. He stopped and stared at its features. The Buddha's eyes were half shut but A. felt his gaze was everywhere. It was as if it could see into his soul. He stood there for several minutes and gazed at the Buddha's face.

The monk saw him standing before the statue. He'd never known an American to enter the temple before. What's more, this one seemed completely captivated by the Buddha's gaze. He walked up and tapped A. and the shoulder.

"Do you speak English?" A. asked.

"Yes. I speak English. How may I help you?" the monk replied.

Instead of answering right away, A. looked back at the Buddha. The monk stood by patiently for few seconds.

"Are you Buddhist?" he asked.

"I have no religion," A. replied.

"Buddhism is more a philosophy than a religion," the monk said. "But that is not why you've come here, is it?"

"No. I made a promise to a dying NVA soldier yesterday and I need your help to fulfill it," A. said as he looked at the monk.

He told him everything that happened, and then gave him the wallet along with a letter he'd written to the family.

The monk smiled.

"I will translate your letter as exactly as I can and make sure his family receives this," he assured him. "I will send it to the temple in his home town. The monks there will make certain his family receives it. This is a great and kind thing you are doing. A most unusual thing, too."

"I'm just a soldier carrying out a promise I made to a fellow soldier," A. said.

"The warrior's bond?" the monk asked.

"Something like that. It's kind of a code I live by," A. said with a smile. "How will I know it reached his family?"

"They will write to you and give you their thanks and blessings. You have no idea what this means in our culture. The letter will come here and I will give it to you," the monk explained.

He looked back up at the Buddha.

"What do you feel when you look into his eyes?" the monk asked.

"I'm not sure. I can't describe what I feel. It's mostly peaceful," A. answered.

"The Buddha has blessed you. He will always bless you," the monk said. "You are one with him."

"Maybe you're right," A. said.

He took out his wallet. He had 4,000 piastas and some military scrip. He gave the piastas to the monk.

"For the temple," A. said.

The monk smiled and bowed.

"Be safe, my friend," he said as they walked out.

"You do the same," A. said as he headed back to the base.

The LT. saw him when he came back and walked over to him.

"I know what you've done. Father Flynn told me all about it. You're the damnedest soldier I ever saw, A. You live by some sort of code of honor that belongs in another time. You're some kind of throwback," he said.

"A girlfriend of mine in Japan thinks I'm a reincarnated samurai," A. smiled.

"Well, considering what you've just done, I'd say she might be onto something. You're a rare bird, A. I wish everyone was like you around here. Since you're so good at keeping promises, I want you to promise me something," the LT said.

"Name it," A. said.

"No matter what happens, don't ever change. Keep to your code of ethics. Don't let the world change you," the LT said.

They shook hands.

"You have my word, LT," A. said.

Nakinagara aruku

M. sat down and turned on the PC. The first thing she did was check her emails for her daily message from A. Not a day went by where they didn't write to each other and their exchanges had grown more and more intimate as time passed.

Very very intimate.

She smiled at his email. He'd had another highly erotic dream about them. As usual, he described it in great, almost poetic detail. She was amazed that anyone would have such dream about her at this stage in her life and she wondered how he'd really feel if he saw her in person.

But this dream was even more erotic than the others. As she read, she grew warm between her thighs. Halfway through it, she opened her shorts and slid her hand down into her panties as she imagined they were together and making love in the very same ways he described.

He had a way of arousing her with his words and compliments. He made her feel so sexy. So desirable. As she read, she massaged herself faster and faster. She soon lay back on the cushion with her eyes closed as she tried to feel him moving inside of her, feel herself moving with him as they made love. She knew if he were there at that moment, she would gladly give herself to him.

Her fingers moved faster and faster. Her breath grew heavy and her chest heaved as her entire body clenched. This was followed by a sudden release of an intense wave of pleasure. She kept rubbing herself until it happened again.

As she came, she sighed, "anata wa aishimasu!"

She withdrew her hand and took several deep breaths to calm down. Her actions, although unobserved, somewhat embarrassed her. When she was by herself, she always thought of him or reread his emails. Especially the highly erotic ones she'd saved. He did things to her with his words that no other man ever could.

"But," she thought. "I am married. I am an old married lady. I should not have such feelings for another man!"

M. had just recovered from her orgasm when K. entered the room. He saw the flush on her cheeks and immediately realized what had happened.

"Were you preparing yourself for me?" he teased as he hugged her.

"Hai," she lied. "Can you handle me?"

She didn't dare tell him the real reason for her ecstatic flush.

"When you are like this, I'm not sure any man can handle you," he joked. "I'm afraid you might injure me or worse."

"Not even a little bit?" she asked as she massaged his crotch in an effort to arouse him.

"We'll see," he said. "I need to shower first. I've just returned from the gym."

He smiled to himself as he walked into the bathroom. After all these years together, he knew all her expressions. He especially knew the way she looked after an orgasm. He also knew that he was not really the source of that orgasm.

His realized that his wife was in love with someone else. He also had some idea who that someone else might be. He didn't worry so much. She was just a silly old woman and no one else could possibly be seriously attracted to her now. Even if he was, they most likely would never actually meet face-to-face. He decided to let her have her fun for now.

Toyotomi's year-long campaign to conquer Korea proved to be a disaster. To save face, he declared victory and returned to Japan in "triumph". Date found this more than a bit amusing.

"The 'God of War' lost his ass in Korea," he told Koinu. "The Koreans proved to be our match and then some. When that bitter winter came, I knew it was over. I've never felt so cold in my life. It was if my very bones had turned to ice inside me. We lost many good men to the cold and sickness. When the Koreans launched their spring campaign against us, I knew it was the end.

So I advised Lord Toyotomi to declare victory and return home before we lost any more samurai. After some urging, he finally agreed. I think the only reason he did so was because he, too, was ill at the time and I feel he wanted to die here at home instead of in that Hellhole."

Toyotomi followed his advice, too.

Although their initial military campaigns had been highly successful, mostly due to date's unique and adaptable strategies, the vast empire of China which viewed Korea as a vassal state, had a seemingly endless supply of men it could keep throwing at them. Within months, the invasion had become a deadly and tedious defensive war with neither side making any great gains.

Then came the extremely bitter Korean winter.

The invaders were not prepared for nor had they ever experienced a winter like that. The heavy snows and fiercely cold winds had brought most of the fighting to a standstill. Then influenza struck. So did pneumonia and other diseases. These took a heavy toll on the Japanese and their cemetery began to fill up.

The heavy spring rains melted the ice and snow and turned roads and paths into muck. Toyotomi's spring campaign turned into a stalemate as the Chinese and Koreans countered almost every move. Then some illness struck the God of war himself and rendered him too weak to lead his men into battles and too feverish to think clearly. Command effectively passed to Date while Toyotomi recovered.

Date launched a two pronged attack on a large concentration of enemy troops and scattered them in all directions within a few hours. He tried to pursue the main body but again the Korean weather forced him to return to their base.

Date knew the weather would enable the enemy to regroup and bring in reinforcements. They were already badly outnumbered and he saw no use in wasting more good men in what was steadily proving to be a futile campaign. That's when he advised Toyotomi to declare a great victory and return home. This way, he could save face and his honor and reputation would be elevated.

Toyotomi saw the wisdom in his counsel and wrote a letter to the Emperor announcing his great victory. Then he ordered his army to make the necessary preparations to leave Korea.

Toyotomi never fully recovered from his illness.

Although he put up a brave front and carried out his plans to complete the unification of Japan, he slowly wasted away.

Date was astute enough to observe this.

So was Tokugawa. And the crafty daimyo quietly began laying the foundations for a takeover after the God of War expired.

M. finished reading the book. As she set it aside, she thought about the vivid depictions of the inside maneuverings at the high court in Kyoto. A. grasp of 17th century political events intrigued her. He wrote about them as if he'd observed then personally. He added extra dimensions to the personalities of each major player and managed to add a somewhat Shakespearian angle to it all.

As she sat there thinking, K. came in from his gardening. He saw the pitcher of iced tea on the counter and poured himself a glass. Then he walked over and sat beside her.

"You're not reading?" he asked.

"I have just finished another chapter. A.-san has remarkable insight into our history," she said. "In fact, I think he could teach it at a university here."

He raised an eyebrow.

"His words draw you into the story. He makes the past live again," she continued.

"Oh?" K. said. "Maybe I will read it when you are finished then."

"Please do so," she urged. "I think you will find it fascinating."

"You have found yourself a most unusual American," he said with a smile. "He is very unconventional—just like your friendship. I was not sure if I should be jealous or angry at first, but when you told me he was married and showed me the photos of his wife, I realized I was safe. He would be judged as quite insane if he left her for you. Such an act might even get him committed to an asylum!"

"Since you think I look so terrible, why do you stay?" she asked.

"I stay because of pity," K. replied.

She glared at him.

Her glare made him wince.

"I do not need yours or anyone else's pity. How could you say such a mean thing to me?" she snapped. "Perhaps I should be pitied because I have been stuck with you all these years! If that's how you feel about me, you should leave!"

"I don't stay because I pity you. I stay because I pity the next man who might marry you. No one deserves such a sharp-tongued wife!" K.

smiled. "Not even I— but I am willing to bear the burden for the sake of humanity."

"That's very noble of you," she said.

"I think so, too," he smiled.

M. decided to go for a walk. It was a pleasant morning and she needed some exercise. As she walked along the waterfront, she thought back to her first few days with A. in Yufuin. He told her that he decided to visit her because his baseball season had been brought to an abrupt halt by an injury. Since the team doctors told him to take the rest of the year off to heal, he decided to visit her.

"How were you injured?" she asked.

"I was playing the outfield. A batter on the other team hit the ball. I chased it back to the wall and dove into the seats after it. I missed it completely but I landed between the fence and a row of seats so hard that I dislocated my shoulder," he explained. "So, instead of staying home to heal, I decided to visit you."

She smiled.

"I was going to come and see after the season ended in late September," he said. "This worked out better because I got to meet you faster."

She was flattered that he'd rather spend his time with her than staying home to mend his shoulder.

"You don't appear to be injured," she observed.

"The team doctor snapped it back into place right after it happened. It only hurts when I try to lift heavy things or throw a ball too hard," he explained. "I haven't tried to swing a bat since it happened. I'll give it another try next season."

"Are you a good player?" she asked.

He smiled.

"I like to think so," he said. "Maybe you'll get a chance to see me play soon. Then you can decide for yourself."

"I would like to see you play very much," she replied.

M. sighed.

He had found a higher calling than baseball—although she never knew about it. In fact, he'd had a most colorful life. He'd gone everywhere and did things she never would have imagined he'd do. She really had no idea just how adventurous he was—until his first novel was published and she read his bio on the back cover.

She wondered if he would have done all those things if they had married. Or would A. have played it safe and settled down to a more traditional, even mundane life?

She sighed.

There was no way she'd ever know.

Hitoribotchi no yoru

Koinu, Watanabe and Buntaro were honing their archery skills by shooting arrows at a target some 100 yards away. As they fired arrow after arrow into the target, M. came out of the house to see if they'd like something cool to drink.

She watched them practice for a few minutes. She then walked over to her husband and touched his arm.

"May I please try?" she asked.

"What do you know about using a bow?" Buntaro asked almost scornfully. "You're a woman."

"Are you afraid that I will embarrass you?" she challenged with her usual smirk.

Buntaro laughed.

"Not at all. I doubt that you'll even be able to draw it. Go ahead and let her try, Koinu-san," he said confidently.

Koinu winked at her and gave her the bow. Then he stepped aside. She knocked the arrow to the string, raised the bow and slowly brought it down while drawing it. When the arrow was on the target, she let it fly.

It struck the target dead center.

Buntaro and the Watanabe gaped in wonder.

Koinu just smiled as M. handed the bow back to him.

"That was an incredible shot. An excellent shot," Buntaro said. "Please try another."

She grinned at him.

"There is no need to," she said as she walked away.

Buntaro turned to Koinu.

"How is she with a katana?" he asked.

"I'm afraid to find out," Koinu replied.

M. laughed at the scene. It was typical of his other novels. His female characters were always more than they appeared to be on the surface. While they were very feminine and sexy, they were also intelligent, resourceful, strong and fiercely loyal.

They were the type of women A. was obviously attracted to. She wondered what about her had attracted A. Did he see those traits in her? If he did, she wondered how he knew as she'd never considered herself to be anything that. Especially back then.

It was Sunday.

Flynn had held his usual morning mass for the usual handful of believers. A. had slept in like he normally did on Sundays. He went to the chow hall, got a tray full of SOS and tepid coffee and gulped it down hungrily. The SOS was about the only thing edible on Sundays. The eggs always tasted like Styrofoam and the pancakes soaked up gallons of syrup and somehow managed to stay dry and tasteless. Even the coffee was becoming an adventure lately.

After breakfast, he walked across the compound to where a group of his buddies were gathered. They had set up a target near the edge of the perimeter. It had a red bull's eye painted on it and the men were taking turns trying to hit it with a Montagnards bow and arrows Simmons had procured. They were also drinking beer and laughing at their wild misses.

Simmons handed him a beer.

"We're having some target practice," he said.

"But we ain't too good at it," George added as his shot missed by at least eight feet.

"So far, we haven't hit anything but the sandbags behind the target," Simmons said.

"Wanna take a shot?" asked George as he handed A. the bow and an arrow. "It's a lot harder than it looks."

He looked at the weapon. He'd never shot a bow in his entire life, but he'd watched a lot of samurai movies. He handed his beer to Simmons.

"Hold my beer and watch this shit," he said with a grin.

He stepped up and fit the arrow to the bowstring, and then he raised it above his head and brought it slowly downward until it was centered on the target. At the same time, he drew the bow until it was as taut as he could get it. He exhaled and let the arrow fly.

The guys laughed and hooted as the arrow struck the bull's eye dead center. A. handed the bow to George. Simmons handed him the beer.

"That was some shot," he said.

He nodded and walked away as if he'd done nothing special.

M. laughed at a passage in the novel.

Koinu's wife had accompanied him to a gathering at Date's manor. She stood by and listened as two of his captains discussed possible strategies with Date. Something about what was proposed by Captain Sukiyori struck her as being imprudent and she told him so. Her interjection brought their conversation to a quick stop.

When Sukiyori asked her what was wrong with his idea, she stood her ground and told him. She concluded that although he was an experienced and able samurai, he had failed to consider the consequences that would befall him if he took such actions. She also said that if she could see the flaws in his plans, his enemies would see them, too.

Sukiyori left without uttering another word, but Koinu could see that he wasn't pleased to have a "mere woman" point out his mistakes. The other captains stood by and smiled.

Koinu decided to head off any possible trouble and quickly apologized to the captains.

Date smiled and placed his hand on Koinu's shoulder.

"Do not apologize for M.-san. She spoke what was on her mind," he said.

"But still, she spoke out of turn," Koinu said.

"Let her. She spoke the truth—same as you do. She is honest, loyal and intelligent. I value her advice as much as I do yours and that of my wife. Never apologize for her. Treasure her. No matter what happens, she will be at your side—and mine," Date said.

He looked at his officers seated cross-legged against the wall and laughed. His laugh was more than a little derisive.

"I wish some of you were like her and Koinu. You tell me only what you feel I want to hear. You're more concerned with saving your own stations than telling me what I really need to know. Maybe I should appoint M.-san my chief advisor! She has more balls than the lot of you put together!" he said.

He stood up and scowled at them.

"Now get out of here! I'm tired of seeing your faces!" he shouted as he pointed to the door.

Koinu and M. watched as they shuffled out. Date had shamed them. Again.

Koinu chuckled.

Date patted his back and smiled at M.

"I've always said that you married well!"

R. watched as A. opened the letter from his publisher. After he read it, he smiled and handed it to her.

"Pack your bag. We leave in five days," he said.

She looked it over.

There were two book signings, a magazine and a TV interview in Tokyo. Another signing in Sendai and an interview with the local TV station. Signings in Osaka, Kyoto, Nara and Fukuoka. In Tokyo, they were going to be in a suite at the Imperial Hotel for one week.

She looked at him.

"That's a busy schedule," she said. "Are we going to have time to sightsee and shop?"

"Sure we will. We'll also make a side trip to Hachioji to meet M.'s family and tour the ruins of Hachioji Castle. We may even get lucky and hit a matsuri or two," he said.

"Matsuri?" she queried.

"Festival," he said. "They are always very large and colorful and each has some sort of historic significance. Most go back hundreds of years."

"I can hardly wait!" she beamed. "You'd better email M. so she knows your schedule."

He nodded.

"I'll do that right away," he said.

J. spotted the announcement in the book section of the Asahi Shimbun the next day. He smiled and showed the paper to his mother.

"That's less than a week from today!" she said as she felt her hear skip a beat.

"That's right. It says he will be at the Imperial Hotel and that he will attend a cocktail party the next evening in the hotel ballroom, during which he will gladly autograph copies of his book for anyone who brings it to him," J. pointed out.

"Isn't that a very private affair?" she asked.

"Hai. It's only for members of the publishing and newspaper professions. It's by invitation only," he said.

"Oh," she said in a disappointed tone.

He smiled.

"Were you planning to go there?" he asked.

"I'm not sure," she replied. "But there will be so many people there. He will not notice me."

"You could always go either before or after the party," J. suggested. "I'm sure he would be happy to see you again after all this time."

She nodded but kept quiet.

He could tell the idea intrigued her but she was too nervous to actually do it. He touched her hand.

"He will be in Japan for five weeks. Please consider trying to see him again. It will do you both much good," he said.

"I will think about it," she said.

Toyotomi Hideyoshi lay dying.

After many years of hard-fought campaigns, his body had given out. Date went to visit him just hours before he died. He knelt by Toyotomi's bed and recited a Zen poem. Toyotomi gave Date an approving smile, and then closed his eyes.

It was 1598.

The funeral was attended by all of the daimyo and the Emperor. It was a grand, yet solemn and dignified affair. A very traditional send-off, befitting a man who had lived a dignified, traditional life.

His son, Hideyori, was named to succeed him. Although the choice was logical and expected, Hideyori was merely an infant at the time.

This opened the door for Tokugawa and he began plotting Hideyori's downfall.

Another powerful daimyo and close ally of Toyotomi, Mitsunari Ishida had similar ambitions and began plotting his own rise to assume Toyotomi's place. The two men's ambitions had been held in check by their alliance with Toyotomi. Now that he was gone, the gloves had come off and they began making alliances to go against each other.

The ever-astute Date had anticipated this. Ever since they'd returned from the Korean campaign, he'd watched Tokugawa's machinations with an eye toward his own survival. He almost immediately arranged for one of his sons to marry into Tokugawa's clan. That cemented the connection between the two families.

Koinu had observed Date's maneuverings. He had seen the handwriting on the wall and knew that something big was coming on the wind.

Tokugawa was strong, determined, a good tactician and above all, hungry for power. He had his eyes focused on the Shogunate. Date had his eye focused on survival and began to build up his army and fortify his holdings.

As Koinu watched the latest company of bushi march through the castle, he glanced at Date who was standing a few feet from him. Date nodded.

"Tell me what is on your mind, my friend," Date said.

"We have nearly doubled the number of bushi since Toyotomi Hideyoshi's death. More men come every day and our smiths are working day and night to equip them. You have also added several guns to our arsenal. Are you preparing for war?" Koinu asked.

"Perhaps. I feel war will be thrust upon us and soon. So, we must be ready to defend ourselves or march into battle when we are summoned," Date explained.

"Are we still allied to the Toyotomi?" Koinu asked.

"For now," Date said with a smile.

"And if war does come?" Koinu asked.

"If war does come, I will support Lord Tokugawa," Date replied.

Koinu nodded.

"You think he will win?" he asked.

Date laughed.

"With me at his side, how can he possibly lose?" he said.

Simmons and A. were walking toward the chow hut when a series of loud clicks caught their attention. They stopped in their tracks and looked behind them to see what was making the sounds. They stood and stared as a black, shiny beetle about the size of a football helmet clopped its way across the compound. It walked past them, totally oblivious to their presence, and headed toward the perimeter.

He turned to Simmons.

"What the Hell was that?" he asked.

"Beats me, man. I've never seen anything like that before," Simmons said.

"Do you think it's dangerous?" A. asked as they watched it climb slowly up the sandbag barrier.

"I don't know and I don't wanna know," Simmons replied. "Out here, I've learned not to fuck with anything unless it fucks with you first. And I'm leaving that thing alone!"

The next time they saw that beetle, someone had glued a tiny American flag to the top of its shell and let it run across the camp. All the men who saw it stopped and saluted smartly as it ambled past. Ever since that morning, it was dubbed the Patriot Bug. It hung around the camp for about a week then was never seen again.

It's a good thing, too.

The LT was planning to grab it and glue sergeant stripes to the shell. If the beetle had stayed much longer, it might have ended up in charge of a platoon or even the entire company. Apparently, it knew what was up and didn't want any part of it, so it left.

After all, one the men had made friends with a small monkey the year before and had even outfitted with an entire Army uniform, minus the jungle boots. When he rotated out of the company, he took the monkey with him. By then, it was wearing LT bars.

When A. heard the story he laughed. By now, it was probably a colonel.

Omoidasu aki no hi

Flynn got to be good friends with A. and the old priest proved to be a valuable source of information on local language and customs. He'd been in Vietnam for five years and knew just about everything worth knowing.

"What was the craziest thing you remember?" A. asked as they sat outside and drank beer.

"When I was first in-country, I was with a battalion up in the DMZ. We were always out in the field and under fire. One Sunday, one of the men asked if I was going to give mass. Well, I had an assistant chaplain back then and we had a portable altar. So, I set this up in the middle of a clearing, put on my white shawl and laid everything out nicely," Flynn said with a grin.

"You did that in a combat area? Wasn't that dangerous?" A. asked.

"You betcha! A few of the men gathered around. As soon as I started with the opening prayer, the enemy lobbed a mortar round into the clearing and sent us running in all directions. It landed about eight feet from the altar and blew it to pieces. God must have been with us that morning because no one got hurt—or that was His way of telling me how stupid that was," Flynn replied.

They laughed.

"That was the first and last time I ever tried to hold mass in a combat zone like that," Flynn said with a grin. "I didn't want to risk it after that first time."

"I don't blame you," A. said.

"The CO showed me your file and I've read a couple of your dispatches to Stars and Stripes. You're a damned good writer, A. and you get your facts straight. The Stars and stripes prints your articles exactly as you write them. But when I saw those same articles in a copy of the L.A. Times, I couldn't believe the changes that were made to them. Those bastards back home are doing a real hatchet job on your stories. They make it look like you're some kind of anti-American, anti-war nut," Flynn said.

"I know. And there's not a damned thing I can do about that from here. I've sent letters of complaint to UPI because they're the ones who edit and feed my articles to other papers, but no one responded. What's worse is, after UPI sends them to the papers, those liberal bastards edit them again. Those people want us to lose this war, Padre. They want America to fail," A. said bitterly.

"You plan on doing this for a profession after the war?" Flynn asked.

"I'm going to give it my best shot," A. said.

"Good luck with that," Flynn said as they clinked bottles.

"Amen!" A. said.

Date and Koinu sat at the table playing "Go" and drinking sake while their wives watched. They had just finished their evening meal. As Koinu moved his black marker, Watanabe rushed in and knelt before Date.

"I bring news from Kyoto," he said.

"Oh?" Date queried as he moved to counter Koinu's piece.

"Lord Tokugawa has uncovered a conspiracy to assassinate him and he has accused the allies of the Toyotomi clan of being behind it," Watanabe said.

Date smiled.

"Knowing Ieyesu, he probably started the rumor himself. That way, he has an excuse to go against Toyotomi," he said. "Anything else?"

"Lord Tokugawa has ordered several of Toyotomi's allies to submit to his authority of face punishment by the Emperor," Watanabe said.

Date laughed.

"Ieyesu is the real power behind the throne. The Emperor does as he is told. How many daimyo have caved in to his demands?" he asked.

"All but Kagekatsu Uesugi and Mitsunari Ishida, the closest allies of the Toyotomi clan," Watanabe said. "Kagekatsu has refused to obey Lord Tokugawa and is rumored to be building up his army to oppose him."

"And so it begins," Date smiled. Return to Kyoto and keep me appraised of events as they unfold."

He looked at Koinu.

"A storm is coming. We had best prepare ourselves to withstand it," he said as he made another move.

"What's the weirdest shit you've seen or done since you've been here?" A. asked Gonzalez.

"That's an easy one, man. But you're not gonna believe it," Gonzalez said.

"Try me," A. said as he opened another bottle of 33.

"Well, it happened at the hospital in Pleiku. I went down there to get a growth saved off the bottom of my left foot. So the docs assigned me to a ward that was down the hall from the cold storage lockers. You know, the place where they keep bodies and body parts? On the night before my operation, I had trouble sleeping so I decided to walk around. When I got close to the unit, I heard men laughing inside. I got nosy and went in. Man it was crazy!" Gonzalez said.

"Go on," A. urged.

"When I walked in, I saw a bunch of the medics sitting on the floor and smokin' weed. I mean, the air was thick with it, too. They had drawn a circle on the floor and were making bets on what I thought was a marbles game. I mean, they looked like they were playin' marbles. I watched and saw that the marbles were really crazy lookin'. So I asked the docs what kind of marbles they were," Gonzalez said with a smile.

"What did they say?" asked A.

"One of them looked at me after he took another drag on the roach. Then he sorta smiled and said those weren't marbles," Gonzalez said.

"So what were they?" A. asked.

"He said they were human eyeballs, A. He told me they froze them overnight, and then took them out to play with them. Then he picked one up and tossed t to me. When I caught it, I dropped it right away. It really was an eyeball, A. Those dudes were fuckin' sick! I got out of there fast and went back to my bed. I didn't want to know what other crazy shit those guys did there after that," Gonzalez said.

He took a swallow of beer. A. looked at him. His expression never changed, either.

"Wow!" A. remarked. "That is some weird shit!"

"The weirdest, man. Those guys were so high on weed, they couldn't see anything wrong with what they were doing. It was like a scene from some kinda horror movie. I'll never be able to get that outa my head for as long as I live," Gonzalez said.

"What about you?" he asked Simmons.

"I don't have anything as weird as that. But when I first got in country, I was assigned to the 101st unit at Da Nang. I went to the supply to get the rest of my gear. When I opened the door to the supply sergeant's office, he scared the shit outs me. I ended up staring at a .45 with a silencer attached to it. He looked at me; then motioned for me to step aside. As soon as I did, he fired the weapon. When I turned to see what he was shooting at, I realized he was shooting at these big roaches that were crawling up the wall," Simmons said.

"'That makes six so far this week,' he said. Then he asked what I wanted. I gave him my orders and he gave me my shirt and I was out of there like a shot. That guy was psycho!" he finished.

They all laughed.

Weeks prior to the battle, Tokugawa used all of his skills to persuade the powerful Mori clan to fight under his banners. To do this, he focused his attentions on the young Kobayakawa Hideaki, who had just risen to commander status. Kobayakawa was related to clans on both sides of the upcoming battle and h was having trouble deciding whom to support. Despite Tokugawa's efforts and cajoling, the young daimyo remained uncommitted and indecisive.

Date observed Tokugawa's efforts while visiting him at Edo.

He knew that the Mori clan held the keys to victory. If they remained loyal to Mitsunari, the other minor daimyos would also remain loyal. If the Mori's defected, the others would follow.

He thought that trying to persuade the young and indecisive Kobayakawa was a mistake. The man had never had to make an important decision in his life. Date wondered if he'd even show up at Sekigahara, much less choose which side to fight for.

Tokugawa wondered the same thing.

When Kobayakawa left, Date shook his head. Tokugawa shrugged.

"Do you think he'll switch sides?" Date asked.

"What do you think he'll do?" Tokugawa asked.

"I truly don't know," Date replied.

"Neither do I," Tokugawa said. "I have done all I can to persuade him. When the day comes, we will know."

He looked at the map of Sekigahara. It was the perfect place for a battle.

"This is where it will happen," he said. "This is where we will decide the fate of Japan."

"How many men will we have?" Date inquired.

"At least 60,000," Tokugawa replied. "Mitsunari will have about the same. The Moris are the key. Whichever side they choose to support will win."

"What of Kagekatsu?" asked Date.

"I expect him to strike elsewhere as a diversion. Whatever he does, I want you to keep him in check," Tokugawa said.

Date nodded.

M. was asleep in her dorm room when she sensed a presence in the room with her. Cautiously, she opened her eyes. When she did, she saw a figure seated on the floor next to her futon. She sat up.

"Who are you?" she asked in a shaky voice, afraid that someone had broken into her room to rape her or worse.

The figure turned his head and stared at her. That's when she realized he was in a military uniform. They sat and stared at each other for what seemed like an eternity, and then the soldier faded into nothingness.

M. was left shaken and scared.

Too scared to return to sleep.

"Who are you? What do you want from me?" she asked in the darkness.

The storm rolled across Japan quickly.

Furious that Kagekatsu had refused to obey him, Tokugawa demanded that he come to Kyoto and explain himself before the Emperor.

Kagekatsu's advisor, Kanatsugo Naoe, issued a condemnation of Tokugawa and accused him of defying Toyotomi Hideyoshi's rules. Several other daimyo chimed in and allied themselves with Toyotomi and Mitsunari.

And both sides began building massive armies.

Date observed these maneuverings with great interest. After a little soul searching, he broke his alliance with Toyotomi and sent a letter to Tokugawa pledging his support in the event of war. Date's support emboldened Tokugawa. He reissued his earlier demands to Kagekatsu and received the expected rebuff.

Events unfolded quickly after that and the nation plunged headlong into yet another civil war.

M. put the book down to rest her eyes. His descriptions of the events leading up to the battle were detailed and vivid. His narrative drew her into the story so thoroughly that she felt as if she were witnessing them first hand. And A. wrote like he'd been there personally.

"How could he write of our historical events as if he'd lived through them?" she wondered as she sipped her tea. "How can he make them feel so real?"

Her son entered and saw her seated in the living room. He walked over and sat down. He noticed the book on the table.

"How far have you gotten?" he asked.

"I'm up to Sekigahara," she replied.

"He's written of the battle?" he asked.

"Hai. He seems to know very particular details of the events that led up to it. It is as if he was there personally and knew each of the men involved. The battle itself goes on for many pages and it is so vivid, I could feel a katana in my hands as I read," she said.

"He has a gift for writing about battles and wars," J. said.

"This one is especially realistic," she said.

"Please allow me to read the book when you are finished," J. said.

"I will," she promised.

When he left, she returned to her reading.

Hitoribotchi no yoru

Date paced as he read Tokugawa's letter. Koinu, Buntaro and Watanabe watched and waited until the daimyo made his decision.

Date stopped pacing and looked at the messenger.

"Inform Lord Tokugawa that I will do as he asks," he said.

The messenger bowed and left the room. Date smiled at the others.

"Kagekatsu has attacked Hasebo. Lord Tokugawa has asked me to ride to Hasebo and take Kagekatsu down while he marches to meet Mitsunari's army at Sekigahara. He has also requested that I provide him with 5,000 bushi for his upcoming campaign. I want you three to join Tokugawa. I will go to Hasebo and checkmate Kagekatsu. The remainder of our men will stay here to defend Sendai," he said.

He smiled and placed a hand on both Koinu's and Watanabe's shoulders.

"Don't waste your lives or the lives of our men. If things go badly for Ieyesu, you all know what to do," he winked.

On October 21, 1600, the two great armies collided at a place called Sekigahara. The ensuing bloodbath broke the back of the Toyotomi alliance and scattered them in all directions. The great victory was followed by three more years of sporadic battles that ranged from Honshu to Kyushu. Three long years for Tokugawa to consolidate his power through war, political maneuverings, and making and breaking alliances as he saw fit.

When he felt he had assembled a large enough army, he marched them to the small valley that would become famous as the greatest and bloodiest battle ever fought on Japanese soil.

He was lying on his bunk reading a comic book when the LT walked in.

"I got this letter for you. It's from your grandmother," he said as he handed it to him.

He put the comic book down and opened the envelope. The letter was short and he smiled then laughed as he read it.

"Dear A.—

I know you're alright because Buddy keeps going to the door each day at four to wait for you to come home. Is it what you expected? You don't have to tell me anything if you don't want to. After sending five sons off to war, I understand. Just write to let me know you're okay.

Love, Ma"

He handed the letter to the LT.

"Cats know those things," the LT said. "Dogs, too."

"Ulysses had an old dog named Argus who waited 20 years for him to come after the Trojan War. I have Buddy," A. said. "You ever have any animals waiting for you?"

"I have a cat named Toby. He's been with me since high school. My wife says he's waiting for me, too. It's funny how they know," the LT said. "You planning to stay in?"

"I don't know yet," A. shrugged. "I like what I'm doing here, so I'll probably hang in until the end of the war. After that, who knows? What about you?"

"Hell, A. I'm a lifer," the LT said. "I've been in eight years. There's nothing waiting for me back in Arkansas. The Army's all I know."

"Your wife good with that?" A. asked.

"Sure," the LT said. "Hell, we met in Korea after I first enlisted. She doesn't mind that I'm a lifer. It's as good a job as any other out there."

"I'm hungry. What time is it anyway?" A. asked.

"Almost seven. If you're planning to eat, you'd better go into the village," the LT advised.

"I usually eat at the Lon Huoc Café. Care to join me?" A. offered.

"Don't mind if I do. I like that place," the LT said as they left the barracks.

M. placed the plates on the table in front of her husband and sat down across from him. He looked at each of the dishes, and then glanced up at her.

"What is this?" he asked.

"That is salmon steamed with green onions, ginger and garlic," she replied as he picked at the fish.

"And the green stuff?" he queried as he nodded at the bowl next to it.

"Spinach from America in shoyu, vinegar and brown sugar sauce," she replied.

He hesitated then helped himself. She watched as he tried a bit of the fish. He smiled and took more.

"This is quite good," he said. "In fact, you've outdone yourself this time."

"Arigato. I am glad that it pleases you. What do you mean by 'this time'?" she said.

"It's better than what you usually cook," he said.

"Oh? Are you implying that my other meals aren't any good?" she asked.

He swallowed his salmon and chose his words carefully.

"Of course they're good. I always eat what you prepare—don't I? I simply meant that this is one of your masterpieces," he said.

M. smiled.

"Are you planning to serve this to A.-san and his family when they visit us?" he asked.

"Do you think they will like it?" she asked.

"Of course they will. I think they will be very pleased and impressed by your expertise in the kitchen," he assured her. "Better this than what you normally prepare. I would not want you to poison our guests and send them to the hospital—like you did me."

"That was many years ago. It was when we were first married!" she reminded him.

"True. But that was one of your more memorable meals," he said. "Please do not make A.'s meal that memorable!"

She laughed.

She recalled watching him try valiantly to finish that abomination she'd created so as not to offend her. A half hour later, they were in a taxi cab and headed for the nearest emergency room. She thought she had nearly killed him and was more than a little mortified when they had to explain what happened to the doctors.

Even since that night, he always viewed her meals with suspicion.

"I always tell A.-san what I cook for dinner. He says my dishes sound simple and delicious and he has even prepared some of them himself. So far, he hasn't had to rush to a hospital," she said.

"He's been very fortunate," K. smiled. "But didn't you tell me he tried to eat something very hot recently that actually did send him to the hospital?"

She laughed.

"Hai. He and his best friend attempted to win a contest by eating the hottest sandwich in St. Louis. He said it was so hot, they could only finish half and it caused him great pain and suffering for the remainder of the night. It was so painful, his wife took him to the emergency room," she said. "He said he suffered no permanent damage to anything but his pride."

"That was very foolish of him. I never would have done such a thing!" K. said.

"Of course not. You are not as adventurous or daring as A.-san. I admire the fact that he tried—which most men would not have done. And I am almost sure he will attempt something like that again one day," she said.

He looked at her.

"You admire him for doing something stupid?" he asked.

"No. I admire him because he dared to try it. It shows he is alive and vital," she said. "Have you ever done anything that required great risk and courage?"

"Of course I have!" he smiled.

"Oh? And what was that, may I ask?" she queried.

"I married you!" he replied. "That took a great deal of courage! It was like jumping into a dragon's lair."

She squinted at him.

"You're calling me a dragon?" she asked.

"Well, maybe a little bit of a dragon," he hedged.

"So I'm dangerous?" she asked.

"All women are dangerous—especially very beautiful ones," he replied.

"So I'm beautiful?" she smiled.

"You were. Now, you're becoming less dangerous," he said. "I don't have to draw my katana to defend myself."

"And how on earth could you defend yourself with something that small?" she shot back.

"I only need a small katana to deal with a small lizard," he replied.

"I like dragon much better than lizard," she said. "It sounds less insulting."

"We are what we are," he said. "You are my lizard and I am your pocket knife."

They laughed.

Early in the morning of October 21, 1600, the two sides assembled on either end of the mist-shrouded field known as Sekigahara. When the fog finally dissipated at eight a.m., both sides launched their initial attacks.

Tokugawa watched as Kobayakawa arrived on the field and took up a position on the hills to the west. Tokugawa expected him to lead his 15,000 men into the battle. Instead, he just remained seated on his horse and watched the battle unfold.

Both sides had suffered horrific losses. Despite Tokugawa's best efforts, his forces were slowly being driven back. Both sides now looked to Kobayakawa. Mitsunari signaled the young commander to attack but Kobayakawa did nothing. He was still wavering.

Mitsunari again signaled.

Kobayakawa just sat there, watching.

That's when he realized that Mori clan had abandoned him. He decided that he'd teach them a harsh lesson after he dealt with Tokugawa.

Tokugawa also signaled Kobayakawa to attack. When he didn't respond, he took a gamble. He ordered his musketeers to open fire on the Mori troops to force the issue. He realized that this could have worked badly and the attack might have caused Kobayakawa to attack him.

The gunfire stirred the young commander into action and he led his fresh troops into the battle. They attacked Mitsunari's forces from the flank and all but drove them from the field. Tokugawa regrouped his forces and attacked again.

An hour later, the battle was over.

The valley was now filled with clouds of dust and smoke and the screams of the dying. Over 40,000 samurai were killed that day and Tokugawa's victorious horsemen chased after Mitsunari's fleeing troops and cut them down with a vengeance.

Mitsunari was taken prisoner and executed by an order from Tokugawa. He was not allowed to commit seppuku as befit a man of his station.

Koinu sat astride his horse and looked out upon the horrific aftermath of the battle. Bodies of dead and wounded men and horses lay everywhere in pools of their own blood. Scattered throughout were helmets, (some with heads still in them), broken banners, bits of yoroi, and battered weapons of all types and limbs that had been blown, shot or lopped off. There were thousands of bodies. Some lay three or four deep and it was nearly impossible to walk across the field without stepping on bodies.

He sat there, shaking with exhaustion and battle shock. He was unable to focus his mind on anything. Unable to process the slaughter he'd participated in. His entire body ached and he was bathed in sweat and covered with blood and dust. Even his horse was exhausted. He had loosed every last arrow and engaged countless samurai in one-on-one combat. He didn't know how many men he'd killed.

He didn't want to know.

He just sat there, trembling.

Staring.

He vaguely was aware that Tokugawa had won.

That didn't matter to him.

All that really mattered was he had survived.

After a while he was a weary-looking samurai riding slowly toward him.

"Buntaro!" he shouted. "You're alive!"

The samurai stopped and stared at him.

"I am?" he asked. "Arigato for telling me. I wasn't sure. Now this was a battle that will be written and talked about for all time. I have always dreamed of fighting in such a battle. Now that I have, I hope I never see another."

Koinu nodded.

"I've never felt so tired, so numb in my entire life," he said as they turned and rode back to Tokugawa's pavilion. "I feel as if I could sleep for days."

Along the way, they passed hundreds of battle-weary men and horses staggering across the field. Some helped wounded comrades. Some carried wounded on litters. The air was filled with the sounds of heavy, shuffling feet, coughs, moans and heavy breathing.

No one spoke.

Nor smiled.

"My father told me that I would not like war," Koinu said.

"Your father was a very wise man," said Buntaro.

When they reached the top of the hill, they saw Watanabe and Kenshin seated on the grass. Their helmets were on the ground between their legs and their horses were grazing nearby. They smiled wearily up at them as they dismounted.

"I think I'll retire after this war," Kenshin said.

Kanashimi wa hoshi no kage ni

Kagekatsu was no match for the wily Date, who not only drove him from Hasebo but chased him back to his castle at Shiroishi. Date encircled the castle and quickly destroyed it. Kagekatsu was taken prisoner and marched to Kyoto. When he was brought before Tokugawa, he immediately swore allegiance to him. Tokugawa spared his life and allowed him to rebuild Shiroishi.

"That was wise of you, Ieyesu-san," Date said.

"I learned that from you," Tokugawa smiled. "You always said to keep your friends close and your enemies closer. I don't trust Kagekatsu. I know he swore allegiance to me just to save his own skin. But he may yet prove useful to me."

He laughed.

"Besides, if I kill all of the daimyo who opposed me, there'd be no one left to rule or help maintain order. I'll just punish those who directly opposed me. The rest will fall in line rather than follow them into Heaven," he said.

"What of Toyotomi?" Date asked.

"I think I can afford to be generous there," Tokugawa said.

"Are you sure?" Date asked.

"No. Right now, he is merely a child. We'll see what happens once he becomes a man," Tokugawa said.

Tokugawa congratulated Kobayakawa for his actions during the battle and placed him at the head of the Mori clan. But the young samurai was unable to live with his betrayal of Mitsunari. A few months later, he committed seppuku.

When Tokugawa heard the news, he simply shrugged.

Kobayakawa had served his purpose.

Date cast a wary on Tokugawa's reaction. He had discarded the samurai like so much trash. True, he had elevated him to a higher station, but he showed no emotions of any kind when he learned of his suicide.

Tokugawa, he decided, is very pragmatic.

And he despised ambitious men and feared anyone he felt was strong enough to challenge him. Date was indeed strong enough, but he had no desire to rule Japan or any other place but Sendai. His only ambitions centered on survival.

Right now, Tokugawa trusted him. He was determined to maintain that trust.

True to his word, Tokugawa was generous in victory. He allowed Toyotomi Hideyori and his mother, Yodogimi, to retain their residence at Osaka Castle along with large tracts of land in three neighboring provinces. In effect, he'd put Tokugawa out to pasture. With nothing but a small contingent of samurai to protect him, he had been neutered.

But he wasn't so generous to the other daimyo who had opposed him. He confiscated the lands, castles and other properties of more than 90 rival daimyo and also greatly reduced the holdings and power of many others.

Being on the losing end of the war, they had no choice but to submit to his authority.

In 1603, the Emperor declared Tokugawa Shogun. His family would effectively rule Japan until 1868. Tokugawa's rise to power finally ended the "warring states" era in Japan and unified the nation.

Even so, pockets of resistance remained. There were other attempts on Tokugawa's life, which led to reprisals that were awesomely brutal. He also ordered all of the holdouts to be hunted down and crushed without mercy. This task fell into the hands of Koinu and others like him.

Over the next few months, he and his friends found themselves involved in so many smaller skirmishes that they felt as if they were wading through blood.

M. was working in the small garden when her friend, Y. walked up. They greeted each other then M. invited Y. inside for some iced tea and a chat. Y. had a copy of the Asahi Shimbun with her.

"How old did you say your friend is?" Y. asked.

"He is four years younger than me. Why?" M. asked.

Y. unfolded the newspaper and pointed to a photo of A. that his publisher had sent to the editor.

"He looks much younger than that!" Y. smiled.

"I know he does. He takes very good care of himself. He works out almost every night and still plays baseball with men half his age and younger. But that is the way her looks now," M. said with a touch of pride.

"And he thinks you are look much younger that you are," Y. observed.

M. blushed.

"K.-san best be careful or he may lose you to A.-san," Y. joked. "If he hasn't already lost you, that is."

M. laughed.

"Have you had any more of those dreams about him?" Y. asked.

"I had a different sort of dream last night. I saw an American soldier in a worn out uniform. He had a helmet on his head and a rifle in his hands. His face was covered with dirt and he looked like he had been in a terrible battle. The soldiers walked toward me. He had a big smile on his face as I ran to him. Then we embraced and he picked me up in his arms and carried me into my bedroom," M. said.

"How exciting and romantic!" Y. teased. "I wish I could have such dreams! Mine are so boring all the time. Did you do it in the dream?"

M. nodded.

"I could feel each deep thrust, too. I clung to his arms and moved with him and begged him to keep going. When I woke, my hand was between my legs and K. was standing in the doorway," she said. "I was so embarrassed! I didn't say anything. I just rolled over and covered myself until he left. Then I finished what I'd started."

"Did you write A.-san about it?" Y. joked.

"Hai. I told him everything," she admitted. "Then he said he would love to make all of our dreams come true one day."

"I am sure he will try to do just that when he gets here—if you let him," Y. said. "And I'm sure you will."

It was a very warm day in late August. The three samurai rode along the dirt road that wound its way into the mountains. When they came to a flight of steps cut into the hillside, they stopped. The other two watched as Koinu dismounted and climbed the steps to the small shrine atop the hill.

When he got there, he removed his dusty helmet and walked over to the small well. He picked up the ladle and scooped water from the well then poured it over his hands to purify them. Then he walked to the front of the shrine and clapped three times.

Ten minutes later, he climbed down the stairs and mounted his horse.

"I didn't know you believed in gods," Buntaro said as they continued riding.

"I usually don't," Koinu replied.

"Then why did you stop there?" asked Watanabe.

"We have just fought the hardest battle of our lives. I thought it only proper to stop and give thanks," Koinu said.

"For our victory?" Buntaro asked.

"For our survival," Koinu smiled.

"Survival? Don't you care that Lord Tokugawa won today?" Watanabe asked.

"No more than you nor any other samurai who has ever fought. I only cared about fighting well enough to survive so I can return to my wife and family," Koinu said honestly. "That's all any bushi needs to care about."

"What if Lord Tokugawa had lost?" Buntaro asked.

"That's simple. I'd have done what most bushi do when their side loses," Koinu grinned.

"Switch sides?" Buntaro asked.

"Exactly!" he replied. "Let's go home!"

As A. packed for his trip, he thought about his first wife. S. was either the right person at the wrong time or the wrong person at the right time. Either way, he met her when he was at an emotional nadir.

She was thin, sexy and sensuous and Chinese. The moment they met on a subway platform in New York, they were attracted to each other. She was older than him by eight years but that didn't matter to either of them. After a few dates, he decided to pursue her.

Or she decided to let him so she could catch him.

After a ten month courtship, A. proposed. To his delight, she accepted and they decided to get married the following month.

There was still the matter of M. They had kept in touch the entire time. But she had made him aware that he had a rival for her affections.

Since she had never told him exactly how she felt or committed herself to the relationship in any way, A. went after S.

It proved to be a decision he would later regret—in spades.

M. didn't know this.

When A. told her he was getting married, the news almost tore the heart from her chest. She cried and cried for days on end when she realized her mistake. She never did have the courage to call him and tell him she loved him and she wanted to marry him.

She didn't realize that had she done so, he would have broken off his engagement and flown to Japan to marry her. Maybe he didn't realize this himself at that time.

But by the time he'd realized his mistake two years later, M. was already married. She had given herself to another man; even though it was A. she really wanted. She wrote him off as a lost cause and attempted to move on with her life as best as she could.

And each time she looked up at the drawing on her bedroom wall, she wept in silence for what might have been…

The marriage was stormy and passionate at times. A. and S. had their ups and downs. The downs were becoming more and more frequent as their relationship unraveled. After 19 years, he divorced S. and married R.

M.'s husband died in an auto accident while driving home drunk from his favorite club. Neither she nor her son, J., missed him.

It was about that time she had accidentally discovered A.'s novels online. She was feeling lost and bored one night and went online to kill time. As a lark, she typed his name into the search bar. To her surprise, hundreds of references appeared. All had to do with novels he'd written, too. She searched deeper. One search led her to his web site. It listed all of his novels and had an order link. She clicked the link on the first novel and decided to buy it.

It was just before dawn as the column of mounted samurai approached the small, secluded village in the mountains near Yunohira.

At the head of the column rode Koinu, Buntaro and Watanabe.

As they rode through the mist shrouded field, they became nervous. On either side of the road were dozens of corpses tied upside-down to cross shaped boards. The crosses lent the area an eerie, almost terrifying atmosphere. The rolling morning mist served to heighten that effect

Koinu noticed that each dead man bore horrific wounds. Most were deep gashes. They looked rough and slovenly. Although some wore pieces of yoroi, they could tell they weren't samurai.

"Bandits?" he asked.

Buntaro nodded.

"Most likely, they scavenged the yoroi and weapons from battlefields. Or some might have been bushi of a defeated daimyo. They probably made their living plundering small villages like this one," he said.

"It looks like they chose the wrong village," Watanabe said.

"Definitely!" Koinu said.

When they entered the village itself, the streets looked deserted. The doors and window of each building were shut tight, yet they all felt as if a hundred eyes were on them each step of the way. The quiet made them more nervous. They stopped in the middle of the village.

Buntaro stood in his stirrups and shouted for the villagers to come out and show themselves. Then he sat down. They waited.

And waited.

The doors of several buildings slid open. They watched, hands on katana hilts, as the villagers emerged one-by-one. The men were ragged and weary looking. They were armed, too.

Some carried pikes and naginata. Some carried spears. A few had yumi across their backs. Some had pitchforks and hatchets. A few even wore helmets or breastplates. The women and children also emerged. They looked worn out, as if they hadn't slept for a few nights.

All were dirty.

Tired.

Fed up.

An older man, dressed in full yoroi, strode toward them. Ten feet away, he stopped and bowed his head respectfully.

"We came out because we saw you are not bandits—like these others," he said as he nodded at the men on the crosses.

"Of course we aren't bandits. We are samurai. What is this place called?" Koinu asked.

"Yufuin," the man said. "Who do you serve?"

"We serve Lord Date Masamune. He serves the Shogun," Buntaro said.

"Then you are most welcome here. All of you," the man said graciously.

"What of them?" Koinu asked as he pointed back at the slain bandits.

"Those fools came here three days ago and demanded all of our food, our money and our women. They got butchered instead. We put them up there as a warning to other would-be marauders," the man said as they followed him into the largest structure.

"This is my ryokan. I came here because of the onsen. I decided to retire here and I had this ryokan built to earn some extra money," he said.

He smiled at the three of them.

"You and your men are welcome to stay and refresh yourselves here. We have an onsen in back of the ryokan. Please feel free to make use of it," he said. "I know what it is to be a samurai. I know how you feel after a hard-fought battle. I used to be a samurai. In fact, I also served Lord Date. But that was almost ten years ago," he said.

"What is your name?" Buntaro asked.

"Shimizu Hideyoshi," the man said. "And yours?"

They introduced themselves.

"Many of us old samurai have retired here," Shimizu said. "Many active samurai also have their houses here. Even though all of the young men are off fighting in the war, those bandits learned that we "retired" bushi have not allowed or skills to decline with age. They never stood a chance."

Buntaro laughed.

"Maybe you should come back and serve Lord Date again," he suggested.

"Even though I am retired, I still serve Lord Date," Shimizu replied. "This time, it was mostly indirectly."

The Montagnards, which is French for mountain dwellers, occupied a large swath of the Central Highlands from Saigon in the south to Da Nang in the north. Their territory was just east of the Laos-Cambodian border and they considered themselves to be separate from the Vietnamese, whom they disliked.

They lived in neatly arranged villages of stilted hooches. Each village had a longhouse where they met to discuss things that affected them or to hold ceremonies. Although each village was led by an Elder or chief, everyone had a say in how to run things.

The Montagnards had been mostly Christianized by missionaries, but many still clung to their old tribal religions or practice a blend of both.

No one knew exactly how many Montagnards there were or how many villages they had. The Vietnamese called the "moi" (savages) and avoided dealing with them for the most part. There were more than dozen Montagnard tribes and they even had a "capital city" called Ban Me Thout.

The Americans considered them to be their most loyal allies in Vietnam and trusted them completely. In the early part of the war, Special Forces teams trained the Montagnards and provided them with modern weapons and even uniforms to counter the VC who had been trying to force the Montagnards to fight for the Communists. Their "recruiting" methods only made the Montagnards despise them even more.

The Rhadi tribesmen were especially loyal and tough. They were tenacious fighters and completely ruthless in combat. And the Montagnards never took prisoners unless the Americans asked them to.

This particular village belonged to the Sedang tribe.

It sat on a high point overlooking a river about 20 miles from base camp. Although A. had seen several of the Sedang in the village near the camp, this was his first visit to a Montagnard village.

The village was surrounded by a high stockade fence. It had two gates. One faced the river. The other the mountains in the opposite direction.

"The fence serves two purposes," the LT said. "The first is to keep the livestock in. The second is to keep Charlie out."

As they approached the fence, A. noticed that the area appeared to be eerily quiet. He felt as if hundreds of pairs of eyes were watching his every step.

"Neither Charlie nor the NVA fuck with the Montagnards," the LT said. "That's why."

He pointed to the four bloated bodies dangling upside down from the cross beam of the gate. Their ankles were secured with heavy ropes. Two were headless. All looked as if they'd been through meat grinders.

"These people despise the VC more than anyone. They hunt them down and kill them on sight. I've heard that even the Japs didn't fuck with them during World War II," the LT said as they drew closer.

"What about their women?" asked one of the new guys.

"They're shy and cute. And they're off limits. If you mess with one of their women, you'd better be ready to get married on the spot and settle down," the LT said.

"And if we don't want to?" the guy asked.

Simmons nodded at the bodies above.

"You end up like them," he said.

The village was very neat and picturesque. There were about 40 or so neat hooches up in stilts. They had thatched roofs and one large opening that served as a door and four windows for ventilation. They did their cooking outside on communal fires and pigs and caribou roamed freely. As did their children who rushed toward them the second they entered the village.

The men gave the kids candy, a few small toys and other things as they walked happily and noisily beside them. A. took out his camera and snapped several photos of the village and a few of the woman in their colorful dresses. The men wore loin cloths or shorts. Some had shirts. A few sported the traditional head cloths. A. spotted a half dozen men in camouflage uniforms, hats and jungle boots. Each carried an M-14 or M-16 and bandoliers with ammo cartridges.

One walked up to the LT. The shook hands.

"Hello, Ben," he said.

"Hello, LT. Long time no see. Is this a social call or are you after something?" Ben asked as they walked toward the large central hooch called a longhouse.

Several dozen of the Sedang men were gathered outside. All were armed with rifles, crossbows or spears. A few had painted their faces. A. thought they resembled Apache warriors from the American southwest.

A burly man dressed in an elaborate head cloth came out of the longhouse. He saw the LT and waved for them to come inside.

"What's up, Ben?" the LT asked.

"You'll see when you get inside," Ben replied as they walked up the wooden steps.

The longhouse was darker and cooler. The men sat down with their backs against the walls while Ben, the LT and the chief talked. While they watched, four Sedang women passed out cups containing a milky liquid. A. sniffed it.

"Durian juice," he said as he drank it down.

The woman who gave it to him seemed surprise that he liked it. She refilled his cup immediately and smiled. He watched her walk away and smiled as he drank.

"You really like this stuff?" Simmons asked.

"Yeah. This stuff is great once you get used to it," A. said.

Simmons watched him drink and followed his example.

"You're right. It's not bad at all," he agreed.

After a half hour or so, the LT came back. A. handed him a cup of the juice. The LT gulped it down and wiped his lips with the back of his hand.

"The chief told me that his men captured a VC just outside the village. Actually, there were five. You already know what they did to the first four," he said.

"Why'd they take this one alive?" asked George.

"So we can interrogate him," Ben replied with an almost evil grin. "I was about to start when you guys arrived. Now that you're here, you can watch."

They followed Ben and the chief outside and watched as four Sedang warriors dragged a badly bruised VC across the open ground to two poles standing side-by-side. They tied his ankles and wrists to the poles and stepped aside so Ben, the LT and the chief could approach the prisoner.

They watched as Ben rammed his rifle but into the VC's ribs as he asked a question. When he didn't answer, they took turns punching him in the face and kicking him in the balls. The LT would shout a question. Every non-answer elicited a violent response.

"Looks like their playing 20 questions with that bozo," Simmons said.

"I'm sure glad I'm not him!" A. said as they watched the beating continue.

No one cared how brutally VC captives were treated. Most didn't survive the interrogations anyway. Since Charlie liked to torture and rape innocent civilians and never took prisoners, no one gave a shit how they were treated. In war, mercy begat mercy. Brutality was answered with even more brutality.

A few minutes later, Ben and the LT turned away from the VC who hung limply from the ropes on his wrists.

"What you find out?" asked Simmons.

"Maybe. Troy, get home base on the horn for me now. I know the perfect way to find out if our prisoner told us the truth," he said.

Troy unpacked the radio and called HQ. When he got someone who sounded like he was in charge, he passed the phone to the LT. The LT took out his map and read off a series of coordinates.

"You got that?" he asked. "Read it back to make sure. That's it. How soon can you make the drop?"

He smiled and tossed the phone back to Troy.

"You might as well relax for a while, men. Kick back, eat and watch the show," he said.

They found shady spots to rest under. A. opened a can of peaches and leaned against a tree to eat. As he did, the woman who had served him the durian juice earlier, came over to him with a large wooden cup and a bowl of boiled rice. She placed it down in front of him.

"You eat now," she said.

As he ate, he watched the children playing a game that resembles soccer. At least a gang of them were kicking this large, red, rubber ball around in between two hooches while their parents watched from the porches.

He didn't care what the Vietnamese thought of them. The Sedang certainly weren't moi.

That's when he heard the jest fly over. He stopped eating and watched as they swooped low over the jungle and dumped their cargo about six miles from the village. A few minutes later, he was the balls of flame and black smoke mushroom over the tree line. Seconds later, the jets made a second pass and did it again.

He was glad the village was downwind from the napalm.

Immediately after, Ben and his group, accompanied by at least 50 Sedang warriors raced out of the village and in the direction of the napalm smoke. The LT sat down next to A.

"We going with them, LT?" he asked.

"There's no need. We'd only slow those people down. If any VC lived through that, Ben and his men will make them wish they hadn't," the LT said.

He stood up and raised his voice so the others could hear him.

"Settle down and get some sleep, men. We saddle up at sunrise," he said. He sat back down under the tree and pulled his helmet down over his eyes. A. finished his meal and did the same.

The Sedang returned to the village just before sunrise and were greeted by the rest of the villagers with shouts of joy and victory. The LT woke and walked over to Ben. Half of his men now carried Ak-47s and lots of ammo they had taken from the VC.

The LT laughed, slapped Ben on the back to congratulate him and walked back to the platoon.

"Ben told me they killed 23 VC and the chief has called for a celebration. He also insisted that we stay to celebrate with them. Since we are to maintain good relations with these people, I accepted his invitation. I'm sure you guys won't mind staying for the party," he said.

Kanashimi wa tsuki no kage ni

Watanabe turned to Koinu.

"There are woman there and sake. Please join us," he said.

"You two go ahead. I'll wait until we home. M.-san is the only woman I need or want," Koinu said.

"If she's that good, maybe I'll give her a try," Watanabe joked.

"You do and Koinu will cut your dick off!" Buntaro said.

Koinu laughed.

"I won't have to. M.-san is very good with a katana. She'll slice it off as soon as you take it out," he said.

They all laughed.

"She must be a very special lady," Watanabe said.

"She's the best," Koinu said.

"You're a lucky man," Buntaro stated.

"I know," Koinu smiled.

M. smiled as she read the passage.

Koinu's love for his M. was boundless. While she lived and breathed, there could be no other woman in his life. Not even for a second.

And he knew she felt the same about him.

Complete trust and a deep, strong love. It made them strong. It made them feel alive.

She wondered if that was another subtle message he'd written for her benefit. Was this his way of telling her that this is the way it would have been?

She sighed.

She put down the book and walked to the window. It was raining again and quite hard. In fact, there wasn't even a trace of sunshine anywhere.

"If this is what you felt back then, then why didn't you propose to me? Why did you give up like that?" she asked as she looked up at the clouds.

She shook her head.

The questions were rhetorical.

And stupid.

She already knew the answers anyway.

"You got a girlfriend, A.?" George asked as they walked the perimeter to check the mines.

"Not really," A. replied as he stooped and turned a mine around.

When he'd set it a week earlier, it was faced toward the jungle. The mine had been turned toward the camp. A sure indication that Charlie was in the neighborhood. He got up, looked around and smiled.

"I know you're out there, assholes," he said under his breath.

"What do you mean by not really?" asked George. "You either have one or you don't. So which is it?"

"When you put it that way, I guess I don't," A. said.

"I bet you'll have one before you leave this place," George said. "It wouldn't surprise me if you married one of these little honeys and took her home with you. You gotta admit they look real sexy in those dresses."

"I can't argue with that," A. agreed. "Those slit dresses are certainly attention-getters. They leave just enough to the imagination to make it interesting, too."

"Roger that!" George said. "So, when are you going to go out and get yourself one of them?"

"I don't know, man. I'm too damned young to even worry about that. I'm not interested in any romantic entanglements," A. said.

"We'll see," George grinned.

"It ain't going to happen," A. said.

"I'll bet you fifty bucks it does," George challenged.

"Deal!" A. said as they shook hands. "You realize, of course, this is a sucker's bet?"

"Yeah. And you're the sucker who's going to pay me!" George avowed.

Koinu and Buntaro stood on the wall and watched as a company of young, faceless bushi lined up in the courtyard below as their captain barked orders.

"Replacements," Koinu said.

"Oh? And who have they come to replace?" asked Buntaro.

Koinu smiled.

"Us-if we fail to survive our next battle," he said.

They watched as the captain put them through their paces and reminded them of their oath to Lord Date and of the code they served under. Most were around 20 years old. Some were younger. They would be trained in the mist basic fighting techniques. It would be up to them to improve upon that.

Most would never get that chance.

"Are any of them from important families" Buntaro asked.

"Maybe a handful," Koinu said. "Most have joined us to escape poverty or life on the farms. Some are here to make names for themselves. Most will die in the next battle instead."

"And more will come to replace them," Buntaro sighed. "Oh, well. There's a certain glory to dying in battle."

Koinu smiled.

"There's no glory in death. Death is just death. It doesn't matter how we die. All that matters is how well we're remembered and by whom," he said.

"And dying gloriously in battle is the best way to be remembered," Buntaro said.

Koinu laughed.

"You're impossible!" he said.

Simmons, George and A. watched as a group of fresh-faced kids got off the bus and lined up. A. smiled.

"Looks like we've got some fresh meat today," he said.

"Yeah. Fresh meat for the grinder," Simmons said.

The kids, as they were referred to, were between the ages of 18 and 22. There were 16 of them, fresh out of AIT, too. Their uniforms were still neat and almost spotless. Hell, even their boots were spit polished.

"What do we have here?" asked another squad member who had just arrived.

"Replacements," A. said.

"Yeah? Who are they replacing?" he asked.

"Us—if we get stupid out there," A. said with a smile.

One of the newbies was a Midwestern kid named Johnson. He was fresh out of infantry school and looked almost awed by being in country. A. walked over and shook his hand as he introduced himself.

"Glad to meet you, A.," Johnson said.

"Since you're new, I'd better show you the ropes," A. said. "This isn't Kansas and there's no Oz. We got the NVA and Charlie and there's a big difference between the two. I'll show you where to bunk and what to do so you don't go home in a trash bag."

"Thanks. I really appreciate that," Johnson said as he followed him to the barracks.

Over the next two weeks, A. showed Johnson everything he'd learned since he arrived at base camp and showed him around the village. A couple of the other new guys tagged along. A. told them everything Simmons and the LT had told him and warned them about the booby traps, spider holes and how not to piss off the locals.

"These are good people. You treat them with respect and respect their culture and they'll be your best friends for life. Piss them off and they'll throw you under a bus. They have no use for assholes and neither do I," A. said.

The kids, as A. called them, were fast learners. If they had any questions, they asked him or the LT. The CO saw this and called A. into his office.

"Thanks for taking care of the new guys. The LT assign them to you?" he asked.

"No. I just thought they should know how to act out here," A. said.

"Any look like trouble?" he asked.

"No, Sir. I think they'll do just fine if they pay attention to shit around them," A. answered.

"Since you're so good at this, I'm going to have you take care of all of our replacements from now on. That okay with you?" the CO asked.

"No problem. I'll be glad to do it," A. agreed.

"I have to confess that I had my doubts about you when you first came here. You've proven yourself time and again and the locals love you. You're a damned good soldier, A. And a fine human being," the CO smiled.

"I know you don't hear this much, but I enjoy being here," A. said.

"You gunning for a Section 8?" the CO asked.

"No. I really do like it here," A. said.

"Wanna know a secret? So do I!" the CO smiled. "So do Simmons and George. They're both on their second tour here. Most of our guys are volunteers. I think only a handful of them were drafted. This place gets under a man's skin. It makes you feel alive 24-7. Where else can you feel like that?"

"Noplace I've ever been," A. agreed.

"You plan on staying in?" the CO asked.

"I'm considering it," A. replied.

"If you decide to stay in, I'd like to be the one re-upping you," the CO said.

"I wouldn't have it any other way," A. said.

Koinu looked at Date.

"Why can't I go?" he asked.

"You would be away from home for several years. You might even be lost at sea. I don't want to sit and watch your wife worry herself sick about you while you're gone. Besides, I value your counsel too much. You are one of the few I know I can trust. I know that you have my back as I have yours. I need you here, not running around Europe as part of the trade expedition," Date said.

When put in such a manner, he could hardly argue or feel slighted. Date's explanation made him feel honored.

Date paced awhile, then stopped and sat beside him.

This showed that the daimyo considered him not only a friend, but an equal.

"Trade commissions are for diplomats and ass kissers. You are samurai. Such a long, tedious trip would bore the life from you," he said.

Then he winked.

"And I really don't want you to leave M.-san alone here. Not with all of these wolves around," he joked. "Even though I am certain that anyone who attempted to seduce her would be quickly neutered!"

They laughed.

"She doesn't want me to go, either," Koinu said.

"There you have it! You cannot go against her wishes. That would bring you nothing but bad karma," Date said.

They rose and he walked him to the door.

"You and M.-san will dine with us tonight. My wife insists, so you must accept the invitation. If you don't, you will upset her. When she becomes upset, she makes me upset. That would not go very well for you," Date said.

"In that case, we will be honored to join you. What time shall we arrive?" Koinu asked.

"Come at five—and please be prompt," Date smiled.

Two weeks later, Date's trade commission, headed by his retainer Hasekawa Tsunenaga and the Jesuit priest, Padre Sotelo, whose release Date had obtained from one of Tokugawa's jails, set sail for Rome on the newly built Date Maru. The Date Maru had a crew of 180. Sotelo carried with him a letter from Date to Pope Paul V, asking to open better trade and diplomatic relations. It was the most daring, audacious and highly successful expedition ever launched by a daimyo.

The Date Maru made stops in the Philippines, Mexico, Spain and Rome and became the first Japanese expedition to circumnavigate the globe.

"I don't fear gaijin or their ideas. I embrace them. I take from them what I can use for my own purposes and discard the rest," he explained. "You should do the same, Koinu-san. Always be aware of who and what you are, but keep your mind open to new ideas and technologies. If you don't, you'll be bitten in the ass by them later."

M. smiled.

K. noticed her expression and asked about it.

"It's the way he describes things. People. Places and even conversations. He writes about such things as if he knew them personally. He seems to be very insightful when it comes to Date's personality. He brings him to life," she explained.

"Really?" K. asked.

She nodded.

"He has even written about Date's trade commission. Our own history books don't even mention that," she said.

K. nodded.

"How did he know?" he asked.

"How does he know anything? He writes as if he was there to witness it all," she said. "Are you going to read the book when I'm finished?"

"Perhaps. Your comments have made me very curious," K. said.

Date's wife had developed a very close friendship with M. Upon observation, Date decided they were very much alike.

Like mother and daughter.

His wife, in turn, said that Koinu reminded her of him when he was younger. Date saw this, too, and had also developed a close friendship with Koinu. Since both Koinu's parents and M.'s were dead, Date sort of adopted them. His wife had no objections to this, either.

"M.-san is like a fresh breeze compared to all of the other wives I've met," she said. "She has a wonderful personality and I adore her frankness and sense of humor."

Date nodded.

"She reminds me of you in many ways. You were never afraid to speak your mind or wield your sarcasm like a katana. So it's only natural that you and she would become friends," he said.

The Dates took the news of M.s pregnancy with great joy. Date's wife hugged them both, and then Date invited Koinu to sit and drink with him.

"So, you are about to make me a grandfather," he said with a grin. "Now you definitely can't go on that trip. Since you will soon be a father, I'm promoting you and raising your pay."

"That is very generous of you, Masamune-san," Koinu said as they toasted each other with sake.

"Not at all. As you will soon discover, children are expensive and the first is often quickly followed by others. You will need the extra money. By raising your pay, I'm making sure that you don't leave because you need more money."

Ue o muite arukou

The new 2nd LT walked to the village with A. and S. When they came to a wooden bride that spanned a sluggish stream, the 2ndLT walked across it. A. and Simmons walked across the stream instead. The 2nd LT watched them and waited on the other side until they crossed.

"How come you guys walked through that stream?" he asked.

"We walked through the stream because the bridge might be booby trapped," Simmons replied.

"Or not," A. added with a grin.

The 2ndLT laughed. But he knew they were right. Here in Nam, one should never take things at face value. Not even the people. They used the bridge as an example. It was their way of showing him to keep his eyes open.

"Thanks, guys," he said. "I needed that."

"You just got here, Mike. I don't want to have to ship you home in a black bag," A. said. "Watch us. Learn from us and just maybe, we'll all get home alive."

"I'll do that," the 2ndLT said.

The kid was fresh out of ROTC. He was sent to Nam with little or no practical training. A. felt sorry for kids like him. ROTC officers were treated like shit by the West Pointers and field officers. And nobody seemed to give a rat's ass if they survived.

When A. and Simmons saw the 2nd LT, or "butter bar" as they were called, he knew the kid felt lost. So they decided to teach him the ropes. They always tried to help the new guys any way they could. After all, they were all in this together.

"What's your MOS, A.?" the 2nd LT asked.

"I'm a 73 Quebec," he replied.

"What's that?" the 2nd LT asked.

"Journalist," A. said. "I write dispatches for Star and Striped and UPI. I take photos whenever practical."

"Any of your stuff get printed?" the 2nd LT asked.

"Some," A. said.

"Do they change anything?" the 2nd LT asked.

"Hell yeah! Those left wing editors at UPI twist everything around to make it sound like we're the bad guys out here. I hardly recognize anything after they print it. That shit pisses me off, too. The press back home is doing a real hatchet job on what we do here. According to them, everyone out here is a dope smoking slacker who goes around raping women and killing innocent civilians. We're all nut jobs. It's nothing like that at all," A. ranted.

The 2nd LT laughed.

"Sounds like I hit sore spot," he remarked.

"Sore and infected," A. said. "Those so-called journalists back home are a disgrace to my profession. They're going to cost us this war, too, because the morons who read and hear that shit actually believe it."

"Do you really think we can win this war?" the 2nd LT asked.

"That all depends on your definition of winning," A. replied. "We win if we get home alive. These people here win when this freaking war comes to an end. If you ask the locals, they don't care which side wins. They just want to live their lives in peace."

"This is really a civil war, Mike. Somehow or other, we ended up in the middle of this shit and no one's ever been able to explain why to my satisfaction," Simmons added.

"As far as Ho's concerned, he's just trying to kick out another colonial power and unify Vietnam. To him, we're no better than the French. Those people don't hate us. They really don't want to kill us any more than we want to kill them. They just want us gone," A. explained.

"The CO told me that you enlisted and insisted on coming here. That true?" the 2nd LT asked.

"It's true," A. said.

"Why in Hell did you do that?" he asked.

"I come from a long line of soldiers. We go all the way back to 12th century Germany. But I'll say this, I sure as Hell hope I'm the last one in my line who ever goes to war," A. said.

His grandmother watched as A.'s cat, Buddy, woke up and stretched. He then jumped from the couch and walked over to the door and sat down.

It was four p.m.

Each day at this exact time, Buddy waited by the front door for A. to come home. Just as he'd been doing since A. brought him home as a kitten years ago. A, and Buddy were inseparable. She knew that Buddy would wait by the door for one hour, then give up and wander into A. s room. Each night, he curled up an A.'s pillow, as if he were keeping it safe for him.

She smiled.

She knew that as long as Buddy waited at the door each day, A. was safe.

Koinu knelt beside the futon and beamed as he cradled his new-born son. M. smiled up at him.

"What shall we name him?" Koinu asked.

"I have named him Hiroshi," she replied.

He laughed. It was her father's name.

"So you've named him without first consulting me? He teased.

"I didn't think you'd mind," she said.

He laughed again.

"I don't," he said as he looked into the baby's eyes. "Konnichiwa, Hiroshi-chan!"

Hiroshi replied with a belch.

He stood in the delivery room and watched as his son pushed his way out of R.'s vagina. The doctor picked him up, snipped the umbilical cord, and handed the boy to him. A. held him close and swelled with pride. The nurse handed him the birth certificate. He cradled the baby in his left arm, looked at the certificate, and filled CSW in the name blank.

As he did so, he had the strangest feeling that he'd gone through this before, but in another place. Another time. He handed the boy back to the nurse, kissed his wife on the forehead and staggered home in the bitter December cold.

It had been a very long night.

When he got home, he picked up the phone and called his wife's family in Manila to tell them good news. The he fell into a deep sleep...

When word reached Kyoto that Toyotomi Hideyori had refortified Osaka Castle, Tokugawa took notice but did nothing. But when word got out that the young daimyo was recruiting an army of ronin and assorted enemies of the Shogunate, Tokugawa called it an act of treason.

He amassed a force of 164,000 men and marched on Osaka to deal with the upstart. Among them were Kagekatsu and Date.

Toyotomi wasn't worried.

He had one of the best generals and strategists in Japan on his side, the almost legendary Sanada Yakimara, whom he put in command of all of his armies.

On November 19, 2015, Tokugawa personally led a force of 3,000 across Kizu River to attack a small fort Toyotomi had constructed there. The fort fell quickly. The following week, Tokugawa's forces attacked the village of Imafaku and burnt it to the ground.

For the next three weeks, Tokugawa's Easter Army took several more small forts and villages and the ring around Osaka gradually tightened.

Toyotomi had constructed a strong earthwork wall around most of the castle. It was here that Yakimara placed his 7,000 men. Tokugawa attacked the earthworks three times. Each time, they suffered heavy losses and were forced to retreat.

Tokugawa then realized the castle could not be taken that way. He brought up over 300 artillery pieces and began pounding the castle with shells. On January 22nd, asked for a truce and promised he would not rise up in rebellion against Tokugawa again.

To ensure this, Tokugawa ordered that his outer walls be demolished and that the moat surrounding the castle be filled in.

This didn't last.

In the spring, Toyotomi began recruiting an even larger army and sent his troops out to halt the filling in of the moat. Tokugawa was enraged.

He became even more enraged when Toyotomi launched a series of attacks against Tokugawa's forces that were stationed near Osaka.

The entire Kansai region became awash in blood. Battle after brutal battle erupted that left the countryside in ruins and the ground littered with bodies. The fighting spilled into villages and even the city of Osaka itself.

Date found himself once more in the thick of things.

On June 2nd, his forces tangled with Sanada's during the fiercely-fought battle of Domyoji. Date's men mauled Sanada's forces and forced them to retreat toward Osaka Castle. Neither Date nor the other Tokugawa commanders bothered to pursue him as they were too busy licking their own wounds.

The Summer Campaign, as it was called, came to a head during the ill-fated and badly run battle of Tennoji. The Eastern Army was led by Tokugawa's son Hidetada who had assumed the Shogunate in 1605 but still fell under his father's shadow and influence. The Western Army was commanded by Toyotomi Hideyori himself.

A series of misread signals and tactical blunders almost sent the battle into chaos. During the battle, Sanada was killed and news of his death totally demoralized his men, who began fleeing the battlefield. Toyotomi ordered them to fall back to the castle.

This time, Tokugawa pursued and the castle fell hours later and was put to the torch.

Toyotomi committed seppuku. His son, Kunimatsu, age 8, was captured and beheaded in Kyoto by order of Hidetada. His daughter, Naahime, was spared and she later became a nun.

This ended all major opposition to the Tokugawa Shogunate.

But pockets of resistance still lingered in remote places. And those pockets had to be eradicated.

Another patrol.

This time, they followed an obscure, narrow foot path south and west of the camp. The path led them up a gentle slope and down into a shaded glen of close-knit trees and mosquitoes. The damned things were everywhere in Vietnam. A. never got used to them, either.

And he hated them.

Not a day went by that he didn't get bitten.

The path ended at a small cluster of apparently long-abandoned huts. The LT held up his fist and pointed. A., Simmons and Gonzalez went to the left. The LT and the others circled to the right. They moved slowly and watched the ground for mines, trip wires and punji pits. Charlie had once occupied this place.

Word had it that he had returned.

They checked the grounds for an hour. The LT found a spider hole next to one of the huts. He pulled the cover away and tossed an incendiary grenade down into it. He and the others stepped back and watched it go off.

Nothing.

"Check it out," he told Cruz.

Cruz nodded and jumped into the hole. He came out a few seconds later.

"Nothing," he said. "It looks like it hasn't been used for a while."

The others assembled around the hole.

"Let's torch this place. Burn everything to the ground. Leave nothing behind for Charlie to make use of," he ordered.

They tossed incendiaries into each of the huts. The old, dry timbers went up quickly and became totally consumed by the flames. Within minutes, the entire cluster was on fire and the sky above became tainted by the clouds of white and black smoke.

They watched it burn for a little while, and then headed back to camp.

"How did that place become a ghost town?" A. asked.

"We went in there a year ago to flush a bunch of VC out. It took us a couple of hours. When it was over, they had two dozen dead and we had five wounded. Then I had one of the locals spread the word that the place was haunted so nobody would try to live there again. They're real superstitious, so it worked.

There were a lot more huts there at the time. We burned most of them down," the LT explained.

"Any civilians get killed?" A. asked.

The LT shrugged.

"When you're dealing with VC, you can never be sure. You just go in and kill anyone who points a weapon at you. Sometimes, even that doesn't work," he said. "In cases like that, you just have to hope you make the right decisions, but the primary thing is to make sure you get your men in and out alive."

"You ever make the wrong decision?" A. asked.

"I hope not—but then again, I don't dwell on that shit, either. If you let it get to you, you'll go nuts," the LT replied.

When they got back to camp, A. saw Flynn seated on the steps of the hut that he used for a chapel. As usual, he was drinking beer. He walked over and sat beside him. Flynn handed him a cold one.

"You drink a lot for a priest," A. smiled.

"I wasn't always a priest. Certain habits carry over," Flynn said. "I'm Irish. We like to drink. It's part of our genetic makeup."

He laughed.

"How as the patrol?" asked Flynn.

"Nothing special. We just put the torch to an abandoned village," A. said.

"I know the place you're talking about," Flynn said. "I was there when we drove the VC out. That was a nasty little fight, too. I went there for moral support and ended up fighting. It wasn't the first time. I'm sure it won't be the last."

"Father Flynn: Warrior Priest. That'd make a good title for a movie," A. said.

"I'm sure they'll make lots of movies about this war when it's over. Most of them will a pack of lies written by people who were never here," Flynn mused.

"Like history itself," A. said.

Flynn nodded.

"What do you hope to get out of this?" he asked.

"I thought I knew when I first came here. Now, I'm not sure," A. admitted. "What about you?"

"The same," Flynn said. "Maybe memories?"

"Good or bad?" asked A.

"Both," Flynn said. "Vietnam will remain a part of me for the rest of my life. Yours, too. You can't just forget about it, A. This will either toughen or break you. There's no middle ground."

K. and M. sat in front of the TV watching the movie "Platoon". As the movie progressed, M. imagined A. as the "good sergeant". That would be the character he would identify with. The others were too extreme.

K. turned to her.

"Your friend was in Vietnam?" he asked.

"Hai," she replied.

"How much did he tell you about it?" he asked.

"He told me much but not everything," she replied.

"Was he ever in a battle?" K. asked.

"He told me that he had been in two battles," she said. "One was very bad."

"Did he kill anyone?" K. asked.

"He said that he didn't know. He also said that he didn't want to know and he always hoped that he didn't," she replied.

"You said he volunteered, didn't you?" he asked.

She nodded.

"He said he felt it was his duty," she replied.

He nodded.

"The more I learn about your friend, the more I respect him," K. said. "I am starting to understand why he fascinates you now. He is very different from other gaijin you've met, isn't he?"

"Very much so," she said. "I have never known anyone like him. I feel that his wife is a very lucky woman."

"Is my wife also a very lucky woman?" he asked.

"I think so—but in a different way," she said with a smile.

R. was fairly oblivious to A.s past. She did know that he'd bee to Vietnam, but didn't know any of the details of his stay. This was fine with A. S. didn't know, either. That didn't matter at the time and it didn't matter now.

He'd gone there and returned in one piece.

That's all that mattered.

She did know about M.—both of them. And of course she knew about S. And she was jealous of all of them. A. like the fact she was jealous, too. It let him know there was still a lot of love and passion in their marriage. She was especially jealous of M. at first. But she was married for a long, long time and was a grandmother. So, she didn't feel really threatened by her anymore.

She knew that A. like her a lot and she liked him.

But they were just internet "pen pals". Still, that's how he'd met the first M. and her.

As for his past—she figured she knew all she needed to know about that. She was more concerned with the here and now and their future. The past was already gone forever and no longer mattered.

Koinu was sitting on the front steps of their house polishing his katana with a white cloth when M. walked out.

"Must we attend the funeral?" M. asked as wrapped her arms around him.

"We have to. Lord Date said that since he and his family are attending, we all must attend it. He said we should think of it as an honor to attend the funeral of such an important man. Of course he almost laughed when he said that."

"Did you like the Shogun?" she asked as she sat in his lap.

"I respected him—and that's all I'll say on the matter," he replied.

"Ah, so you didn't like him?" she asked.

He smiled.

"He was a difficult man to like. He always wore his yoroi. He was always too consumed with his self-image. No one really got close enough to know what he was really like. I don't think his own family ever knew him well. He was distant.

And arrogant," he said with some thought.

"You like Masamune-san," she teased.

"Hai. I like and respect him. He has his flaws and he does not put on false face to hide them. He is who he is and he's a survivor. That's not easy in these times," he said.

He looked into her eyes.

"But there's no one else on earth or in Heaven that I love, respect or need more than you," he smiled. "I am very fortunate that you chased after me when you did."

M. thought about that afternoon in her house. A. had come to visit her after she got home from school. As they chatted, they heard a motorcycle outside. They went to the window and A. saw her parents pull up in front of the house.

"Your parents are dressed kind of formally. Where have they been?" he asked.

Unsure of the English word, she picked up her dictionary. After shuffling through a few pages, she pointed to 'funeral'.

"Soshiki" she said.

They went down to greet them. Her father saw him and smiled. He knew he had come all the way to Yufuin just to see his daughter. After a brief almost chat, he and M. went for a walk, during which he tried to teach her his language and she tried to teach him hers.

She smiled.

They were both so shy then. So awkward.

And so very young.

She sipped her iced tea and continued reading.

Tokugawa Ieyesu had been appointed Shogun by the emperor 13 years earlier. Actually, the emperor had little choice in the matter. Tokugawa had already seized control over much of the country by crushing his would-be challengers in a series of bloody battles.

Now that he was dead, his third and most pragmatic son, Hidetada, would succeed him—as per the late Shogun's wishes. Hidetada was well respected. Like his father, he was determined to eliminate all traces of Christianity from the nation and close Japan to all foreigners.

He and Date didn't see eye-to eye on these matters, but the daimyo had given up such battles years ago when Tokugawa outlawed Christianity. He'd learned to pick his battles carefully. He knew he had enemies. Those who only pretended to be his friends while they secretly coveted his stronghold at Sendai.

Even he had to laugh at the irony of that one.

Tokugawa had banished him to Sendai for arriving late during the siege of Odawara. At the time, it was just a remote stretch of swamp to the north and west of Edo. But Date had seen its potential. He knew what the region had and how to make the best use of it. Within five years, he built Sendai into one of Japan's wealthiest fiefdoms—much to the chagrin of the Shogun who had banished him.

Now, everyone envied him.

Everyone wanted to take Sendai from him.

M. watched as Koinu moped about the house. Like everyone else, he had been ordered to attend Tokugawa's funeral. He had to pay his respects to a man he cared very little about.

"Everyone will be at the funeral," M. said.

"Everyone has to be there. It was his final command," he said. "I understand that he had a most elaborate tomb constructed at Nikko. It supposedly outshines those of even the emperors. I have heard that his body will be encased in jade like the emperors of China. The man's ego knew no bounds!"

"That may be interesting to see," M. said.

"We can look at it later—if you really want to," he promised.

A., along with three of his uncles, carried the small white casket down the steps of the church and slid it into the back of the hearse. The casket held the body of his grandmother who had died only a few days before after a long illness.

Up until now, he'd been too busy with funeral arrangements to allow himself to weep. Anyway, it wasn't like him to do so in public.

That day, he was in his Army dress greens and he felt that it wouldn't look good for a soldier to cry.

His first wife S. walked up.

"Was it heavy?" she asked.

He thought it was a monumentally stupid question, even from someone as insensitive as her.

"It was the heaviest thing I've ever carried in my entire life," he said.

After they drove to Lutheran Cemetery and buried her in the family plot, he allowed the tears to flow on the drive home. His grandmother had raised him. She raised him to be smart and tough and honest and honorable. She taught him right from wrong and that there would be consequences for doing the wrong thing. She had laid the foundations of his persona.

Now she was gone.

He felt like a ship lost in a stormy sea without a rudder. His wife was no help.

No comfort.

In essence, he felt alone.

He thought about M. and wished she were at his side. She'd know how to comfort him. She'd be his anchor.

Poor S. didn't know how to be any of that. She didn't show any sort of real human emotion. If she had any emotions, she kept them hidden deep inside her outer shell.

That's why he often pitied her.

"Where is my M. when I need you most?" he thought as he felt the hole in his heart grow larger.

After the great Shogun's funeral, Koinu and M. begged leave of Lord Date and headed for Hachioji. It was time to pay their respects to a man they both liked and respected far more than they ever did Tokugawa.

They arrived early the next morning and checked in at a small ryokan. After eating and bathing, they walked over to the ruins of the castle. M. had purchased some prayer beads at the local temple. Koinu brought along a bottle of sake and three small cups.

When they arrived, they saw that much of the castle had been leveled and the area felt unusually quiet. After the castle was taken, rumors spread quickly that the ruins were haunted by the spirits of the slain samurai and members of the Hojo clan. No one came there anymore.

They walked to where the main gate once stood and into the ruins. They followed the road up the hill and off to the left. There was an old shrine there. Or part of a shrine. It, too, had been destroyed along with castle. The grass had grown tall now. They looked around until they saw the wooden grave marker. Koinu cut the grass away from the grave with his katana while she watched. When he had cleared an area large enough for them sit in, she gathered up the cut grass and carted them off to the side.

Koinu and M. knelt by the grave. She placed her beads on the head board while he opened the sake and filled the three cups. He placed one at the base of the marker. Then he and M. raised their cups.

"This one is for you, my friend," he said as they drank.

M. put the book aside. He had described Tokugawa's funeral in minute detail, even down to what the important ladies wore. He had even captured the somber mood of the attendees and the hints of the political in-fighting that might begin among the most powerful daimyo. It was as if he'd actually been there.

J. entered the room and turned on the TV. The Yomiuri Giants were playing the Whales at the "egg", which is what they'd nicknamed the domed stadium in Tokyo. M. watched with him. As they did, she told him of A.'s dream of playing professional baseball in Japan.

"Really?" he asked in surprise.

"He grew up watching yakyu on TV in New York. They had a Japanese language station there and he and his uncle would watch the Giants games each Sunday evening. His favorite players were Oh, Nagashima and Kaneda. They inspired him to play baseball and he always felt that Japan was the real major leagues," she explained.

"How unusual," J. said.

"A.-san was and perhaps still is, a most unusual man. I have always thought that he acted more Nihon-jin than American—but an older type. I think he would have felt very much at home with the samurai he wrote about," she said with a smile.

He laughed.

"It's true!" she said. "He didn't like modern Nihon. He preferred ancient Nihon. That's why he liked Yufuin so much. He said he felt at home there."

"Perhaps he is a reincarnated samurai?" J. suggested.

She nodded.

She then told him of a very unusual incident that occurred during his first visit.

They were walking along a narrow path that wound through Yufuin. When they came to a flight of ancient steps that led up to the top of a small, rocky hill, A. stopped.

She watched as she slowly shook his head.

"What is wrong? Do you feel alright?" she asked worriedly.

"At the top of this is hill is a small wooden shrine that is very old. In front of it is a well with two wooden ladles. The well has a roof that looks like the roof of a temple," he said.

Her eyes widened at his description.

"Please follow me," she said as she led him up the steps.

When they reached the top of the hill, he was stunned to see the exact shrine he had described. He stared at it, dumbstruck.

"How did you know about this shrine?" M. asked.

"I don't know. I just did. I saw it in my mind. I felt it somehow," he said as he walked around it.

"This is very old. It goes back to a time before Tokugawa Ieyesu. This was used by samurai. They prayed here before going into battle. No one ever comes here now," she said.

"It seems to be well maintained," he observed.

"The local bokushi takes care of it out of respect for the god," she explained.

"How could I know this was here?" he asked.

"I think I know. I think you were a samurai in another life. You knew this was here because you came here once a long time ago. Perhaps you prayed here just before going into battle," she suggested.

"Reincarnation?" he asked.

"It is the only way to explain this," she said.

"Were there battles near here?" he asked.

"There were several battles in this area. Many samurai also lived in Yufuin and other villages nearby. Their houses still stand today. They go all the way back to the Edo Period," she said.

"Was your house on of them?" he asked.

"Yes. It was built by a samurai," she replied.

"Maybe that's why it feels so comfortable to me," he said. "Why it feels like home."

J. looked at her.

"That really happened?" he asked.

"Hai. It was a very strange experience for us. We were so young. There was so much we did not understand yet. When I told this to my parents, they didn't seem very surprised. Father said he believed that A. had the soul of an ancient samurai and he was trying to find his way home after wandering so many centuries," she said.

"Do you think he was right?" J. asked.

She nodded.

"How many Americans have you met who have read Musashi's Book of Five Rings or adhere to a personal code of honor that is similar to Bushido? A.-san knows more about Musashi than most Nihon-jin. That is why he is in his book," she said.

"Musashi is in "Bushi'?" J. asked.

She nodded.

"Maybe I should read it when you are finished," he said.

"I think you should. I'm sure you will enjoy it very much," M. said.

Namida ga kaborenai youni

Ikawa and a few other officers watched as M. and Koinu walked past them to speak with Date. Ikawa, who was disdainful of strong-willed women, muttered under his breath.

"There goes Koinu-san and his bitch again!"

He didn't think he'd said it loud enough for her to hear, but he was wrong.

M. turned and glared at Ikawa.

"I am not Koinu's bitch. I am his wife. You are just jealous because your wife is fat, lazy and stupid and you are too ugly to ever have anyone like me," she shot back calmly.

Ikawa scowled at Koinu as M. walked away.

"She just insulted me! I demand se apologize," he said.

"You'll get none from her. You started it. You insulted her first. She just defended herself," Koinu said.

"Either have her apologize or draw!" Ikawa shouted as the veins in his neck bulged.

Date stepped between them.

"I advise you to apologize sincerely to M.-san," he said softly.

"Why should I?" Ikawa asked.

"If you don't, I will allow Koinu-san to defend his wife's honor. I will allow you attempt to draw you katana. Before you do so, please tell me what you'd like done with your corpse," Date said.

Kenshin stepped behind Ishikawa and whispered in his ear.

"I highly recommend that you do as Lord Date said."

"Why? Is he that good?" Ishikawa asked.

"I made the mistake of drawing against him many years ago. Because of that, I am forced to wield my katana left handed. The choice is yours. I advise you to make it a wise one," Kenshin said.

Date nodded.

"I think the only man who can stand a chance against him is Musashi," he said. "He is that good."

Ishikawa looked at Date who nodded again. He took a deep breath, exhaled and calmed down. He looked at M. standing next to Koinu. He walked over, got on his knees and bowed his head in supplication.

"Forgive me, Lady. I spoke without thinking. Sometimes my mouth gets the better of my brain and I say things I don't mean," he said.

M. looked at him and bowed her head slightly.

"I forgive you, Ishikawa-san. Next time, think before you speak aloud, neh?" she said.

"I will endeavor to do so, Lady," Ishikawa promised as he got accustomed to the taste of the crow in his mouth.

Date leaned close to him.

"I hope you realize that Kenshin and I just saved your worthless life. Another such incident and I will insist that you do the honorable thing. Understand?" he said softly.

Ishikawa nodded.

He felt truly humbled now. Never in his 54 years had ever been forced to apologize to anyone—especially a woman. It was a most enlightening experience.

He laughed.

"Why are you laughing?" Date queried.

"Lady M. is correct. My wife is fat, lazy and stupid and I am far too homely to have anyone better," he said.

Everyone laughed.

Koinu glanced at M. and winked.

It was about eight in the evening. A. had just gotten off watch and was headed for the mess hall. As he walked past the supply hut, he noticed that the doo wad slightly open. Thinking it might be a VC trying to booby trap the place, he checked the magazine in his rifle and crept up to the door.

He heard something shuffling around inside. He took a deep breath, stepped back, and kicked the door open all the way. Then he charged in with his rifle pointed forward.

To his surprise—and hers—he came face-to-face with a young and very frightened girl. She was standing there with a bunch of cans in her arms, shaking like a leaf and staring at the weapon that was now aimed right at her.

He lowered his weapon.

"What are you doing here?" he asked.

The girl touched her lips and stomach to indicate she was hungry.

"Can you speak?" he asked.

She shook her head.

"Do you understand English?" he asked.

She nodded. A. smiled.

"Are you taking that food to your family?" he asked.

She nodded.

"Well, you don't want that crap. Besides, the cooks count those cans every day and they'll know some are missing. Put those cans back on the shelf," he said.

She sighed and did as he said. She started to leave but he held up his hand. She thought she was under arrest or worse. Instead, he took out his wallet and gave her all the piastas he had.

"Give that to your parents," he said. "Tell them to buy food with it."

She smiled and hugged him tightly, then ran toward the village. He watched until she was out of sight and smiled.

Simmons walked up.

"I saw what you did. That was really nice of you," he said.

"She needs it more than I do," A. said. "It's only money."

To his surprise, the girl returned the next evening carrying a small, lidded iron pot. When she saw A. she ran over to him and handed him the pot. He sat down on some sandbags and removed the lid. Inside, was a dish made of rice and vegetables and it smelled good. He motioned for her to sit with him.

To her surprise, he took two pairs of chopsticks from his shirt pocket and handed her a set.

"Please join me," he said.

They sat and ate together. She signed about where he learned to use the sticks.

"In Japan," he said. "Where did you learn?"

She laughed at his question.

"This is delicious," he said. "Did you cook this?"

She nodded.

"You're a great cook. This is the best meal I've had in weeks," he said.

She beamed and signed "Thank you."

"What's your name?" he asked.

She wrote Ma Li in the dirt with her finger. Then Molly next to it. She pointed at him.

"A.." he said

She wrote it in the dirt. He nodded. They shook hands.

"Where did you learn English?" he asked.

"Nuns taught me. Where did you learn?" she wrote.

They both laughed.

They finished eating. Molly covered the pot and prepared to leave. Then she touched her head to show she'd remembered something. She reached into her pocket, took out a piece of paper and gave it to him.

"You wrote this?" he asked.

She nodded.

It was an invitation from her father to come to their house the next night for dinner. He smiled and nodded.

"I'd be honored," he said. "What time?"

She held up four fingers and pointed at the gate. He nodded. Molly hugged him and walked off.

He ran into Father Flynn on the way back to the hut.

"I see you've made friends with Molly Kwa," Flynn said. "She goes to the Catholic school on the other side of the village. The Ursulines run it. They teach the girls all sorts of stuff. They taught her how to sign and understand English. Maybe one day, she'll be able to get out of this country."

The Ursulines originated in Quebec when it was under French control. They also opened a chapel and convent in New Orleans during the 1750s. These particular nuns were from the New Orleans convent.

Flynn stopped and lit a cigarette.

"Simmons told me what you did yesterday. You made yourself friends with her family for life. You know how they think. That money you gave them should go a long way, too. From now on, you'll be part of their family," Flynn explained.

"How old is Molly?" A. asked.

"She 14," Flynn said.

"I thought she was only nine or ten. She looks so young," A. said. "Her family invited me to their home for dinner tomorrow. What should I bring?"

"Small tokens of appreciation for everyone in the family. Molly has two younger brothers and her father likes Marlboros," Flynn replied. "You'll like them. They're good people. And you're one of the few G.I.s I know who won't make a jackass of himself with the locals," Flynn smiled.

"This is their country. We're the foreigners here and we need to learn and respect their traditions," A. said.

Flynn smiled.

"That's right. It's too damned bad that most of our guys tend to forget that," he said.

The Kwa house was on a busy street a few blocks from the church. Molly met him at the gate at four and they walked to the house. As they did, some of the locals greeted them. One woman said something to Molly which caused her to blush. A. could only guess what she'd said.

The house was a small wood and concrete structure that had an almost French look to it. It had shuttered windows and was painted white with a red tiled roof. It was a fairly old house, too.

She escorted him inside and introduced him to her parents and two younger brothers. They all bowed and welcomed him in English to make him feel at ease. The house was neatly furnished and well kept and decorated with vases filled with flowers.

Mr. Kwa was short, thin and walked with a bad limp.

"I was in the army, he said. "I got wounded very badly by an NVA mine several months ago. I have been trying to make ends meet with my military pension but it is quite small. When we ran out of money, then food, I didn't know what would become of us. Then Ma Li met you. You saved us from going hungry," he said as they sat down at the table.

His "pension" was about 1,200 piastas a month—when it actually arrived. Barely enough for one person to survive on much less a large family like theirs. Before he was drafted, he was a teacher. He hoped to get back into the profession one day.

Mrs. Kwa was an older version of Molly with a ready smile and good nature. Her brothers were typical small boys but far more polite than the average American kids their ages.

The visit went very well. Molly's parents spoke in English and her father had a great sense of humor. They ate, or rather feasted, on prawn steamed with beer and eggs, the traditional noodle soup, steamed vegetables and sticky rice. Molly had even bought beer and some ice to keep it cold.

After dinner, A. showed her brothers how to play checkers while the parents watched. He asked Molly to play after she said she knew how. Then she proved it by beating him three straight times. Each time they joked and laughed.

As he prepared to take his leave of them some five hours later, her father shook his hand.

"Please return to eat with us tomorrow," he said. "And please do not disappoint my daughter by refusing our invitation."

"I will be delighted to accept your invitation," A. agreed.

Molly smiled and signed that she would cook.

"And I look forward to eating it," he smiled.

On the way back to the base he thought to himself that he could really get to like Vietnam if it weren't for the war.

When he entered the barracks, Simmons was lying on his bunk reading a comic book.

"How was it?" he asked.

"It was nice. We had a real good time. They're good people," he said as he sat down.

Simmons smiled.

"What's so funny?" A. asked.

"I think you've been adopted," he said. "You're part of the family now. Did they invite you back?"

"Yes. I'm eating with them again tomorrow," A. replied.

"Yep. You've been adopted alright," Simmons said as George and the others who were nearby laughed.

Koinu's presence had been requested by Shogun Tokugawa Hidetada. So on a clear spring afternoon, he and M. arrived at Hidetada's residence in Kyoto. M. waited outside while Koinu had his audience with Tokugawa.

The Shogun walked over to him and placed his hand on Koinu's shoulder.

"I need to surround myself with good men. Men I can trust. Men who are not afraid to speak their minds and who will tell me the truth. I have heard that you are such a man. I asked you to come here so that I may offer a position as my aide and advisor," he said.

Koinu was stunned.

He looked at Tokugawa. The Shogun noticed that his gaze was steady and direct. He liked that.

"I am already employed by Lord Date," Koinu said.

"I am aware of that. In fact, I have gotten Lord Date's permission to speak with you," Tokugawa said with a smile.

"I see," Koinu mused.

"What do you have to say about my offer?" Tokugawa asked.

"I am honored that you think so highly of me, but I must respectfully decline out of loyalty to Lord Date," Koinu replied.

Tokugawa raised an eyebrow.

"I am offering a high position. One that will more than double what you earn now. Do you understand this?" he asked.

"Hai. Still, I must decline your offer," Koinu said.

"That's a lot of money to turn down. You could become a very wealthy man," Tokugawa pointed out.

"There are far more important things than money," Koinu said. "Lord Date is my friend. He relies on me and trusts me. Such things cannot be bought at any price."

Tokugawa smiled.

"I expected you to say that. So did Lord Date or he would not have allowed me to make you this offer," he said.

"You are a better man than I have ever known before. While I sincerely would like to have you at my side, I understand and highly respect your position. I am honored to know you, Koinu-san. Lord Date has a strong right arm in you. I envy him—and you," he added as he walked him outside.

M. was seated on a bench when they came out. She watched as Tokugawa and Koinu exchanged jokes and laughed as if they were of equal rank. The Shogun saw her and bowed in her direction. Surprised, she returned it.

"You have an exceptional husband, M.-san," he said as they walked over to her. "And I am sure that he has an exceptional wife to stand at his side. May the Gods bless you both with long and happy lives."

He bowed to Koinu, who returned it respectfully.

Tokugawa stood and smiled.

"You need never to bow before anyone," he said. "Not even me."

He turned and went back inside. Koinu told M. what had transpired at the audience. She beamed and clutched his arm as they walked.

"I am even more proud of you than ever!" she said happily.

"My loyalty to Date-san cannot be bought at any price," he said. "The Shogun said he admired and respected me for that."

"As I have always!" M. said.

She lay on the bed and opened her thighs as she watched him disrobe. His prick was long and thin and very erect. He moved between her thighs. She bent her knees and smiled as he eased his prick into her already moist cunt. He went in slowly, too. As he did, she felt his prick deliciously massage every nook and cranny of her cunt and send tingling sensations racing through her body.

He smiled at her exquisite tightness then fucked her. He made sure to go all the way in and pull nearly completely out of her with each hard thrust. He fucked her nice and slowly. She soon picked up his rhythm and began to fuck him back.

In---out.

In---out.

Faster and faster.

Her entire body was on fire now as she gripped his arms and thrust with him. They fucked faster and faster. She sighed and groaned with each deep stroke of his prick. It was proving to be a wonderfully exciting fuck.

"Faster! Do it faster! Use me good. I love it!" she ranted.

He grinned and leaned into her. She almost jumped out f her skin as he thrust faster and faster. She'd never felt anything like it before.

"Oohh yes!" she cried. "Harder. Make me all yours now!"

He fucked her as fast as he cold now. She screamed as he came but kept fucking with him back with even more enthusiasm. Then she came a second time.

And a third.

He just kept fucking and fucking like there was no tomorrow. She shivered and cried out as she came again and again. She'd never come so many times from just one fuck. His prick was like magic inside of her.

"Yes! Yes! Yes! That's wonderful! I love it!" she moaned as she thrashed around.

"Now!" she heard him say.

He began ramming in and out her faster and faster. On each inward thrust, she felt a warm liquid jet into her cunt. Stream after stream filled her cunt but he kept fucking and fucking until she thought she couldn't take any more. Then he stopped and eased his still partially erect prick out of her cum-filled cunt. She smiled and closed her eyes to catch her breath.

As she read the highly descriptive and erotic love scene, she felt herself grow warm all over. She was getting especially warm between her thighs. The scene was so vivid and so well-crafted that it excited her. The more she read, the warmer she grew.

She hadn't had sexual release for a long time. Since she was alone in the house, she stopped reading and slid her jeans off. The she leaned back against the cushion and continued reading. This time, she decided to pleasure herself and slid her hand down into her light colored panties. As she did, she parted her legs and gently massaged her already swollen clitoris.

The written scene went on for several pages. Each paragraph seemed hotter and more erotic than the one before it. And she massaged herself faster.

Faster.

As she did, she put the book down and allowed her imagination to take wings. Now she was the woman in the novel and she was making love to her samurai. She was making love to A. She began breathing harder and harder. Her pulse quickened as she felt him enter her. Her legs were wide apart now as if she were receiving him.

She rubbed faster and faster.

She kept going until she climaxed.

It was a powerful one, too. One she hadn't felt the likes of in years. She sighed and moaned and kept rubbing herself until she came again.

And again.

Just before she let herself fall asleep, she whispered:

"Anata wa aishimasu, A.!"

When she woke, the sun was sinking in the west. She sat up and thought about what she'd done. She looked at the clock on the wall and realized that J. would not be home for at least two more hours. She smiled to herself and peeled off her panties...

He stood by the gate talking with Simmons when they saw Molly approaching. Simmons grinned

"Looks like you've got yourself a girlfriend, A.," he said.

"She's just a kid," A. said.

"She doesn't think she is," Simmons pointed out. "This war makes kids grow up fast and she's got her eyes on you, my friend."

The meal was even more superb than they last. Molly had curried a duck and served it with a spicy salad made of greens, water chestnuts, bamboo shoots and red peppers. There were several smaller dishes like boiled noodles in a brown sauce and steamed vegetables.

And of course, cold beer.

Molly personally served him each dish and waited anxiously to learn what he thought. She proved to be an exceptional cook, too. A. told her that each dish was delicious and perfect. She beamed happily and seemed to feel more and more at ease as the meal progressed.

After the meal, the boys played checkers while Mrs. Kwa cleaned up. Mr., Kwa handed A. another beer and they went into then parlor to chat.

"What do you think of my daughter?" he asked.

"She's very pretty and intelligent," A. replied. "I like her very much."

Molly smiled then held up her left hand. She then used her index finger of the right hand and made a circling motion around her left ring finger. Her father laughed.

"My daughter said she wants to marry you. What do you think of that?" he asked.

"Maybe if she were older," A. hedged unsure of how to handle this situation.

"This is not America. We marry young here and our marriages last forever. My wife and I were married when we were just 16. That's normal here. Sometimes, we marry younger—if the parents give their consent," her father explained.

Molly beamed at A.

There was no doubting the look in her eyes, either.

"If you wish to marry my daughter, I give you my consent and my blessings. This is war, A. There is no way to tell how long this will last or what will happen. We must live every moment as if it might be our last. We must seize life," her father said.

Molly signed that she would wait until he was ready—but to please not take too long. A. was also aware of the custom that dictated if he married Molly, who was the oldest child, he would also be expected to take care of her family. He was just 21 years old himself. He wasn't sure he could handle that kind of responsibility yet.

"Most people see my daughter's inability to speak as a handicap but you don't. That tells me that you are a very exceptional young man. You are someone who is worthy of my daughter. You are also comfortable with our traditions and culture and you have a good heart and fine sense of humor. I know that you will be good to her," her father said.

He noticed that A. and Molly never broke eye contact and laughed.

"When do you leave Vietnam?" he asked.

"In six more months. I can stay longer if I request it," A. replied.

"Why would you do that?" he asked.

"I may have a good reason to stay now," A. admitted. "A very good reason."

Her father laughed.

"My daughter will be 15 in two days. Can you stay one more year after that?" he asked.

"I think so," A. said.

"Good. We will plan the wedding for her 16th birthday," he said as he slapped A. on the back. "I will be proud to give her to you."

Molly blushed a deep red and signed "I'm sorry".

"Don't be," A. said.

After dinner, he and Molly walked around the village. Some of the women smiled at them as if they knew. Their smiled made A. a little nervous.

"I guess we're engaged now, huh?" he asked.

She nodded.

"I didn't have a choice, did I?" he asked.

She shook her head.

He laughed.

Nakinagara aruku

Date laughed when Koinu told him about his meeting with the Shogun. He pounded him on the back.

"I should have bet that bastard you wouldn't take his offer. I could have made a lot of money," he said as he invited him and M. to sit and drink with him.

"I knew you were a man of great character when I first met you. I had no doubt that you'd turn down his offer. You can't be bought because friendship, honor, trust and loyalty mean more to you than all of the money on Earth. You are the true embodiment of a samurai," Date said as he raised his cup.

He smiled at M.

"And I give equal credit to you, M.-san," he said as he raised his cup to her.

He poured each of them more sake.

"A man with your character should be rewarded. I have decided to promote you to my second in command. Starting now, your pay is doubled!" he said.

"I am honored!" Koinu said.

"You've earned it. There's no one I trust more," Date said.

"May I request that Watanabe and Buntaro also be promoted? They, too, are loyal and deserving men," Koinu suggested.

"Consider it done! If you vouch for them, that's good enough for me. Besides, the three of you are inseparable. I'll double their pay as well. You can tell them the good news yourself," Date readily agreed.

He smiled.

"If Kenshin were alive, I'd do the same for him. He was a trusted friend. I've missed him greatly since he was killed in the attack on Osaka Castle," he said.

"I have also missed him," Koinu said.

When he broke the news to the LT, he laughed.

"I think everyone saw that coming but you," he said. "You could do worse. The Kwas are fine people and Molly's real pretty. I kind of envy you now. You actually have something in this country worth fighting for now. You will always be connected to this place in one way or another for the rest of your life. I hope you have a long, happy life with her."

Flynn saw them and walked over.

Without saying a word, he hugged A.

"God bless you, kid!" he said.

"How'd you find out?" A. asked.

"Hell, A. It's all over the damned village already. This is a big deal here. But I did see this coming," Flynn said.

"How come everybody else saw this coming but me?" A. asked.

The LT and Flynn laughed.

Even Simmons and George gave him a hard time about it. He took all of their ribbing good naturedly and gave some back to them.

And each day, Molly waited at the gate for him. They walked to her house and had dinner and he got to know and like the Kwa family very much. They made him feel comfortable and at home and he and Molly grew closer and closer.

She was a sweet, gentle soul with a beautiful smile and melodic laugh. She was bright, a quick learner and had a good sense of humor. There was a certain sexy innocence about her, too. When he was with her, there was no war.

Just the two of them.

Whenever Simmons, Gonzalez or George saw them together, they'd hum the wedding march. A. always smiled when they did this. Even the CO and LT got into the act later on. Ma Li asked him what the song was. When he told her, she laughed and grinned at him.

"I like it," she signed.

"Me, too," he said. "Anh yeu em."

When he said this, she gripped his hand tighter and beamed.

M.'s heart leapt to her throat when she received A.s email about his book tour of Japan. When he asked if they could meet as his hotel the day after his arrival, she eagerly agreed.

After years of exchanging sometimes very intimate and high-charged erotic dreams, she was finally going to meet him face-to-face. But she was also worried about the way he would perceive her. She was slightly older than him, but he'd always told her she looked young, pretty and sexy to him. He said this so often, she had almost believed it.

Exchanging flirtations on Facebook and through emails was one thing. Meeting him in person was quite another. She decided to ask her friend, Y. to come with her for moral support. Y. knew about her exchanges with A. and was also curious to meet him. Just in case things did not go as well as she hoped, M. wanted Y. there to lean on.

Just to be on the safe side, she decided to ask her husband, K., if she could meet him. To her surprise, he gave his approval.

Since A. was bringing his wife with him, he knew M. would be safe. Y. would also be an additional layer of protection.

"A.-san has asked about you and the rest of our family. He said he would like to come to Hachioji and meet us as he wants to see the castle ruins as he has written about the battle in his book," M. said.

"I think I would also like to meet him. You can make reservations for him and his wife at the ryokan a few streets from here. I'm sure he will enjoy it there. It is very well run," K. suggested.

M. was ecstatic.

K. had approved everything without an argument. Apparently, he was curious about this gaijin who had befriended his wife. Theirs was, to say the least, a rather unconventional friendship, too.

"I will email him right away," she said.

"Please do so. You must really be eager to meet with him after all these years. I have not seen you look this happy in a long time," he joked. "Just don't throw yourself naked at him. If you do, you'll frighten him away."

She slapped him on the arm playfully.

"Men!" she said with indignation.

He laughed and left the room.

As she sat down at the computer to write her response, she allowed her thoughts to drift back to their accidental meeting.

She recalled the day she was seated at her PC, looking at her FB page when she received an unusual query from a man in America asking if she was the young woman he had known many years ago because she had the same and last name as she did.

Curious, she responded that she was indeed in Osaka at that time. She then inquired if he was Swedish as she had known a man from Sweden then.

"I'm an American," he wrote along with other things.

His response intrigued her, so she replied.

"If I did not know you were an American, I would think you were a Japanese man. Your way of writing things seems very Japanese," she wrote.

He wrote that he had spent much time in Japan and that he'd even read Tales of Genji and Musashi's Book of Five Rings and that his friends even said he acted more Japanese than American. This led to another exchange of letters and another.

They had been in almost daily contact since and their correspondences, at his suggestion, became email exchanges to maintain their privacy.

And their friendship blossomed into an attraction.

This was very unusual by Japanese standards, especially for a married woman of her generation. Such daily exchanges with a man other than her husband would be considered highly improper. But they kept writing each other daily.

He discussed subjects with her as if she were his equal. Things like politics, world events, family matters and even complimented on her English and the way she looked and her sense of humor. He said he admired her enthusiasm and intelligence as they discussed things and ideas that most men in Japan considered too complicated for women to comprehend.

This was new for her.

They exchanged cards on holidays.

And small gifts.

And a lot of photos.

He sent her a manuscript from a book he'd written which was based on Japanese mythology and ancient history. She was surprised at how much he knew and understood. And he wrote about things as if he'd lived through them.

He was a very unusual and fascinating foreigner.

One day, he wrote to tell her about a dream he'd had. It was about a young samurai and his lady. There was more than one dream and they were vivid. Each seemed to be another segment of the samurai's life and his lady was by his side the entire time. He said he'd never had such dream before, but each one he had he wrote down. Before long, he had enough for an entire book. A very detailed book.

M. felt the dreams were memories of his past life. Was he, in fact, a samurai during Tokugawa's reign? That would explain his fascination for ancient Japan and attraction to Japanese women.

Then she began to dream.

It was a very odd dream, too.

She dreamt she was standing on a foggy plain, peering into the mist and waiting. After a while, the mist parted and she saw a man dressed in ancient European armor approaching her. At his side was a small black cat.

She woke.

She knew that A. had two cats and one was black. And that cat followed him everywhere her went.

In the dream, she was wearing a simple blue kimono that seemed to be from another time. She wondered if she was the lady in A's dreams. Were they two souls who had found each other again after so many centuries? If so, why now?

He wrote her about a similar dream involving the samurai. He had just returned from a very hard won battle many miles away. It was a dark, foggy night and the samurai was following the light from a lantern he saw dimly glowing in the mist. When he drew close to the light, he smiled and his heart was filled with joy when he saw the lady standing in the road, waiting for him, with a lantern on the end of a stick.

And they had the dreams at almost the exact same moment!

Their exchanges continued and became more and more intimate. Soon, he wrote her about another kind of dream he'd had. This was about him and her as they are now. And it was highly erotic. Curious, she asked him to describe it.

He did.

In detail.

But he did so almost poetically. It was erotic but also romantic. And so vivid that it triggered long dormant feelings inside of her and led her to dream a similar dream that very same night. While she dreamt, she reached between her thighs and touched herself.

And she made herself climax.

It was a strong climax, too. In fact, her sighs of pleasure woke her husband K. who was sleeping on a futon a few feet away. When he asked her about it, she said she was dreaming of their honeymoon. He smiled and hugged her and said maybe one day, they would have another such trip. But she knew that would never happen.

K. had changed too much. She told A. about his mood changes and the way he had become. A. urged her to have him examined to make sure there wasn't some physical cause. She said she would try, but he didn't like wasting time and money on doctors. A. said he was pretty much the same way. She also realized that he shared some similar traits with her husband. Neither of them liked the way modern society was heading and both wished they could return to more simple and more humane times. But unlike K., A. loved travel and adventure.

They flirted even more after that.

And he wrote her of more erotic dreams, which triggered similar dreams for her—and more climaxes. She now wanted to hear his voice.

One week, K. was out of town helping their daughter set up for an exhibition of her paintings. M. woke at four a.m., Tokyo time, and called him. His voice was not what she expected. He spoke slowly and clearly to allow her to understand and he used what little Nihon-go he remembered.

She liked what she heard.

He thought her voice was sweet and soft and oh-so feminine and sexy. In fact, it gave him an immediate erection. A good one, too.

After their brief chat, he emailed her and told her what happened. When she read it, she was shocked—and elated that he'd gotten such a reaction simply from hearing her voice. The idea excited her.

So much, in fact, that she called him again the following day. He told her loved her voice. It was soft and sweet and very sexy. He complimented her on her ability to speak English. Then he told her she was very pretty.

And sexy.

Even K. had never said such things to her. She also felt he was very sincere when he said those things. He actually did think she was pretty and sexy.

"Imagine," she thought. "A man who is younger than me saying such things to me!"

She enjoyed hearing it, too. A. made her feel young and attractive again. And his voice excited her, too, as she imagined his reaction the day before. They talked for more than 10 minutes.

And he got another good erection.

Their talk was followed by another exchange of emails.

"I enjoyed hearing your voice again," she wrote. "Did you have the same reaction?"

"Yes I did," he admitted. "You do things to me no one else ever has."

"I had a similar reaction. It was like the one in my dream. I was very aroused," she admitted.

"We have a very strong attraction to each other," he wrote.

"I am almost embarrassed to say this, but I touched myself while we talked," she replied.

"Wow! Now I'm hard again!" he responded.

"If you will not think badly of me for saying so, but I feel very happy to be the cause of that. It has been such a long time since my husband has reacted to me in that way," she wrote. "I feel very flattered."

"I'm flattered that I excite you in the same way," he answered. "I can imagine you touching yourself while on the phone. How long did you do that?"

"I did it until I climaxed," she replied. "Oh, I feel so embarrassed to admit such things, but I can't help it with you. You must think I am a very silly old woman!"

"On the contrary, I think you are a young, kawaii and very sexy woman," he assured her.

When K. queried about her exchanges with the foreigner, M. said they had made friends by accident, then half-lied about him helping her with her English. K. told her it was alright to continue but not to spend too much time on the computer as she had other, more important things to attend to.

Like take him to his gym and other places.

That was another thing A. and K. had in common. Neither drove or wanted to learn how to drive. A's wife, R. (a very cute Filipina that was several years younger than him) was the driver in their family just like she was the driver for K. Both had grown up in major cities and never saw a need to learn how to drive. So both now relied on their wives to get around.

She had to smile at that.

R's driving sometimes scared the Hell out of A. just like hers often scared the Hell out of K.

"Yes, they are somewhat alike in that respect," she thought.

When her daughter, A. read the article about A.'s upcoming book tour in Japan, she immediately phoned. M. told her about the plans and A. laughed. She knew all about their emails and obvious infatuation with each other.

"Of course I would like to meet him. You have told me so much about him and I have seen his photos and emails. I think he has a very big crush on you, Mother," A. said.

"That's silly. What would he want to do with an old woman like me?" M. asked.

"Everything!" A. said.

M. blushed. She often thought about how improbable her relationship with A. He was an artist, writer, world traveler, and gourmet chef. He knew about the paranormal, science and history and religion. He'd been a soldier and a professional athlete.

In short, he was a modern day Renaissance man.

And she was a simple housewife in Hachioji.

And they were both married to other people. Yet, they'd been drawn to each other from the very start. She had developed very real and deep feelings toward him. Feelings she should not have for anyone other than her husband.

But she had them.

And they were growing stronger.

Only two other people knew how she felt. They were her daughter A. and her best friend Y. Her husband knew she had an American friend who she contacted online. But he apparently didn't think anything of it because he hardly asked her about him. He commented when he sent photos and cards, but that's as far as it went.

She went upstairs to see about K. When she got there, he was fast asleep on his futon. She smiled and went back downstairs. She picked up the copy of A.'s book and settled down to read.

On Ma Li's 15th birthday, A. bought her flowers and a cake. They celebrated at the Kwa house, and then he gave her 3,000 piastas to go shopping. She threw her arms around his neck and they exchanged their first kiss. Her mother blushed at this display. Mr. Kwa simply smiled and nodded.

Ma Li insisted that A. accompany her on her shopping spree. After some cajoling, he relented and walked with her to the market. He watched as she explored store after store. Finally, after three hours, she settled on two skirts and two blouses and a pair of sandals. She tried each of them on and modeled them for him.

He smiled approvingly.

Everything looked so cute on her.

They stopped to eat at one of the village's two cafés. She took a pen from her small handbag and wrote on a napkin:

I love you.

"I love you, too," he said.

"Really?" she wrote.

"Really!" he assured her.

He escorted her back home and watched while Ma Li showed her parents what he'd bought her for her birthday. Her mother smiled and made a huge fuss. A. and Mr. Kaw just had a beer and talked a while.

"That was very generous of you. I have never seen her look so happy before. The two of you make a fine couple. I'm sure your marriage will be a strong and happy one, too. I am proud she has chosen you and that you have chosen her. Where do you plan to live after you leave Vietnam?" Mr. Kwa asked.

"Well, I'm from Brooklyn. I guess we'll start there and see how it goes. I'll live anywhere that makes her happy," A. said.

Ma Li looked at him and signed that she will live wherever he feels comfortable. A. nodded and signed "I love you". She beamed.

"How many grandchildren do you plan to give us?" her father asked.

Ma Li blushed.

"We'll work on that as we go along," A. smiled.

After another hour or so, A. bade her and her family good-night. As he walked through the gate, he saw Flynn sitting on a pile of sandbags, drinking a beer. A. walked up and sat next to him.

"How'd it go?" asked Flynn.

"Very nicely," A. smiled. "I'm starting to get used to the idea of marrying her now."

Flynn nodded.

"You could do worse. Ma Li is a really sweet girl," he said. "So you're really going through with it?"

"Definitely," A. said.

"You want a Buddhist or Catholic wedding?" Flynn asked.

"How about both?" A. asked.

"That can be arranged, A," Flynn assured him.

M. woke with a start. She sat up on her futon and looked through her open window at the stars. She'd had the strangest dream about a young soldier coming into her room in the middle of the night. The soldier squatted beside her as she slept, then smiled and gently touched her cheek. The sensation felt so real, she woke.

She got up and walked to the bathroom. She threw cold water on her face and looked in the mirror. As she did, she saw that same soldier looking over her shoulder. Frightened, she turned to confront him but no one was there.

She looked at the clock.

It was two a.m.

She had to go to class in four more hours. She walked back to her futon and lay down. Seconds later, she fell into a very deep sleep until the soldier reappeared to disturb her. This time, she decided to stay up. She showered, brushed her teeth and dressed. Then she sat down at her desk to study. But every time she tried to concentrate on her subject, the image of the soldier entered her mind.

She sighed and closed the book.

"Who are you?" she asked. "Why are you bothering me?"

Simmons woke A. up early one morning.

"Get yourself decent, A. You've got company," he said.

He stretched and yawned, then sat up.

"Who?" he asked.

"The Mother Superior from the church," Simmons replied.

He dressed and brushed his teeth. The nun, in her white habit, was standing outside the barracks. She smiled at him.

"Are you A.?" she queried in a soft Louisiana accent.

"That's me," A. replied as he held out his right hand.

She shook it and smiled.

"My name is Anna LaRoux. I run the convent and school here in the village. I am also Ma Li's teacher. She has come to me with remarkable news. I just want to verify that it's true," the nun said.

"What did she say?" A. asked.

"She said that you and she are engaged to be married on her 16th birthday and that you have the blessings of her parents. Is this true?" she asked.

"Every bit of it, Sister," A. replied.

She looked amazed.

"Would you mind telling me how this all came to pass?" she asked as they sat down on the steps.

He told her everything. Even she had to laugh at how he became engaged. When he was finished, she hugged him.

"Bless you!" she said with tears in her eyes.

"I think I've already been blessed a thousand times over," he said.

"You are not bothered by her inability to speak?" she asked.

"Ma Li speaks. You just have to listen with your heart," he said.

"That is the most beautiful thing I have ever heard. You must be a poet," she said.

"No. I'm more of a journalist. Ma Li brings the poet out in me," A. said.

"So you will extend your tour here so you can be married?" she asked.

"Definitely," he said. "I have a good reason to stay now. A very good reason."

"When Ma Li told me the news, I just couldn't believe it. She told me to ask you myself, so I decided to do just that. I must say that I approve of her choice. I have often prayed she'd find someone. It looks like my prayers have been answered," she said.

"Or mine and hers," A. said.

"I must get back to the school now. Please be sure to invite me and the other sisters to your wedding. I would hate to miss it," she said as she stood.

"I'll come over to the church and invite you personally, Sister," he promised as he escorted her to the gate.

Just before she left, she turned and smiled at him.

"I'm just happy to know that Ma Li will be in very good, loving hands," she said. 'I'll see you around, A. Don't be a stranger."

"I won't," he said as he watched her leave.

Simmons, George and Gonzalez were waiting a few yards away. They all grinned at him.

"You better be good to Ma Li, A. Or the God Squad will come down hard on you," George said.

"Yeah. You wouldn't want the sisters to bring the wrath of God down on you" Simmons joked.

"So you're really gonna extend for another year just to marry her. I can't let you do it alone. We Brooklyn guys have to stick together, so I'm gonna extend just so I can be at your wedding," Gonzalez said as he slapped A. on the back.

"Let's get some chow," Simmons said.

"Yep. There's nothing like greasy powdered eggs and stale coffee to get you going," George said.

"And keep you going," A. said.

"And going…"

"And going…"

Hitoribotchi no yuru

After another fine meal at the Kwa house, A. and her father sat on the porch and talked as they usually did. The two had become good friends. Mr. Kwa trusted him with Ma Li and was very happy that she chose "such an exceptional young man to marry."

"What surprised me most about you is that Ma Li said she wanted to marry you, you acted surprised but didn't try to talk her out of it. Most other Americans would have done everything they could to avoid marrying her. You did not," he said.

"That's because I really care for Ma Li," A. said as he accepted another beer from him. "She's a very special young lady. A very sweet, intelligent and caring young lady. I'm looking forward to spending the rest of my life with her."

He beamed.

Ma Li walked out and sat beside A. She leaned into him. He put his arm around her and kissed her on the forehead. Mr. Kwa smile and went into the house.

Ma Li looked up at the stars as A. caressed her hair.

"I wish we were married now," she wrote in her pad.

"So do I," he said.

"Will your family like me?" she asked.

"They will adore you," he assured her.

"Why?" she asked.

"Because I adore you," he replied. "Don't worry about a thing. It will be just fine. You'll see. I promise."

"I'm not worried when I'm with you," she signed.

M. looked at her reflection as she brushed her shoulder-length hair. It was still full and thick. Still mostly black, even after so many years. Although she dyed it occasionally to hide the silver threads, she really didn't get too concerned about her looks.

Not at this stage in her life.

She stopped and put the brush down. She wondered if A. would still recognize her. Would he find her attractive?

She blushed at her "silly" thoughts. Even if they met again and he did recognize her, he was married. Surely, he would not be attracted to her now.

Or would he?

Her name was in most of his novels. That was not coincidental. And she was always the main female character. The big love interest.

They were smart, pretty and strong and very loyal.

"Is that what he originally saw in me?" she wondered.

He had tried to encourage her to speak her mind several times. Instead, she followed tradition and kept her thoughts to herself, believing that he knew how she felt. Or if he didn't, that he'd figure it out sooner or later.

She realized too late how wrong she was.

She thought about the character in "Bushi" and how outspoken and fiercely loyal to her husband she was. It was the way he had hoped she would be.

Was her son right?

Did A. still have strong, deep feelings for her? Was his the kind of love that never dies?

The newspaper article said that he would stay at the Shimizu Ryokan in Yufuin for six nights. It was

Where he had stayed during his first trip to Nihon and he'd always wanted to return to it.

M. smiled.

That was so much like him. It was something she'd expect him to do. She sighed and thought back to those days.

Being an inexperienced traveler, he took a JAL flight to Fukuoka instead of an ANA flight to Oita. Once he got to Fukuoka, he made matters worse. He took the bus to Oita when the train would have been much faster.

When he arrived at Oita Bus Station several hours later, he was surprised to see M. waiting for him when he got off. He was amazed and grateful for her patience and he apologized for making her wait so long.

But he also fell madly in love with her the moment he saw her. She wore a pretty, medium blue dress with white shoes and a small matching purse. Her hair was straight and dark and shoulder length. Her eyes sparkled and she had the prettiest smile he'd ever seen.

"Have you eaten" she asked.

"Not yet," he replied.

She checked his suitcase at the station then showed him to a small café. They had various snacks and small dishes. To A.s surprise, plastic models of each dish were on display in the window. They selected two things and placed their order. They sat down outside and talked for awhile. The language barrier was obvious but both thought they would eventually overcome it.

At that time, he was clueless about Japanese cuisine. In fact, at that age, he was fairly naïve about a lot of things. She tried to teach him how to use the chopsticks and they laughed over his efforts. The food looked great and she tried to explain what it was. His initial encounter with Japanese cuisine didn't go very well.

At all.

"I made reservations for you at a very nice ryokan, but your room will not be available for two days. Tonight, you will stay at our home—if you don't mind," she said.

When Koinu returned on a rainy night, he found that M. was still awake and waiting for him. She rushed to the door and threw her arms around him. They held each other closely as they exchanged greetings.

"Why are you up so late?" he asked as he sat down on the floor.

She hurried over with a bowl of rice and some steamed fish and vegetables and placed them before him. Then she went and got the sake and two cups.

"Kenshin-san told me you were on your way home and should be here this evening. So I waited," she said. "I knew you would not mind. I have even prepared our bath."

"Our bath?" he asked with a smile.

"Of course. We have much time to make up for. That is the perfect place to begin," she smiled.

M. sat by the window as she read the scene. While she read, she had her hand between her thighs. His love scenes were sexually charged yet poetic. And since she knew the female character was based on her, she imagined she and A. were making love as she read.

She was so engrossed in what she was doing that she failed to notice that Y. had come in. She stood by the door and watched while M. pleasured herself. Her hand moved faster and faster. She heard her breathing grow louder and louder. M.'s head fell back and she closed her eyes. Y. smiled when she saw her quiver all over.

She waited until M. caught her breath, and then knocked on the door jamb. M. almost jumped out her clothes, then blushed deeply when she realized she had been watching.

"How long were you standing there?" she asked as Y. sat down.

"About ten minutes. That looked like a good one," she teased.

"Oh, it was," M. admitted. "They are all good."

"I hope you don't cripple A.-san when he arrives. You may prove to be too much for him to handle," Y. joked. "That was very interesting. I've never watched anyone do that before. It was very erotic and stimulating."

"You should have called out when you entered," M. said.

"I did call out. When you didn't answer, I thought I would check up here. Now I know why you didn't hear me!" Y. smiled. "It's good that K-san didn't see you!"

M. nodded.

"That would have been very difficult to explain," she agreed.

"When does he arrive?" Y. asked.

"In three more days. He has emailed me the flight and arrival times. He's staying at the Imperial Hotel," M. said as she showed her his email.

"In a suite! His publisher is sending him in style. That's one of the best hotels in all of Nihon, too," Y. said. "Call me when you want to meet him. We'll take my car. I'll drive because you'll be too nervous to concentrate. Your mind will be on something else," Y. said.

M. nodded.

"I am so happy that you're going with me," she said.

"I am your friend. I can't allow you to make a fool of yourself alone. Besides, I want to meet him. You've made me very curious about him," Y. said.

"Just don't steal him from me," M. teased.

"I don't think that would be possible, even if I should try," Y. said.

Ue o muite arukou

There were three of them.

Rockets.

The first shot landed in the open space between the huts of the base camp and did nothing but kick up clouds of dust and dirt.

The next two hit the village and caused all sorts of mayhem and chaos. Then, everything went quiet. After waiting for the next barrage that never came, the LT led the men into the village to see who and what got hit and to help out wherever possible. The men had a good relationship with the villagers and the CO wanted to keep it that way.

The second rocket had landed in the marketplace. It was a direct hit that left the market in ruins. Produce, meat, small animals and debris lay everywhere. Amid it all were several bodies of women and children who had been shopping for their evening meal. They saw several women cradling their dead and wounded children and sobbing hysterically while others scrambled through the rubble in search of missing relatives and wounded.

A few of the men jumped in to help while the medics raced to the aid of the wounded. The scene was tragic.

Horrible.

They found a small boy with blood running down the side of his face crying at the mutilated body of his mother. The poor woman had been blown to bits and was lying there in a pool of blood. One of the med tried to comfort the boy by picking him up but he just kept wailing and reaching for his mother. It was the kind of thing that stays with a man. Something that haunts his dreams forever.

He hurried over to Molly's house. To his horror, he found that the once neat little house was now a pile of smoldering wood and thatch.

The third rocket had scored a direct hit on the place and the blast leveled Molly's house and the houses on either side. Locals were frantically scouring the wreckage for survivors. A. joined in. After a few frenetic minutes, he found her two brothers. They were laying side-by-side beneath part of the roof. He checked their pulses and sighed.

They were dead.

Several other villagers shouted. He watched as they carried the bloodied body of a woman out into the street and placed her on the ground. He walked over and shook his head. It was Molly's mother. She had a long piece of bamboo stuck in her chest. The blast had sent it flying right into her. She never had a chance.

As he searched, he called Molly's name several times. But there was no answer. After an hour, he gave up. Since he didn't find her, maybe, he thought, she was alright. Maybe she wasn't in the house when it got hit.

But he also knew that this would have been the place she immediately ran to after the attack. She'd be working with the villagers, crying and wailing when they pulled her family out of the rubble.

But she wasn't.

He left the scene and wandered around the immediate area. Every few seconds he called her name. Dejected, he decided to return to base camp. Instead of taking his normal path, something in the back of his mind led him down an alternate path into the nearby jungle. As he passed a large tree, he saw a small form huddled against it. He rushed over.

It was Molly.

She was scorched and bloody. Her school uniform was dirty and torn and her eyes were shut tight. He knelt beside her and cradled her in his arms.

She felt cold and stiff.

He stayed there for several minutes and wept.

He did his best to compose himself and picked her up. With tears streaming down his cheeks, he carried her through the village. He passed several of his men along the way. They stopped what they were doing and watched silently. Several of the villagers did the same. No one spoke. No one moved for a few seconds.

He carried Molly to the temple and placed her on the steps. The monk came out. He saw the sorrow and pain in A.s eyes.

"Give Molly and her family a proper burial," he said. "I'll pay for everything."

The monk nodded.

"Please bring her inside," he said.

He picked her up and placed her in front of the Buddha. Then he fell to his knees and wept. The monk knelt beside him and prayed, both for Molly's soul and his. No words were necessary. No words would make things better.

He eventually made it back to base camp.

The war had suddenly gotten personal. Simmons was sitting on the bench outside the hut drinking beer. He handed one to A.

"I'm sorry, man. I'm truly and deeply sorry," he said.

"War sucks," A. said as they drank.

M. returned from shopping and saw K. seated on a cushion near the window, reading a book. She was surprised to see he was reading "Bushi"—and that he was halfway through it.

"You are reading A.-san's book?" she asked as she sat in front of him.

"Hai. I started this morning. I picked it up out of curiosity and just kept reading. It's very good. He has a real feel for our history and his characters ring true. All but the woman," he replied.

"Oh? What's wrong with her?" she asked.

"She is too strong and opinionated. I think he modeled her after you," K. said.

"So you think I'm opinionated?" she asked in mock indignation.

"Definitely. And you are becoming more so. You never bothered to verbally spar with me until recently. Now, you don't hesitate to do so. You're becoming quite good at it, too. Just like the woman in this book," K. said with a grin.

"Does that bother you?" she asked.

"More like it worries me. It shows that you are growing stronger and more independent. I'm afraid that soon, you will no longer have need of me," he teased.

"You worry for no reason, K.-san, "she said with a hug.

"Then perhaps A.-san should also be worried about you?" he suggested.

"I don't think I would worry him at all. He likes strong, intelligent women," she said with a giggle.

"Now I'm really worried his mental health," K. said.

"Why?" she asked.

"Because he thinks that you are intelligent! He must be delusional," K. joked.

Before she could respond, he told her she had a letter on the table from A. She hurried to open and read it. She looked so happy; he asked what he'd written.

"He has finalized his plans to come to Nihon," she beamed. "He said he will email his itinerary as soon as he gets it from his publisher. He will also email his flight and arrival time so we can all get together."

"All?" K. asked.

"Hai. He would like to meet our entire family. That also includes you," she said.

"Ah, so. What A.-san really wants is to meet you," he said. "If it makes you happy, I will welcome him and his wife to our home when they arrive. I admit that I am curious about him. Are you excited that you will finally meet him in person after all these years?"

"Of course I am!" she beamed. "Oh my! I think I had best have my hair dyed. I show too much gray now," she added as she glanced into a nearby mirror.

"Why bother? He already knows that you are an old woman," K. teased. "I'm sure your gray hair will not matter to him."

"You don't understand. I'm a woman. Such things do matter to me!" she said.

Flynn saw A. sitting in the shade against the side of the barracks drinking beer. He walked over. A. reached into the ice bucket, took out a bottle, popped off the cap and handed it to him. Flynn took it and sat down next to him.

"I'm sorry about Molly and her family. They were good people. Really good people," he said as he sipped.

"Why them? All those houses and that fuckin' rocket hit theirs. Why?" A. asked sadly.

"That's the tragedy of war, son. Innocent people always get killed. It's just random shit. Call it bad luck, if you want. Or God's will," Flynn said.

"If that's God's will, you can stick him up your ass, Padre," A. said bitterly. "Shit, if there really was a god, he wouldn't let shit like this happen. Either that or he really doesn't give a rat's ass about this rock we live on. If this really was his will, then he is a very sadistic, uncaring bastard."

Flynn nodded.

"War is insane. Nothing good ever comes from it. When I was your age, I enlisted to fight in Korea. My first real action was at a place called White Horse Hill. Ever hear of it?" Flynn asked.

"Sure. I've heard of it. That's where my old man got killed," A. said. "All they ever found of him was his left foot inside a combat boot."

Flynn looked at him.

"What was his name?" he asked.

"According to my grandmother, his name was Andrew Vaness," A. said. "My mother said she wasn't sure. Who cares? After all this time, what does that matter?"

Flynn shook his head. He'd actually known a soldier by that name but only for a couple of days. He thought about the weird way the world worked sometimes.

"Anyway, I just barely survived that battle. Before that night, I was an atheist. I didn't believe in shit. But while all Hell was breaking loose around me, I prayed. It might have been the first time in my life I ever prayed. And I prayed hard. I promised God that if he got me through this one, I'd serve him the best way I could.

When the sun came up, I was still alive. I looked up at the sky and thanked God. After the war, I decided to enter the seminary and become a priest. That night, I became a believer—but with more than a little touch of skepticism and suspicion," Flynn said.

"You don't sound like you're 100% sure," A. pointed out.

"Let's just say I like to hedge my bets. Maybe you should do the same," Flynn said.

"I'll tell you what, Padre—if you can answer one question to my satisfaction, and without all of that faith crap, I'll think about it," A. offered.

"That's fair enough. What's your question?" Flynn agreed.

"Did God create man or did man create God?" A. asked.

"Wow! That's a good one!" Flynn admitted.

"I'll say. Now, what's the answer?" A. pressed.

Flynn shrugged and finished the beer. A. opened another and passed it to him.

"Beats the shit out of me, A.," he said. "I have to admit I can't answer that one. You know, I've got to stop talking to you. If this keeps up, you'll have me questioning my faith," Flynn said with a smile.

"Do you?" asked A.

"All the time. Then I see things that reinforce my belief," Flynn said.

"Like what?" A. asked.

"Like what you've done for Molly and her family and that young NVA soldier," Flynn said. "If that's not God's handiwork, I don't know what is."

"God has nothing to do with that. I just do what I feel is right," A. said thoughtfully as he opened another beer.

"Are you sure?" Flynn asked.

"Shit, Padre. You keep talking like that and you'll have me questioning my lack of faith!" A. laughed as they clinked bottles.

Namida ga kaborenai youni

When J. got home, he realized that the house was empty. There was a note on the table from his mother advising him to microwave the meal she'd prepared before eating it. He put down his briefcase and pulled off his tie just as he heard her enter.

She was dressed in a white t-shirt and running shorts and sneakers. She was sweating and breathing hard, too. He gave her a questioning look.

She smiled.

"I was out jogging. It has been a little while since I did that," she said as she poured herself a glass of ice water.

"I didn't realize that you had such a nice figure. If I weren't your son, I'd ask you out," he smiled.

She actually did have a nice figure. She liked to keep herself fit and she had never smoked and drank very little. Mostly she walked or jogged for many miles at a time. But she hadn't done so for a few weeks due to an ankle injury.

"If your old friend saw you now, he'd carry you away with him," J. said as he nuked his dinner.

"You're being silly," she said with a smile. "I'm an old woman now."

"You don't look or act like an old woman," J. pointed out as he took his dinner out of the microwave and sat down at the table to eat.

She smiled.

She weighed exactly the same as she did the last time she'd seen A. Only now, she was more health and fitness conscious. She'd been that way for several years.

"I think you and he would make an excellent pair. The newspaper stories say he is into cross training and even plays baseball. You could even work out together—at the gym, I mean," he said.

She laughed.

When he got his orders to leave Vietnam, he felt a mix of emotions. They roiled around inside of him and, in the end, they left him feeling empty.

Hollow.

Drained.

He had four days left at base camp. He walked over to the locker and took out a white envelope that contained a simple gold wedding band. He placed it into his pocket along with a photo Simmons had taken of him seated next to Molly outside the gate. He put this in his pocket with the ring. He left the base and walked out into the market. He saw an old woman selling bouquets of various flowers. He pointed to the dark, red roses.

"I'll take those," he said.

"How many?" she asked.

"Twelve," he replied. "Bundle them up nicely."

She smiled and made them into a beautiful bouquet. He handed her 500 piastas.

"Keep the change," he said as he walked off.

He walked over to the temple. The bokushi greeted him outside. When he saw the flowers, he nodded.

"I will walk there with you and pray if you like," he offered.

"I'd appreciate that," A. said.

They walked to the local cemetery and along a path and stopped at the plot that was the resting place for Molly and her family. A. placed a single rose on the graves of her mother, father and young siblings. Then he placed the rest on Molly's grave. The bokushi watched as she took out the ring and photo and placed them on the grave, too. This done, he dropped to one knee and wept while the bokushi prayed for them both.

After a little while, they walked back to the temple.

"The Kwa family were good friends of mine. I will tend to their resting place for as long as I am able. Their souls are at peace now. I will pray for yours to find peace as well," the bokushi said as they shook hands.

He met Flynn not 100 yards from the temple.

"I thought I'd find you here. Molly's teacher at the Catholic school gave this to me. She thought you'd like to read it. It's a poem Molly wrote about you," he said as he handed him a folded slip of paper.

He watched as A. read it. When he finished, tears were running down his face. He smiled and handed the poem back to Flynn.

"Do me a favor, Padre. Place this on Molly's grave. And while you're there, say a prayer for us both," he said.

"You want me to pray for you?" Flynn asked.

"Let's just say I'm hedging my bets," A. grinned.

Flynn laughed.

M. woke and sat up.

She'd dreamt about the soldier again. Only this time, she saw him kneeling on one knee and weeping over a grave. The dream was so real, it gave her chills.

She lay back down and tried to sleep, but she just couldn't get that dream out of her mind.

"Who are you? Why do you haunt me?" she asked aloud.

After an hour passed, she gave up and got ready for school. As she brushed her teeth, she glanced up and saw him standing behind her. Frightened, she stopped brushing and slowly turned her head.

He was gone.

Just like before.

"Who are you?" she asked.

She turned back to the mirror and stared at the capital letter "A" that had been drawn on the glass.

Da Lat was the capital of Lam Dong Province. It sat on the edge of the crystal clear Xuan Huong Lake on the Langbien Plateau in the southern part of the Central Highlands. One reached it by either driving the twisting roads through the pine forest or you took the train to the ornate station in the center of the city.

Because of the pine trees, the locals named it the "city of thousands of pine trees". Because of its cooler climate, abundance of colorful flowers and mist shrouded valleys, it was also known as the "city of eternal spring."

Da Lat was constructed by the French for use as a resort in 1907. They laid the tracks and built the railroad station. The wealthy colonials soon moved in and added French-style villas along wide boulevards, a health care complex, schools, churches, parks and other amenities. Most of the architecture was of the French Colonial style.

During the 1920s, the train station was expanded and remade in the then popular Art Deco style but with the high, pointed roofs characteristic of Vietnamese architecture of the Central Highlands.

In 1922, the Da Lat Palace Hotel, with its 39 suites, ornate lobby, and finely furnished dining room and other facilities, was completed and the city began to swell with tourists. The Da Lat Palace was considered to be among the poshest hotels in Southeast Asia.

In 1943, the ornate façade was changed to give it a more, sleek, modern appearance and the interior workings were upgraded.

During the war, the hotel still swarmed with tourists. It was also the meeting place for the international press corps, the CIA, a company of Special Forces people, and assorted soldiers on R&R who had come to Da Lat to enjoy its famous bistros, cafes, night life and beautiful women.

Going to Da Lat was almost like going to Paris.

To a newcomer like A., Da Lat seemed almost surreal. As he sat in the back of the taxi he had hailed at the station, he was amazed to see people seated at outdoor tables in front of cafes, and strolling along the boulevards, talking, laughing and joking as if the war was a million miles away. He saw French holdouts, other Europeans and even American couples enjoying what the city had to offer.

But what amused him most were the locals.

Seated outside the cafes with their perfectly tilted berets and wearing their French-cut clothes and smoking cigarettes attached to plastic holders or puffing on pipes, they looked and had even taken on the characteristics of typical Frenchmen. The only thing that's that reminded him that he wasn't in Paris was the fact that the locals spoke Vietnamese and the women wore those gorgeous body-hugging, colorful silk dresses with the leg slits and carried light, colorful parasols or wore the wide, round hats to shield them from the sun.

He had decided to come to Da Lat for a week's leave. It was fairly close to base camp and the LT had told him it was someplace he just had to see while in country. He booked the train and hotel through a local travel agent in the village the month before.

And although the LT had described Da Lat to him before he left, he quickly realized that no verbal description could do it justice.

It was clean.

And safe.

And remote.

It was French but Vietnamese.

It was beautiful and colorful and oh so very unique.

And it was lost in space in time like no other city on Earth.

The taxi stopped in front of the hotel. A bellman ran out and unloaded his bag while A. paid the cabby.

"Follow me, please," the bellman said as the uniformed doorman let them into the lobby

It was stunning.

It had highly-polished, patterned marble floors, ornate Persian carpets, comfortable French colonial furnishings and ornately Baroque brass and crystal chandeliers. People of all nationalities, including a few uniformed officers, meandered through the lobby. He followed the bellman to the front desk. The clerk, dressed in a white jacket with black tie greeted him with a smile. A. showed him his ID card.

The clerk handed him the register and a set of keys that looked like they belonged in a museum.

"Take Mr. A. to Suite 317," he said.

The bellman nodded. He led A, up two wide marble flights of stairs and down a wide, carpeted hallway to a large, hand-carved door. The bellman took A.'s key, let him in and placed his bag in the large closet.

After a quick tour of the suite, the bellman held out his hand. A. smiled and handed him 20 piastas. The man smiled and thanked him.

"If you need anything special, please call the front desk. We will do our best to make your stay a most pleasant and memorable one," he said.

The suite had French doors that led out to a balcony. A. opened the door and stepped outside to look out at the city. He faced the wide city center with his tall trees and well-trimmed parks. Two other hotels were on the other side of the square. They looked smaller and newer.

"Am I still in Vietnam?" he wondered.

When they were fully naked, she grabbed his rigid prick and led him to the bed. Just before they climbed in, she knelt and engulfed his knob with her mouth. He sighed dreamily at her obvious expertise.

His prick tasted almost salty-sweet. As she sucked, she also beat him off. After a few minutes of this, she let him go and got onto the bed with her legs wide apart and her knees bent.

"Fuck me like you did before. Make me yours again," she said.

"Your wish is my command," he said as he rammed his prick deep into her cunt.

They again settled into a good, deep, satisfying fuck. This time, it felt even better and waves of intense pleasure surged through her, lapping over her like waves hitting a beach. They fucked faster and faster.

Harder and harder.

She moaned and matched his every stroke with incredible passion as she soared higher and higher. This was now the most incredible fuck of her life. And she fucked him back with a zest that surprised even her. Her body was trembling with desire and she was bathed in sweat.

"Ooooh yes!" she screamed as she came.

Like before, they just kept fucking. And she came again.

And again.

And again.

"I'm yours now! Fuck me! Fuck me forever!" she moaned as she shook harder.

She felt his cum spurting into her on each inward stroke and fucked him as hard as she could to milk him of every last drop. They kept at it for what felt like an eternity. She came more times than she could count and fell limp.

"My God that was nice!" she said.

M. sat back to catch her breath. Just like the last scene, this one had aroused her. This time, however, she prepared herself better. She stripped off her skirt and panties and got out her favorite "toy". Then she sat back with her legs apart and read the scene. As she did, she moved the toy in and out of herself. After a while, she stopped reading and just closed her eyes and imagined she was the lady and A. was the samurai and they were making wild, passionate love.

When she finally climaxed, she moved the toy in and out faster and faster until she climaxed a second time.

And a third.

Satisfied, she stopped.

She looked at the clock. It was four p.m. Her son had just left work. He'd be home in about two hours. That was just enough time to shower and prepare dinner. She got up went into the bathroom. As she washed her toy, she smiled.

"If I ever do get the courage to see him again, I'm going to wear him out!" she said to her reflection.

That's when she saw the reflection of someone standing behind her and froze. She watched as trembled as she recognized the soldier who had haunted her during her college years. The soldier smiled at her then slowly vanished.

When he returned to States, he never told anyone about his experiences in Nam. Hell, his best friend never even knew he went there. Neither did his family. As far as they were concerned, he was off playing baseball or traveling around. The only ones who knew he was there were the guys he served with.

He put the war behind him.

When he did think about Vietnam, he thought about the good times he'd had and the crazy practical jokes the men played on each other or the bizarre incidents and places he'd experienced. He even managed to avoid the nightmares.

But it would remain part of him forever.

He spent the next year honing his baseball skills in a semi-pro league and trying to decide what he'd like to do for a living. He took a job at a bank and worked as a stringer or part-time reporter for several publications. When he thought he was ready, he decided to find M.

M. thought about her relationship with A. She was always amazed at how much he knew about Nihon. He knew its history, its politics, its legends and myths. He admired their customs. He knew details of the lives of individual samurai and daimyo and loved the wood block paintings of Hiroshige.

His thoughts were more Nihon-jin than Western. His personal philosophy leaned toward Buddhism and he lived his life by a code of ethics and honor that mirrored Bushido.

She became fascinated with him.

So much so, that she felt compelled to keep writing to him every single day. She looked forward to his emails and, after a few weeks, she knew they would be friends forever.

They exchanged photos and cards.

Gifts.

He sent her brochures and postcards from his many travels.

Their chance connection had quickly developed into a deeply intimate, affection and quite unconventional friendship. It was something that would have been frowned up years ago. And she knew her husband would become angry if he found out.

But she couldn't stop.

She didn't want to stop.

Neither did he.

They began to flirt with each other more and more. She soon realized that A. had become enamored with her, too. He'd even told her this. What started as a search for the original M. had brought them together at a when she needed such support the most.

Now, after so many years, he was coming to Nihon. She would finally get the chance to meet and speak with him in person.

And she was a nervous wreck!

Her friend, Y. noticed her agitation and assured her that all would be well.

"You have corresponded for a while now. Has his interest in you ever weakened?" she asked.

"Not that I have noticed," M. said. "In fact, he seems even more interested in me than ever."

Y. smiled.

"You are acting like a lovesick schoolgirl waiting for her prom date," she teased.

"Am I so obvious?" M. asked.

"You are very obvious," Y. said. "In fact, I have always been able to tell when you have heard from him. You look so happy afterward."

M. laughed.

"I can't help that," she said. "He is the only man who ever made me touch myself while thinking or dreaming of him. Oh, I can't believe I even admitted that!"

Y. laughed.

"And you have said that he always has such dreams about you. So you have nothing to worry about. The two of you will get along famously— like the lovers you plan to become," she said.

M. nodded.

Yes, she did plan to become his lover. Even if it was for only one night. But how was that even possible with A.'s wife coming with him? She looked at Y.

"Don't worry. I'll try to help you get some time alone with him. We'll think of something to make that happen," Y. assured her.

Omoidasu haru no hi

M. thought about what she had said to A. on the last day of his first visit. It had been a silly schoolgirl kind of test to see if he really had an interest in her. Now, she wished she hadn't said such a thing at all. She should have allowed things to take their natural course, regardless of their ages.

"I will be too busy with my studies to write you," she told him.

It was a test to see if he'd keep writing anyway.

A week after he left, his letter came. She read it but didn't answer.

Another came a week later.

Then another.

She let them both go unanswered.

Then no more came after that.

Weeks passed.

Then months.

She buried herself in her studies, took the entrance exams and passed them and went on to Osaka to attend the Kansai Junior College for Foreign Languages. As time passed, she thought that A. had found someone else or was so angry with her that he decided not to write again.

But A. had not given up.

He, too, had been busy in ways she never imagined. Ways that would have shocked her had she known about it.

In any case, she thought it was over for them.

Then something remarkable happened.

When M. received his letter at college, she was surprised. It had been nearly 3 years since he'd written. That had been mostly her fault.

Although she was attracted to him, he also scared her a little bit. When he said he loved her and wanted to marry her, she thought they were both too young to be serious about such things.

At least she didn't think he was.

She was wrong.

Not only did he still have interest in her, he had persistently attempted to locate her.

Somehow, he managed to track her down.

She read the letter several times, and then decided to write back. She apologized for not being able to write to him but also told him she was finished with her studies and working for the Osaka Grand Hotel chain. She was living in a dormitory of sorts for the time being.

Two weeks later, he phoned. When she heard his voice, she became so excited that she could barely speak or breathe. He told her he was returning to Nihon and he wanted to see her again very much.

She asked if he'd made hotel reservations. When he said that he hadn't, she said she would get him a nice room at the Royal Hotel. Since she was employed by the chain, she would also get him a good discount. He thanked her and said he'd be arriving on Japan Air Lines on August 18th.

"And this time, I'll make sure I get on the right plane," he promised with a laugh.

"That would be very nice," she replied as they both laughed about his first trip.

Koinu looked up into the serene face of the Daibutsu and felt a wave of peace and calm wash through him. He had survived yet another battle and had gone to Todaiji Temple to rest his weary body. As he gazed at the Buddha, he felt the pain, tension and weariness slowly leave him. He then took a deep, almost purifying, breath.

Koinu had never given much consideration to religion, but the Daibutsu filled him with a sense of awe and wonder. It smiled peacefully down at him and its eyes seemed to peer deep into his soul.

Without realizing it, he knelt. And he could not take his gaze off the Daibutsu's face.

A bokushi walked over and touched his shoulder. Koinu turned his head. The bokushi smiled and nodded to show he understood.

"Is it always like this?" Koinu asked in a hushed voice.

"For some," the bokushi said. "What do you feel inside now?"

"Peace. And calm. A deep sense of calm," he replied. "Is the Buddha real?"

"He is as real as you wish him to be. Are you Buddhist?" the bokushi asked.

"I'm not sure," Koinu said. "I don't know what I believe."

"There is time," the bokushi assured him. "The Buddha comes to each of us in different ways. Open your mind and heart and he will come to you, too."

"You make it sound so easy," Koinu said.

"It is as easy as you make it to be," the bokushi replied.

"How will I know?" he asked.

"You will know when he helps you to know," the bokushi replied.

He walked up to the JAL service counter and asked the young lady to page M. She called out her name several times. A few minutes later, M. arrived. When he saw her, his heart nearly stopped.

She had gone from very cute to downright beautiful.

She had allowed her hair to grow longer and fuller and wore just a hint of makeup. And her figure had truly blossomed. For several seconds, he didn't speak. He just stood there and admired her as if he were seeing a great work of art for the first time. His gaze made her nervous.

"Gomen nasai for staring, but you are truly beautiful," he said after he'd collected himself.

She almost blushed.

"I got you a room in the Royal Hotel. It's very nice and I managed to get you a good discount," she said as they walked out to the taxi stand.

"Arigato. That was very nice of you," he said.

"It was no trouble. I am happy to see you again. I work five days each week until five, so we can only get together in the evenings and weekends. What are your plans for the afternoons?" she asked as they got into the first taxi.

"Since I'm here on vacation, I'll take a few tours. Do you have any suggestions?" he said.

"Please take a tour of Osaka Castle while you are here. You can also go to Kyoto. I'm sure you will enjoy both. On the weekend, we can take the train to Nara for the day. I want to show you Nara. It is very beautiful," she said.

"This is Saturday. Do you have any plans for today?" he asked.

"None yet. What would you like to do?" she replied.

"Anything you like. This is your country, M.-san. I'm the gaijin here. Take me to your favorite places," he said.

"Alright. I will give you time to refresh yourself at the hotel. Then we can go and have something to eat. Do you still use hashi?" she asked.

'Hai," he smiled.

"Are there things you do not like to eat? Things you want to avoid?" she asked.

"I'll eat anything but liver. I'm willing to try everything—and I've developed a real taste for Asahi and Sapporo beer and plum wine," he smiled.

"I'm surprised. You did not seem to enjoy Japanese food on your last visit. I did not know what to feed you," she laughed. "But you liked our ice cream!"

"I still do. I've eaten a lot of different foods since you last saw me. You could say that my taste buds have expanded their horizons. I've concentrated mostly on Nihon-jin cuisine lately, especially since I've discovered that it's very good," he said.

"I see you have changed toward some things," she smiled.

"But not all things," he said. "Some, very important things, are the same."

M. put aside the book and leaned back as she thought about the last chapter. The ending had struck a chord deep inside of her.

It was so sad.

So purposeful.

Yet filled with happiness.

His words were so vivid. In fact, he'd painted each and every scene as if he'd lived it.

J. entered the room. He saw the tears on her cheeks and sat beside her as he picked up the novel.

"Are you crying because of the book?" he asked.

She nodded.

"It was beautiful. It's the best book he has ever written," she said as she sniffed back more tears.

"So it is not like his other novels?" he asked.

"Not at all. He put his heart and soul into it. He allowed his emotions to run free and he did it so perfectly," she said.

"You still love him, don't you? Even after all this time, you still love him," J. said as he smiled at her.

She nodded and wiped her tears with a tissue.

"Then go and see him, Mother. You know his itinerary. Pick a place that is convenient and visit him. I'm sure he'll be very happy to see you again," J. urged again.

"Why do you think so?" she asked.

"That's very plain. He has always used you as the main female character in his novels. Your name is everywhere. This tells me that he always thinks of you and that he misses you very much—as much as you miss him. Go and see him, Mother," J. said.

"Have you read 'Bushi'?" she asked.

"Not yet. Should I?" J. replied.

"Hai. I would like to know what you think of it," she said.

He nodded.

"I'll read it on the train while I commute to work," he promised. "Please think about what I've said. Go and see him."

He rose and left the room. She looked up at the poster on her wall and smiled as she remembered the day he bought it for her.

It was beautiful, warm and sunny.

They were walking hand-in-hand along one of the busier streets of Osaka. It was late afternoon and they had just come from a local theater where they had gone to see "The Sting". This had been their first actual date and they were just walking along and discussing the movie.

The soon came upon a young foreign artist who was selling his drawings in the street. They stopped to look them over. They were drawings of cute, large- eyed children. A. watched as she looked them over.

"These are very nice," she remarked.

"Pick one," A. said to her surprise.

She looked them over and pointed to one of a little girl standing in the street of what might have been a city in France.

"That one," she said.

"How much is it?" A. asked.

"Eight hundred yen," the artist replied.

"We'll take it," he told the artist as he counted out the money.

The artist rolled the drawing up, put a rubber band around it and gave it to her. A. gave him the money and they went on their way. She was happy, not because he had bought her the drawing, but because he bought it for her without hesitation, even though she had not expected him to do so.

His gesture spoke volumes to her.

"I'll buy you anything you like as long as I can afford it," he promised.

She had kept that drawing ever since. She even framed it so it wouldn't deteriorate with time. And each time she looked at it, she recalled that very happy afternoon.

She got into a taxi a few minutes later and returned to her boarding house. He returned to his hotel to get cleaned up for their next date that same evening.

As she relived that day in her mind, the tears once again rolled down her cheeks.

"Arigato," was all she could say. She wanted to say much more but her poor command of English caused her to keep quiet.

"I don't want you to buy me things. I only want you," was what she wanted to say.

What she should have said. She didn't know that men needed to be told such things and were terrible at reading emotions.

She heard footsteps behind her and smiled as her son entered.

"I forgot my briefcase," he said. "Why are you crying?"

"I was just remembering," she said. "Forgive me. I get sentimental at times."

He nodded.

He looked up at the drawing. After all this time, she still thought of him. He then looked across the room at the small bookshelf. There were 50 books on it. All were written by him. He had also read them because she urged him to. He was surprised to find her name in almost all of them.

He'd never forgotten her either.

Even though she knew where he was, she had never once tried to contact him. Yet she still loved him. He admired her loyalty. And he silently pitied them both.

"I have to go. I'll see you tonight," he said as he left.

She nodded.

As Koinu, Watanabe and Buntaro walked down the street, a tall, broad-shouldered young samurai purposely shouldered Koinu aside. The samurai stopped and glared at him.

"Gomen nasai," Koinu said.

"Is that all you're going to say?" the samurai asked haughtily.

"What more do you want? After all, it was you who purposely ran into me," Koinu said.

"How insulting! How dare you accuse me of being so rude!" the samurai said as he took a defiant stance.

Koinu just laughed at him.

"You think this is funny?" the samurai almost screamed.

"I do, actually," Koinu smiled. "I find it amusing that you are so eager to die."

"Me die? You'd best be careful what you say, old man or I'll send you to the undertaker!" the samurai said.

"If I go to the undertaker, it will be to purchase a coffin for you," Koinu said.

The samurai attempted to draw. Koinu grabbed his wrist and gave it a painful twist. The samurai heard it snap and he screamed in agony and Koinu drove him to his knees. He looked at him with tears in his eyes as the pain increased with each passing second.

"You broke my wrist!" he grunted as he clutched it with his left hand.

"And yet, you still live," Koinu said as he walked away.

Buntaro squatted next to the samurai.

"Be thankful that he did not draw on you or you would be lying in a pool of your own blood right now," he said.

"Just who the Hell is he anyway?" the samurai asked.

"He is the best," Buntaro said.

"And he's so good, he feels no need to prove it to ones like you," Watanabe added. "Now go back to that farm you escaped from while you still have a head on your shoulders. Next time, be more respectful of those you don't know. Understand?"

"I understand," the samurai replied.

He struggled to his feet and walked down the street. As he did, he saw three locals grinning at him.

"Who was that samurai?" he asked. "Do any of you know him?"

"We know him alright. That is Koinu-san. He is the right hand man of Date Masamune," one man replied. "They say the only one better than him is Musashi."

He turned and looked up the street. He realized then he was indeed fortunate to still be alive.

"Why do you suppose that samurai wanted to pick a fight with me?" Koinu asked.

"He must be new in town and perhaps he wanted to make a reputation for himself," Buntaro guessed.

"Well, he does have a reputation now. But not one he hoped for," Watanabe said.

"Funny how life works sometimes, isn't it?"Koinu smiled.

It was the third day of his second visit. They were seated in the back of a taxi. They had just come from having dinner together. It might have been considered their first actual date. On the way back to his hotel, he reached over and took her hand.

She was so surprised, she blushed.

But she didn't pull back.

His move, she thought, was unexpected—and welcome.

And so very sweet.

They were both very shy but he had made the first move. His touch excited her. No, it thrilled her. She looked up at the driver and saw him smiling in the mirror.

The next day he met her outside her hotel after work. She smiled at him.

"You surprised me yesterday. I did not expect you to take my hand in the taxi," she said as he took it again. "You are the first to hold my hand like this."

"I'm sorry if I startled you," he said softly. "I just had to let you know."

"I think you have not changed toward me," she said hopefully.

"Never. I can't help it, M.-san. You are all I've thought about for the last three years. I'll never change how I feel about you," he said.

"I'm glad," she smiled.

She was amazed and thrilled. His feelings had withstood the separation. They had passed the test of time. And he had returned to be with her.

M. stood in front of the mirror after returning from the beauty parlor. Her hair was black again with some strands of dark brown for highlights. She frowned at the lines around her mouth and wished she could erase them.

K. walked into the bathroom and saw her gazing at her reflection.

"I see you had your hair dyed," he observed.

"Do you like it?" she asked as she turned to face him.

"From behind, you look very young and sexy. From the front, not so much," he said. "How much did you pay the woman at the shop?"

"I paid her 3,000 yen," M. replied.

"You should return to the shop and demand your money back," he said. "You still look the same."

"Doesn't the dark hair make me look a little bit younger?" she asked.

"No. You look like an old woman with dyed hair," K. joked. "If you did that to please me, it didn't work."

"It is not you I want to please," she said with a sly smile.

"Ah, so. I don't think you will please A.-san, either. Not unless you break his eyeglasses," he said. "That way, he will not be able to see you clearly."

M. "humphed" and walked past him.

He smiled.

"She actually does look good with her hair colored," he thought. "Perhaps too good."

As M. finished dressing, she wondered what A.'s old love looked like. How would she look compared with her? M. was eight years younger than her. She was still young and most likely, very pretty. If she showed up where A. happened to be, would he even notice her? Would he ignore her and go with his old friend instead?

"I cannot change who or what I am," she thought. "He has always said that I look young, pretty and sexy to him and always will. I'm sure he means that so I shouldn't have anything to worry about. Should I?"

Hitori botchi no yoru

M. was cleaning the second house like she did every week. Her mind, however, was miles away as she thought about A.'s impending visit. As she slid the door open to another room, she was surprised to see her eldest son, R. seated on a chair next to the window reading a book.

"Gomen nasai. I didn't know you were home," she apologized. "What are you reading?"

"Bushi," he replied. "I thought I'd read it before I met your friend. He's an excellent writer. He uses his words to paint very vivid pictures and his characters seem true to life. I notice that the main female character has the same name as you. Were you his inspiration?" R. asked.

She blushed.

"You can tell me, Mother. I won't let anyone else know," he assured her.

She sat down.

"He said that I inspired many scenes in the book. But I think his female character is a combination of me and his first love in Nihon. She also had the same first and last name as me," she said.

R. smiled.

She had told him how they met on FB and how their accidental connection had led to a long, strong friendship that was very unusual for a Japanese woman of her generation. He also knew they were very close and intimate friends and both got strength from each other.

"Didn't you say he was a soldier?" R. asked.

"Hai. He was in Vietnam," she replied.

"That might explain his vivid battle scenes. Was he conscripted?" R. asked.

"No. He volunteered. He said it was his duty," she replied.

"Just like a samurai," R. smiled.

"Hai. He told me that 'Bushi' is based on a series of dreams he has had. The way her said he felt as if he was remembering instead of dreaming, made me think he was a samurai in a past life," M. said.

R. nodded.

"That would explain his deep understanding of those times," he said. "You two have grown very close. Would you have married him had you known him before you met Father?"

"If he had asked me, I would have happily done so," M. said.

R. laughed.

"What if he asked you now?" he teased.

"You are incorrigible!" she said as she playfully hit him with the dust towel.

He grinned as she left.

He didn't tell her that he'd accidentally read one of their more intimate emails in which A. described a very vivid, highly erotic dream he'd had about the two of them. Her response had been just as vivid and erotic. That's when he realized their friendship had deepened beyond anything he ever imagined. Perhaps they even loved each other now.

M. finished cleaning and returned to the other house. She saw K. snipping branches from the tree out in front and greeted him. He smiled.

"Your friend's book is at the top of the Best Seller list here in Nihon. I saw it in today's paper. The article said that all of his other novels are now being translated in Nihon-go. He should become very wealthy soon," K. said. "You must feel very happy for him."

"I do. He and his family deserve it," M. smiled.

"Has he told you when his flight will arrive?" K. asked.

"Not yet. It has only been two days," she said as she poured them each a glass of iced tea.

"The day is getting close. Why not email him and ask?" he suggested.

"I will later. It is the middle of the night where he is," she said.

"Do so anyway. He'll respond when he wakes—like he always does," K. said.

She looked at him. He smiled at her expression.

"I know that you exchange emails every day," he said. "Who else would you be contacting if not our children?"

"You've known all along?" she asked.

He nodded.

"It bothered me at first. I wanted to forbid it, but I realized that if I did so, you would resent me. And you would find a way of continuing your contact. So, there was no sense trying to stop you. Since he is married to such a pretty young woman, I have no need to be jealous or worry about him trying to steal you away from me—even if my katana is nothing more than a small kitchen knife that is rusted and without much use," he said as he quoted one of her emails.

She stared at him and blushed deeply.

"You read that?" she asked.

"Hai. In fact, I have read many of your exchanges," he said. "I thought that one was very amusing. So did he. And I agree that you have a very amusing and colorful way of insulting people."

He handed her the empty glass and returned to his trimming. She took the glasses into the house and wondered exactly how much K. knew.

But K. said nothing more.

K. wasn't too crazy about his wife's friendship with another man, but he reasoned there was no way to prevent it. Forbidding her to contact him would only make A. more attractive in her eyes and might even drive M. into his arms. That would cause too much needless trouble for everyone.

A. was helping her with her English and he had even sent them a jazz CD from New Orleans because she told him her husband liked the older styles of jazz. But there were changes in M. he never expected.

Her humor had emerged. And he discovered she was both sarcastic and funny. She was becoming more assertive but not in a confrontational way. And she was more willing to express her opinions on a wide variety of subjects he didn't know she even paid attention to.

He wasn't exactly sure how to handle her now, but he began to rely on her more and more. He now realized that she was indeed the rock that the entire family had been anchored to all these years. Like most Japanese men, he'd been too busy to see that.

He'd stopped reading their emails after the first two years. What intrigued him most was the fact that A. actually thought of M. as young and sexy. He was very attracted to her and her to him. He just didn't understand that. To most other men, M. was just another elderly woman. Someone they wouldn't give even a first glance to.

He was stunned to read one email in which A. declared that if he and M. were both single, he'd be kneeling before with a ring as quick as a jet would fly him to Japan. In other words, he would not hesitate to ask her to marry him. Her reply shocked him even more.

She wrote back that she would not hesitate to accept his ring.

Were they in love? If so, what did they plan to do about it? That's as far as their flirtations ever went, though. A. had given her advice of eating more vitamin packed fruit like blueberries and ways of figuring out ailments. She had followed his advice and, at one point, it had helped head off what could have been a serious health issue for K. So, in a sense, his advice had saved his life.

He also picked up on A.'s sense of honor and commitment. In both, he was more samurai than American. Despite himself, he began to like A.

He just wished he hadn't become a rival.

J. had taken his mother out to dinner that evening. As usual, he steered their conversation toward A.

"Does your old friend follow a particular religion?" J. asked.

"I always felt that his soul was too free for such things. He never said what he believed or if he believed. But when we were in Nara, something happened that makes me feel he is a Buddhist. Not the pacifistic type. He is more like a warrior-monk," she said.

"What happened in Nara?" he asked.

"It was very strange and unexpected," she said.

They had taken the train to Nara. It was a gorgeous summer day

When they entered the famous Todaiji Temple which was the home of one of the Daibutsu, or Great Buddha. The interior was somewhat dark and cool. Around them he saw monks at prayer as tourists snapped photos. He took several himself then walked up and looked into the face of Great Buddha.

It was almost like the experience he'd had in Vietnam only far more powerful.

More dramatic.

He became overwhelmed by a sense of awe and inner peace that was so profound, he began to weep. The tears were not tears of sorrow, but of deep personal joy. He stood there, transfixed, for several minutes. He felt as if time itself had been frozen. The Buddha's gaze penetrated every corner of his soul and filled them with light. He didn't know if he should kneel.

Or stand.

Or pray.

He decided to kneel.

Then he clapped three times and began to pray silently.

M. was dumbstruck. A. told her he didn't bother with religion, yet there he knelt. What really surprised her was that he knew exactly what to do in a temple.

His actions caught the attention of one of the bokushis. He walked over and knelt beside him. A. smiled at him.

"Are you enlightened?" the bokushi asked.

"Is anyone?" A. responded.

"It is said that only the Buddha ever reached Nirvana. He was the first. He showed us the way. I sense that your soul is in torment," the bokushi said.

"It is," A. said.

"Are you bushi? Were you in the war?" he asked.

"Hai," A. said softly so M. couldn't hear.

"The past is gone. You must stop reliving it. Let it go. The future has not yet happened, so do not worry about it. We all live in the present. Enjoy this moment. Embrace it."

M. shook her head.

"I have never seen anyone else act like he did that day. When I asked him what had happened, he just smiled at me. He said he understood now. I asked what it was he understood. He said more than he expected," she said.

"He seemed to be lighter and easier going after that. His experience at Todaiji changed him. I did not realize what had happened then. But I did see that he was completely awed by the Daibutsu," she added.

J. thought about it for second or so.

"The more you tell me about him, the more I feel the two of you should have married," he said. "He is not what we think of as the typical American. But you knew that at the time. There were things about him that surprised you all the time. I think you would have had a very happy and exciting life together."

"I cannot go back and change anything. At the same time, I cannot let it go," she said with a sad smile.

"From what I've read in his book, he can't, either," J. pointed out. "If anything, I think that he loves you even more. That's why you need to go and see him, Mother. For both your sakes."

"I am afraid if I did, it would make our lives too complicated," she said. "He is married. I don't want to ruin that for him."

"I'm not asking you to destroy his marriage. I'm asking you to go and see him. What happens after that is up to the gods," J. said.

M. watched her husband eat.

He stopped and smiled at her.

"Do you ever weary of my cooking?" she asked.

"Of course not. You an excellent cook. You can work magic with the simplest of ingredients. You are able to turn anything into a feast for the eyes and tongue. I feel honored and fortunate that you have been preparing meals for me all these years," he said as he refilled his bowl.

"I will never grow tired of you, either," he assured her. "In fact, I love you more with each passing day and you are younger and more beautiful now than the day we first met."

She laughed.

"I think your eyes grow dim with age," she said.

"I assure you there is nothing at all amiss with my eyes—or any other body part," he smiled.

It was a beautiful, clear summer night in Osaka. They had just finished dinner and the night was still young. They walked along the narrow river hand-in-hand. Passersby looked at them and smiled. Some bowed and greeted them. A couple of older women giggled to each other. M. & A. didn't care. They were in love. They came to a foot bride that spanned the river and walked over it. Halfway across, they stopped and leaned on the rail to watch the city lights dance in the ripples of the water. The evening was warm and pleasant. He reached out and put his arm around her waist as she sidled closer.

Everything felt so right.

Perfect.

It was the most perfect moment of her life.

Three young men passed them as they staggered across the bridge. The one in the middle was so drunk that his two friends had to help him walk. He looked at A. and grinned.

"Hello, American!" he shouted happily.

"Hello," A. said with a smile.

"I like Americans! Good-bye, American!" he shouted as he friends took him across to the other side.

They watched them walk away and laughed. A. pulled her closer and looked into her eyes. She felt her knees quake.

"Anata wa aishimasu," he said.

She felt her heart beat faster and faster. She smiled at him.

"I know," was all she managed to say.

She hoped he understood how she felt, too. A. was about to say something else. Perhaps he was about to ask the expected and longed for question. Before he could say anything, an elderly couple appeared out of nowhere and walked up to them. The man was in his 60s with short cut, gray brown hair. The woman was Japanese and around the same age. Both looked strangely familiar to her and A. but they couldn't understand why.

The couple stared asking a lot of questions about sights in and around Osaka. Ever polite, M. answered each of them as best as she could while A. added some comments of his own.

The conversation dragged on.

Long enough to spoil that particular moment.

The couple thanked them and continued across the bridge. As the man passed, he turned and nodded at them. They watched until the couple melted into the night crowd.

"Do you know them?" M. asked.

"Although they look very familiar, I'm sure we've never met. Do you know them?" he asked.

"I don't think so. Yet, I feel that I should know who they are. That's very strange," she said.

Just then, a heavy shower came out of nowhere and just about drowned them. A. looked around and saw a taxi stand. They ran over and jumped into the first cab in the line. She told the driver to take her back to the dormitory then to take A. to his hotel afterward.

"What would you like to do tomorrow?" A. asked.

"I have to work until five. Why don't you tour the castle in the morning and come to the hotel where I work after? Then we can go out somewhere for dinner," she suggested.

"How about after dinner?" he asked.

"Do you want to go to the amusement park? It's a lot of fun," she asked.

"We can go anywhere you like, M.-san," he said. "Anywhere at all."

When the taxi stopped in front of her dorm, A. escorted her to the door. They hugged for a little while.

He smiled at her.

"Tomorrow," he said.

"Tomorrow," she repeated.

She watched as he got back into the cab and drove off. Then she went up to her room and sighed. What was he about to say when that old couple interrupted?

"Next time," she smiled.

Ue o muite arukou

When M. returned from shopping, she heard jazz music throughout the house. She went into the living room and saw K. leaning back in a chair with his eyes shut as he listened to the music. She smiled. He was listening to the CD A. had sent him years before. It was old-style New Orleans jazz.

He opened his eyes and smiled at her.

"Did you leave any money in our bank account?" he joked.

"Not a yen. I spent it all on a mink coat and diamond earrings," she joked back.

"It's too warm for a mink coat and I won't look good in the earrings," he smiled.

"You?" she queried.

"Hai. Since you used my money, I assume you purchased those things for me," he said as he sat up. "Your friend has excellent taste in music. What does he normally like to listen to?"

"He told me that he likes everything buy rap and something called hip-hop. He says that both are ghetto noise, not music," M. replied.

"After seeing the photos of his wife, I know he also has excellent taste in woman," K. said. "Although I do question his taste when I know he likes you. Perhaps his eyesight is failing?"

She scowled at him.

"He told me that there is nothing wrong with his eyesight and he likes what he sees," she said. "You used to."

"That was a very long time ago. You once looked elegant and grand like a great ocean liner. Now, you seem more of a ship wreck," he teased.

"And that makes you the reef I became wrecked upon!" she retorted.

"I think I look rather fine," he said.

"You're not so bad for an old, rusted out rowboat with broken oars," she said. "Many years ago, you were like a powerful warship or submarine. But that was before your torpedo stopped working," M. said.

He winced.

"I think I'll quit while I'm behind," he said.

"I think that's one of your better ideas," she agreed as she went to put the groceries away.

The amusement park reminded him of Coney Island in many ways. It had about 30 different rides, mostly of the roller coaster variety, but was better organized and much, much cleaner. And the food was better.

At least that's what A. told her.

There was a "tunnel of love" style ride. The attendant helped them climb into the front of a small boat like car and advised them to hold on. There was no one else in the back seat. The ride slowly moved into the tunnel and they soon found themselves snuggled together in total darkness. He put his arm around her and held her close. She felt his heart beating and smiled. It was strong and steady. And she felt so right in his arms.

The ride, like its American counterpart, was misnamed. At certain intervals, lights flashed and images of demons. Accompanied by Hellish laughter, leapt out of the darkness at them. M. jumped a few times and clung to him even tighter while he just laughed.

"Does nothing frighten you?" she asked.

"Not anymore," he said.

She didn't understand it at the time. She just thought it was a natural part of him becoming more mature. At one point, the ride went into a very slow mode. There were no flashing lights or demons. It was quiet.

Romantic.

"Anata wa aishimasu," he whispered.

Her heart beat faster. This was the perfect place and time.

That's when they heard something in the car behind them. They turned around and saw the same elderly couple they had met on the bridge.

But where did they come from?

The seat behind them was empty when they entered the tunnel. M. was sure of that. She didn't see anyone else get on with them and no sounds of any kind had come from that seat until now. The woman smiled knowingly at her.

"I remember you. We met in the bridge," she said.

"Hello again," A. said, obviously miffed they had interrupted him. "We didn't know you were back there."

"When did you get on?" M. asked.

"The same time you did. You were so wrapped up in each other that you didn't notice," the woman said.

The mood spoiled, they just chatted with the couple until they finished the ride. Just before they reached the end of the tunnel, A. looked back and asked the couple who they were. The man winked and tapped his shoulder.

"You'll understand one day," he said.

The tunnel opened back up into the bright lights of the amusement park. As A. and M. disembarked, they looked back only to discover that the couple was gone. They looked at each other in puzzlement.

Where had they gone?

M. sighed as she thought about that evening.

That had been the second time that couple had shown up to ruin the mood. Unfortunately, it wouldn't be the last.

They got on a few more rides, but the meeting with the couple stayed in their thoughts the entire evening. They talked about them and wondered how they'd appeared without being seen by them. And both wondered why the couple had looked so very familiar.

A sudden shower came in from nowhere and soaked the amusement park. A. and M. took cover in a food stand. They ordered sodas and waited for the rain to lessen. Several others had also taken shelter there and the place became crowded. When they finished their sodas, the rain had lessened.

It was now almost midnight and the park was shutting down. They walked to a taxi stand and got into the first one. She told the driver where to take them. He drove to her dorm first.

And they held hands the entire time.

As the taxi pulled up in front of the dorm, she smiled at A.

"Tomorrow is Saturday. Let's go to Nara," he said.

"That will be fun. I will be at the hotel at nine," she said happily.

He watched from the taxi until she was safely inside, and then told the driver to take him to the hotel.

R. beamed as she sat down.

"I can't believe that we're going to Japan! I'm so excited. This is your big chance, A. You're famous now. Your book is selling all over the world," she gushed. "Did you tell M.?"

"I emailed her. She said that since our flight won't get into Tokyo until 10 p.m., she'll meet us at our hotel the following morning. I told her that I'd phone her after we check into our hotel," he said.

"Where are we staying?" she asked.

"The Imperial Hotel. It's one the finest in all of Tokyo. The publisher got us a suite, too," he said.

He took the schedule from his pocket and looked it over.

"I'm going to be real busy, too. I have three book signings around Tokyo, two newspaper interviews and an appearance on a late night talk show. After a three day break, we head for Osaka, Kyoto, Nara and Fukuoka, Matsumoto... we'll be all over the place. The last stop is in Osaka. After that, I'm going to Yufuin for a week. You'll fly to Manila from Osaka and we'll meet there," he said. "We'll be traveling for five weeks."

"One day, I might get around to reading your book," R. said. "But you know I'm not much of a reader."

"Yes I know. If it doesn't have anything to do with Philippine movie stars and their private lives or stupid soap operas, you're clueless about it. That's why I've insisted that you not be interviewed. You have no idea what 'Bushi' is about, so you'd be no help to me at all."

He smiled.

"Maybe if it was on your cell phone, you'd read it? Your nose is always buried in that thing anyway," he said with more than a little irritation. "I'm glad we'll be off the grid in Japan. Your stupid phone won't work. When I get there, I'm going to have to rent a cell phone so I can make and receive calls. I'll rent one for you, too. But it won't be a smart phone."

"You really love Japan, don't you?" she asked.

"Yes. I do. So will you once you experience it. It's a wonderful country with warm, friendly people. It's clean and safe and it has a unique culture and fascinating history. But it's getting too modern for my taste. I prefer the older places of Japan. I'm more comfortable there," he said.

Nijinda hoshi o kazoete

Pike stepped out on the front porch of his long ranch house and looked up at the deep, cloudless blue sky and took a deep breath. He reached into his vest pocket, took out his silver watch and checked the time.

Eleven a.m... A perfect autumn day in Wyoming. He stepped off the porch and walked casually to the large corral where a young Army officer stood leaning against the rail fence watching the horses canter about. Pyke smiled as he drew close to him.

"Well, how do they look, Lt. Thompson?" Pyke asked nodding toward the horses.

"Mighty fine, Mr. Pyke. Best I've seen in the Territory so far. What are you asking for them?" Thompson replied. Pyke grinned.

"The usual--two hundred a head. Is it a deal?" Pyke asked. Thompson nodded his approval.

"No problem. I'll have the money here tomorrow morning around seven. How many do you have?"

"Twenty two, Lieutenant. They're all saddle broken and of the best stock we could find. Same as always," Pyke said. Thompson nodded. Pyke stepped up to fence and studied the young officer. Cal Thompson was from back east. A Philadelphia man and had joined the U.S. Cavalry just after the War. He was young for an Army horse buyer--just around 30--but had a good eye for horses and the Army trusted him. So did Pyke. In fact, he liked Thompson a lot and admired his honesty.

"You're the best horse breeder in these parts, Mr. Pyke and it's a pleasure to do business with you. I always feel that the Army is getting its money's worth from you," Thompson said. His eyes went to a snow-colored pony at the far end of the corral and stayed there. He had never seen a horse so pure in color before. In fact, it almost gleamed in the morning sun.

"That's the most beautiful pony I ever saw, Mr. Pyke. What kind of horse is that?" asked Thompson.

"A white one," said Pyke a broad grin on his face. Thompson laughed. The old rancher sure had a weird sense of humor.

"You got me there, Mr. Pyke. He sure is a beauty. How much you want for him?" asked Thompson.

"He's not for sale. It took me three generations to breed that one. He's an exact copy of his grandfather; a horse a I had over 30 years ago. There isn't another like him anywhere in the Territory," Pyke said.

"Too bad. I'd sure love to have him. What's his name?"

"He doesn't have one just yet. I'm not sure what to call him. But he's real special to me," Pyke said.

Thompson looked longingly at the pony and sighed. He was an incredibly beautiful horse. Special--just like the old man said. He shrugged.

"Oh, well. I guess a man can't have everything he wants," Thompson said as he held his hand out. Pyke gripped it firmly to seal the bargain. Thompson saluted him, climbed onto his brown cavalry horse and smiled at Pyke.

"Tomorrow then. Bright and early," he said as he galloped off toward the south. Pyke watched until the lieutenant faded from sight then returned to the ranch house. It had been a good day for business.

Pyke rose at dawn and bathed in the stream that ran near the back of the house. The water was crisp and cold--a real eye-opener that made him shiver. He toweled down and headed back inside to shave. He mixed his shaving soap in the large crock mug and stood before the mirror as he lathered his face. As he scraped the razor across his deeply tanned face, Pyke studied his reflection casually.

"Not bad looking for an old man," he thought. "Not a line on my face. I look almost as young as I did 20 years ago when---" He dropped the thought and finished shaving. He sighed. Those days were long gone now. It was better to keep his mind on more practical matters.

Two hours later, he heard the clatter of hoof beats and horse-drawn wagons outside the house. He stepped out onto the porch to see twenty mounted troopers with and Eighth Cavalry guidon and two heavy covered wagons. One was laden with supplies for the troops. The other was a family of settlers. A burly young man with yellow hair and his chubby wife sat in the front of the wagon while a thing, sandy haired boy leaped out and raced to the corral to see the horses. Pyke greeted Lt. Thompson as he dismounted. The men shook hands and headed into the house.

Thompson reached into his shirt and took out a stack of 44 $100 bills and handed them to Pyke. The old man put them into a drawer.

"Aren't you going to count them?" asked Thompson.

"I don't have to," he said as he headed to the corral. Thompson followed. Pyke looked at the boy who was now seated on the fence and smiled. The boy smiled back.

"My name's Kitt Browne. What's yours?" the boy said.

"John Pyke. What's that you have there, Kitt?" Pyke asked as he noticed the book in the boy's pocket. Kitt pulled it out and handed it to him. Pyke grinned. It was a dime novel. They were pretty popular these days. Just about all the kids read them--and many adults as well. Pyke looked at cover. It featured a masked man astride a rearing white horse blazing away with two six guns.

"The Lone Ranger?" Pyke asked, a tone of amusement in his voice.

"He's my favorite. I've read everything I could find about him. A lot of folks told me that he was real and that he disappeared nearly twenty years ago. But my Dad says that's a lot of bunk. That there never was a Lone Ranger. But I believe there was. Do you, Mr. Pyke?" Kitt said. Pyke smiled broadly.

"Oh, he was real all right. As real as you and me. A lot of people around these parts claim to have seen him. A lot of them are still in prison, too," Pyke said as he handed the dime novel back to Kitt.

Kitt returned it.

"You can keep that one, Mr. Pyke. I have two more just like it," he said as he leaped from the fence and trotted back to the wagon.

"Nice boy. Quite a group you have there, Lieutenant. Where are you headed?" Pyke asked as several soldiers entered the corral and began herding the horses out of it. Thompson watched and barked a few orders before he sat down on the porch. Pyke sat next to him.

"We're headed up to Fort Laramie to drop off the horses and the monthly payroll," Thompson said.

"What about them?" Pyke asked nodding toward the Brownes.

"They'll hook up with a wagon train headed west into the Oregon Territory. They plan to try their luck in Portland. They're fine people," Thompson said.

The door creaked open. Pyke's partner, a tall Cherokee Indian a couple of years older than him, stepped out and handed each of them a cup of coffee. Thompson sipped it as he watched his men tie up the horses.

"That's at least a week's travel from here through some pretty barren country. What about the Comancheros? I heard they were operating up in these parts now," Pyke said.

"I'm not worried. I have a full troop of good men with me. If the Comancheros are way up here, I doubt they'd be crazy enough to attack an armed cavalry troop. They usually steer clear of soldiers anyway," Thompson said. He drained his cup and placed it on the porch rail. A sergeant trotted up to them and saluted. Thompson returned it.

"The troop is mounted and ready, Sir!" the sergeant barked. Thompson stood, shook hands with Pyke and his partner, then mounted his horse. He looked over at the corral at the pure white pony again and wished it was his.

"Well, gotta go now, Mr. Pyke. I'll see you on the way back," Thompson said. Pyke nodded. Thompson barked a few orders and they whole troop headed west. Pyke and his partner watched until the troop was out of sight then sat down on the porch again.

"We made $4400 today, old friend," Pyke said to his partner. The Indian whistled.

"That is much money, Kimosabe," the Indian replied. Pyke smiled. After nearly 45 years together, his partner still called him that. Some things never change and this was one instance where Pyke was glad of it.

"Half is yours, old friend. After all, you did most of the rounding up and your sons helped break them. You've earned it," Pyke said.

"I thank you on behalf of my family and myself, Kimosabe," he said, a genuine tone of gratitude n his deep voice. He noticed the dime novel rolled up in Pyke's hand. "What's that?" he asked. Pyke handed it to him.

"The Lone Ranger?" his partner asked. Pyke nodded. "They are still writing these things?"

"Apparently so, old friend," Pyke said. His partner smiled.

"Then many people still remember?" he asked. Pyke nodded. His partner smiled. "It is good they remember,"

"Why?" asked Pyke.

"Because people need a hero. Someone or something to believe in. It gives them hope," his partner said.

Pyke sighed. He looked at the Indian and smiled. Forty-five years and they were still the best of friends. Hell, they were closer than brothers. He looked up into the cloudless sky and took stock of his life. A big ranch. Lots of money and a good, strong friend. What more could any man want?

The phone rang.

M. turned the volume down on the TV set and answered it. Her heart nearly sang when she heard his voice.

"Where are you?" she asked.

"We've just checked into the Imperial Hotel. It's kind of late. I hope I didn't wake you," he apologized.

"You did not. I am watching a movie on the TV right now. I've been waiting for your call," she replied.

"R. and I are going to get something to eat at the ryorya around the corner then shower and turn in. Let's get together tomorrow," he said.

"That would be perfect. We can meet at your hotel. What time is good?" she asked.

"Anytime after ten a.m. It will be wonderful to finally meet you in person," he said.

"Can I bring Y.?" she asked.

"Of course. You've mentioned her so often, I'd like to meet her," he agreed. "We'll see you tomorrow. Konbanwa!"

"Konbanwa," she said as she hung up.

She turned the sound back up on the TV. Try as she might, she was unable to concentrate on the movie

They stood on an observation deck at Kansai Airport while they waited for A.'s flight number to be called. It was another beautiful night.

He put his arm around her as they talked. And she silently waited for those words she longed to hear.

Then something happened.

Again it was totally unexpected.

He asked if he could kiss her. She nodded, expecting him to kiss her on the cheek, even though it was not a Japanese custom. To her surprise, he took her in his arms and gently kissed her on the lips. Despite her surprise, she let herself enjoy the moment. The kiss was pleasant and a little exciting.

And it was a first for both of them.

"Anata wa aishimasu," he said.

She repeated the words to him and held him close as he stroked her hair. The moment was perfect again. She heard him clear his throat and smiled.

But the gods were playing their cruel games again that night.

Before he could pop the question, that same elderly couple they had met on the bridge and at the amusement park suddenly emerged from the doorway. They saw them and said hello and asked A. if he was on the flight back to Tokyo.

He politely said he was, despite his obvious annoyance.

And the couple talked on and on and on like they had the last two times. A few minutes later, the boarding call for A.'s flight crackled over the loudspeakers. He had just 15 minutes to board. He sighed and smiled at M.

"I have to run now. I'll call you when I get to Tokyo," he said.

She watched him hurry back into the terminal and smiled. She looked for the couple but they had vanished as suddenly as they had appeared. She didn't recall seeing them leave, either.

She was becoming frustrated.

She imagined that A. was, too.

Each time the perfect moment arose, the elderly couple appeared to ruin it. They always seemed to be there at the wrong time, like they were following them for the sole purpose of stopping A.'s proposal in its tracks.

And they looked so familiar, too.

She felt she should know them from somewhere.

She watched another flight leave the runway and wept. She really wanted to scream at the top of her lungs to vent her frustrations. Instead, she took a taxi back to her dorm.

Along the way, she came up with an idea. Something that would get A. to propose marriage to her. She thought it was quite clever, too.

It would prove to be the mistake that would haunt them both forever...

Omoidasu haru no hi

"Are you sure you won't join us?" she asked as she picked up her purse.

"I'm sure. I'll get to meet him when he comes to Hachioji. You and Y. go and meet him. Have a nice visit and call me later if you have a chance," K. said.

"Are you afraid he might try to steal me away from you?" she teased.

"No. I can't imagine him giving up his pretty young wife for an old woman like," K. joked. "He would have to brain damaged!"

He watched her expression, expecting one of her sarcastic barbs. None came.

"Besides, his wife would probably kill you both if she suspected anything," he said. "Then I'd be left all alone and I'd really miss you."

"You would?" she asked.

"Of course. If you weren't here, I'd have no one to drive me to the gym or my favorite pub or any other appointments. I would also have to clean this place by myself. That would be far too exhausting," he said.

"Men!" M. huffed.

He laughed.

"I might have to hire a pretty young maid to help me," he said.

"She'd be perfectly safe with you. Your katana hasn't left its sheath in years," M. slashed.

He winced, then laughed.

"That's because I haven't had a reason to lately. I only draw my katana for beautiful young women—not grandmothers," he shot back.

"It's so rusty now that if you drew it, the blade would fall off," she returned.

Before he could fire back, M. saw a dark green car drive up.

"Oh, there is Y. I must leave now. We should be back this evening," she said as she hurried out.

He walked to the door and waved as they drove away.

M.'s last barb had been one of her best. He knew that her friendship with A. had brought out her stronger, tougher and more sarcastic tendencies which she had kept submerged all these years. He was now confident that his wife would be able to survive without him—if she had to.

This made him breathe and sleep easier.

He heard the email tone go off on the PC. He walked over and clicked it on. It was from A. Although M. and Y. expected to return that same evening, A. had emailed M. that he had booked a suite for them for the next two nights so they wouldn't have to make the long, hectic drive to and from Tokyo each day. M. had left before she saw it.

He smiled.

Her friend A. was very generous and practical. He wanted to save them some time and trouble. They would be staying at the most glamorous hotel in Tokyo, a place M. had always wanted to spend one night at, just to experience its legendary luxury. A. was about to grant her that wish.

He smiled.

M. was going to be very surprised.

"You have to see him, Mother," J. insisted.

"I am afraid to. It's been such a long time. He might not remember me," she argued.

He laughed.

"He remembers you. I think he will never forget you. He has used you as the model for the female characters in his books. In a way, he honors you. He has put you on a pedestal," he said.

"You think he idolizes me?" she asked.

"Hai. I've read all of his books. Mostly I did this because you've read them. I was curious as the why this American author fascinated you so much. Now that I've read them, I know," he said.

He looked at the poster on her bedroom wall.

"You've kept this since you were 20 years old. You told me of the day he bought it for you. I think he'd be pleased to know that you've kept it all this time and that you think about him each time you look at it. Would you have married him if he'd asked, Mother?" he said.

She nodded.

"What happened to spoil it?" he asked.

"Many things. One stupid thing led to another and it ended," she said with a deep sadness in her voice.

"Tell me about it," he said as she sat down.

"There is another man here. He has asked me to go out with him. He is very persistent," she said.

"Oh. I have a competitor now?" he asked.

"Maybe. I'm not sure," she said, as she hoped to get him to ask the question.

"Is he handsome?" he asked instead.

"I think so," she said in an attempt to make him feel threatened and jealous. Jealous enough to propose.

"I see. Do you like him?" A. asked.

"A little bit," she replied. "Should I go out with him?"

She wanted him to say no. To tell her that she belonged to him.

Stupidly, Art said the wrong thing because he didn't want her to feel that he was trying to control her in any way.

"That's up to you—but only if you really want to," he said.

She was stunned. She wasn't expecting that and she was at a total loss as how to respond. She remained silent for a few seconds. She wanted to say that she had made it all up. That there was no other man but she didn't want him to feel she was trying to trap him into proposing. She was afraid he'd become angry.

So, she said nothing instead.

He didn't either.

They ended with some chit-chat and he said he'd try to return to Japan as soon as he could afford it.

He never did.

He wrote her every week. She had plenty of chances to tell him the truth. Instead, she kept playing the jealousy angle in an effort to get him to propose. But the more she played it, the more he began to give up.

They were two young people who were very much in love and caught up in a misunderstanding that was slowly strangling their budding love to death.

Instead of returning to propose as she'd hoped, A. wrote her several weeks later to tell her he was marrying someone else. Then he wished her a happy life with her new boyfriend. When she read the letter, her heart shattered. Too late, she realized her mistake. There was no going back. A. was lost to her now and it was all her own doing.

She cried for weeks afterward.

She'd been so stupid. Instead of getting jealous and proposing, A. wrongfully reasoned that her new "suitor" had the distinct advantage over him by being close enough to see her every day. That nearness would only bring them closer and closer and enable them to know each other better.

He was 9,000 miles away.

Much too far away to have any kind of fair chance of winning her. He didn't know that all he had to do was pick up the phone and ask her to marry him and she'd fly into his arms.

Instead he gave up.

Her gamble had completely backfired and left her alone and heartbroken.

She looked down at the lights shimmering on the water and wept. After all this time, it still haunted her. She knew that it always would.

"I wept for many days after that. I wanted to write and tell him I was sorry. I wanted to beg him to marry me, but I was afraid that he'd think less of me if I acted like that. I was so stupid. So very, very stupid," she lamented.

"He was, too. Instead of acting immediately as you expected, he gave up. That's so sad. Now all either of you do is mourn for what might have been. You wish for a past that can't be recaptured," J. said.

"If I had married him, you would not be here now to hear my story," she said.

"It's a good story. You should write a book about it," he said.

She wiped her tears with a tissue and smiled.

"Someone already has," she said.

He leaned closer.

"Go to him, Mother. Don't be afraid. Just do it," he urged.

He got up and left the room. She waited until she heard him leave, then broke down and cried for a little while longer.

She used to blame him for the misunderstanding. As time passed, she realized it was both their faults. If she could take it all back and start anew, she would without hesitation. But would he?

Unlike her, he'd had a very exciting, very full life. Would he trade all of that in just to be with her? Would he feel she was worth it?

"What would you have done if we had never met?" M. asked as she and Koinu enjoyed the hot, soothing water of the onsen.

"I think I would have failed miserably at everything I tried to do," he said without hesitation.

"Really?" she asked.

"Really. I can't imagine life without you. You are everything to me. You are more precious than the very air I breathe. Without you at my side, I am nothing but a hollow shell. And I mean every word of that," he said as he pulled her to him.

"I really love to hear you say those things. I would be lost without you, too," she said. "There would be no spark or passion or peace in my life."

"We are the most perfect couple in all of Nihon—the world!" he smiled.

Even Date Masamune thought that.

One of the things he liked most about them was that neither of them was pretentious. They dressed simply and comfortably. He never bothered with any of the top knots that were fashionable among samurai or dressed to show off his high rank. He kept his hair cut very short (M. often teased him about looking like a monk) and he was honest, likeable and had high standards of honor and morals.

M. preferred simple, but pretty, cotton kimono to the more elaborate silks and wore her hair long and tied at the base of her neck with a colorful ribbon. And her character exactly mirrored Koinu's.

Date had to smile because their way of dressing and speaking had rubbed off on their closest friends, Watanabe, Buntaro and to some extent, Kenshin.

And he knew he could trust all of them.

There was no doubting their loyalty. All had turned down offers from the Shogun for higher rank and greater pay to remain with him. He felt honored by their decisions.

"Loyalty begets loyalty," he said.

Hotoribotchi no yoru

M. was so nervous that her knees shook. There she was, in the lobby of the magnificent Imperial Hotel, waiting like a terrified child to meet the man she had been corresponding with for several years.

Although they had exchanged several photos over the years and had become quite intimate with their daily communications, she still worried what he'd think of her.

Would he find her too old?

Too short?

Unattractive?

She watched as the elevator opened and A. and his wife walked across the lobby to greet her and Y.

Both bowed respectfully to A. and R. A. smiled at them and bowed in the traditional manner then said in his quaint, old-fashioned Japanese that he was delighted to meet her after all these years and that she was even more beautiful and sexy than he ever imagined.

He greeted Y. warmly and said that he was delighted to meet her. Then he introduced his wife. They sat down in lobby to chat for few minutes. During their conversation, Y. noticed that M. never took her eyes from A. She was obviously infatuated with him and his greeting and friendly manner had put her at ease.

They spoke about A's book tour and his heavy schedule and what he planned on doing between commitments. A. said that since this was R's first visit to Japan, he thought they would take a tour of Tokyo.

"I'd really like to visit the National History Museum. I understand it's very large and it takes more than one day to see it all," A. said.

Y. suggested they go there after lunch. If it was what he expects, they could always return the following day to explore it further.

"I don't know if we'll be able to go with you tomorrow. It is a long drive to Hachioji," Y. said.

"You needn't worry about that. I've booked a suite here at the hotel for you and M. You can stay the night. That way, you'll be good and rested tomorrow. In fact, I've booked it for two nights. That way, we can all get to know each other better," A. said.

"That is a wonderful Idea—but this hotel is so expensive. We cannot possibly accept such a gift!" M. said.

"I insist," A. smiled. "You both came all the way over here to meet us. The least I can do is make your trip worthwhile. Besides, it will give us more time together. After I finish my commitments here in Tokyo, R. and I will come to Hachioji for few days and you can show us around. It will give us a chance to meet K. and the rest of your family."

M. beamed.

It took all of her self-restraint to keep from hugging him.

"I was not expecting this," Y. said. "I did not pack anything. I will have to shop for toiletries and other things."

"Me, too," M. said. "This is a wonderful surprise! Domo arigato gozaimasu!"

Y. echoed her thanks. Art just smiled.

"I think you should phone K. to let him know you won't be home for a couple of nights. I don't want you to cause him to worry or cause you any trouble," A. suggested.

"I will do so later," M. promised.

She was still stunned by his generous gift. He hadn't even hinted at it in his emails so it was a complete surprise. She smiled nervously at R.

"Did you know?" she asked.

"Yes. He told me last week," R. replied. "Since you are such good friends, I agreed it would be a nice gesture and very practical. And I would also like to get to know you better and I have so many questions about your country!"

They decided to have lunch at a traditional ryoriya a few blocks away, so R. could experience something uniquely Japanese.

As they ate, M. explained what she and Y. had planned for the rest of the day. A. had mentioned he would like to visit the extensive National Museum.

"Their collection is huge," Y. said. "They have more than 80,000 exhibits. It would take more than one day to see everything."

"You can purchase a multiple day pass," M. suggested. "That way, you can save about 1,000 yen per ticket."

"I don't have anything going until tomorrow evening, so I think I'll do that," A. said.

"I don't want to spend two days in a museum. I want to shop for souvenirs," R. said.

"After today, we can try something different tomorrow. A.-san and I can return to the museum while you go shopping with Y," M. suggested.

"That's fine," R. agreed.

"The Museum is several blocks from here," Y. said.

"Let's take the train. It will be a good experience for R.," A. said.

J. had just finished the chapter about Sekigahara. The scene lasted for several pages and was amazingly detailed.

J. put the book down and looked at his mother.

"Your old friend writes battle scenes that are so real, so vivid; it is like he actually lived through them. As I read, I could almost smell the sweat of the horses and samurai and taste the dust they stirred up while fighting. In fact, I could almost feel the hilt of a katana in my hands. He is a master with words," he said.

"All of his battle scenes are like that," M. said. "Some go on for many pages but they are so detailed and exciting one cannot stop reading."

"Was he a writer when you knew him?" J. asked.

"Not yet. He was more of an artist or cartoonist then. I think he has found his true calling as a writer," she replied.

"He's on television Friday night. He's the only guest on Mr. T.'s Late Show. It comes on at 11," J. said. "Will you watch?"

"Hai. I want to see what he looks like now. I want to hear how he talks and if his mannerisms have changed and how he handles himself during the interview. He used to be very introverted," she said with a remembering smile. "I found that very attractive."

"I don't think he's introverted now," J. said. "He has been on talk shows before in America."

"Will Mr. T. interview him in English?" she asked.

"You will have to watch and see," J. answered.

They walked to the far side of the room and down a narrow aisle of display cases. When he was certain no one could see them, he pulled her close and held her. She wrapped her arms around him and sighed. His arms felt strong.

Safe.

And dangerous.

As they embraced, she felt something press against her. It was about waist high and growing. The longer they held each other, the longer and harder that something grew.

She was surprised, scared and delighted. She realized that holding her excited him. Aroused him. She never expected such a reaction. No one had reacted this way to her in years.

K. had lost interest in her a while back and she thought of herself as a plain, little old woman that no one ever noticed. Now here she was in the arms of a slightly younger man who was very obviously aroused by her.

"I feel you pressing against me," she whispered.

He stroked her hair gently. His touch aroused her.

"I excite you?" she asked.

"Hai," he replied.

"Why?" she asked, almost fearful of the answer. "Why are you aroused by such an old woman?"

"You're not old to me. You'll never be old to me," he said softly.

She blushed.

She'd never been with anyone else but her husband. She never imagined such a thing could happen. That any other man would have such feelings about her.

"You are very hard," she said.

"You make me hard," he said.

"And you make me feel things I have not felt for a long time. You make me feel young and attractive," she said happily.

"You are young and attractive and so very sexy," he said.

She looked up at him.

"Anata wa aishimasu," he said softly.

Her heart almost stopped.

No one had said that to her for many years. She knew he meant it, too. She could tell by the way he held her and by the hardness that now pressed against her.

"Anata wa aishimasu," he whispered.

She was surprised again. A. had said the very words she wanted to hear more than anything else on Earth. Curious about the ever growing hardness below his belt, she ran her fingers over it. It was big, she thought. Bigger than she expected.

"I want you," he said.

"I am yours," she replied as her heart beat faster and faster.

"Now what do we do?" he asked.

"Y. and I will meet you in the lobby tomorrow morning. We will have breakfast together then Y. will take your wife shopping while we go to the National Museum. While they are shopping, we can return to my hotel room together. No one will know but us—and Y," she said.

As she said the words, she felt so wicked. This was something she never imagined she'd ever do. But A. had said the words she wanted to hear and she knew that he meant them.

"Call us when you are ready," he said. "Are you sure you want to do this?"

"Hai. I have wanted to do this for a long time now. I must feel you inside of me," she said softly.

She was elated. A. was slightly younger, athletically built and handsome. She could not believe that he wanted her. Until that moment, something like this had been a remote fantasy, something she never thought would actually happen.

Now, as they held each other close and she heard his heart beating in his chest and felt his warm breath on her cheek, she realized that her fantasies were about to become a reality.

Shiawase wa kumo no ue ni

J. boarded the morning train for work. He looked around and saw there was only one seat in the car. He walked over and sat down. Then he opened his briefcase, took out the novel, and started reading. The woman seated next to him smiled.

"I see that you are reading 'Bushi', she observed.

"I started yesterday. What do you think of it?" J. asked.

"I think he writes very well. It's rare that gaijin can capture the essence of our culture and history so well. He paints in vivid colors and makes me feel as if I am there witnessing the events in his novel. I think it is a beautiful piece of work but the ending is very sad. It made me cry," she said.

"My mother said the same. She's a big fan of his. She has all of his novels. They were friends a long time ago," J. said. "In fact, I think he uses her as the model for all of his main female characters."

The woman thought for a moment.

"Is your mother's name M.?" she asked.

"Hai," he said.

"If you don't mind my saying so, but he must love her deeply. I have read other novels by him and he always writes of her in favorable ways," she said.

"So, you see it too?" he asked. "I've told my mother the same. I've even urged her to contact him, but she never has."

"I think she should," the woman said. "Oh, here's my stop. Thank you for speaking with me. Sayonara!"

He watched her get off. Their chat had made him even more interested in the book. He opened it and started reading. He became so engrossed in it that he not only missed his stop, but he didn't even notice it until he'd reached the end of the line some two hours later. He looked at his watch and scowled.

The day was half over. He saw no sense in going to work at this hour. He took out his cell phone and called in sick instead. Then he found a nice quiet park, sat down on a bench, and continued his reading.

"Who are you?" Musashi asked.

"People call me Koinu," he replied. "I serve Date Masamune. I fought at Sekigahara."

"So did I," Musashi said.

"But I was on the winning side," Koinu smiled.

Musashi laughed.

"That was a bad day," he said. "I was young and foolish. In fact, I was just 13 years old. I went to fight because I thought if I did well in the battle, I could make a name for myself. I barely escaped with my life," he said.

"But since then, you have made yourself into the most famous swordsman in all of Nihon. Your two sword technique is a work of beauty and your duel with Sasaki is legendary," Koinu said.

Musashi sized him up as he scratched his chin whiskers.

"I've heard of you," he said. "Some people say that you're very good with a katana. Some say that you are better than me."

Koinu shrugged.

"People like to exaggerate," he said.

Musashi laughed.

"Hai. They do. They like to make comparisons. What about you? Do you think you are better than me?" he asked.

"What does it matter? I feel no need to prove myself to you or anyone else. Besides, I'm not a fencer. I am bushi," Koinu replied.

Musashi grinned.

"I like you. I also respect you. Only one who has confidence in his own abilities feel no need to prove himself," he said.

"I am satisfied with the path I've chosen," Koinu said.

"I think I have also reached that place, Musashi said. "I am finally at ease with myself."

"Do people still challenge you?" Koinu.

Musashi smiled as he looked at the ground.

"Not like they once did. Not since my duel with Sasaki. In my younger days, I challenged people to fence me. Now, I discourage them," he said. "My reputation is such that I rarely get challenged."

Koinu laughed.

"What's so funny?" asked Musashi.

"Challenging you would be like committing seppuku," he said. "Yet you have had several matches since Sasaki. I've heard of them."

"Hai. But most were not to the death," Musashi pointed out. "I rarely kill. I find it far more satisfying to embarrass my challengers now. What about you? How many men have you killed?"

"I've never bothered to count," Koinu replied. "I've never sought nor desired any sort of fame or reputation. I just serve Lord Date to the best of my abilities. That suits me perfectly."

"What is your favorite technique in a one-on-one duel?" Musashi asked.

"The drop and draw," Koinu replied. "I also like the drop-spin-and draw."

"Those are two good techniques. Very good techniques. Maybe we should fence just for the fun of it? We could use wooden swords so neither of gets hurt," Musashi suggested.

Koinu smiled.

"Only if we can do so without anyone watching," he said.

"That can be arranged easily enough. Buy why?" Musashi asked.

"That way, no one will ever know we did or who won. We won't be challenged by would-be Musashis everywhere we go," he explained.

They agreed to meet the following morning in private. Neither ever said they met and neither ever said who won. The two never met again but Koinu spoke fondly and respectfully of Musashi to the end of his days.

His wife looked at him.

"Can I go shopping with Y?" she asked hopefully.

"Sure," A. said as he took his credit card out of his wallet and handed it to her. "Have fun. Buy whatever you like. Just be back here at six so we can all go out to dinner. M. and I will return to the museum and finish touring the exhibits, then we'll have lunch. We'll see you back here."

R. smiled, took the card and hugged him.

They walked out to the car with them and watched them drive away. A. turned and smiled at M.

"We now have the entire day to ourselves," he said as he took her hand.

She was trembling nervously. He pulled her close.

"You don't have to do this if you don't want to. I'll understand," he whispered.

"If I don't do this now, I'll spend the rest of my life wondering what it would have been like. I don't want that. I don't want to end up like her," she replied referring to his old love.

"Let's go up to your suite," he said.

They returned to the hotel and went up to M's suite. Her knees trembled as she opened the door and let him inside. This was the moment she'd been hoping for.

Dreamt about.

Wished for.

Her heart beat uncontrollably as he took her hand and led her to the bedroom. She briefly wanted to flee because she was afraid of letting him see her naked. He pulled her close and kissed her cheek.

"Anata wa aishimasu," he said again.

"And I love you, too," she replied in English. "Let's do this before we lose our courage."

He smiled and removed his eyeglasses. She did the same. They looked deep into each other's eyes and smiled. Her eyes, he thought, were lovely. He almost became lost in them. He pulled her to him and kissed her on the lips.

It was the very first time she had been kissed that way. And she was surprised at how pleasant and arousing it felt. And how much she had been missing for all these years. Kissing, she decided, is a good custom.

He kissed her cheek.

Then her neck.

As he did, he slowly unbuttoned her blouse. No man but her husband had ever done this and she began to tremble with desire. She let him slide the blouse off her shoulders. Then down her arms. Then off her body altogether. She let it fall to the floor and quivered as he gently played with her nipples through her light bra.

She was trembling all over now.

Like she had on her first night with K. many years ago. He reached behind her and unclasped her bra, then slipped it off her and tossed it onto a nearby chair. She moaned as he leaned over to lick and suck each of her nipples until they were straight and hard and she tingled all over.

She felt him undo her slacks and slide them down her legs. As he did, he kissed his way down her flat, smooth belly and slowly peeled down her panties, which were small and surprisingly sexy.

M. closed her eyes and moaned as his tongue explored her pleasure garden. It had been a long time since she'd felt anything like this.

A very long time.

He was now making love to her with his tongue. And she loved every second of it. She quivered and moaned as it moved along her swollen lips. She sighed and gripped his shoulders as it dipped inside of her and she shook like a leaf on a tree limb in a storm when he sucked her love button. She was so excited, so elated, that she climaxed within seconds.

He caught her just as her knees buckled and carried her in his strong arms and placed her down on the bed. She watched as he quickly disrobed and admired his lean and muscular body. A. worked out almost every day and still played baseball. And it showed.

But what really caught her attention most was the long, swollen member dancing between his thighs. She wondered if she could take all of it inside of her. It seemed much too big for her tiny body. As he climbed onto the bed, she opened her legs and beamed up at him.

He stopped to admire her body. She was smooth and compact and tight. Her legs were perfectly shaped and the beautiful garden between them looked even better than it tasted. He lay next to her and ran his hand all over her body. She reached down and wrapped her fingers around his ember as her heart soared higher and higher.

"I am yours," she whispered. "Take me."

He moved between her legs and eased his member only halfway into her. He knew it had been a long time for her and he didn't want to hurt her in any way. But even though he was in only halfway, it felt so wonderfully warm, tight and exiting.

He saw a look of concern on her face and comforted her.

"Relax, M-san," he whispered. 'I'll be gentle. If it hurts, tell me and stop. I don't want to cause you any pain. Ever."

He moved in and out of her slowly. After a few halfway thrusts, she began to feel warm and wet and she tingled deliciously. His thrusts awakened sensations within her body she hadn't felt for a long while and she began to move with him. Each thrust went a little bit deeper. Each thrust felt a little bit better, too.

She was on fire now.

"You see? I don't have to go all the way in," he whispered.

"Oh—yes—you-- do!" she moaned.

Although she knew that A. was taking it easy so as not to hurt her, her libido suddenly kicked into high gear. She wrapped her arms and legs around him and drove her hips upward as hard as she could until his entire member was buried deep inside of her.

"I want to feel all of you inside me!" she groaned as the first wave of pain surged through her. "I want to give myself to you completely! Forever!" she said as she thrust her hips up and down several times. Each time, it hurt less and any pain she felt was quickly made second to the pleasure she received.

"Are you alright?" he asked.

"Hai! I feel wonderful. Love me!" she gasped.

They moved together faster and faster. She was on cloud nine now. She was feeling things she never thought she'd feel again and she was making love with the man of her dreams. She didn't mind the pain which grew less and less with each wonderful thrust of his katana. All that mattered now was the fact they were doing it.

And it was exciting.

Incredible.

Perfect.

They made love for several minutes. Then, as if their actions were blessed by the gods themselves, they both climaxed at the exact same instant. As they did, she moved her hips faster and faster and reveled in the way his love liquid fertilized her garden. He held on and allowed her to take control, loving the way her inner muscles polished every inch of his blade. They kept going until both were totally spent and bathed with sweat.

They held each other close for several minutes. She felt good all over. Thrilled beyond words that he found her so sexy and exciting.

She was happy, too.

Inside and out.

He propped himself up on one elbow and ran his hand over her body. It felt so smooth and sexy. And it looked flawless.

M. always thought of herself as an old woman with small, sagging breasts. But she realized that A. saw her in a completely different light. He saw her as an alluring, vibrant woman with compact, slender body and perfect legs

"You really like my body?" she asked.

"I love your body," he said. "Anata utsukushii desu."

"I think you need new glasses," she joked as she enjoyed the compliment.

"My glasses are fine and I really like what I see," he assured her.

"I wish my breasts were larger and more firm," she said.

"They are perfect just the way they are. Everything about you is perfect," he complimented.

"Am I what you expected?" she asked.

"You are much better than I ever imagined," he said as he kissed her cheek.

"I still can't believe this really happened. I am still up in the clouds. You make me feel young and beautiful again. I feel alive now. Like a real woman again," she said.

"That's because you are alive and beautiful and sexy," he assured her.

"Only you would say such a thing and mean it," she smiled.

They got up and dressed and cleaned up as best as they could. They still had three hours before they were to meet Y. and R. for lunch. There was still time to walk over to museum and finish the tour they'd started the day before. That way, they could honestly say they were at the museum that morning.

Just before they left the suite, they kissed again. This time, she tasted herself when their tongues met. When she realized this, she giggled.

"So that is how I taste," she smiled.

"What do you think?" he teased.

"If you like it, I like it," she replied. "We are one now, A.-san. Forever."

At three, J. got back on the train. On the way home, he saw the same woman he'd spoken to earlier get on. He motioned to her to sit next to him. She smiled and walked over.

"Hello again," she said cheerfully.

J. decided she was quite pretty, especially when she smiled.

"It's nice to see you again," he said.

"How far have you gotten with the book?" she asked.

"I'm nearly finished. I read all day. I just couldn't stop," he admitted.

She laughed when he told her how he'd missed his stop because he was so wrapped up in the novel.

"So, what do you think of it?" she asked.

"It's excellent. This is his best work yet. He writes as if he has actually lived in those times," he said. "Oh, by the way, my name's J. What's yours?"

"I'm afraid if I tell you, you say that I made it up," she said.

"No I won't. Please tell me," he said.

"My name is M.," she said shyly.

He laughed.

"I am very pleased to meet you, M.-san," he replied.

"I feel that your mother is the most fortunate woman in Nihon," she said.

"Why do you say that?" he asked.

"Any woman would feel fortunate to have a man love her so strongly and deeply for such a long time," she said.

"I don't know if she feels that way. When they were in Osaka together in 1973, he bought her this poster. She still has it on her bedroom wall. I think it's her most precious possession," he said.

"How romantic!" M. said. "Oh, there's my stop coming up."

"I'd like to see you again," J. said.

"Are you asking me for a date?" she queried.

"I guess I am," he smiled.

"Okay. Here is my phone number," she said as she took a pen and paper from her purse and wrote. "Call me tonight if you like. We can talk more."

"What time will be good?" he asked as the train rolled into the station.

"Anytime after seven! Sayonara!"she said as she hurried from the train.

He smiled and watched her race across the platform. Then he wondered if the gods were playing a trick on him.

Shiawase wa sora no ue ni

Her son looked at her.

"Did you know he had been in the war?" he asked.

She shook her head.

"He never told me. I think it was my fault in a way. He'd asked me what I thought of soldiers. I told him I didn't like soldiers and I would never marry one. He said nothing more after that," she said.

"What would you have said or done had he told you? Would you have felt differently toward him? Would you have walked away?" J. asked.

M. shrugged.

"I don't know. What does it matter now?" she said.

"What if he had asked you to marry him? Would you have said yes?" he asked.

"Hai. I would have. I wanted him to ask the question more than anything else on Earth. But he never did," she said sadly. "Then I made what proved to be a terrible mistake. I tried to get him to propose by telling him that another man had asked me out."

J. shook his head.

"When did you realize it was a mistake?" he asked.

"Several months later when he wrote to tell me he was getting married. Instead of getting him to propose, he gave up. He believed the other man had a big advantage over him because he was here with me and A. was thousands of miles away. I cried for weeks afterward and wrote him about it. But it was too late," she sighed.

"I had hoped to make him jealous enough to propose. I thought that I was being very clever. Instead, I turned everything into ashes," she said.

She smiled at him.

"There is a bright side. Had my plan worked like I'd hoped, you would not be here now," she said as she pated his hand.

"Perhaps not. But someone else would," J. said.

That night when they had returned to their suite, Y. turned to M.

"Did you really do it?" she asked.

"Hai," she smiled.

"How was he?" Y. asked.

"Masterful. Gentle and wonderful. He makes me feel very young again," M. said with a big grin.

"He must have been something very special. I haven't seen you smile like this for a long time. Are you madly in love with him now?"

"Very much so," she said. "Oh, I can't believe I even said that! You must think I'm such a bad woman!"

"No, I don't. You told me all about him and your dreams many times. I knew that you would join with him if you ever got the chance. So, are you going to do it again before we return to Hachioji?" Y. asked.

"Again and again and again. If we get the chance," M. replied happily.

"Will you need me to distract his wife again?" Y. asked.

They laughed.

A few minutes later, M's daughter, A. called.

"Did you really meet him?" she asked.

"Hai," M. replied.

"What is he really like?" she asked.

"He is just like his letters and emails. He is warm, and funny, and intelligent and romantic. He is everything I imagined he would be," M. almost gushed.

"Is he handsome?" A. asked.

"I think so," M. said.

"Well? Did you do it?" A. asked.

"Do what?" M. hedged.

"You know, Mother!" A. said.

"Hai. I had to. I had to find out what it was like," M. said.

"How as he?" A. asked.

"Wonderful! I want him again," M. replied happily.

"So he is your Prince Charming?" A. asked in jest.

"He is my shining samurai-poet. He makes me feel so young and pretty. Please keep this our secret," M. answered.

"I promise. If he's so good, maybe I should try him?" she teased.

"Don't you dare!" M. said.

They both laughed.

The limousine arrived at seven to take A. to his first book signing. The bookstore was several blocks from the hotel and since his arrival had been well-hyped for several days, there was already a crowd waiting.

Most of them were young woman. A. smiled and greeted each customer who came to have his or her book signed and he even stopped to chat with a few afterward. Most were impressed that he spoke Japanese. A few of the woman had their photos taken with him, too.

The signings ended when the last of the books were sold. A. was even surprised by several male fans that had purchased copies of "Realm of Blood" for him to sign.

A young female TV reporter who had covered the event asked him for an interview which he agreed to.

"I have noticed that your latest book, 'Bushi' has become very popular with young women here in Nihon while your last book, 'Realm of Blood' is very popular with men. Why do you think that is so?" she asked.

"That's easy. 'Realm' is essentially a fantasy and war novel while 'Bushi' is more romantic. Men like to read action-adventure stories. Women are into the more romantic stories, so naturally, there's a big difference in the type of readers they attract. Have you read either one yet?" he teased.

"Actually, I have read 'Realm'. I prefer your adventure novels. I do plan to read 'Bushi' but that is because my mother insists on it," she replied.

"Arigato to both of you. I hope you enjoy 'Bushi'," he said.

The next day, they went on a general tour of Tokyo. They visited the Imperial Gardens and the Asakusa Shrine. As they approached the shrine, they saw a path leading from the torii directly to the steps.

R. was about to step on the path when A. grabbed her by the shoulders and pulled her to the side.

"Don't walk on that path," he said.

"How come?" she asked.

"Only the god is allowed to use that path. We must walk to either side," he said.

Y. and M. smiled.

"How does he know that?" Y. asked.

"A.-san knows many of our customs," M. said with a sense of pride. "And he respects all of them."

They stopped at the well outside of the shrine. A. used the wooden ladle to scoop water from the well and poured it over his hands. Then he did the same to R.

"What's that for?" R. asked.

"We must purify ourselves before entering. Normally, we would also wash our feet, but they have provided shoe covers for us," he said as he sat down and slipped the protective covers on.

R. followed his example and they went into the shrine.

When they entered the sanctuary, A. lit two sticks if incense and placed them on the altar. He looked up at the god and clapped his hands three times. Then he knelt and said a short prayer. M. and Y. did the same while R. stood by and watched. They left the shrine a few moments later. A. removed his shoe covers and placed them in a wooden box that was on the front steps.

"Why'd you clap?" R. asked.

"To get the god's attention so he could hear my prayers," A. explained.

Y. pulled M. aside.

"Is A.-san a Buddhist?" she asked.

"A.-san claims to have no religion but he admires the Buddhist philosophy," M. explained. "I told you he was very different."

"Do you want to be with him again tonight?" Y. asked.

"Hai!" M. smiled.

"I will arrange it," Y. assured her.

When they returned to the hotel after their morning tour, a car and driver arrived to take A. to his next book signing. M. and Y. said they would take R. to lunch and meet him in the lobby afterward. R. waved as A. drove away.

"You must be very proud of your husband," Y. said.

"I've always been proud of him. Now I'm proud for him," R. said. "Where shall we go? I'm hungry."

Somehow, Y. arranged to take R. someplace for some "interesting" shopping. A. and M. said they would walk around the general neighborhood a while and meet them in the hotel lobby afterward. Then they would all attend the Grand Kabuki.

This also surprised Y.

She didn't realize that A. was a fan of kabuki. Then he said he'd been introduced to Noh and Bunraku as well and that he enjoyed them all. She glanced at M. who simply smiled and nodded. She wasn't the least bit surprised that A. had purchased four tickets to the Grand Kabuki. He'd told her that he tried to see it whenever he was in Tokyo.

As soon as R. left with Y., A. and M. took the elevator back up to the suite…

M. walked over to her bookshelf and selected one of A. most erotic novels. She leafed through the pages until she came to the scene she wanted and stopped. She then walked to her drawer and took out another of her "toys'. This one was quite longer than the last and made of soft gel. She smiled as she coated the end with aloe vera, and then took it and the book to her bed. She removed her shorts and panties and lay down. Then she leaned on her elbow and read. As she read, she ran her fingertips over her moist lips. By the time she'd gotten halfway down the page, she was moving her toy in and out of her slit. By the time she'd reached the bottom of the page, she was on her back with her knees bent and legs wide apart doing it faster and faster as she imagine she was making love with A.

She climaxed moments later and shook all over.

But she kept going and going.

Faster and harder.

She climaxed again and let out a long, deep moan as the waves of pleasure surged through her body. She laid still for a while to catch her breath, and then started up again. She did this several more times. Until she was totally spent and covered with sweat. When she woke, it was already well past midnight. That's when she realized that she had left her door wide open. Since J. room was down the hall, he had to pass by hers to get to it.

That means he saw her!

She felt herself blush several shades of crimson—especially when she realized that her toy had been nestled deep inside of her the entire time.

The next morning after breakfast, M. and Y. bade A. and R. good-bye.

"I must return to Hachioji before K. has a cow," M. joked. "Please don't forget to visit as you promised. I will make reservations at a nice ryokan a few streets from our house. My entire family is eager to meet you and they have all read your book."

"I have two more signings here in Tokyo tomorrow. I'll call you when we're on our way to Hachioji. Then we can go to the castle," A. said.

They all exchanged polite bows.

On the way back to Hachioji, Y. quizzed M. about her liaison.

"Was it as good as the first time?" she asked.

"It was much better," M. smiled. "Much better. He let me lead so I showed him a few things I used to do with K. a long time ago. He told me I was a wonderful lover, too."

"Do you feel guilty about this?" Y. asked.

"I did the first time. Not so much last night. There was no one else in the universe but him and me and we both wanted to make it special," M. said.

"Did you?" Y. asked.

"There are no words to describe how it was," M. said. "He makes my heart sing!"

"Just don't start singing now. I've heard you sing. I would have to put you out of my car!" Y. joked.

Ue o muite arukou

K. looked her over carefully.

"You must have had a really wonderful time," he said.

"I had a really good time," she said as she put her bags in the closet.

He noticed the near-lilt in her voice and smiled.

"You look so happy and relaxed. Younger, too," he observed. "And there is a bounce in your step."

"Stop that. You're imagining things," she countered.

"The last time you looked and acted this happy was when we were on our honeymoon," he joked. "Did you and your friend have a little honeymoon together?"

She threw a small figurine at him. He caught it and laughed. She acted offended, but a smile eventually forced its way to her lips—which looked fuller to him now.

K. winked at her.

"You remind me of my obasan," he said.

"I remind you of your grandmother?" she asked as if she couldn't believe he'd said that.

"Hai. She was a small, elderly lady," he replied.

"You think I am small and elderly? How old do you think I am? May I remind you that you are older than I am?" she responded.

"Maybe so, but I don't look as old as you," he said.

"Well, maybe you need to look more closely at your reflection the next time you shave," she retorted.

"I think I look quite handsome. You just look old," he teased. "I should trade you in for a younger woman."

"You wouldn't be able to do anything with her if you did," she said.

K. winced. He realized then he'd hit the wrong button. He'd forgotten that his once-docile wife had become excellent at verbal warfare. He was now looking for an avenue of escape. But M. wasn't finished.

"Go ahead and trade me in if you want. I know someone who will take me just as I am and who doesn't think I look like his obasan," she said. "And he is much younger and more virile than you."

"Gomen nasai. I did not mean any of what I said. I concede this round to you," he apologized. "You do not remind me of my obasan."

"Arigato," she said coldly.

"Actually, you remind me more of my grandfather," he said as he hurried from the room.

She picked up a nearby cushion and hurled it at him just as he ducked out. She heard him laugh as he walked upstairs.

Then she laughed, too.

K. was right. Her time with A. did feel like a honeymoon, albeit a far-too-short one. But he would soon come to Hachioji. Then she planned to continue the honeymoon.

Afterward, A. planned to spend a week in Yufuin at the same ryokan he'd stayed at many years ago. She planned to join him there, too. They would have the entire week together. Then, it would really become a honeymoon.

He arrived at the NHK Studios at ten p.m. and was greeted by a pretty production assistant who showed him to the waiting room. It proved to be a small, comfortable lounge with a bar, wide screen TV, a small round table and three chairs. A. thanked her and walked to the bar. He saw a bottle of Ashi beer in the fridge and picked it up. It was good and cold, too.

Just as he popped the cap of with the built-in bottle opener attached to the bar, the door opened and the show's host, Mr. T. walked in.

He introduced himself and they shook hands.

"I thought we'd have a chat before the show to put you at ease," Mr. T. said. "You will be my only guest tonight. Your novel has become so popular in Japan that I wanted to devote the entire program to you."

"I'm honored," A. said.

"I see you like Asahi beer," Mr. T. observed.

"This was the very first beer I ever drank and it's been one of my favorites ever since. Of course, I also like the other Nihon-jin brands and sake," A. said.

Mr. T. laughed.

"I always try to make my guests feel at home. Would you prefer to be interviewed in English or Japanese?" he asked.

"Either is fine," A. replied in Japanese.

Mr. T. smiled

"Are you fluent in our language?" he asked.

"Somewhat. I learned it several decades ago, so I may come across as old fashioned or stuffy," A. said.

"I see what you mean. Your Japanese is a more formal, older style. Our audience may find that quaint or amusing. How about we do the interview in both languages? That way, if you have difficulty with certain questions, we can switch to English to make it easier?" Mr. T. suggested.

"That sounds perfect. I would hate to be perceived as some stuffy, pompous gaijin. That might put some people off or offend them," A. agreed.

"Excellent. Just relax until show time. If you need anything, my assistant, R. will get it for you. Just push that button on the bar," Mr. T. said.

M. watched the interview on the late night talk show with great interest. She normally didn't bother with such shows, but the host, Mr. T., had a most unusual guest.

It was A.

She smiled at the TV.

When she first met him, she never imagined that he would become a famous writer. If anything, she'd expected him to become a professional baseball player. He was very passionate about the game.

And very good at it.

Now she realized that he had an equal passion for his writing. Most likely, he would have shown that same passion for her.

But he was more subdued then.

So shy.

So was she

M. studied his features with great interest. His hair was short now and sort of silver and the lines on his face were slightly more pronounced.

But he was still recognizable. He had the same infectious smile and laugh. The same mannerisms and the lines added character to his face.

They said: I've lived.

His voice was also the same. He still had a distinctive Brooklyn accent but now, it was infused with great confidence. He spoke like a man who was very comfortable in his own skin. He was dressed neatly but casually as always, and he looked every bit the world traveler-writer-soldier he'd been.

As she watched, her heart beat faster.

The interview was carried out in a mixture of Nihon-go and English. She was amazed at his mastery of her language, even if it was a more stilted, old-fashioned version. Then T. asked who the M. in his novel was based on.

She watched as a sort of sad smile came to A.'s lips.

"She is based on someone I met and fell in love with many years ago. In fact, she is in all of my novels as the female lead and still holds a very special place in my heart," he said.

"You mean you still love her after all these years?" T. asked.

"Hai. She was very special. She was my first true love," A. replied.

M. almost stopped breathing when she heard this. She realized her son was right now. A. still loved her. She didn't know what to think now. She kept watching.

"Would you like to see her again?" T. asked.

"Hai. I would like that very much," A. said.

T. smiled.

"Perhaps she is watching at this very moment. If you are watching, M., please call us at 0764834 now. Someone would like to speak with you again," he announced.

This made A. blush a little. He had not expected this.

M. jotted down the number. She picked up her cell phone and punched in the numbers.

It rang once.

Twice.

On the third ring, she turned the phone off and chided herself for being so silly.

T. looked off stage and nodded.

"I have just been informed that our phone rang three times. When my assistant picked it up, she heard someone hang up on the other end.

If that was you, M., please call again. Your first love wants to speak with you again," he said into the camera.

M. reached for the phone, hesitated, and withdrew her hand.

A. finished the interview. T. thanked him. They stood and bowed to each other, then shook hands. M. turned off the TV and wiped the tears from her eyes.

M. watched the interview. To her surprise, K. watched with her. When they saw T. ask M. to call the show, K. turned to his wife.

"Are you going to call?" he asked teasingly.

"I would—if I were that M.," she replied.

"Oh? You are not?" K. asked.

"No. By coincidence, she and I share the exact same name. It is because of this, that A. and I became friends on Facebook. He did a name search and mine came up. Then A. contacted me to ask if I were her. We have been friends ever since," she explained.

"You never did tell me how your friendship blossomed," K. said as he gave her his "tell me all about it" look.

She smiled and told him everything that transpired that first few times and how, over time, she and A. grew closer and closer. When she was finished, he smiled.

"I feel sorry for your friend," he said.

"Why?" she asked.

"He is still searching for his M. while I found mine a long time ago," he replied.

She was surprised.

That was very romantic and insightful of him. It was something she'd never expected to hear him say. K. touched her hair.

"Although he has a very young and beautiful wife and they love each other greatly, he still wonders about his first love and that has led him to you and you to him. It is 'en'. It was meant to be. If not, then there is no logical explanation for any of it. I am just happy that you did not know him when you were young and single," he said.

"Oh? Why do you say that?" she asked.

"Because if you had, he would be seated here with you now instead of me," K. smiled.

When A. and his wife returned to their hotel room after the interview, the phone rang. He picked it up.

"Moshi-moshi," he said.

M. laughed. Hardly anyone said that anymore.

"I watched your interview. We all did. I thought it went very well, but I was surprised that you opened yourself up like you did on TV. That was very touching and courageous," M. said.

"Arigato. I just felt it was best to be as truthful as I could. I was sort of embarrassed when T.-san asked her to call the show if she was watching," A. said.

"We could tell that you were somewhat uncomfortable. Did R. like your interview?" M. asked.

"We mostly spoke in Nihon-go so she didn't understand what was said. I'll explain it to her later if she asks. Are we still set for tomorrow?" he asked.

"Hai. I have arranged for you and R. to stay at a very nice ryokan here in Hachioji. I will pick you up in our car tomorrow morning. After you check in, we can visit the ruins," M. said.

"Excellent. We'll see you tomorrow. Konbanwa," he said.

"Konbanwa," she replied as he turned off her phone. She turned to K.

"Will you go with us?"

"No. I have been to the ruins many times. A.-san and I will go to my favorite pub afterward," K. said as he grinned at her.

"Why are you looking at me in such a way?" she queried.

"Is his katana sharp and straight?" he asked.

She reddened.

"How could you ask such a thing? How would I even know that?" she asked.

He sensed the nervousness in her voice.

"I just assumed that you experienced it while in Tokyo," he teased. "I saw the look in your eyes when you watched him on TV. I know that look, M.-san. I know it very well."

She blushed deeper.

He laughed.

"I have no idea what you're talking about. Neither do you!" she said.

"So his katana has not found its way into your sheath?" he joked.

"Of course not! What kind of woman do you think I am?" she asked defensively.

"I think you are a beautiful, vibrant woman whom I have sadly neglected for a very long time through no fault f my own. You want and need something I may no longer be able to give you. For that, I beg your forgiveness," he said softly as he touched her cheek.

"Oh, that's not so important anymore," she said as she tried to assure him.

"You are very kawaii when you try to lie," he said as he held her.

He let her go and walked away. Just before he left the room, he looked over his shoulder at her and smiled.

"I can understand why you are attracted to him. I just cannot understand why he is attracted to such an old woman!"

She picked up a soft cushion and threw it at him. He laughed and ran down the stairs. M. turned and looked at her reflection in the mirror. A. didn't find her old at all. If he did, he certainly didn't show it in the hotel suite. In fact, he made her feel like she 20 years old again.

K.'s remarks had caught her off guard. He was a very perceptive man and he knew her moods and expressions better than anyone else. He'd teased her about having an affair with A. But he wasn't harsh or insulting. In fact, he'd been humorous and playful and even hinted that it was alright. She decided not to fret over it. At the moment, she was plotting ways to have another romantic interlude with A. before he left for Osaka.

Namida ga koborenai youni

M. turned on the radio to break the silence. After some idle chatter, the DJ played the first song. He said it was requested by an American visitor who liked to listen to it in his younger days. When she heard the familiar tune, she froze and listened.

The song was: Ue O Muite Arukou

As she listened to it, her eyes flooded with tears. It had been one of his favorite songs.

Ue o muite arikou
Namida ga Kaborenai youni
Omoidasu haru no hi
Hotoribotchi no yoru

Ue o muite arukou
Nijinda hoshi o kazoete
Omoidasu haru no hi
Hotoribotchi no yoru

Shiwase wa kumo no ue ni
Shiwase wa sora no ue ni

Ue o muite arukou
Namida ga kaborenai youni
Nakinagara aruku
Hotoribotchi no yoru

Omoidasu aki no hi
Hitoribotchi no yoru

Kanashimi wa hoshi no kage ni
Kanashimi wa tsuki no kage ni

Ue o muite arukou
Namida ga kaborenai youni
Nakinagara aruku
Hitoribotchi no yoru

She buried her face in her hands and sobbed. An hour later, her son found her lying on the sofa and staring up at the ceiling. Her eyes were puffy and red.

"You've been crying," he observed.

"I have been reminiscing. It's silly of me, I know. I'm a foolish old woman," she said.

"Why are you crying?" he asked.

"I heard a song on the radio. It was a very old song. One he always liked," she said.

"You mean the Sukiyaki Song?" he asked, giving it the American title.

"Hai. Whenever I hear it, I cry for what might have been," she said softly.

"Stop torturing yourself, Mother. Go and see him. I've read 'Bushi'. The woman in his story is you. Just like the women in his other novels. Each of them is modeled after you and only you," J. said.

She sniffled.

"Please go and see him," J. urged.

"What could I possibly say to him after so many years?" she asked.

"You could start by saying 'hello'. Then you could tell him how much you've missed him and have thought of him all this time. I'm sure he would be thrilled to hear those words from you," J. said.

"Why would he want to see such an old woman?" she asked.

"You are not old. I remind you that he, too, has aged. You saw him on TV didn't you?" J. said.

"He still looks much younger than his age. He still looks almost the same as he did before but his hair is gray and cut very short," she replied.

"He is a little older than you. You've told me that. Go and see him. Pick a place that feels right to you and see him. Let yourself live, Mother," he pressed.

She looked at him and smiled.

"I think I shall," she said softly.

He shook his head. He disliked seeing her this way. It was as if she were mourning for a life she never had.

"Please do so," he said.

The ruins of Hachioji Castle were vast. Although it was now a park, the area was eerily silent. They heard no birds overhead. No insects buzzing. And not even a breeze stirred the leaves on the branches of the trees.

"This is very strange," M. said. "Normally, there are many birds in the branches and they make very much noise. The ruins are very quiet today."

"I think I understand why," A. said.

"Ghosts?" R. asked.

"Yes. They are all around us now. Today is June 23rd. This is the anniversary of the battle," A. said. "The spirits have come here to remember."

He and M. were in the lead. As the crossed over the bridge, the others stopped to take photos. For some reason, A. kept moving. M. stayed with him and wondered why he seemed to be in such a hurry.

As they approached the remains of the gate, the ghostly image of a tall, barrel-chested, older samurai materialized. He was holding a spear. A. stopped in his tracks as they made eye contact. Then the old samurai smiled at him in recognition. A. realized who the spirit was. Then he heard a familiar, albeit distant voice in his head.

"I see that you've returned to pay me a visit, Koinu-san. It's been a very long time," it said.

"Hachiman?" A. whispered.

"Hai. It is good to be remembered by an old friend. I see that your lovely wife is still at your side—just as she was meant to be forever," the old samurai said without actually speaking.

For the next few seconds, A. carried on a conversation with him in perfect Nihon-go. M. peered into the empty space and touched his arm.

"Who are you speaking with?" she asked.

"A dear, old friend from a past life," he replied. "He said he remembers you, too. He remembers the day you first came here with me and he invited us to dine with his family," A. said.

She stared at the space and watched as something began to take form. Then she saw him, too.

The old samurai smiled and bowed his head respectfully. She stood and stared at A. to let him know she saw him.

"Your dreams were not just dreams," she said.

"They were memories of a past life. Memories that had remained buried deep inside my soul until our friendship brought them back. It was a life that we both shared so many centuries ago," he said as the old samurai nodded approval.

M. slipped her hand in A's. He pulled her closer and smiled. The old samurai bowed his head, turned and walked up the path. They watched as he melted into thin air. He knew that they'd find each other again. Now that they had, he could rest.

M. blushed and looked around to make sure no had seen them. A. smiled.

"I understand now why you wished to come here," she said.

"This is why I was drawn to this place. Why I was drawn to you. This is why I returned," he said.

"So you are the young samurai? The one you wrote about?" she asked. He nodded.

"And I am your lady?" she asked in wonder.

"You are my lady," he assured her. "And we are back where we belong."

"Do you believe in reincarnation?" she asked.

"I'm not sure," he replied. "Do you?"

"I did not believe in it before. Now, I am not sure," she answered.

Seconds later, the rest of their group walked up the path. As usual, R. had a bag from the local souvenir shop. A. laughed.

"Now that you're finished shopping, we can explore the rest of ruins," he said.

They followed the main path upward through the ruins. The others were now far behind. A. noticed a side path that wound off into the distance. He took M.'s hand and led her down it. After a few minutes, they found themselves alone amid a clump of bamboo. A. pulled her close and they kissed. She beamed happily and melted into him.

"I must have you again," he whispered.

"When?" she asked as her heart raced.

"Tonight," he said.

She nodded.

"I will arrange for Y. and my daughter to take your wife out somewhere. Then I will come to you," she said. "I am yours now. I will be there for you whenever you need me. Forever."

They lucked out that day and the next.

In Hachioji, as I was in other parts of Japan, the start of summer signaled the start of the matsuri or festivals. This gave M. and Y. a perfect way to hatch their plan. Y. suggested they all go to the matsuri. R. was all for it. She loved festivals and this would be her first one ever in Japan. The festival was to begin that day around noon and last the entire weekend.

And just about everyone in town would be there.

There'd be parades and musicians, and games and dancing, and hundreds of food stalls, souvenir stands, and many other things that are only seen at a matsuri in Japan. R. was excited by the idea. She wanted to go everywhere and see everything.

"It will be very crowded," M. warned. "We may become separated. It would be very difficult to find each other if that happens."

"We'd better pick a place and time to meet later, just in case," A. suggested. "Someplace that's easy to get to."

"We could meet here at the ryokan. What time will be good?" Y. said.

"How about six?" R. suggested. "That will give us plenty of time to see everything."

"Good idea. If we become separated, we'll meet back here at six. Don't worry about getting lost. This is Japan. You'll be perfectly safe here," A. said.

"Don't worry," A. said. "Y. and I will stay close to her."

They left for the festival around noon. They watched the opening parade, which featured traditional drummers and rows of kimono-clad dancers moving down the main avenue for nearly two hours. Then they stopped at a drink stand to quench their thirsts before wandering off to explore the various stalls and shops.

As planned, A. and M. slowly "got lost" in the crowd when the others didn't notice. They quickly returned to the ryokan and entered through the back door. After making sure that no one could see them, they hurried up to A.'s room.

M. giggled.

"I feel like I am a teen age girl who is disobeying her father," she said.

"You look like a teenager to me," he said as he led her to the futon.

While at the matsuri, R. was standing looking over some silk scarves at one of the stalls. As she looked over her shoulder, she saw a rather pretty woman standing a few feet away. She also noticed that she seemed to be looking her over. After a few seconds, the woman walked over.

"Pardon me for staring, but you look familiar to me. Have we met before?" the woman asked.

"I don't think so," R. replied.

The woman smiled at her accent and realized she was a foreigner.

"I don't think we have met, either. But I know I have seen you before," she said. "You have an accent. Where are you from?"

"I'm from the United States. I was born in Manila but I moved to St. Louis when I married my husband," R. explained.

"Oh, I know where I saw you. It was in the Asahi Shimbun. Are you famous?" the woman asked.

"I'm not but my husband is. He's here on a book tour," R. replied with a big smile.

The woman's expression changed. She looked as if she had been doused with ice water. She now knew exactly who R. was. What's more, she knew who her husband was. She seemed to become flustered and a little bit nervous.

"Your husband wrote 'Bushi'!" she said.

Just then, R. heard her name being called. She turned just as Y. and A. walked over.

"It's good that we found you. We've been looking all over for you," Y. said with relief.

"I'm alright. I was just talking to this lady—"R. turned but the woman was gone.

"What lady?" Y. asked.

"I don't know her name but she recognized me from our picture in the newspaper," R. said. "She's gone now. She acted funny after she found out who I was."

"In what way?" A. asked.

"She acted kind of nervous," R. said. "Like she wanted to run away."

Y. and A. looked at each other as R. told them about the chance meeting.

"What does she look like?" Y. asked.

"She was your mom's height but her hair was wavier. I couldn't tell how old she was," R. said.

"That describes many women in Nihon," A. said.

"But why would she approach you then suddenly leave after she found out who you are? That doesn't make sense," Y. said.

"I don't know. It doesn't matter anyway. How much time do we have before we need to find A. and M.?" R. asked.

"Two hours more," Y. said as she looked at her watch. "What would you like to do next?"

"What I always like to do," R. said.

"In that case, there are some very nice shops over there that sell things that are hand made by local craftspeople." Y. said.

"Let's go!" R. said.

She looked up at the sky and sighed. She felt content now.

Happy.

He walked up behind her and wrapped his arms around her. She responded by leaning into him. She reached up behind her and caressed his cheek.

"When I am with you, there is no other. I am your lover. Your wife. Whatever you wish me to be. All that matters is that we are together," she whispered as ran his hands slowly and gently over the front of her chest.

Everything felt so right now.

So perfectly right.

She shivered as the opened her blouse and caressed her breasts through her bra. He then pulled the garment from her shoulders. She allowed it to slide from her body to the floor where it came to a many folded rest at her feet. He unclasped her bra and removed it. As he did, he kissed her cheek, her neck, and her shoulders.

She trembled as his fingers danced playfully over her nipples. His touches were like magic and they ignited the fires deep within her. She felt his hands slide down her belly to her slacks and sighed as he undid the top button and eased his hand down into her panties. When she felt him explore her pleasure garden, she quivered and leaned into him.

There was no past.

No future.

All that mattered was this time. This place.

He picked her up and carried her to the futon. She smiled as he laid her down and eased off the rest of her clothes. Then he, too, undressed. As he removed his pants, she was please to see his katana standing straight and sharp—and even more pleased that she had such an effect on him.

This made her feel young again.

Beautiful.

Wanted.

He leaned over and kissed her on the lips. Kissing had seemed so alien to her until he came into her life. It was something that was not a custom of her generation. Now, it seemed so natural. So exciting.

Intimate.

She was elated that she aroused him so. That he found her sexy and irresistible. She reached out and stroked him to make him even harder while he gently swirled his tongue over her nipples. After a few seconds, he kissed his way downward. When he reached her garden, she parted her thighs and sighed and moaned as he made love to her with his tongue.

"Now," she sighed after a few moments.

He moved between her legs and eased his katana into her hot, moist sheath. She trembled as he went in deeply, then wrapped her arms and legs around him and moved with him as they made love. It was a nice, deep love, too.

The first two times they had done this, it had hurt when he entered her. She was again using a part of her body that had been long neglected. He understood and took it easy on her. He let her call the shots so she could become comfortable.

Now, each time they made love, it had become easier.

And more exciting.

Wonderful.

It felt as it had before and she felt young and sexy again.

M. headed straight for the train station. She didn't know why she'd fled. Something lent wings to her feet, too. It was as if she'd been compelled to run away from the matsuri as quickly as she could.

"So that was A.-s wife! She thought as she boarded the train. "She's absolutely beautiful. With a wife like that, why would he even think about me?"

Nakinagara aruku

He woke up first and spent a few moments watching her sleep. There was something almost magical about M. and the way the felt toward each other. They had made love three times that afternoon. Each time, they tried a different position. M. proved to be exciting, inventive and flexible.

She opened her eyes and smiled up at him.

"What time is it?" she asked.

"It's 5:15. We have to get dressed so we can meet the others in front of the ryokan," he said as he ran his hand over her smooth, creamy thigh. "You are so utsukushii. So sexy."

"I still think you need new glasses," she joked as they kissed.

They got up and dressed. Then they retreated to the sink and rinsed their mouths out and wash up a little bit.

"It's time," he said.

They left through the back door and walked around the block. When they turned the corner, they saw the others walk up to the front door. R. waved as they approached and asked where they were.

"We've just been wandering around, looking at things and sampling some snacks and drinks," A. replied. "We tried to find you guys at first, but gave up. There are too many people out here."

"Now that we are all here together again, what shall we do?" Y. asked.

J. was watching TV when he heard M. come home. She shouted the traditional greeting as she removed her shoes and changed to house slippers.

"Tadaima!" she said.

"You're home early. I thought you were going to matsuri in Hachioji," J. said.

"I went for a couple of hours then decided to come home," M. said.

J. noticed she seemed kind of nervous.

"What's wrong? What happened there?" he asked.

She sat down next to him and took a deep breath. Then she told him about her chance encounter. J. shook his head.

"Why did you run?" he asked. "I'm sure that if you had explained who you are, she would have taken you to see him. I'm sure that she knows all about you by now and is very curious about you. You should have introduced yourself."

"I was too afraid. I didn't want to cause any trouble between them. I know, I'm just being silly. I can't help it," she said. "I can't help it."

He nodded.

"I think that you need to see him again. You know his itinerary. Use that to accidentally bump into him. Or just be more direct. Go to his hotel one day and call him from the lobby. Or better yet, go to his room and knock on his door," J. suggested.

M. nodded.

She didn't even have the courage to call him that night. Her son's suggestion almost terrified her. She knew she would never be that bold. She never expected to meet his wife at the matsuri. She didn't even know they were in Hachioji. Yet it made sense for A. to go there. After all, he wrote about the battle at Hachioji Castle in his book. It would be only natural for him to want to see it in person.

And she just happened to go there at the same time.

"Thousands of people at the matsuri and I run into his wife! The gods are playing games with me," she thought.

Then she had another thought.

What if he had been with her?

What would she have said?

Would he even recognize her now?

That's when she realized that she had actually been talking to herself. She looked at J.

"You'd better go and meet him, Mother. If you don't, you'll just make yourself crazy," he said. "And me, too."

When K. awoke the next morning, he heard M. singing in the kitchen. He dressed, brushed his teeth and walked downstairs. She smiled happily and greeted him with a hug.

"Ohayo!" she said cheerfully.

She went back to the stove to finish preparing the meal. He listened to her hum and smiled. She put the food onto plates and walked to the table. She also placed a pot of tea and some blueberries on the table. The blueberries were A.'s suggestion. M. had described K.'s health problems a few years ago and how he refused to take vitamins. A. suggested she give him fresh berries each morning instead. He'd been eating them every since. A. had made many suggestions over the years concerning his and M's health. All of them had actually worked.

"A. should have been a doctor," he thought as he ate the berries.

"You seem especially happy this morning. Did you have a nice time with A. and his wife yesterday?" he asked.

"We had a wonderful time. We went to the matsuri then had a delicious dinner at the ryokan. I wanted to tell you about it last night but you were asleep when I returned," she said. "I invited him and R. to our home for dinner this evening. I already phone O. and S. They said they will be here as both are anxious to meet A. O. has read several of his books and he wants to discuss them with A."

"That sounds good. I'm eager to meet them, too. Afterward, A. and I can go to the pub and get better acquainted," K. said. "I have much to discuss with him."

"Oh? Like what?" M. asked.

"It's man stuff. You wouldn't understand," he replied, knowing that she probably would.

She shrugged.

"A. and I are going shopping this morning. I have to buy the ingredients for our meal," she said.

"Maybe I should take him to the pub before dinner. After he samples your cooking, we may have to rush him to an emergency room," K. joked.

She laughed.

M. and A. had exchanged many recipes and ideas over the years. Her style was simple, nutritious and attractive. A. had even prepared her recipes at home and he'd been delighted with the outcomes. He even suggested subtle ways she could make them more exciting. She followed his instructions but K. never seemed to notice.

She sighed.

"My cooking only sent you to the emergency room once," she said.

"That is because I have a stomach of iron, although you did scare me a few times," he said. "In the beginning, you seemed to be completely lost in the kitchen. But you have steadily improved to where your meals are at least tolerable if not edible. At least you didn't cause any permanent harm to our children."

"I am sure no one will be at risk this evening," she smiled."Oh. I must get fresh seaweed. A.-san loves seaweed salad."

K. seemed surprised.

"Are you sure he's not Nihon-jin? I've never met an American who likes seaweed," he said. "Well, that is yet another thing he and I have in common—besides you."

She blushed but remained silent.

K. and A. hit it off almost immediately. The first few minutes, K. sized A. up. He asked all sorts of questions. To his surprise, A. answered each directly and in Nihon-go. It was a somewhat old-fashioned and formal style that wasn't used anymore. For some reason, that pleased K. It showed that he had a respect for Japanese culture.

He also discovered that they saw eye-to-eye on many topics and that, like him, A. didn't care for modern times very much. He preferred the older Japan to the modern and was afraid that the country y was sacrificing its soul and culture in its pursuit of technology.

He liked A.'s wife, R.

He thought she was cute and funny and very friendly. She also seemed awed with what she'd seen so far in Nihon. A. and R. got along well with O. and S., their daughter R. and A. and R. A. was surprised that all of them had read "Bushi".

The evening passed by quickly.

At nine, O. announced that he had to leave as they had a long train ride home. They took their leave and shook hands with A. and R. A. invited them to stay at his home in St. Louis if they ever decided to visit the United States. O. said he would be honored.

M.walked them out. Just before they left, O. leaned over and whispered in M.'s ear. She blushed noticeably and pushed him as he laughed.

Around ten, K. invited A. to accompany him to his favorite pub to get better acquainted. A. agreed without hesitation. M. said she would walk R. back to the ryokan. As she watched A. and K. leave, she wondered what K. really had in mind.

When they reached the pub, the woman who owned it greeted K. warmly. He introduced A. and she was pleased when he greeted her in Japanese.

They walked over a table and sat down. The woman brought them two cold beers. K. picked his up and saluted A. with it. A. returned it.

"My wife thinks very highly of you. Ordinarily, I would disapprove of your friendship. You know yourself that this is highly unusual in our culture, especially for people of our generation. When I found out, I was thinking of putting an end to it. I did try, but she continued to correspond with you anyway. So I let her do so. You are married and so far away that I thought you two would never actually meet. Now, much to my surprise, here you are," K. began as he poured beer into his glass.

"I must admit that I never expected M. and I to become such good friends, either. But once we started writing, I could not stop. I was drawn to her from the start. It was like we'd met before, a long time ago," A. said as he sipped his beer.

K. looked A. straight in the eyes. It was a direct, almost challenging glare. Penetrating. He was surprised that this gaijin didn't flinch.

"He has nothing to hide," he thought. "He is exactly who he is. I like that."

"Such a thing was unthinkable and improper a few years ago. A married woman is not to have a close relationship with another man. It is not considered proper," he said.

K. smiled as he sipped his beer.

"But in this case, I will grant the exception. Your friendship makes M. very happy. You support and encourage her to be stronger and to allow her inner personality to come out. She has shown me a side that I find intriguing—to say the least. She is more decisive. Her sense of humor is wittier and sarcastic and she even dares to disagree with me lately," he continued.

"I doubt this would have happened if you two had not become friends. I must admit that I like the new M. I feel she can handle life without me if she has to. So, I am happy for her and grateful to you. She could not have made friends with a better man," he said as he held up his glass.

"Arigato, K.-san. I appreciate your candor," A. said as he returned the salute. "I also think she chose the perfect man for herself many years ago."

K. smiled.

"But that was very long ago. Over the years, I have become more demanding and irritable and far less romantic. Of course, I was never very romantic to begin with. I didn't compliment her. I didn't tell her how I felt. I thought there was no need for such things after so many years. But I forgot that women like to hear such things—and M. is definitely a woman," he joked.

"To be honest, M. was becoming bored and frustrated with me. I think she was about to leave me. But I understand that you helped her to understand what was wrong with me and urged her to be patient and to get me the medical attention you thought I should have. I think in many ways, you brought us back together," he said. "At least, that is what I feel after reading your email exchanges."

He laughed.

"How many did you read?" A. asked.

"About half. I usually read them before she does. I must admit, you two surprise me. Because of that, I know how you feel about each other. That is why I would like to ask a favor of you."

"Anything," A. assured him.

"Please continue to be her friend. Promise me that if anything ever happens to me, you will take care of her and help her if she needs it," K. asked.

"You have my word, K.-san," vowed. "I will always be there for M. You too, if you need me."

K. smiled and ordered another round.

"Every decent husband wants to be assured that his wife will be taken care of after he's gone. I now have such assurance, although a few years ago, such a thing would have upset and angered me to no end.

Times are different now. We must learn to accept help and friendship, even from unusual places. I know that you are a strong, honorable and good man. You follow a personal code that is much like Bushido. You might have been a samurai in another life. I know I can trust you to keep your word," he said.

He ordered another round.

"I have read your book. You have an understanding of our history and culture that astonishes me. I feel you are more Nihon-jin than gaijin. And you have old-fashioned ideals and a sense of honor that is rare in this world," he said.

He leaned closer and smiled.

"I also know that M. loves you very much. I can see it in the way she looks at you and the way she acts when she is near you. You make her heart sing. You make her young and happy and pretty again. And I see by the way you look at her that you feel the same. I see a true passion between you. You see things in M. that I had forgotten. Please keep that passion burning. Don't ever let it die out," he advised.

K.'s words didn't exactly surprise A.

K. was a very perceptive man. He'd expected him to be jealous. Instead, he was understanding.

It was as if he felt resigned to the situation.

K. laughed.

"Just don't marry her until after I am gone," he joked. "Until then, she is still mine."

They drank for another hour or so. They laughed and joked and grew to be good friends. Around one a.m., K. and A. parted at the train station. K. took the train back to the house. A. took a taxi to his ryokan.

It had been a most interesting night.

R. was still awake when A. returned. She noticed he was stumbling around drunk and laughed.

"It guess you two really hit it off tonight," she said.

"Yes we did. We're good friends now. Very good friends," A. said as she helped him undress.

M. opened the door to let the very inebriated K. inside. He staggered into the house and grinned at her.

"I really like him. He is a good man," he said as he undressed.

"I am glad you approve," M. said.

"You have chosen very well," he said. "Better than I expected. I like him but I did tell him that he could not have you until after I am gone."

She stared at him.

He laughed.

"And you are entitled to only one husband at a time," he said as he hugged her. "Just as he can have only one wife at a time. But you can still be lovers!"

"You're crazy. You're drunk, too," she said.

"Hai. But neither changes anything!" he replied as he sat down and fell back onto the futon.

Hitoribotchi no yoru

M. asked A. if he'd like to accompany her to the nursing home to visit her mother. Since she'd written him about her so many times and even sent him photos, he said he'd be happy to meet her.

When they went into her mother's room, she smiled when she saw M. Then she sort of squinted at A. M. introduced them.

"I am pleased and honored to meet you, O-san," he said with a respectful bow.

Her mother smiled.

"I am honored to meet you as well," she replied. She glanced at M. "Is this your new husband? He is quite different from K."

M. blushed.

"It is nothing like that, Mom. This is my good friend from America," she explained.

Her mother laughed.

"Sometimes my mind wanders from my body, but don't be mistaken. I am still very observant. I know each of your emotional expressions. I can tell when you are in love—like you are now. If you are not married, I know that you will be one day," she said.

M. was speechless.

She looked at A.

He smiled.

Her mother looked straight at him.

"I see the love for M. in your expression, too," she said. "Although my body does not always work the way it should, my mind is still sharp at times and my senses are good. You love my daughter, don't you?"

"Hai," A. replied.

"In that case, I give you my permission and blessing to wed her when the time comes," she said.

When they left the home M. chuckled. She smiled up at A.

"I guess we are so very obvious that we no longer can conceal our feelings for each other. I hope your wife isn't so good at reading our expressions. I don't wish to have my head cut off!" she said.

"Your mother is exactly what I expected her to be," he said. "She knows you very well after all these years. She might know you better than you know yourself. But I feel much better now that we have her permission to marry."

She laughed.

"That is something that K. would say!" she said.

From there, they returned to the ryokan. R. was out with A. and Y. again and would not be back for at least three hours. They discretely went around the corner and came in the back door. Then they quietly walked upstairs to the room.

They made love slowly and warmly. Each too time to find out what pleased the other. As they made love, they changed positions a few times. M. guided him to all of her most erotic spots and he found a couple she didn't know she had. She did the same with him. It became a wonderful, erotic ballet that ended in a strong, quivering, mutual climax.

They held each other closely afterward.

When her heart rate returned to normal, she sighed happily. She used to believe all of her most erotic days were long past. Now, she realized they were about to begin anew

"This is like a wonderful fairy tale," she said. "I thought such things were gone from my life forever. Then you came into it and my life began all over again."

"You're an amazing woman, M.-san. Truly amazing," he said.

"This is your last night in Hachioji," she said sadly. "I wish it would never end."

"We'll have more such nights in Yufuin," A. assured her. "But first, I have other signings and interviews to go to. I leave for Osaka tomorrow. I have one signing and a magazine interview there. Then I have signings in Nara and Kyoto. In between, R. and I will take several tours. Then I'll fly to Oita and she'll fly to Manila. I'll have ten days in Yufuin to relax at the Shimizu Ryokan. You can join me there and we'll treat it like our honeymoon," A. said.

"I can hardly wait!" she said softly.

M. looked at the morning paper. She turned to the book section and saw that A. and his wife had taken the Bullet Train to Osaka. Ironically, the publisher had gotten them a suite in the Royal Hotel—the same hotel where she had booked a room for him on his second visit.

His life was moving in a full circle.

Of course, the hotel had recently been completely renovated and was considered to be quite elegant. That's probably why the publisher selected it.

A large part of her wanted to go to Osaka and visit him at the hotel. An even larger part was telling her to let things be.

Her accidental meeting with R. had scared her. If R knew about their past relationship, she was most likely very jealous and protective of A. She might not like one of his old flames dropping by. Most likely, she'd be going everywhere with him on this part of his trip, too. And M. wanted to try to see A. when no one else was around.

She knew he'd be flying to Oita for a ten day stay at the Shimizu Ryokan in Yufuin. She also knew that his wife would not be joining there. She decided that if she did get up the courage to see him again, it would have to be there.

Where it all started so very long ago.

"You'll really like Osaka. It's very different from Tokyo. It's smaller and more relaxed. I've always enjoyed it more. The people are friendlier and the cuisine is better, too. Don't worry about shopping. You'll have more than enough places to go for that," A. said as they sat on the Bullet Train and watched the scenery zip by.

"I'm glad M. and her friend aren't coming with us. I finally have you all to myself," R. said as she snuggled close.

He laughed.

"I'm sure that K. wouldn't have let M. come along with us," he said. "He doesn't need some gaijin monopolizing all of his wife's time."

"I like your friend. She's very nice—just like you said she'd be. I hope we get to see her again one day. Maybe you can invite them to visit us in St. Louis?"

"I already have," A. smiled.

"Good. Do you think they'll come?" R. asked.

He shrugged.

"That all depends on their circumstances," A. said. "She has to talk K. into it—which won't be easy."

"She's very different from the young people here," R. said.

"Different generations breed different attitudes," A. said. "I'm kind of sorry to see their old traditions going away. This will be a very different country in another 50 years."

When K. returned from the gym, he saw a very cheerful M. preparing their dinner in the kitchen. He watched her for a few moments and smiled at the obvious lightness in her movements. She turned and started when she saw him.

"I'm sorry that I startled you," he apologized. "Did you see your friends off at the train station?"

"Hai. They are on their way to Osaka now. Our lives can now return to normal," she said as she put their food into dishes and carried them to the table.

"I hope not," he said as they sat down.

"Why?" she queried.

"You are acting young and cheerful right now. I prefer to keep you that way," he said. "But in order for you to stay this way, I know that A.-san would have to divorce his wife and marry you. Unfortunately, I don't think he will ever do that, so I fear that we are stuck with each other for a few more years."

"Is that so bad?" she asked with a smile.

"I'm not sure. I am sure of this: A.-san is exactly what you needed. You met him at the right time. It's as if the gods arranged it. What I don't understand is why? What did he ever do in this life or a previous life for them to do this to him?" he said.

"Do what to him?" she asked.

"Punish him with you, of course!" he smiled. "But at least now, I have someone I can share the burden with."

She laughed.

He looked at her expression. She looked so serene. So content.

"No snappy comeback this time?" he asked.

"None," she smiled.

"Wow. He must be very good then!" he said with a fake touch of "awe".

The book signings went better than expected as did his interviews. In between, they managed to tour Osaka and Himeji castles, and Kyoto and Nara. On Friday morning, A. and R. parted company at Kansai Airport in Osaka. She took a flight to Manila. He took a flight to Oita on Kyushu.

M. smiled when he told her his plan.

He had also given her a plane ticket to Oita. She would arrive two days after he did and they would "honeymoon" in their suite at the Shimizu Ryokan. If K. would allow her, that is.

"A. is going to Yufuin. He is staying at the same ryokan that he stayed in during his first trip to Nihon many years ago. It sounds so very romantic!" she said.

"He is far too sentimental for my taste," K. said. "But you find such things attractive, don't you?"

She nodded.

"He is not afraid to remove his yoroi and allow his real self to breathe," she said. "He only dons his yoroi when he truly needs it. He does not hide behind it. You said this yourself."

"So I did," he smiled.

He had to admire A. While he was often too fearful of showing any signs of weakness, A. didn't worry about such things. He was who he appeared to be.

"Let me guess. You and he made arrangements to meet in Yufuin?" he asked.

She nodded.

"And just how are you going to get there?" he asked.

She showed him the e-ticket. He laughed.

"So, even if I say you can't go, you will do so anyway?" he asked.

"I am not sure. You are my husband and I feel that I should obey you—within reason," she hedged.

He sighed.

He knew that if he forbade her, she'd obey him but she'd feel miserable. That would lead her to making him feel miserable in return. Also, he reasoned that such a thing might break her newfound spirit. He liked the new M. She was funny and challenging and strong. He didn't want her robotic, obedient self to return.

He also knew that they loved each other.

And their love ran true, strong and deep.

He smiled at her and stroked her hair. She held his hand to her cheek.

"What time is your flight?" he asked.

Omoidasu aki no hi

When A. landed at Oita airport, he retrieved his bag from the luggage carousel and walked out of the terminal. The airport had been expanded since he last saw it. The terminal was longer and more modern and the runway was able to accommodate jets. He saw a black car parked just outside the building with a middle-aged man in a white shirt and shorts leaning against it.

"Are you A.-san?" the man asked.

"Hai," A. replied.

"Please get in," the man said as he took his bag and placed it into the trunk.

"I am S.," the man said as he got into the driver's seat.

"The last time I saw you, you were about ten years old," A. said.

"You were here before? When?" S. asked.

"In 1970. You have an older brother and sister. I forget their names. Your father is K," A. replied.

"Your father told me that I was only the second gaijin ever to stay at the ryokan. You, me and a bunch of your friends played catch behind the ryokan after M.-san told you I was a baseball player."

S. smiled.

"Hai. I remember now. That was so very long ago. I am happy that you decided to stay at our ryokan again," he said.

"It was my most enjoyable stay anywhere. Your family treated me more like a relative than a guest. I have never felt more at home anywhere else I've stayed and I always promised myself I'd return," A. said.

"My wife, O. and I manage the ryokan now. My brother lives in Hiroshima. My sister married and moved to Sapporo. I have a son named K. He is ten years old now. We named him after my father," S. explained as they got onto the long, scenic road that wound its way into the mountains.

"How is your father?" A. asked.

"I am sorry to say that he is no longer with us," S. replied. "He died eight years ago. He was 101 years old," S. said.

"I am sorry to hear that. He was a very fine man," A. said sadly.

"Arigato. He always spoke well of you, too. He liked to tell the story of what happened at the party that night. It amused him to think of it," S. smiled.

"That was the very first time in my life that I'd ever been drunk. Most of that night is a blur to me. Just what did I do that was so amusing?" A. asked.

S. smiled.

"Even after all these years, it is still not polite to say," he said.

"That's exactly what you father said when I asked him!" A. said with a laugh.

"Are you the author of 'Bushi'?" S. asked.

"Hai," A. said. "Have you read it?"

"My wife has. I've read part of it. According to the back cover, you have done many things during your life. You were even a bushi yourself," S. said.

"It's all true," A. said.

When they arrived at the ryokan, O. and K. came out to meet them. S. introduced them to A. who bowed politely and said he was honored to meet them and happy to stay at the ryokan once again.

K. smiled at him.

"I know who you are! I even know what room you stayed in," he said.

"My father has told him about you many times," S. explained. "He said he wished he could meet you one day."

"Well, you've got your wish, K-chan," A. said as the boy picked up his bag.

"I'll show you to your room!" he said cheerfully.

A, S. and O. followed him up the steps and down a long hallway to a set of open doors. They went into a large, two room suite with tatami mat floors, and a large window that opened onto the beautiful garden below.

There was a small sink, low table and cushions with backs and another smaller table with two chairs set up by the window.

"This is perfect," A. said. "Beautiful!"

"You asked for our best room," S. said. "How long will you be with us?"

"At least ten days," A. said as he placed his bag on the luggage stand.

"We would be pleased to have you join us for dinner each evening," S. said. "My wife is an excellent cook."

"I will be honored to join you," A. said as he opened his bag.

K. watched as he took out an old first baseman's mitt and a baseball. A. smiled at him.

"Why did you bring your glove?" K. asked.

"I always bring it with me—just in case someone asks me to play," A. said.

They laughed.

"You didn't have one with you the first time," S. said.

"No. I had to ask your father to purchase one for me. He made a good choice. He selected a Naniwa Rabbit. It was a very good mitt. I kept it for years," A. said. "I've had this mitt since I was a teenager. I bought it in 1969."

O. looked him over carefully.

"Pardon me for asking—but can you tell me your age?" she asked.

When he told her, she looked at him in disbelief.

"How do you stay so young?" she asked.

He smiled.

"I have a very young wife that requires much attention. I also exercise four times a week and I still play baseball," he said as he handed K. the ball.

The ball also looked quite old. K. saw that it had several Japanese autographs on it. He read them aloud.

"Oh Sadaharu, Nagashima Shigeo, Kaneda Masaichi," he looked at A. and his father.

"Those were my favorite baseball players when I was younger. I got a chance to meet them at a spring training camp one winter and I asked them to autograph that ball," A. explained. "I was trying to win a spot on their team but I just didn't make it."

"Wow! Those are the most famous players in Nihon history," S. said.

K. handed the ball back to A. A. smiled and gave it back to him.

"That ball is yours now," he said. "I want you to have it."

The boy stared at him. He looked like he'd been given the greatest gift of his entire young life.

"You shouldn't!" his mother said.

"I insist," A. replied.

"You are most generous. Too generous," S. said.

"Gozo arigato gozaimasu!" K. shouted happily. "I'll put it on my shelf—but I want you to autograph it, first."

"Me?" A. asked. "Why?"

"So I can honor you, too," K. replied.

S. took a pen from his pocket and handed it to A. K. handed him the ball and watched as he signed it. K. beamed as A. handed it back along with the pen.

They played catch-up during dinner, which proved to be a real feast of sukiyaki, boiled rice (gohan) and various steamed vegetables. Each dish was perfectly prepared and seasoned and they washed it down with bottles of cold Asahi beer.

They were surprised at his use of Japanese and they made him feel comfortable by switching to English as much as they could. O. got him to autograph her copy of 'Bushi' and they took several photos.

"You have an excellent feel for our history and culture," O. said. "Your book is very vivid and I love your female character, M."

"Is she based on your old friend?" S. asked.

"Actually, she's based on several woman I've known," A. replied. "But the character is mostly M.-san."

"Why did you ask for our best suite?" S. asked.

"Someone will be joining me in a day or two," A. replied. "Her name is M."

S. looked surprise.

"No. She just happens to have the same first and last name. We met accidentally on the internet one day several years ago," A. explained. 'I've told her so much about this ryokan that she wanted to see it. So I invited her to join me."

"Is she your wife?" S. asked.

"She will be while she's here," A. said with a wink.

After dinner, A. took a long, comfortable soak in the ryokan bath. He first filled a small bucket with hot water from the tub and poured it all over himself until he was good and wet. Then he soaped and rinsed himself off. When he was sure he was completely clean, he got into the bath and allowed the water from the onsen to relax him.

He smiled as he remembered his first time in the bath. K. had to show him how to do it properly. After one or two baths, he got the hang of it and really enjoyed it.

"When in Japan..." he thought.

After the bath, he put on the yukata and returned to his room. As he prepared to brush his teeth, he heard S. call out from the hall.

The door slid open and he and K. entered.

"Would you care to join us for an evening drink before your retire?" S. asked.

"I'd be delighted," A, said as he followed them downstairs and out into the garden to a small metal table surrounded by four chairs.

O. greeted them with a bow. He returned it and sat down while she poured three cups of sake and handed K. a container of orange juice.

"My father told me you were a bushi," K. said.

"Yes. I was," A. said. "That was a long time ago."

"Did you fight in a war?" K. asked.

"Yes I did. I was in Vietnam," A. replied.

"Really?" K. asked.

"Really," A. smiled. "I was just 21 at the time. I volunteered to go."

"You sound just like a samurai!" K. said with a smile.

"I live by the warrior code," A. said.

"Bushido?" K. asked.

"Yes with touches of Chivalry like the knights of ancient Europe," A. said.

"What was the war really like?" K. asked.

"It had its good and bad times--like all things. I prefer to remember the good times," A. said.

"Can you tell me about it? Please!" K. asked.

"I'll try. What do you want to know about?" A. smiled.

"What do you remember most about Vietnam?" K. asked.

"The country or the war?" A. asked.

"The country," K. said.

"I remember the oppressive heat. The daily rains that soaked through everything for 10 minutes then stopped. When they stopped, everything just got hotter and steamier. I remember the mosquitoes, the no see ums that managed to bite you even if you were covered. I remember the two step vipers and the fuck you lizards and the sluggish streams of putrid water and the stench from newly fertilized rice paddies," A. said.

"Is that all?" K. asked.

"No. There are many other things. I remember the beauty of Cam Ranh Bay as I flew over it. I remember night skies lit by thousands of stars. I remember beautiful villages with houses up on stilts and thatched roofs. I remember the smiles on the faces of friendly people and the many wonderful Vietnamese dishes I tried. I remember the laughter shared with close friends and the sound bullets make as they hiss past you during battles—and many other things that are hard to describe," A. said.

"My grandfather was a bushi," K. said.

"I know. Your uncle showed me the katana he carried during World War II. He was an officer in the Imperial Army," A. said.

K. smiled and nodded.

"I really liked your grandfather. He was a good, kind, honest and funny man."

S. beamed at his recollection.

"He always thought well of you, too. He always remembered your stay with us and often wondered what had become of you," he said.

"Were you a soldier when you met him?" K. asked.

"No. Back then, I was a baseball player," A. replied.

"Were you good?" K. asked.

"That all depends on who you ask," A. joked.

"Were you ever in a battle?" O. asked.

"I was in three battles and a couple of small fights," A. said.

"What was it like?" she asked.

He thought for s few seconds, and then told him about the ambush that had gone terribly wrong and how it ended with the napalm strike that scorched everything for a mile in every direction. They listened quietly to his very vivid descriptions. When it was over, S. and O. shook their heads.

"It must have been terrifying!" O. remarked.

"It was—afterward. During the battle, I was far too busy to get scared. It all hit me after the battle, when I saw all those dead men everywhere," A. said.

"That's a good story," K. said. "I didn't know it was like that. Can you tell me more?"

"How about something really weird?" A. asked.

"Okay. What was the strangest thing you ever saw there?" K. asked.

He smiled as he let his memory drift back to that afternoon.

"You're not going to believe this," he said.

After trudging through the dense rainforest for what felt like an eternity, they reached a small clearing. It was partially shaded by the interlocking green canopy above them and had a narrow, clear water stream running through it. They could hear birds of several varieties chirping and singing in the branches above and the air was thick with mosquitoes.

The area felt quiet and oddly safe. Like it was cut off from the rest of the world.

The point man, a young Black Special Forces sergeant named Mac, was the first to enter the clearing. He walked in a few yards, looked up at a tree and laughed.

"Hey you guys!" he called out. "C'mere. You're not gonna fuckin' believe this!"

The y walked up and looked where he indicated with a nod of his head. A. looked up and laughed so hard he nearly cried. So did the others.

There, nailed to the trunk of the tree, was a rusted tin sign that read: DRINK COCA COLA.

They stood and stared at it for a few minutes as they laughed. One of them snapped a photo and said he was going to send it to Stars and Stripes.

"How do you suppose that got way out here?" Mac asked.

"Beats me. There isn't shit for 50 miles in any direction," A. said. "Whoever nailed that to the tree must have had a good sense of humor. Maybe he figured that somebody like us would find it one day and wonder how in Hell it got here."

"I don't think it was done by a G.I. We're the first one to make it through here," one of the other men said.

"Are you sure about that?" A. asked.

"Maybe some VC nailed it up there?" another soldier suggested.

Mac eyed him quizzically.

"What the fuck for?" he asked.

"To fuck with the heads of anyone who found it?" the soldier offered.

They sat down in the shade to rest and eat. A. kept staring at the sign and wondering. It was old.

Real old.

Most of the paint was gone and it was badly rusted but you could still read it.

He wondered if whoever nailed the sign up actually drank Coca Cola and why he had carried that sign out into the middle of nowhere just to nail it to the tree. He knew he'd never learn the answers to his questions. He just chalked this one up to another of the war's oddities.

A young soldier named Franklin took out his camera and snapped a photo of it. Franklin never went anywhere without that camera.

They left the clearing a few minutes later. They left the sign right where it was for some future group of travelers to wonder about.

S. looked at A. as if he were crazy.

"Did you make that up?" he asked.

"No. That really happened," A. said. "For all I know, that sign is still there. A lot of crazy things happened in Nam, but that was by far, the craziest."

S. laughed as he tried to picture the sign in his mind.

"I'd like to see that someday," he said.

"Good luck finding it," A. said. "I know I couldn't find it again if I searched that area for the next 20 years. That wasn't even on any of our maps back then. I know we were about 25 kilometers from the Cambodian border but I don't have any idea where to begin looking."

"Maybe we can look for it together?" K. asked.

"Okay. When you're old enough, maybe we'll give it a try. It might be fun," A. agreed with a smile.

"What happened to the photo?" S. asked.

"I don't know. I never actually saw it," A. said. "After the patrol, Franklin went to Saigon and I never saw him again. I don't even know if he's still alive."

"I wish I could see it," S. said.

"So do I," A. nodded. "There was something else that I thought was very strange. This was a place that most people wouldn't even expect to find in the middle of war zone."

S. and K. looked at him as he gathered his thoughts. He took another sip of the beer and began his narrative.

They were sent about 100 clicks north and west to help the guys at a remote station set up new radio gear. The camp was situated atop a hill that overlooked a village with a narrow stream running through it. Directly across, was another camp. This one flew the NVA flag and seemed to be nearly twice as large.

As A. trained his binoculars on the NVA camp, he saw an enemy soldier doing the same. The NVA soldier waved. A. waved back and laughed. The two were definitely within rifle range, but no one fired a shot. Hell, no one even carried weapons in either camp.

"You've been here before," he asked the LT. "What with this situation?"

"We have an unwritten truce with those guys over there," the LT said. "They don't shoot at us and we don't shoot at them. The village is for R&R purposes only. Both sides use it. So if you go there, the rule is no weapons. Not even a knife."

"Interesting," A. said. "Are there other places like this in Nam?"

"I've heard that Da Lat is like this, but I've never been," the LT said. "You should go down and check out the village tonight."

"Is it worth it?" A. asked.

"I'll let you decide that," the LT smiled.

As he entered the village, A. was surprised to see uniformed soldiers from both sides openly mingling with each other and the locals. The food stalls, cafes and handful of bars provided a respite from the never-ending war.

Here, the war never happened.

Somewhere along the line, both sides had come to an agreement which forbade soldiers from either side to bring any sort of weapons into the village. It was a local tradition now. The soldiers were welcome but weapons were not. The village was a true "demilitarized zone".

The troops were there to gamble.

To eat and drink.

To whore around with the dozens of women who worked the bars and cafes.

One came here to relax and ignore the war for a few precious hours. There were no enemies here.

This was one of the true absurdities of the war.

An anomaly.

He walked into a small, clean eating establishment and sat down at a table. A pretty young woman hurried over and greeted him in English while handing him a bottle Ba mi Ba (number 33), which was the local beer and the most common outside of Saigon. It was sort of warm but drinkable.

Out in the sticks, you drank whatever was available and forced yourself to like it. She went away and returned with a large bowl of noodles with broth, beef balls, vegetables and hot peppers. It smelled and tasted quite good. A. gave her the thumbs up. She smiled.

It was always best never to ask what the meat was in Nam. Since there were no cows, you could be sure it wasn't beef. It could be caribou. Dog. Or even money or rat. If it tasted good, you just ate it and hoped for the best.

As he ate, an NVA officer entered and looked around. The woman showed him to the only empty seat left which was at A.'s table. The officer smiled as he sat down.

"I hope you don't mind my joining you," he said in perfect English.

"Not at all. My name's A." he said as he extended his hand.

"Tranh," the officer replied as he shook it. "I am pleased to meet you. Have you been here very long?"

"Eight months," A. replied. "Your English is perfect."

"Thanks. I went to school at UCLA. I studied marine biology. You have a great country. I would like to see my country become like yours one day," Tranh said as the waitress brought him a 33 and bowl of noodles.

"You like our cuisine?" Tranh asked.

"It beats the Hell out of C Rations," A. said. "I've grown very fond of Vietnamese food actually. Your country is very beautiful, too. If it weren't for this damned war, it would be a great place to vacation. It has a lot of potential and history."

Tranh smiled.

"This war stinks. I detest it myself but after we got betrayed by the Treaty of Paris, I had no choice but to come home and fight. I don't know why the United Nations decided to divide Vietnam into two countries. But they did and that's why we're fighting to re-unite it," he said as they clinked bottles.

"It doesn't make sense to me, either, Tranh. We should have helped you rebuild Vietnam after you drove the French out. This war has become a tragedy in more ways than I can count," A. said.

Tranh nodded.

"When Vietnam was divided, it triggered a civil war. A few years ago, you decided to send weapons and troops here to fight alongside the South Vietnamese soldiers. What I can't understand is why America decided to interfere with our civil war. After all, Vietnam didn't interfere with your civil war," he said.

"Be damned if I know, Tranh. I enlisted and volunteered to come here because I believed the hype about fighting to contain Communism. Now that I've been here, I admit that I have no idea what the Hell we're fighting for," A. said.

"Personally, I just want to get out of here in one piece—and I don't want to kill anyone in the process."

"I feel the same. The difference is, this is my home country and I'd like to see it unified and free from colonialism. I would rather see that done peacefully if possible," Tranh said.

"I like you, A. You're a good man. I hope you stay safe and healthy and get home alive," he added.

"When this is over, I'd like to meet with you again somewhere. We can laugh and drink until we fall down then maybe you can show me the real Vietnam," A. said as he ordered a second round.

Tranh pulled out his wallet and showed A. a photo of a pretty young woman.

"She's my sister. I'd like you to meet her after this war. I think you and she would make a very good match," he said.

"I'd be honored to meet her one day," A, said. "Hell, we might end up as brothers-in-law!"

They laughed.

The woman brought two more bottles of 33.

"Let's make a pact," Tranh said. "Let's meet here one year to the date after the war ends and cement our friendship. I'll bring my sister."

They shook hands.

"You, my friend, have got yourself a deal!" A> agreed.

Tranh took his leave after two more beers. He said he'd be back in the village in two days. They agreed to meet at the same place at four in the afternoon and have a few more beers together.

But A. never saw Tranh again.

He returned to the village as promised. He sat at the same table and had dinner while he waited. But Tranh never showed. Three hours later, A. downed his last beer and staggered out of the restaurant. He never did learn what happened to Tranh.

Even though decades had passed, he still thought about Tranh once in a while. He wondered if he survived the war. He never made it back to the place a year after the war ended as promised, either. Did Tranh show up? If so, did he bring his sister?

"We soldiers are a strange breed," he said. "During combat, we're bitter enemies. When it's all over, we become friends because of the common bonds we share. I hope Tranh made it."

They looked at him then at each other.

"We here in Nihon never gave the war much thought. It didn't concern us and we barely gave it any news coverage unless a major battle had taken place," S. said. "Your stories help to give me a human perspective of what war is like. My father often spoke about the war, but not in the terms you've described."

"I had an uncle who fought in the Pacific campaign. He fought on Saipan and Okinawa. He always said that the Nihon-jin bushi were the toughest soldiers he'd ever seen and their courage was second to none. He came away with a deep respect for your people and the code of Bushido," A. said. "He passed that respect on to me.

Vietnam was an entirely different kind of war. It was mostly small unit engagements and air strikes and ambushes. We never knew who the enemy was or where. The war had two faces. The day face where everything was fine and everyone was your friend. Then there was the night face where nothing went right and everyone was your enemy."

"How do you win such a war?" S. asked.

He shrugged.

"I don't have an answer for that one, S.-san," he said. "No one does."

M. moped around the house as she tried to decide what to do. She knew from reading the newspaper that he had gone to Yufuin alone. His wife had flown to Manila to see her family and he would join her there in two weeks.

So there would be no awkward meeting between her and his wife. That took much of her anxiety away. But she was still a nervous wreck over seeing him again. She was worried what he'd say, how he'd greet her, how he'd react to her. She wondered if he'd like the way she looked.

She'd seen his photo.

Watched him on TV.

He looked good and fit.

Much more so than she remembered.

She exercised and jogged and ate well. She weighed the same as she did when she was 20. But she was older now. There were some strands of silver in her jet black hair and some lines under her eyes and at the corners of her lips.

Did she really want him to see her this way?

Would it be better if he just remembered her as she was back then?

She went to the bathroom to brush her teeth. As she did, she glanced in the mirror. Then she saw her. A very young, petite Asian girl with long black hair.

She turned but no one was there.

She finished brushing and rinsed her mouth with water. Then she leaned over and splashed water on her face. When she looked up at the mirror, the girl was there again. She stopped and stared at her for several seconds. Then the image faded away.

"A ghost?" she wondered.

She thought about the soldier who had haunted her during her college days. Were the two connected? If so, why were they appearing to her? What did they want?

She finished washing and headed to the bedroom. When she got there, she saw her World Atlas lying on the floor. It was open.

"How did you get down there?" she asked as she bent down to pick it up.

As she reached for it, she saw that it was open to the map of Vietnam…

Hitoribotchi no yoru

When A. returned from his walk down "memory lane", S, and his family were just sitting for lunch. S. saw him and insisted he join them. As they ate, K. again asked a lot of questions. A. answered them with humor and some of his replies made everyone laugh out loud.

After lunch, he and S. walked in the garden.

"Please excuse my son for being so inquisitive. Part of that is my fault. My wife says he is just like me," S. said.

"You and your friends were just as curious during my first visit," A. said. "K. isn't bothering me at all, so please don't apologize."

"My father always believed that you and M.-san would marry. He often said that your love was like an old fairy tale," S. said.

"So did I. I think she did, too. Not every fairy tale has a happy ending. Sometimes, things just go very wrong," A. said.

"Has your life been good?" S. asked.

"Hai. It's been better than I expected in many ways. I've had many surprises along the way. Most have been of the good variety," A. said.

"I am pleased that you have decided to return to our ryokan. I did not think you remembered us after all these years. I'm happy that your stay was so memorable for you," S. said.

"This is the very first place I stayed in Nihon. It was my first experience with your culture, your food and the people of Nihon. Of all the places I've visited or stayed, this is the place I loved most. So, you see, I had to come back," A. said.

"You still have no love for very modern things, do you?" S. asked.

"No. That part of me will never change. Your father sensed that about me. He was a very perceptive man," A. said.

"Your wife is very beautiful. I saw her photo in the newspaper. She is your second wife?" S. asked.

He nodded.

"But you are expecting a guest. A woman?" he asked.

Again A. nodded.

S. smiled discreetly.

"I will speak no more of this," he said.

M. returned from her walk and found Koinu doing his sword exercises in the garden. She stopped to watch for a few minutes. He did this each day, along with several other routines to keep himself fit and flexible. She also had her routines. She did them when she wasn't chasing after children and grandchildren.

Or shopping.

Koinu saw her and stopped. He sheathed his katana and walked over to give her a warm hug. She smiled happily as she wrapped her arms around him. Even after all these years together, their passion had never cooled.

"You need a good, hot bath," she said.

He laughed.

"Did you hear the news about Kenshin? He has decided to retire to Kyushu at the end of the year," he said. "He will be 74 soon. He said that is enough time spent as a samurai."

"Hai. His wife told me this morning. They have built a small house in Yufuin," she said.

"That's a beautiful place. He's made an excellent choice," Koinu said as he walked into the house with her.

"Have you been there?" she asked as she helped him off with his sweaty yukata.

"Hai. But it was many years ago. Would you like to see it? We could go there one day if you like," he offered.

"That would be wonderful! How long would it take?" she asked.

"A week, perhaps more," he replied.

"If we did go, where would we stay?" she asked.

He smiled.

"I think I know just the right place," he said.

They were seated in A.'s suite and listening while he regaled them with his memories of Vietnam. He told them of Ma Li.

"I never even thought of killing anyone until that day. If I could have found the men who fired that rocket, I know I would have killed every one of them without batting an eye. But I knew that I'd never find them. That rocket came from a long way off and, looking back on it, they weren't trying to hit the village. They were shooting at the camp. They just missed," he said.

When A. finished his narrative, S. and K. looked at him.

O. was in tears.

"So that's what war is really like?" K. asked.

"That's the way it was for me. Everyone takes something different away with them—and we all leave something behind," A. said.

"When did you leave Vietnam?" S. asked.

"I left on July 4, 1971," A. said. "I was very fortunate. I didn't get so much as a scratch—unless you count mosquito bites."

They laughed.

O. dried her eyes and smiled at him. Then she looked at her son.

"Gomen nasai, A.-san. It is past K.'s bed time," she said.

S. looked at his watch and nodded.

"I did not realize it was this late," he said.

K. jumped and followed his mother out.

"See you tomorrow, A.-san!" he called over his shoulder.

"Tomorrow," A. smiled.

"Would you care to join me for a drink before you turn in?" S. asked.

"I'd be delighted to," A. said as he followed him down stairs.

They sat down in the lobby while S. wife brought them beer. A. smiled at the label.

"Asahi beer. It's still one of my favorites," he said.

"Your descriptions of your war experiences are very powerful. When you speak, you make me feel as if I am there with you," he said.

"And every word is true," A. said. "It was many years before I could talk about them. I'm glad it's something that you never experienced and I hope your son never does."

"Me, too." S. said.

"Were you frightened? O. asked.

"Only until my first battle. After that, the fear went away and I wasn't numbed by it anymore," A. said.

"Would you actually have married that girl you spoke of?" S. asked.

"I think I really would not have had much choice in the matter," A. smiled. "I think about her once in a while. That was the one time I felt any sort of real loss or pain over there. That's when the war really hit home and became more personal."

S. looked at him.

"Your stories are quite vivid. You should write a book about Vietnam," he said.

"Maybe I will one day," A. replied as he sipped his beer.

"Do you dream about the war?" O. asked.

"Sometimes," A. admitted.

"Do the dreams bother you?" O. asked.

"Not really. The war wasn't all combat and blood. I like to sum it up as long periods of inactivity and boredom interrupted by short periods of extreme violence. Also, there were some good things. Even bittersweet things that I prefer to recall. If you dwell on the bad, it makes your life miserable. Bad things shape your life in bad ways. I prefer to allow the good things to shape mine," he said.

"What was the best thing about the war?" O. asked.

He laughed.

"Getting home alive and in one piece," he said.

"I think you were a good soldier," O. said.

"I was just lucky," A. said with a chuckle.

"Did you get medals?" S. asked.

"A few," A. said.

"Do you still have them?" O. asked.

"I think they're in a small wooden box in one of my closets back home along with some other Army stuff," A. said. "I haven't bothered with them in years."

S. smiled.

"I'm sorry if my son has been bothering you," he said.

"He's not bothering me at all. He's good company," A. said.

"But he asks so many questions!" O. said.

"So did his father when I first came here," A. said.

S. laughed.

"I guess I did. I'd never met a gaijin before and M.-san told us that you were a professional baseball player. So, I wanted you to show me how to play," he said.

"So did all of the boys in Yufuin," A. said.

S. laughed as A. told O. how S. and at least ten other boys showed up at the ryokan one morning with gloves and bats. One held up a baseball.

"Can you show us how to play?" he asked.

He spent several afternoons with them while M. attended school. The boys were quick and eager to learn and everyone had a lot of fun.

"It wasn't easy playing on that street. It was sloped and narrow and slippery and the ball kept going into someone's vegetable garden. After that first day, I decided to go out and purchase a glove. Your father actually purchased it for me. It was a good glove, too. It was a Naniwa Rabbit and it was so soft that I didn't have to break it in," he said.

"I remember," S. smiled. "After you returned to the States, you sent me those Roman soldiers. You also sent my brother several Peanuts comics because he told you that he liked Snoopy."

"Are those the soldiers you gave to K?" O. asked him.

"Hai," S. nodded.

"I'm amazed that you've kept them all these years," A. said.

"Why did you send them? Most gaijin wouldn't have bothered," S. said.

"I promised I would send you something after I got home," A. replied. "And I've always tried my best to keep my promises. It's a matter of honor for me."

"You speak like a samurai," O. said.

"I live by a similar code," A. said with a smile.

"My father lived by that same code. I also try to do the same," S. said.

"It's a good code of ethics. The world would be far better off if everyone lived by it," A. mused.

He thought briefly about one promise he had made to M. but never fulfilled. She had asked him to teach her the words to the son "Mrs. Robinson." He told her that he would. But he was shy and ashamed of his singing voice, so he made up excuses to avoid singing. He could see she was disappointed, even though she never said anything. He always wished he would have at least given it a try.

Like rowing a boat.

He, M. and two of her friends were walking alongside a lake. M. asked if he could row a boat. He said he had never tried and was afraid of deep water at that time. So she and her friend T. went out on the lake while he continued to walk with Y.

That was true.

Being an inner city kid from Brooklyn, there were no lakes around to row a boat on. So it was something he'd never even thought about until that day. He hoped that M. understood but was never sure. He learned later on but by them, he was already married to his first wife, S.

"Another opportunity wasted!" he thought.

Kanashimi wa hoshi no kage ni

As the plane touched down on the runway of Oita airport, M. felt excited. The Shimizu Ryokan was the best in the entire region. It was one of the most romantic onsens on Kyushu. It was a perfect place for them to live their fantasies. It was time to throw caution to the wind and do what they'd always dreamt of.

His wife, R. had already flown to Manila to visit her relatives. A. would join her in seven days. That meant seven wonderful days of love, romance and erotic sex. Seven glorious days to do whatever came into their minds.

She felt like a bride on the first night of a honeymoon.

After she landed, she was surprised to see a dark car waiting outside the terminal. She watched as the rear window rolled down and A. smiled at her.

"Going my way?" he asked.

"Hai! I am going your way!" she said happily as the driver came out to get her bag.

"I got us a nice suite at the ryokan," he said. "It's nice and romantic. It looks out over the garden and the entrance to the onsen cave."

"That sounds wonderful. Why didn't you get your old room that you had on your first trip?" she asked.

"It's far too small for two people," A. replied. "This is much better. I wanted something special for us."

She smiled.

Many years ago, he came to Yufuin to visit a young girl named M. Now, here he was again, staying at the same ryokan with another woman named M. The wheel called en had made a full turn but in a most unexpected way.

R. landed in Manila late in the afternoon and was met outside the terminal by her sisters. Her brother-in-law helped her put her suitcase in the van and they headed to the house.

"Where is A.?" her younger sister asked.

"He had to make another side trip in Japan. He'll be here next week," she replied.

"Why didn't you go with him?" her sister asked.

"He asked me to, but I didn't want to. He went back to some small town in the mountains he'd gone to on his first trip. It didn't sound too interesting, so we decided to split up," R. said.

"Aren't you worried he'll spend the week there with that friend of his?" her sister asked.

"I met her. She's real nice and she's married. So I don't have to worry about her," R. replied.

"You really think so?" her sister asked with a laugh.

"I'm positive," R. said with a smile.

S. and his family gave her a warm reception when she arrived. Since it was five p.m., S, invited them to have dinner.

The conversation centered around how she and A. had originally met and how their friendship had steadily progressed to where they were now. When it was over, S, smiled at them.

"That is a remarkable story. It is almost like a novel or fairy tale," he said. "You found each other by coincidence because you have the same name as his first love. Now, here you both are at the same ryokan!"

"Do you know of M.-san?" O. asked.

"Hai. A.-san has told me all about her—and many other things. We have no secrets from each other. And from the moment we started writing, I felt as if I had known him my entire life. And he felt the same about me," M. said.

"Perhaps you are the couple in A.-san's novel?" O. suggested. "Perhaps 'Bushi' is your past life together and you were meant to meet again in this one?"

"I don't know why we met, but I am very happy that we did," M. said as she touched A.s hand.

"So am I. It's as if I finally found something I'd been searching for all my life," A. said.

"A. has told me so much about Yufuin and this ryokan that I just had to see it. I now understand why he loves this place so much," M. said.

They finished their meal and talked some more. Then A. asked if the bath was free for use. S. assured him that it was as no other guest had scheduled it for that time. They thanked them and excused themselves.

They went to the suite and gathered up their robes and towels and walked down to the bath. After spending several pleasant minutes soaping and gently washing each other, they rinsed off and stepped into the warm water. She smiled at his erection. He'd had one since they entered the bath and it showed no sign of going away. She reached over and moved her hand up and down the shaft several times while he gently fondled her.

They knew the bath would not be the proper place to make love, so they got out of the water, dried each other off, dressed and hurried back to the suite.

M. smiled.

The futon lay in the center of the room that also had a large window that looked out over the town and perfectly framed the night sky above.

They were naked.

At first, she was ashamed to let him see her body for fear the sight it might repel him. After that first night in Tokyo, she knew her fear was groundless. That her body excited him.

As he excited her.

They had just finished making love—again. And he was still aroused. She reached out and stroked his manhood with her soft fingers for a moment then pumped it while he sucked her nipples. Before long, his member was inside her mouth and his soft, knowing tongue was caressing her love garden. It all felt so wonderful.

So right.

After a while, she stopped and got onto her hands and knees. He moved behind her and entered her. She shuddered with delight as he went in deeply and began moving in and out, with long, deep thrusts.

He knew what she liked.

What she wanted.

He hit all of the right buttons.

It was as if they'd been making love to each other their entire lives.

After several thrusts, M. felt herself nearing climax. He did, too, and began moving faster and faster. The change in tempo sent surges of delight through her quivering body and sent her into the clouds. He came also—at the exact same moment and fired his seed deep inside of her.

"Anata wa aishimasu!" they both sighed at once.

"May I ask a favor of you?" she said.

"Anything," he said as he pulled her closer.

"Please take me to M.'s old house," she said.

"Why?" he asked.

"You described it so clearly, I feel that I need to see it. S.-san told me that it is still there," she replied.

"Alright. We'll take a taxi there tomorrow morning," he agreed as he rolled over and ran his hand over her smooth, nude body.

"Tonight, we make love!" he whispered as they kissed.

Afterward, they cuddled close and drifted off into a nice, pleasant sleep until the rays of the sun streaming through the window woke them.

As M. sipped her tea, she happened to look down at the dark liquid in her cup. As she watched the brew settle down, she was taken aback by the image of the same young girl reflected in the tea. She turned suddenly but saw no one.

It was her again.

But who was she?

And why was she haunting her all of sudden?

After breakfast, S. got them a taxi. Just before it arrived. A. asked about the house.

"It still stands. It's a strong, very old house with thick walls. A long time ago, it might have belonged to a samurai and his family. Many of the older houses were built for them during the Edo Period. I think the family still owns the house, but I'm sure it has been empty for several years. After their parents died, they never returned," he explained. "I think its condition will sadden you."

"I just feel I have to see it again," A. said.

"I understand," S. smiled.

The taxi pulled up a moment later. S. saw them off and watched until it was out of sight. He smiled. Yes, he did understand. He also understood why M. wanted to see it.

The house was situated on the outskirts of Yufuin. One reached it by driving along a narrow, twisting road through the mountains. In many places, the road was barely wide enough for a single vehicle and the driver pretty much had to hug the mountainside on the right hand side as the left hand side abutted a sheer drop into a rocky and dense wooded area of tall pines, shrubs and loose ground. A. had traveled this road almost every day for three weeks during that first visit and he remarked that it still looked the same as it did then.

The road actually bypassed the house, which was in a small, flat space just to the right of it. The taxi stopped just above the house. A. asked him to wait, then he and M. stepped out and walked back down the road until it met the open space where the house stood.

The house was still there, although badly weathered. Its roof was missing several tiles and the ancient wood trim was pitted and dull. The upstairs window was shut against the elements but the door was partially open.

The front of the house was a gravel covered space about of about 500 square feet. A small pipe still protruded from the hillside and trickled water into a groove. This had been the family's water supply. The old barn/outhouse structure leaned dangerously in two directions and the wooden roof had fallen in. The structure was now a total loss.

The house stood on a platform about three feet high. This was to keep the interior from flooding out during a typhoon. One climbed up onto a narrow porch, and then removed your shoes before entering. The porch seemed solid but it was now covered with dirt and leaves.

All in all, the house looked sad.

Forlorn as if it longed to be lived in again. To be taken care of.

"It looks as if it has been waiting for someone to return," M. said as she looked it over carefully. "It is exactly how you described it. Even though the front is worn, I can still see what color it was painted.

You have a very good memory."

"It looks sad," he said. "Lonely."

"Let's go inside," she urged. "I want to look around."

"Okay. But we'd best keep our shoes on so we don't step on anything unpleasant," he said as he climbed up on the porch.

He reached out his hand. She took it and he helped her up. The large front door was flanked by two narrow windows. Both were shuttered. He walked to the door and slowly slid it open. The sunlight streamed into a large, open room. When they stepped inside, they saw there was a smaller room behind the first and a flight of dusty wooden steps that led to the second floor. The floors were still covered with rotted, molding tatami mats, bits of plaster that had fallen from the ceiling, leaves, dirt and other bits of debris.

As they stood in the center of the room, A. thought he saw M. mother, just as she was that first day, kneeling and bowing before him with a big smile on her face. The vision came and went in seconds. He smiled as he looked around.

M. watched his expression as he walked around. She could tell that he still had such vivid memories of the house. His expression looked almost sad as he kicked at the rubble.

As he stood in the middle of the room, he could still envision M.'s mother kneeling on the floor and touching her forehead to the mat. He didn't expect that and it kind of embarrassed him.

"Why is she doing that?" he asked M.

"You are our honored guest. Please bow to her," M. instructed.

He did and her parents smiled appreciatively.

When he looked at the steps, he recalled seeing M. and her mother lugging his heavy suitcase up them while he conversed or tried to with her father.

He told A. that he actually saw Babe Ruth as a child. It was sometime before the war and everyone in Japan thought Ruth was some sort of baseball god. He was one of the biggest men M.'s father had ever seen, too.

A few minutes later, a bokushi dressed in black robes came to the house. He exchanged bows with the family, then went to their shrine and prayed and burned incense. Afterward, he and A. attempted to chat.

"Are you a Christian?" the bokushi asked.

"I don't really follow any religion. Are you a Buddhist?" A. asked.

"Hai. I am a bokushi at the local temple. I came here to bless the house and shrine as I do each year on this day. This is what we call Obon," the bokushi replied.

"What is Obon?" asked A.

The bokushi explained that Obon or Bon, is a festival during which people clean their homes and the graves of their ancestors. They also set up a butsudan, or Buddhist altar in their homes and light lanterns called chodin to help guide the spirits of their ancestors back home.

"Many families have butsudan. They place offerings of fruit and fresh vegetables on the altar and arrange flowers. They keep the chodin next to the altar and light it each night. I go to their houses to help them pray for the spirits," the bokushi explained.

"Is Obon an ancient festival?" A. asked.

"Hai. It is more than 500 years old," the bokushi replied.

"It sounds similar to All hallows Eve in Europe and the Day of the Dead in Mexico," A. said.

"All do have certain similarities. Perhaps that might be because they all spring from a single source," the bokushi said.

Afterward, they sat down at the low table and her mother brought him a bowl of steamed vegetable and a fork. He was still pretty much a carnivore back then, but he attempted a few forkfuls. He was actually still tired from his trip across Kyushu and begged their pardon.

"Where do I wash up and brush my teeth?" he asked.

M. led him back outside to where water ran constantly from a narrow pipe in the hillside. As he brushed, he though how very different this was from Brooklyn and he also wondered how this worked out for them during the winter.

"I can see why you remember it so fondly. This is a very old and traditional home. It is like the ones you must have saw in those movies when you were younger," M. said. "It must have been very nice."

They walked to the back room. He pointed to the wall on the right.

"This is where they kept their shrine," he said. "They didn't seem to have much furniture. They had a long, black table in the middle of the first room where they ate their meals, talked and watched TV. There were vases filled with flowers, a few small ceramic figurines. Things of that nature. It was very neat and clean and open."

"Where did you spend the night?" she asked.

"In one of the rooms upstairs," he said.

"Let's look," she said.

The stairs were still very sturdy. They didn't even creak when they walked up them. There was a small room with one large window to the left. Inside was a small, dust-covered desk and wooden chair.

In his mind, he saw a pretty young girl in a white midi blouse and light gray skirt seated at the desk. She looked up at him and smiled. Then she faded away like the image downstairs.

He smiled at the memories.

"This was her room, wasn't it?" M. asked. "This was her desk and chair."

He nodded.

He remembered seeing their Calico cat, Mii, chase a moth across the room. Later that afternoon, her older sister visited. She had her daughter with her. The girl was about two years old and very active. He recalled watching her pick up a small cushion, throw it Mii then chase after her. He and M. laughed.

M.'s sister was also pregnant at the time. She was also very pretty and a bit taller than M. He remembered that M. had showed him her sister's wedding photo. She was in a beautiful white kimono with the traditional cap.

"That's beautiful," he said. "What does that cost?"

"I don't know in your money. It is very expensive, so we rent them," she replied. "What do you think?"

"I think you'd look very pretty in that kimono," A. said.

She thought about what he said, and then sort of smiled.

"I spent many hours in this room, talking with M. I'm sure she did her best to understand me but I probably confused her more than I thought," he said.

"Let's keep looking," M. said.

There were two smaller rooms. He walked to the one in the back of the house and nodded.

"This is it. This is where I slept," he said. "They put a futon on the floor and that's where I slept. I'd never slept on a futon before and it was so comfortable, I fell asleep in seconds."

M. smiled.

"You really must have enjoyed your stay to be able to remember so much," she said.

They went back downstairs and walked through the rooms again.

"I feel that this house is weeping," she said. "It has lost its heartbeat."

"I wonder why they keep it. No one's lived here for years. Why didn't they sell it?" he asked as they walked around.

"Perhaps no one wants it because it is too old and too much out of the way?" she suggested. "I like it, though. It has strong bones. It has a history."

"It almost had an even longer history," he said. "It would be a nice place to retire to but it needs to be modernized a bit without ruining its character."

That's when M. spotted an old dusty framed photograph hanging on a wall. She walked over and took it down. The photo inside was a family photo. She showed it to A. He nodded as he recognized the faces.

"I remember this photo," he said. "She showed it to me. These are her parents in the middle. This is her brother O., her elder sister and her husband. Their daughter. And this is M. I guess she was 16 or 17 when this was taken."

M. looked at the photo.

"She is adorable. No wonder you loved her so," she said.

He put the photo back on the wall and dusted it off. It belonged to the house.

"Let's go," he said.

On the way back to the taxi, they stopped to look at the fallen down outhouse. A. smiled as he recalled his first ever run-in with a live cow.

He had gone into the outhouse to relieve himself the next morning when the cow wandered in to check out the strange, new person in its barn. A. hard something behind. When he turned, he was nose-to-nose with the animal and he had no way out.

The cow as too large to get around or over. Being a city boy, he had no idea what to do in this awkward and somewhat comical situation. About that same time, M.'s mother saw his predicament. She went into the outhouse and slapped the cow on the rump to chase it away. Then she and A. laughed.

So did M. and her father when he told them what happened.

"I guess you would not make a very good farmer," M. said as she laughed at his story.

"Guess not," he chuckled.

When they returned to ryokan, S. greeted them.

"Did you enjoy your visit?" he asked.

"We did," M. replied. "It's such a nice home. It could be nice again. It needs a family to bring it back to life."

S. nodded.

"I've offered to purchase it from the family, but never received a reply. It is sad to watch it rot slowly away like that. It's one of the oldest homes in Yufuin. It has a long history, too. A samurai once lived there with his family," he said. "Please dine with us this evening. I will not accept no for an answer."

"We will be delighted to," A. smiled. "I'd also like to ask a favor of you."

"Ask," S. said.

"We'll talk over dinner tonight," A. said. "Right now, M. and I are going for a walk. It's too nice a day to stay indoors."

They walked down the winding streets and stopped to look in shops and took photos. They came to a set of small benches and decided to sit down for a few minutes. M. leaned her had on his shoulder. He put his arm around her.

"What would R. do if she knew about us?" M. asked.

"She'd kill us both and feed our bodies to alligators," A. replied. "R. is very jealous. That's why I'm happy the two of you became friends and she got to meet your family. That put her at ease and she doesn't think of you as a rival."

M. laughed.

"I should be flattered that any young woman would be jealous of me! Here in Nihon, no one even gives me a second glance. Only you think I'm sexy. I'm still surprised at that. I used to wonder why. Now, I just accept your love and enjoy your attentions," she said. "We have a most amazing relationship, A.-san. Even K. accepts it. I think he is still very jealous of you, but he also likes and respects you. And he knows you treat me very well."

He nodded.

They got up and returned to the ryokan. They went up to the suite and spent the next hour making love in as many ways as they could think of. After they climaxed together, they stopped to rest. M. looked up at the ceiling.

"K. knows," she said.

"Hai. We had a long, pleasant and highly interesting chat at the pub that night," A. said. "I always thought he knew. He's more perceptive than you thought. He even told me that he's read most of our emails."

M. blushed.

"He told me the same. I was afraid he would get angry or even strike me, but he just smiled and hugged me. He said that he understands our relationship and our attraction to each other," she said. "I was surprised. He did not seem jealous."

He laughed.

"Oh, he is jealous but he said that unfortunately, he cannot give you what you need and he refuses to deny your happiness. He also said that our friendship has been very good for you. He likes the changes he sees in you. But he said that I can have only one wife at a time," he said.

They laughed.

"And he told me that I am allowed to have only one husband at a time," she said. "And only one lover. Do you think this would have happened if I had been your first M.?"

He shrugged.

"That's impossible to say. You're different from her in many ways, yet similar. You have many fine qualities that I admire and am attracted to," he said.

"Maybe I am not so different as you imagine. I think the biggest difference is that I never would have let you go and, if you did go, I would have followed. Had she done that, I think you and she would still be married today and we would never have met," M. said.

"Nor would I ever have met and married either S. or R. Life would have been very different for me. But had you and I met back then, we would have made a very good team and your life would have been much more adventurous," A. said.

"You have already made my life more adventurous than I ever dreamed it would be," she said as they held hands.

They lay on the futon and looked at the clouds drifting by through the large open window as a soft, gentle breeze wafted over their naked bodies. She cuddled closer.

"I was just wondering," she began.

"About what?" he asked.

"About what you would do or say if M. showed up here. How would you react?" she asked.

"To be honest, I just don't know. I guess I would ask her about her life and how she is. You know, things of that nature. I think if I saw her again, I'd be part elated and part terrified," he said.

"Would you like to see her again?" she asked.

"I'm not sure. A huge part of me says yes but another small part of me is telling me to let things be," he admitted.

"Would you send her away?" M. asked.

"Of course not. That would be very rude and unkind. Even more so, given our history. I would welcome her as sincerely as I could and try to put her at ease," he said.

She smiled.

"You are a celebrity here in Nihon now. You have been on television and in the newspapers. I am sure she knows that you are here as the papers have printed your schedule. I am also sure that she feels the same way you do. She would like to see you again, but she is worried about how you will react to her. Perhaps she does not want you to see her as she is now. Perhaps she wants you only to remember her when she was young and beautiful. We women are like that," M. said.

"Were you like that?" he asked.

"Hai. Until we met in person, I was very afraid of what you would think of me. You made me feel comfortable right from the start. Now, here we are. Just like the samurai and his wife in your book," she said. "But we are only sharing a few precious moments. When all is said and done, we are still like two ships passing in the night. I must return to K. and you must return to your family. That is the way it has to be."

"I know. But until then, we have the here and now. Let's enjoy what time we still have together," he said.

"What would you do with me if she shows up and wishes to share some precious moments with you? Will you send me away? I would not blame if you did. I would understand," she said.

He smiled.

"I think you worry too much over nothing," he assured her as they kissed.

Koinu and M. walked along the narrow street outside their home. As they walked, she held his hand tightly. They always walked like this. They always would.

"Have you ever thought about another woman?" she asked.

"Just one," he said.

"Was she pretty?" she queried.

"I thought she was very pretty," he admitted.

"Oh. Did you love her?" she asked.

"Hai. I loved her very much," he said.

"Who was she?" she asked.

"She was my mother," he smiled. "I think of her often."

She smiled.

"No one else?" she asked.

"Never anyone else. Only you," he assured her. "What about you? Do you ever think of other men?"

"Never," she said. "There is no need to as long I have you."

M. gripped A.'s arms and moved with him as fast as she could to savor each, hard, deep thrust. She was giving him all she had to show him how much she loved him. He, in, turn was going all out to please her.

They moved together faster and faster.

M. sighed and moaned with each thrust as she threw her hips upward. She felt his body tremble slightly and smiled. Then she slowed her thrusts and used her inner muscles to squeeze him tightly. When they climaxed, it was as one.

They kept going until they were spent. Then they kissed.

And kissed.

"What do we do now?" she asked as she returned to Earth.

"Nothing," he said after some thought.

She looked at him and nodded. He was right, of course. They'd gotten the chance to live out their fantasies. After many years of flirting, dreaming and wishing, they finally got the chance to make those wishes come true.

And they had each said the words they longed to hear. Words she never thought he would actually say. Or mean.

"If you ask me to run away with you, I will," she said.

"And you'd regret it for the rest of your life. So would I. We both have families and obligations. We each have people who rely on us, who need us. The gods have given us these moments to enjoy as a gift. They may give us other such moments. Even though I would love to spend the rest of my life with you, I am honor bound to take care of my family. And you are honor-bound to yours," he said.

She sighed.

"You sound like a samurai. You are much more Japanese than American because you place honor and duty to your family above your own desires," she said. "That is why I love and respect you so."

"You do the same," he said. "We think very much alike. Had we met a long time ago, we would have had a very good life together."

She sighed again.

He was right. She could no more leave her husband than he could leave his wife and son. But she could dream.

He had come into her life when she needed him most. Like a knight in old fairy tales, he had arrived on his white stallion and rescued her from a life that had gotten boring and predictable. Their friendship, improbable as it was, had blossomed into a strong and passionate romance, like the kind one sees in movies.

He told her he appreciated her curiosity, her intelligence and sense of humor. He told her she was young, and pretty and sexy.

And he made her believe it.

"There will more such moments," she said. "Y. and I are going to America next year and we will stay with you in St. Louis, like we planned."

"Then we can all go to New Orleans where we can share more such moments," he smiled. "So I guess that means K. has given you permission to travel with Y.?"

"Hai. He said she will be a big help to us—like she is here," she laughed.

They walked through the town hand-in-hand like the true lovers they were. She was still amazed that this was happening. It felt as if was meant to be. Like something she'd been waiting for her entire life.

Or for several lifetimes.

It felt warm and good and so natural.

They stopped at a scenic overlook and leaned on the fence. The entire valley stretched out below them and they could clearly see the green-covered mountains in the distance. M. faced him and smiled. Her smile was soft and pretty, he thought. It made him feel happy all over, too.

"This is like a fairy tale," she said. "I feel as if I am living someone else's life. I am afraid that this is a dream and when I waken, this will vanish and you will vanish with it. How do you feel?"

"I feel at peace with myself. I feel that I have found something again that was long missing from my life. I feel like my long search is finally ended," he said.

She laughed.

He liked the way it sounded. It was soft and sweet. Almost musical.

"So the samurai has returned to his lady?" she asked.

"Hai. I can take off my yoroi now," he said.

"But please do not put away your katana. I want you to keep that nice and sharp for me—forever and ever," she said.

He laughed and pulled her closer.

"Don't worry. My katana will always be ready to serve you. I will never let it become a kitchen knife that is small and rusted and without much use," he joked, referring to an email comment she had made about K's.

"I never dreamed that anything this magical would happen to me again at my age!" she said as she held him tightly.

"A beautiful young lady like you needs magic in her life," he said. "Where would you like to go next?"

"How about another visit to an onsen?" she said with a wink.

M. was half asleep as she sat in front of the TV. The sound of static coming from the set caused her to open her eyes.

The station had gone off the air for the evening. All she saw was static and snow. She reached for the remote to turn it off. As she aimed it at the TV, she hesitated. Then an image slowly took form amid the snow. She stared as the girl appeared and looked straight at her.

She saw her lips move but no words came out.

"Who are you? What do you want?" she said.

The image vanished, leaving nothing but the static on the screen.

She sat on the edge of the pool and dangled her feet in the warm water. As A. moved toward her, she slowly parted her legs. When he reached her, he kissed each knee then playfully kissed his way up her inner thighs. She closed her eyes and sighed as his tongue entered her garden. As he licked her love button, she ran her fingers over his hair. He made love to her with his tongue until she climaxed. She fell back and moaned and trembled as waves of pleasure washed over her. When he was finished, she smiled up at him.

"Your turn," she said.

He climbed up next to her. His katana was long and sharp as always. M. slid into the water and ran her tongue up and down his blade while she stroked his sack. She then engulfed his knob with her mouth and proceeded to suck away.

He erupted seconds later.

M. swallowed every last drop of his love cream while she stroked his member. He gasped and sighed with each pump of her soft, gentle hand as she coaxed all she could from him. Then he slid into the water with her.

For the next several minutes, they played in the water and drank sake from the small "boats" that drifted past them. He soon grew long and hard again. This time, she put her arms around d his neck, lifted herself upward and eased her body down until his entire member was buried deep within her channel.

"Don't move. Let me do the work," she whispered as she slowly moved up and down.

He was in Heaven now. She felt exquisite, too.

So tight.

So hot.

So perfect.

She made love to him in the water for a very long time and he needed to summon every ounce of willpower to keep from erupting too soon. She began to bounce faster and faster. He gripped her behind and moved with her until they both came together in once huge, joyful explosion. They held each other tightly until they returned to Earth.

"I wish we were both young and married so I could bear you children," she said.

"Don't think about such things. Just live in the moment," he said. "Live in this very perfect moment."

Kanashimi wa tsuki no kage ni

J. sat and listened as his mother told him of her plans to visit A. while he was in Yufuin.

"Will you pack a bag?" he asked.

"No. I will only be there for one afternoon. I am returning to Tokyo that evening," she replied.

"What if he asks you to stay?" he asked.

"I don't know," she answered. "It is taking all of my courage just to fly to Oita. I still can't believe that I'm actually doing this. What do I say to him after all this time?"

"You could start by saying 'hello'," J. smiled. "I'm sure he'll take it from there."

"Take what?" she asked.

"Anything that you're willing to give him," he teased.

When A. and M. returned to the ryokan, S. greeted them.

"I spoke with a local craftsman. He said he knew the house very well as he had gone by it many times. He said he could repair the roof and replace all of the rotted exterior wood trim and clean the place up for 200,000 yen," S. said.

"Is he good?" A. asked.

"He is excellent. I call him whenever I need anything done to the ryokan. He is very reliable and his prices are reasonable," S. said.

"Wonderful. When can he get it done?" asked A.

"He can start in one month," S. replied.

"I'll write you a check. You can pay him when he's finished," A. said.

"Very good. I'll call him at once and let him know," S. said. "Will you require a written contract?"

"No. Your word is better than any written contract," A. said.

S. smiled.

"Why are you doing this?" he asked.

"I guess I'm just sentimental," A. answered with a smile. "That house has a history. Part of it is mine. I just want to see it last a little bit longer."

M. smiled and took his hand.

She understood perfectly.

"We will be pleased to have you join us for dinner this evening," S. offered.

"And we'll be pleased to accept your kind invitation," M. said.

J. drove his mother to Haneda Airport and waved as she got out and walked into the All Nippon Airways terminal. When she was safely inside, he sighed and drove home. He wondered if she would actually go to see him.

The flight to Oita would last two hours. Once there, she could take a taxi to the train station and board the train to Yufuin. That should put her at the ryokan by three p.m.

Her knees shook for the entire trip. She wondered what she would say. What he would say. Would their reunion be awkward?

She knew what he looked like from the TV show. What would he think when he saw her again? More importantly, would he be angry with her for what she did? He didn't sound angry on the interview program.

She thought about their lives.

He had been everywhere. He'd done everything. He was a world famous author with a huge following in Nihon. She was a simple housewife. A widow with a grown son. The two had nothing in common. What could he possibly see in her?

M. told the driver to stop several yards from the ryokan. She got out and paid him. A light rain was falling now and the day seemed a little dreary. She opened her umbrella and walked along the ancient street until she came within sight of the ryokan.

She stopped and looked at it for a long time. It hadn't changed at all. She watched as several people passed by the entrance. One or two went into the ryokan.

As she watched, she thought about the day she'd made the reservation for him and how K.-san had asked her all sorts of questions about her American friend. He had even joked with her about one day marrying him. He had known her family for years and years.

Things were so different then.

So pure and innocent.

They had made mistakes which led them to follow different paths. His had been filled with excitement and adventure. Hers had led her to the more mundane life of a Japanese housewife. It wasn't the kind of life she'd wanted or expected.

But somehow, she felt it was all she really deserved.

She saw someone who appeared to be the owner walk outside. There was an American man with him and they were talking and laughing like old friends. Her heart skipped several beats as she realized the American was A.

There he was, less than 100 feet from her but she remained frozen to spot. She became so nervous that she couldn't get her feet to move in his direction. She wanted to call out his name to see if he'd run to her and take her in his arms.

But no sound came from her open mouth.

She was literally paralyzed with fear and indecision.

Then another woman came out. She said something to A. He laughed and took her hand.

M.'s heart dropped.

She turned and walked back down the street to where she had left the taxi. That cab had taken off but another had just pulled up to a small shop. She waited until the passenger got out, and then walked over.

"Are you free?" she asked.

"Hai. Please get in," the driver said.

She got into the back seat and gave him an address. He thought about it and told her she'd have to guide him to it.

Twenty minutes later, she told him to go to the end of a slope and turn. He did as she asked then stopped in from of an old dilapidated house.

"This is it," she said.

M. got out of the taxi and looked at the house. As she did, she recalled the first time A. had set foot inside of it.

"Please wait here," she instructed the driver as she walked down the road and onto the open area.

The house looked lonesome and neglected, which it had been for ~~~eral~~ years. Her and other members of the family had avoided it since ~~parents~~ died. They had all grown up there. She was the youngest. The ~~to~~ reach adulthood there. The last one to leave.

~~he~~ climbed up onto the porch and slid the door open. To her surprise, there were two sets of footprints in the dust on the floor. One obviously a man's. The other small and delicate and obviously a woman's. The prints, she thought were made recently.

By whom?

Who would bother to come all the way out here to look at the house?

As she looked around, she saw the place where the shrine once was and smiled as she reminisced about A.'s meeting with the Buddhist bokushi.

He was very curious but still shy and awkward. She sat by and listened while they chatted and he told A. about Obon.

She was a Buddhist. She even thought that might be a big obstacle for them to overcome. But since he said he had no religious preferences, she felt no need to worry. She knew he'd respect her beliefs and she vowed to herself that she would try her best to adjust to his.

The she glanced up.

That's when she noticed the old photograph hanging on the wall. She walked over to examine it. To her surprise, it was free of dust. It looked as if someone had cleaned it off and hung it back up. The prints led directly to picture and away from it.

Again, she wondered, who was here?

And why did he clean off the photo and hang it back up?

Then it struck her.

"It was A.! It had to be him. No one else would come here. The house had no meaning for anyone else but him," she thought.

She walked upstairs and smiled when she saw her old desk. Then she wept when she saw that someone had wiped the dust from it.

She composed herself and examined the house again.

It had remained virtually unchanged since she last saw it. In fact, it was practically the same as it was when A. first came to Japan. Except now there was debris on the floor and the old metal roof had rusted badly. She looked up at the sunlight which had worked its way into the house through a small hole in the roof and nodded.

"That needs to be replaced," she said.

She walked to the window and looked out at the dilapidated barn/toilet.

"If I had married him, where would we have lived? He really liked it here. Maybe we would be living in this very house. Of course, A. would have added indoor plumbing and a new bathroom to it. But he would have left everything else unchanged," she thought. "I think I'll add a bathroom."

She left the house and returned to the taxi.

"Where to?" the driver asked.

"Oita Airport," she replied. "The ANA terminal."

They finished making love around eleven. A. propped himself up on his elbow and ran his hand over her body. She lay there and smiled up at him. She loved the way he caressed her. He knew exactly how to make her feel excited all over. He was able to read her moods, her likes and dislikes better than her husband.

"I don't want this to end so soon," she sighed. "But my flight leaves in three hours. Let's have a bath together and go to the airport. It will be something more for us to remember."

They put on their robes and went down to the cave onsen. They bathed for a half hour, and then went back to the room. He watched her dress. She smiled and tried to do it sensuously. She liked when he watched. It made her feel sexy.

M. packed her bag. A. carried it down to the lobby. S. took it and led them out to his car. When A. and M. got into the back seat, K. and O. hurried out. K. got into the backseat with them while O. got in next to her husband.

"We want to see you off," O. said.

"That's very thoughtful of you," M. said.

They reached the airport 20 minutes later. The Shimizu family got out and walked with M. to the check-in counter. The attendant checked her name on the computer and smiled. Then he issued her a boarding pass and checked her bag in.

M. turned to them and bowed.

"Arigato gozaimasu! I've had the most wonderful stay of my life," she said.

"Please come back and stay with us again soon," O. said as they bowed then hugged.

M. turned to A. and put her arms around him. Then they kissed. S. and his family smiled at their open display of affection.

"I will see you again soon. In St. Louis," she said.

"I'm looking forward to it," he said. "Sayonara."

She walked into the terminal and headed for the security gate. She showed the guard her boarding pass and photo ID and he waved her through. Her fairy tale honeymoon had ended.

M. walked up the gangway and showed her boarding pass to the flight attendant. The attendant bowed and welcomed her aboard the aircraft and pointed her to a window seat on the left. M. sat down and watched as more passengers got on. At one point, she made eye contact with another woman. They smiled at each other and the woman took the seat directly behind her. M. thought she looked kind of despondent.

"Are you well?" she asked.

"I'm alright, arigato. My mind is elsewhere," the woman said.

She noticed the glow on M.'s face.

"You look quite content," she said.

"My mind is also elsewhere," M. said.

They said nothing more for the rest of the flight.

M. thought she heard the woman crying softly to herself. She wanted to look back to see if she could comfort her, but thought better of it. When the jet landed at Haneda two hours later, the woman hurried past her. As she did, her wallet fell from her purse. M. picked it up and called out to her, but she didn't hear. She just hurried from the plane and into the terminal.

M. ran after her.

She caught up with her just outside of the security area.

"Gomen nasai! You dropped this when you left the plane," she said as she handed her the wallet.

The woman took it and smiled.

"Arigato gozaimasu! I would have been lost without it and might not have been able to get home," she said as she slid it into her purse.

"Where do you live?" M. asked.

"Meguro. And you?" the woman replied.

"Hachioji," M. said. "I'm glad I was able to catch you before you became lost in the crowd."

"Arigato again. You really saved me today," the woman said with a polite bow. "I must hurry home now. It was nice meeting you. Sayonara!"

"Sayonara!" M. replied as she returned the bow.

She went to baggage claim and noticed that the woman didn't not go there with her.

"Perhaps she didn't bring any luggage with her," she thought as she claimed her bag from the carousel.

M.'s son, O. met her at the airport and drove her back to Hachioji. She was tired so she slept on the way. K. was waiting in front of the house when they arrived. She got out of the car and thanked O. again while K. took her bag upstairs.

She went straight to the kitchen and brewed a pot of tea. K. came down a few minutes later and asked her how her flight was.

"I met a woman on the flight home," M. said as she poured K. a cup of tea. "She seemed so very sad and lonely. I felt bad for her."

"Did you speak with her?" K. asked.

"Only a little. She sat behind me. I could hear her weeping the entire flight. Then she dropped her wallet. I picked it up and ran after her. She thanked me and went directly to the train. She had no luggage with her," M. explained.

"Did you ask her name?" K. queried.

"No. I did not have the chance," M. said.

He smiled.

"Would it not be strange if she was A.-san's long lost love?" he mused. "Perhaps she went to Yufuin to see him but lost her nerve and decided to return to her home."

M. thought about that for a few seconds. Could K. be right? That might explain why she had no luggage and her sadness. Had she somehow had a brief encounter with A.'s first love?

"That would be very strange indeed," she said.

K. nodded.

M. arrived at her house an hour later. Her son was home from work and he smiled as she sat down at the table with him.

"Did you see him?" J. asked.

"No. I went to the ryokan but lost my nerve. So I took a taxi to the old house instead. It's empty now. It looks so sad. So lonely," she said.

"Like you, Mother," he pointed out. "Now what? The newspaper said he's leaving Nihon in four days. He's flying to Manila from Kasai. He might not return for years."

"I know," she sighed.

"Go to Kansai and see him off," he urged.

"No. I can't," M. said.

"Are you afraid that you will get on that flight with him?" he teased.

"Something like that. But I don't think his wife would like that," she smiled.

"I'm sure that would stir up all sorts of trouble. Now what?" he asked.

"We still own that old house in Yunohira. I would like to do something with it. I would like to try and restore it. It is a very sturdy house. If I do it properly, maybe I can sell it," she said.

"Father left you a lot of money. You may as well use it for something you really want to do," J. agreed.

"If you build it, he will come," he said under his breath as he left the room.

M. smiled.

"Maybe he will—one day," she said.

When A. found out that his flight from Kansai to Manila was cancelled, he decided to fly to Tokyo and take a connecting flight to Manila the next day. He phone M. and told her of his situation. She just about jumped for joy at the news.

To his delight, she was waiting at the luggage carousel when he arrived.

"I am so happy to see you again," he beamed as they briefly embraced. "I'm staying close by tonight—at the Haneda Tokyu. My flight leaves at five tomorrow evening."

"Good. That means we can enjoy one more night together," she said with a smile.

They took a taxi to the Haneda Tokyu Hotel, where he'd booked a room for the night. The hotel was one of the older ones in Tokyo and close to the airport. It was also one of the nicer ones in that part of the city.

They checked in went up to the room. As soon as they got inside, M. threw her arms around his neck for a long, deep kiss. He picked her up and carried her to the bed...

Later that evening, they strolled along the Sumida River hand-in-hand. The night was cool and the riverfront was brightly lit. They had been chatting about some of A's experiences in Vietnam.

"Did you ever tell M. about your experiences there?" she asked.

"No," he said with a smile.

"Why not?" she asked.

"I was about to. I asked what she thought of soldiers. She said she didn't like soldiers or anything to do with war. When she said that, I froze and decided not to mention it again," A. said. "I didn't want her to dislike me or upset her, even though I did what I thought was right at the time."

"I think she might have understood your choices and accepted them—if she really loved you. If you had told me that when I was her age, I would have been very curious about why you did it and I would have tried to understand and accept what you did because it was honorable to you. That would have made you seem more like a samurai to me and I would have loved you even more," M. said.

"Like you do now?" he asked.

"Hai. Like I do now," she smiled as they stopped and hugged.

"I don't know why I never told her. I thought it would drive her away from me or something. It's all so silly, really. I'm kind of proud of it. In fact, I'd do again if I had to," he said.

"I admire your patriotism and you courage. It fits your personality perfectly. It is part of who you are," she smiled.

"Arigato. I don't think she would have felt that way. She probably would not have understood," A. said.

"Then she was never the right one for you," M. said. "I feel you have made good choices in your life. You made the choices that were best for you at the times. You need have no regrets," she said.

"I have one regret, M-san," he said.

"Oh? And what is that?" she asked.

"I regret that we did not know each other back then," he said.

As they walked along hand-in-hand, the night breeze caressed them and made the moment that much more special. They sat down on a small bench and watched the lights of the boats as they sailed by.

"Your wife is very pretty," M. said. "She's very nice, too. I like her."

"She likes you, too. In fact, the two of you seem to have become good friends," A. said. "I knew that would happen once the two of you met. But I still think she's a little jealous of you."

M. laughed at the idea that such a beautiful, younger woman would be jealous of her at this time in her life. She also giggled because she knew that R. had every right to be now.

"Do you still love your wife?" she asked.

"I love her with all my heart and soul—as I do you," A. said.

"I never believed a person could be equally in love with two other people at the same time until now. But you and K. are so different. He feels safe, familiar and somewhat dull. You feel exciting and dangerous. You are like the heroes in American movies and when I am with you, I feel like the women in those movies. I feel young again. And alive," she said. "Yet, I love you and K. equally."

"I think R. and K. know how we feel about each other. It's almost impossible to hide it and I'm not sure I want to hide it," he said.

"This is your last night in Tokyo. Do you think you will ever return?" she asked.

"Yes. And when I do, I'll return for you," he vowed.

She leaned her head against his chest and smiled. She'd hoped he would say that. Now that he had, she knew that he meant it.

He looked at his watch.

"We have 40 minutes to board the boat for our cruise," he said.

"This is so exciting. I never thought I'd be going on a romantic dinner cruise with anyone. I am so happy that it is with you," she said as they rose and walked down the pier.

"I want this night to be very special. I want you to remember it," he said.

"Every moment we spend together is special and I will put each one of them into my treasure box and keep them forever," she smiled.

"You need to add one more, but very important item to your treasure box," he said.

"And what is that?" she asked.

"Something you captured a long time ago—my heart," he beamed.

"It is already there. It is the most precious treasure in the world to me. Is my heart in your treasure box?" she asked.

"I think that's been there since the first time we made contact," he assured her.

"K. said that you are a most unusual man, A.-san. You are the first gaijin he has liked, admired and respected and he is still amazed that you love me," she laughed.

"And I'm amazed that you love me. The gods have brought us back together. I intend to make sure that we stay together this time," he said. "Forever."

He watched as she untied her robe and allowed it to slide sensuously down her body to the floor. She smiled at the way his body reacted to her nudity; thrilled that she excited him so much. He took her hand and led her to the bed. Then he knelt before her and ran his tongue along her slit. She quivered with each delicate pass. As he licked, he ran his hands all over her lower body. She shut her eyes and sighed as his tongue took her to the realm of sexual bliss. Moments later, she felt her orgasm trigger. She gasped and moaned as he licked her faster and faster.

She came a second time.

As she shook with pleasure, he lowered her to the bed. She parted her thighs and moaned deeply as he entered her. Then she wrapped her legs around his hips and moved with him. They made love gently at first and she matched his every thrust. His thrusts were slow, warm and deep and she sighed and moaned each time. They gradually moved faster and faster. Their bodies merged and became one as she gave herself him.

Totally.

Completely.

As she came again, she thrust faster and faster. He came a split second after and emptied his seed deep into her tight, sexy body.

Like he did several times before.

Like she wished he always would.

He leaned over and they kissed. She used her inner muscles to squeeze his member, which was still buried deep inside her channel. To her delight, it grew rigid once again. As it did, they began moving together.

The night was still young...

This time, she showed him one of her favorite positions. It was one that heightened their pleasure considerably with each thrust of their hips. He was delighted with her flexibility and abilities. And the sensations were exquisite.

She knew how to use her body in ways that surprised and thrilled him like no one else had before. They made love to the very brink of orgasm.

Then she stopped.

When the feelings subsided, she began thrusting again. Again, when he reached the point of climax, she stopped. Then she started all over again. This time, they went all out. It was one of the most explosively prolonged orgasms he'd ever experienced.

She loved it, too.

More than any other. Her entire body shook with pleasure as she climaxed more than once. As they came together, they kept making love.

Slower and slower.

When it was over, they rested in each other's arms and basked in the deep feelings they had for each other.

"You're amazing," he whispered. "Truly wonderful."

She smiled and hugged him tightly. She was thrilled by the fact that she could give and receive so much pleasure and that he loved her.

"I wish this would never end," she said softly. "I wish you were not leaving tomorrow."

"We'll see each other again," he promised.

"I will come to America in the summer," she said. "Y. will be with me. We will fly into San Francisco first then come to St. Louis."

"You can stay at our house. We have lots of room and I can show you both around," he said as he stroked her hair. "Afterward, we can all go down to New Orleans and I'll show the city better than anyone else could."

"I would like that very much," she smiled.

He ran his hand gently over her lean, smooth body. She was flawless, he thought. Perfect. And oh-so sexy.

"I am yours now," she said softly. "I will always be yours for as long as you desire me."

"In that case, you'll be mine forever," he said as they kissed.

They woke hours later in each others' arms and to the rays of the warm sun streaming over their bodies. She sat up and smiled as he stroked her thigh.

"This is a wonderful weekend," she sighed. "I feel like I am 20 years old again and that we are in some magical paradise where we will stay young forever. I still have trouble believing that this all real," she said softly.

"I feel the same way, M-san," he said. "We make a perfect match."

"I wish we had met many years ago. Your old friend does not know what she missed. I used to feel sorry for her. I don't anymore because I've gotten to make love with you and she didn't," M. said.

"At least the gods have allowed us to share these few days. They are moments I will always treasure. I should be satisfied, but I am not. Now that we are lovers, I want to continue being your lover forever," she added as she caressed his cheek.

"We'll have more chances," he promised. "You're coming to America in the fall. I'm sure that we'll have time to ourselves. I'll find a way for us to be together."

"I would like that very much. I must dress now. I have to return to Hachioji. I promised K. that I would be back tonight," she said.

"And I must fly to Manila this afternoon," he said as he kissed her.

M. returned to Hachioji at seven. K. was in the kitchen preparing his favorite curry. He smiled when he saw her.

"Did your friend get off okay?" he asked.

She blushed.

He laughed.

"I meant his flight," he clarified.

"Oh, that," she said as she sat down at the table.

"What did you think I meant?" he teased.

"Um, the flight," she replied.

"What did you two do all night?" he asked as he put some rice into bowls and placed them and the pot of curry on the table.

"We talked and drank tea and sake and we had a nice dinner at the hotel," she said as she chose her words carefully.

"I hope you didn't wear him out. His wife might want to use him when he arrives in Manila," K. teased.

"You're terrible!" she smiled. "Now that he and I have spent some time together, I like him even more. I wish he could have stayed harder—er, longer!"

K. laughed at her faux pas.

M. blushed a deep crimson which made him laugh even louder.

"Maybe he already has a second wife but he doesn't know it yet," he teased. "Or maybe an obasan!"

"A-san does not think of me as an old woman—like you do," she blurted out without thinking.

"I know. He told me himself how he feels about you. He is very honest and honorable, even under such unusual circumstances. That's why I like him," K. said as he picked up some curry with his chopsticks and put it into his mouth.

M. wondered exactly what A. and K. had spoke about that night at the pub.

"What else did he say?" she asked.

"Enough," K. replied. "I would be very angry about this if I did not like him so much or if I thought I could compete with him. I have neglected you for so long and I am truly sorry for taking you for granted like I have. But in my arrogance, I truly thought that no other man on Earth would find you attractive. A.-san sees things in you that I have missed. He finds you beautiful, sexy and intelligent. He sees the same things in you that I did over 40 years ago. At least we both have excellent taste in women!"

He smiled.

"It is good we didn't have to compete for you when we were all young because I know I would have lost," he said.

"Perhaps not. You and A.-san have many of the same qualities. But I admit, it would have been a most difficult choice," M. said with a smile.

"What if he would have asked you to leave with him last night?" K. asked.

"I would have refused. I am your wife. We have been together for all these years. My place is at your side. And A. will stay at R.'s," she replied.

He reached out and took her hand.

"So you are still my M?" he asked.

"I will always be your M.," she assured him.

Ue o muite arukou

As she served breakfast, K. smiled at her.

"You're glowing," he observed. "I haven't seen you look this content in many years."

"You are imagining things again," she smiled. It was the kind of smile she simply could not prevent. Nor did she want to.

"If you say so. How do you feel?" he asked.

"I feel wonderful, Arigato," she replied as she wondered where he was going with this.

"Do you feel happy?" he asked.

"Of course I feel happy," she said.

"Then he must be very good," he teased.

"You're incorrigible!" she said with a giggle she couldn't help.

"Maybe so, but I am right," he said. "When are you going to the United States?"

"When Y. tells me she is ready. We will fly to San Francisco. From there, we will fly to St. Louis to visit A. and his family. Then we will fly down to New Orleans where he will show us the city better than a tour guide can. He knows New Orleans very well. He has spent much time there—and still does. Will you come with us?" she asked.

"No. Having me along might ruin your plans—and his," K. grinned.

She slapped his hand playfully. He laughed. She knew he was right. There was no way she could convince him otherwise now. No way she could lie to him or fool him after all these years together.

He leaned close and whispered.

"Try not to return pregnant," he said.

She laughed and slapped him a little harder. He laughed and left the room.

When M. returned to the old house a month later, she was stunned to see that it now had a completely new roof. Upon closer examination, she realized that the badly weathered window and door frames and porch supports had been refinished or replaced and that exterior had been freshly painted. Completely puzzled, she walked around the outside of the house and saw that all of the weeds had been pulled and a small garden had been replanted.

"Who would want to preserve this house? What does it mean to them?" she wondered as she went inside.

She saw that the water damage from the leaky roof had been repaired and that all of the debris had been removed. All the house needed was new tatami mats, a coat of paint and some furniture. Her old desk and chair were still in her old bedroom and the old framed photo still hung on the wall. The house only needed a new bathroom now.

She took out her cell phone and called her son, but J. was as surprised as she was when she told him about the house. She then called her sister and brother. Both said they had not been to Yunohira in years.

As she thought about it she smiled.

Suddenly, she knew who had repaired the house. It could only be A. Only he would have fond enough memories to want to preserve an old house on the outskirts of the town. She looked at the desk and smiled as she remembered one of his visits. She was seated at the desk studying when she heard a car drive up. A few seconds later, someone called out her name.

She ran to the window and saw him standing next to the taxi. He had a bouquet of chrysanthemums in his hand. No one had ever brought her flowers before and she wasn't sure how to react. She knew that flowers were a sign of courtship in Nihon, but wasn't sure if they meant the same in his country. She asked him in.

He handed her the flowers.

She thanked him and placed them in a small vase, then led him upstairs so they could talk. Before they could start, the taxi driver called out for help. He had attempted to turn around but got stuck in a soft spot of the road. She and A. hurried down to help him.

She and A. attempted to push the cab to no avail. The driver simply couldn't get any traction in the loose soil. A, spotted a rock on the side of the road and instructed her to put it directly behind the rear tire while he pushed. The rock prevented the cab from sliding backward and the driver was able to find solid ground and get going. He waved and thanked them as he drove off. They waved and returned to the house.

A few minutes later, her parents arrived on the motorcycle. He had been surprised they weren't home when he first arrived. M. explained they had gone to funeral by pointing to the word in a dictionary. Her parents saw him and greeted him warmly as he called out what she instructed him to.

He stayed a little while then they went for a walk. They chatted as they walked and as usual, he spoke slowly and clearly to enable her to understand him. She attempted to teach him some Nihon-go and they laughed at his attempts. She liked the fact he could laugh at his own mistakes. He wasn't proud or aloof.

They returned to the house. A. asked her to call a taxi and did his best to talk with her parents while they waited. He was very shy and unassuming then.

The taxi arrived a half hour later. They saw him off. When she went back inside with her parents, her father smiled.

"Normally, I would not like the idea of you being here alone with a young man. But I like him. I feel I can trust him because he is so shy. You can be with him as much you like while he is here. Remember that he is your friend and your guest and a stranger to our country. You must teach him our customs so he doesn't embarrass himself," he said.

M. smiled and nodded.

She was afraid he would scold her. She was relieved that he liked A. and trusted them to be alone.

Her mother saw the flowers.

"Did he bring you those?" she asked.

"Hai," she replied.

Her mother grinned and hugged her. Her father looked at the flowers and smiled knowingly. He knew that A.'s intentions were completely honorable. They knew why he'd come to Japan even if she wasn't sure. They were both young to think of such things and she had to pass her exams so she could graduate from high school and go on to college.

The next day, he was waiting at the train station when she returned from school. It was about a mile from the station to her house and they walked along a two lane highway that wound through the mountains.

The scenery was beautiful, but A. seemed to only have eyes for her. A fact that she found quite flattering.

They talked as they walked side-by-side. She liked the fact he always spoke slowly so she could process his language, even though she sometimes didn't understand what he said. He always did his best to try and explain it to her and they often used a dictionary. A. was trying to make her feel comfortable. That struck her as being very mature of him.

And considerate.

The dictionary helped. She pointed to words she was trying to use. He helped her with her pronunciations and she helped him with his and they'd laugh.

Then, out of the blue, she heard him say:

"Anata wa aishimasu."

She stopped in her tracks and wondered if he knew what he'd just said. She was unsure how to respond.

"I love you," he said. "I want to marry you."

Her heart pounded faster and faster.

Was that a proposal?

"But I don't have a real job now and you need to finish school. We're too young and not prepared enough to take such a big step. We'll have to wait until we're both ready," he continued.

She breathed a sigh of relief and nodded to indicate that she understood and agreed. The idea frightened her.

And excited her.

But he was mature enough to know it had to wait a little while.

Now she wondered what she would have done or said had he actually proposed that afternoon. He had been the first man to tell her that. The first to declare his love and intentions. He had let her know exactly how he felt and what his plans were.

She sat down at her old desk and wept again for what might have been.

Namida ga kaborenai youni

M. returned to the house a little after sunset. When she walked upstairs to her room, she saw a young woman standing in front of the window.

"Who are you? Why are you in my house?" she asked.

The woman turned and made eye contact with her. M. felt her entire body turn ice cold as she recognized the intruder as the same girl who had haunted her in Meguro. She stood and studied the girl.

She was young.

A teenager perhaps.

The girl smiled.

It was a sad, mournful kind of smile.

"Who are you?" she asked again. "Please tell me what you want."

The girl turned back to the window and vanished.

M. felt her knees trembling. She sat down on the floor and looked at the window.

"Who are you?" she called.

M. chatted with A. as she watched him work out on his Solo Flex. She knew that he worked out at least four times a week. Until now, she wasn't aware of the intensity of his exercises.

"The older I get, the harder I have to work out to stay in shape," he explained. "I have to stay strong to keep up with the women in my life. I don't want to disappoint them."

She laughed.

She watched his muscles tighten and flex as he did a set of presses. He had almost no fat on his frame. He was lean and athletic.

Sexy, she thought.

She also did various stretching exercises and yoga to stay flexible and strong. She also wanted to stay in shape. A. applauded her efforts. He told her she looked younger and sexier than ever.

That's what mattered to her now.

She was staying in shape for him.

She and Y. had flown to the U.S. a week earlier. They stayed three nights in San Francisco then flew to St. Louis where A. and R. welcomed them into their home. They had spent the last two days touring the city. Right now, R. was out shopping with Y. This had been pre-planned by M. and Y. so she and A. could spend a few hours alone.

"In a way, I'm sorry that K. didn't come with you," A. said as he sat up.

"He said he did not wish to get in our way," M. smiled.

He looked at her shapely legs. In the miserable summer heat of St. Louis, she had taken to wearing shorts like everyone else in the city. And he liked what he saw.

"You look great in those shorts," he said. "You have the legs for them."

She blushed.

"K. would be shocked to see me like this. He'd say it's not proper for a women my age to show her legs in public," she said. "But since everyone else here wears shorts, I don't feel so strange. I must admit that I like the way you look in shorts, too."

And the fact that he grew an obvious erection the moment he saw her in the shorts.

He finished his last set and toweled off.

"That's that," he said. "I'm going to shower now. Care to join me?"

As he stood under the shower, the curtain moved and a very naked M. stepped into the tub. As his erection grew and grew, she took the soap and rubbed it between her hands until she created a lather then she wrapped her fingers around his manhood and pumped it nice and slow. Each pump caused his foreskin to roll back and forth over his knob. And each pump caused him to sigh with pleasure. After a few more pumps, she knelt and slid his member into her mouth. He gasped as she worked it with her tongue until he fired his seed into her mouth. She quickly swallowed every bit of it and stood up. He leaned over and sucked each of her nipples while he massaged the space between her thighs. Her heart raced as her passion ignited and her soul soared upward.

He stopped and reached behind his back to turn off the water. They slowly, erotically dried each other off. When they were finished, he swept her up into his arms and carried her into the bedroom. He sat her down on the edge of the bed and knelt between her open thighs. M. sighed happily as made love to her with his tongue. She gasped and moaned then cried out as he brought her to a good, deep climax. She fell back on the bed. He moved between her thighs. She bent her knees and moaned as he entered her garden and wrapped her legs around his hips. They began thrusting in perfect rhythm. Just as they had each and every time.

They made love.

Sweet, wonderful and beautiful love.

Like before, they climaxed together. Into one big, explosive ball of pleasure. M. arched her back as they continued thrusting. On each inward thrust, she felt his love juices spurt deep inside her chamber. They kept making love until both were totally exhausted and they finished with a long, deep, passionate kiss.

She smiled as they dressed.

And she positively glowed. It was a happy, youthful glow, too.

"Each time we make love is better than the last," she said.

"Much better," he agreed. "I'd better start dinner. R. and Y. will be home soon."

They went to the kitchen. She watched while A. gathered up the ingredients and started dinner. As he worked, he explained what he was doing and about the various spices he liked to use. They had exchanged many recipes over the years. A. was a gourmet chef. He had a passion and real flair for cooking and had once owned a restaurant in the Netherlands.

He was a chef, an artist, a writer, a world traveler, an athlete and a warrior. He would have been considered a true Renaissance man had he lived at a different time. All these things made him that much more attractive to her. And she was still amazed that he was equally attracted to her.

He even said she was perfect and he wouldn't change a single thing about her. And she knew that he meant it.

When R. and Y. returned with bags full of souvenirs and clothes, dinner was already on the table. He called it a Cajun-Philippine fusion and he served a white wine from a Missouri winery with it, which Y. and

M. found to be quite delicious. M. and Y. complimented him several times on his meal. Then he surprised them by explaining it was the signature dish of a restaurant he and R. had recently opened in New Orleans.

"It's really caught on with the locals, who were the clients I was aiming for. It's something familiar to them but different and they went crazy for it," he explained. "Our menu features a blend of Cajun, Creole, Philippine and Japanese dishes. We even have our own style of sushi made from all local ingredients."

"What do you call your restaurant?" asked Y.

"We call it Pacific Bayou," R. said with a laugh. "We even have local musicians entertain there on Fridays and Saturdays. We opened it last month and we're surprised at how popular it became."

"Are you moving to NOLA now?" M. asked.

"Maybe later. I go there every month to check on the restaurant and to visit some friends. I have a very good manager running the place for me and he makes sure the food and service are top-notch. Of course, I hired and trained the cooks to make sure they stick to our recipes. The manager keeps track of the money and what dishes sell best," A. explained. "Still, I have to keep an eye on it once in a while."

"We are thinking of opening a similar place here in St. Louis," R. added.

"When are we leaving for NOLA?" M. asked.

"I booked our flights for the day after tomorrow. R. and I own a small townhouse in the French Quarter so we'll all stay there. That way, you won't have to waste money on a hotel," A. said.

M. smiled.

"You are full of surprises!" she said.

He laughed.

"It keeps life interesting," he said.

The bokushi nodded after he listened to M. explanation of the haunting.

"Spirits often attach themselves to the living. There are many reasons for this. She may have been attracted to you because you share some sort of common wish or desire. Or there is something in common that you both feel strongly about. Perhaps she is trying to get you to do something. Perhaps she is trying to prevent you from doing something," he said after some thought.

"You have told me that she does not appear to be malevolent. That means she is not motivated by a desire for revenge. She is not weeping or wailing either. That means she has not come here due to sorrow nor is she drawn to any personal sorrows that you might project," he added,

"It doesn't make any sense," M. said.

"Such things never make sense to the living until the spirits make their desires known. Only she knows why she is here. We can only guess until she decides to speak," the bokushi said.

"She first appeared during Obon," M. said.

"That part makes some sense," the bokushi said. "Sometimes a wandering soul finds a similar soul to commune with. You must have projected similar thoughts or emotions that attracted her."

"I see. How do I make her leave?" M. asked.

"You can't. She will leave when she finds another to attach herself to. Until then, you must continue to try to communicate with her, to learn who she is and what she wants," he said.

They suddenly heard something heavy hit the floor in the next room. They got up to investigate. They found the heavy Atlas lying in the middle of the room. As before, it was open to the map of Vietnam.

M. picked it up. She told the bokushi about the first time this happened.

"There is your first clue. I believe she is telling us that she is from Vietnam," he said, "Do you know anyone in Vietnam?"

"No," she said.

"Do you know someone who has been there?" he asked.

"Hai. A man I loved many years ago was in the war there," she said softly.

"A man? He was an American soldier?" he asked.

"Hai. Among other things," she replied. "He's a famous writer now."

The bokushi looked at the books on her shelf. Almost all were from the same author. He spotted 'Bushi' and nodded.

He walked over and took it from the shelf.

"He is your old friend?" he asked.

She nodded.

"Would you like to talk about it?" he offered. "I am free for the rest of the afternoon. It will do you good."

She nodded.

They returned to the adjoining room and sat down. She poured him more tea...

New Orleans proved to be everything A. always told her it was. They flew down on a Wednesday and took a taxi to his home on Royal. When the taxi stopped, both she and Y. were stunned by the size and age of the Creole townhome. He opened the door and showed them upstairs to a large guest room with a king sized four poster bed with a silk canopy. The room was furnished in the style of the 1860s and had French doors that opened onto a balcony that overlooked a rear courtyard.

"There's a large bathroom two doors down and there are towels, soap and shampoos in the linen cabinet there. Make yourselves at home," A. said as he placed their bags on the high-backed chair. "Our room is on the other end of the hall. I'll give you a tour of the house after you've settled in."

Y. walked around the room. She seemed awed.

"This house is ten times the size of any house in Nihon," she said.

"It's the largest, most elegant mansion in the French Quarter," A. said. "It was built by a wealthy French doctor and his wife in 1820. Their name was LaLaurie and the house was supposedly the most haunted in all of New Orleans. It has a long, interesting history and an unfounded, false legend attached to it. I'll tell you all about it on the tour."

After the tour, they walked down to the Court of Two Sisters for dinner. A. introduced them to Cajun cuisine at its finest and they finished off the evening with a stroll along Bourbon Street. Both M. and Y. wanted to see the WWII museum, so they began their second morning there. They stayed until closing time then headed to NOLA's for dinner then over to the music clubs on Frenchman. They crawled back to the mansion after midnight.

The next day, Y. said she'd like to explore the aquarium then shop at the River Walk mall. M. said she'd like to tour some of the Creole townhomes instead. They agreed to meet at Pere Antoine's at five that evening.

As soon as R. and Y. left for the aquarium, A. and M. walked back upstairs, hand-in-hand…

The rest of their stay in New Orleans was a whirlwind of history tours, plantation tours, cemetery tours, swamp tours and music and fine dining. On the last day, Y. asked R. to accompany her down Magazine Street so she could explore the shops and boutiques there. Magazine was the longest street in New Orleans and it had six miles of shops and other stores. A. knew they'd be gone most of the morning. This enabled him and M. to spend most of the morning making love in as many ways as they could imagine.

The next afternoon, they parted at the airport. M. and Y. took a flight to San Francisco and a connecting flight to Tokyo. A. and R. stayed another week in New Orleans then headed back to St. Louis on a riverboat.

On the flight back to Tokyo, M. couldn't stop smiling. Y. teased her about it the entire way home. The trip had been exciting beyond her wildest dreams. She felt as if she were an actress playing a role in a romantic adventure movie. Or a character in one of A.s books.

But she was also a little bit sad.

She didn't know when or if she would see A. again. They would always write. And they would call each other. She already missed being with him. After so many weeks of fun and romance and love, she was returning to her oh-so ordinary existence in Tokyo.

"At least you got to be with him for a while," Y. said as if she could read M.s mind. "This is a trip I will never forget. He and R. are the perfect hosts and he seems like an exceptionally wonderful man. But you already know that, don't you?"

M. sighed and nodded as looked down at the vast country called America. There was so much to do. So much to see there. But the only place she wanted to be was at A.s side.

Forever.

"I understand why you love him," Y. said. "I almost fell in love with him myself. Don't feel sad. You will see him again. I'm sure of that."

"I know. But when? I don't know if I can be without him now," M. said. "I keep thinking about his first love and how foolish she was. She would have had a wonderful life. A very happy life. I feel so sad for her. And him."

"You need not feel sad for A.-san. He has two women who love him more than anything else. He is truly blessed," Y. pointed out.

"And I am also blessed to know that he loves me as I love him," M. said with a smile. "Our time together was very special. Very precious. Nothing will ever take that away from us. No matter what happens, I now we belong together."

"Like the samurai and his lady?" Y. asked.

"Hai. Like the samurai and his lady," M. said with a smile. "When you were with R., did she say anything that made you think she knew about me and A.?"

"No. If she knows, she is keeping quiet about it. I don't think she suspected anything. She did say she likes you and me very much and she understands how you and A. became friends. Other than that, she views you as a cute but harmless little old woman," Y. replied.

"I'm happy that A. doesn't think of me that way!" M. laughed.

"Of course he doesn't. To him, you are far from harmless," Y. joked. "I think he looks upon you as a dangerously sexy woman."

J. studied his mother's face. She was starting to look tired and pale. Even worried.

"There's a spirit in this house. She's the same one I saw in Meguro. She's followed me here," M. said flatly.

"Are you sure?" he asked.

He knew from her demeanor that she was telling the truth. She would never lie about such a thing.

"I'm positive. She shows up on different times and days. She just looks at me. She never speaks or even gestures. Then she just vanishes. I see her by the window. She is always staring out. It's like she's waiting for someone. I've seen her in my mirrors and even reflected in my tea cup. Sometimes I wake in the middle of the night and see her next to my futon," she said.

"Does she threaten you in any way?" he asked.

"No. She just appears for a few seconds. She's more annoying than anything else," M. said.

"Do you have any idea who she is?" he asked.

She shook her head.

"She isn't the least bit familiar. She's starting to drive me crazy," M. said.

"What are you doing about it?" he asked.

"What can I do?" she asked.

"Have you asked a bokushi to come here?" he suggested.

"Do you think he could help?" she asked hopefully.

"I don't know. But at least it's worth a try, don't you think?" he said.

"I'll go to the temple tomorrow," she agreed.

M. and Y. arrived in Tokyo late the next evening. They got into Y. car which she had left at the airport garage and headed back to Hachioji. To M. surprise, K. was up waiting for her when she got home. She greeted him with a warm hug and said she'd missed and gave him regards from A. and told him that A. was sorry he didn't come along.

Then she took her bag upstairs to the bedroom.

He watched her unpack as he leaned against the door jamb.

"Did you get it all out of your system now?" he asked.

"To be honest, I don't think I will ever get him out of my system," she replied.

She closed the suitcase and smiled at him.

"Domo arigato gozaimasu for being such a wonderful, understanding husband. You must really love me deeply to have allowed me to do this," she said as she hugged him.

"I did this for purely selfish reasons. I just wanted to save what was left of my sanity," he said.

She stepped back and looked him in the eye. She saw that familiar twinkle and knew he was joking again. After all this time, they knew each other's moods perfectly.

"Oh?" she queried.

"Hai. I reasoned that if I had not allowed you to be with him, you would have grown more frustrated and sullen. Then you would have gotten cranky and started taking it out on me. We would have started to argue more and more and I just did not want to be put through all of that.

So I felt that allowing you to make love with A. would be the lesser of the two evils," he explained.

She laughed.

"Whatever you reasons, domo arigato," she repeated.

He smiled.

"Besides, it is very quiet and peaceful around here when you're away," he said.

"Maybe I should go away more often then," she said.

"Maybe. But I like A.-san. I don't think I could do such a thing to him!" K. said.

Nakinagara aruku

When Date Masamune died in 1636, Koinu openly wept. He and his entire attended the funeral, which was a relatively simple and sedate affair. When all was finished, they gave their personal and most sincere condolences to Date's eldest son, Tadamune, and to the rest of his family.

Tadamune had the same temper and demeanor as his father and he had proven himself on the field of battle time and again. On several occasions, he and Koinu had fought side-by-side. The two men grew to like and respect each other greatly.

"Arigato gozaimasu, Koinu-san," Tadamune said as they walked together. "My father thought very highly of you—as do I. Now that he is gone, I hope you will continue to serve our clan instead of retiring."

Koinu smiled.

"I will continue to serve you and your family, faithfully and with honor, for as long as I am physically able to do so," he vowed. "Your father would have wished that."

"As do I. He considered you a trusted friend and advisor. I do, too. I have learned much from you and I feel confident to know that you have my back," Tadamune said.

"Always," Koinu assured him.

He had just turned 65 and his hair had become streaked with strands of silver. Other than that, he still looked, acted and felt the same as he always had.

Todamune was his junior by four years. As such, he looked up to Koinu and considered him to be an older brother. He had also learned something from the samurai that became the code Tadamune lived by. As had his father.

"The best battles are the ones never fought."

"Your father was a great man. Someone should erect a statue in Sendai to commemorate his deeds," Koinu suggested.

Tadamune smiled at the idea.

"Perhaps someone will—one day," he said. "I've been meaning to ask how you still manage to keep yourself in such fine condition at your age?"

Koinu grinned.

"I have a beautiful who keeps me fit," he said.

"So, the passion still burns between you?" Tadamune asked.

"It burns brighter than ever," Koinu replied. "There is no other like her."

"Even after six children?" asked Todamune.

"Hai. That's why I have never once thought of straying. There is no one better. No one who catches my heart like she does," Koinu answered with a sense of pride.

"She is a very lucky woman," Todamune said.

"And I am a very lucky man," said Koinu.

M. unpacked the aging poster and hung it up on the wall above her old desk. The poster, she thought, looked at home there. And it breathed life into the old house.

She looked around.

The workers had done an excellent job. Under her guidance, they had restored the original colors to the walls and re-lacquered the woodwork. Outside of the upgraded electrical system, and new bathroom and kitchen that were added to the back of the house, it looked exactly as it did the day she'd left.

"A. would recognize it now. He'd feel comfortable here," she thought.

She walked to the window and looked up at the sky. They would have been married in this very house. Just as her sister had. It would have been a traditional Japanese wedding, too. She knew he would have wanted it that way, too.

But it all went wrong.

So very, very wrong.

And it was all because of what she'd said.

She heard a car drive up. She watched as it stopped in front of the house and her son, J. got out. He smiled at her as she waved. She waited until he came upstairs.

"This place looks wonderful! How much did you spend?" he asked.

"Almost everything I had in the bank," M. answered. "I think I'll spend a few months here. I've really missed this house. More than I thought I did."

"Did you ever find out who paid to have the roof repaired and the place cleaned up?" he asked.

"Shimizu-san would not tell me, but I'm sure it was A.-san," she said. "No one else cares about this house. Not even our own relatives."

"I think he is still very much in love with you. You should have seen him when you had the chance," J. said.

"I know. But perhaps he will come back here one day. And he will find me here, waiting for him," she said hopefully, although she felt that day would never come.

M. never returned to Tokyo.

She moved into the old house and spent the rest of her days looking out of her window, watching cars go by and hoping that one would stop and he would step out and smile up at her. Her son visited often and even brought her A.s latest novels.

She read each several times over.

And kept looking through the window.

Waiting…hoping…

And weeping…

K. walked in and handed M. a book. She smiled when she saw it was A.'s latest novel.

"I saw this at the bookstore so I thought you would like to have it. It's in Nihon-go, so I'd like to read it when you're finished. The back cover aid it's based on his experiences in Vietnam," he explained.

She smiled.

He had told her of his experiences. Most of them, anyway. The book might provide further insight into A.'s personality. K. left and returned with a pot of fresh brewed tea and cup. He placed it on the table before her. She nodded and opened the book.

She read all night and most of the following day. When K. returned from his workout at the gym, he saw her wiping tears from her eyes. He squatted in front of her.

"Is it the book?" he asked.

"Hai. It's so sad. So terribly sad. I don't know how he can carry so much pain inside himself," she said.

"Are you finished?" he asked.

She nodded.

"May I read it?" he queried.

She handed it to him.

"Arigato," he said softly.

"Why do you want to go back to Vietnam? What's there for you now?" R. asked as they lay in bed.

"It's something I can't explain. Not verbally. Things happened there," he replied.

"What things?" she asked as she cuddled closer.

He put his arm around her.

"Read my book," he said. "If you really want to know, read my book."

"You know I don't like to read," she said.

"In that case, you'll never know," he replied. "It's just as well. It was long before I even knew you. It really has nothing at all to do with us now."

"Then why go back?" she asked.

"Read the book," he repeated.

She just closed her eyes and went to sleep like she usually did. She never did read the book—or any of his books. That was fine with him. He knew all that really interested her were Philippine soap operas and variety shows, shopping and playing with her cell phone. R. was an eternal 16 year old. He always thought it was funny that she'd helped to promote his novels but had never read any of them. But that was just R.

"Did I tell you?" he asked.

"Tell me what?" she asked sleepily.

"An anime studio in Tokyo is turning "Bushi" into a movie. I received a letter from the publisher about it this morning."

"Anime? You mean a cartoon?" she asked.

"Uh-huh. I can hardly wait to see the finished product. They've offered me a million U.S. dollars and one percent of the worldwide sales and distribution. Naturally, I accepted it," he said. "They also want to do the same with 'Realm of Blood.' That's the first book that got translated into Japanese. I told them to go for it."

"We're going to be rich!" she said as she bounced up and down on the bed.

He laughed.

M. put the book down and wept for hours. Had she known then, she would have reacted differently when he asked about soldiers. She had no way of knowing any of this because she had closed her mind to it. She wiped her eyes and sighed.

The house seemed even emptier now.

Bleak and sad.

"Please forgive me, A.!" she cried.

It was then she realized who the soldier in her visions was. And how after all of that, he had come back to her. He had gone out of his way to locate her, contact her, and had returned to see her. Somehow, it all went wrong.

She thought about the girl in the book and wondered what she had looked like. He'd described her in general terms. She could have looked like any one of thousands of young girls back then in any Asian country. But he also wrote about her with a sentimentality that was deeply genuine.

And he had come back to her afterward.

And she had ruined everything.

R. put down the novel and looked at A. with tears in her eyes. This time, it was a novel of his experiences in Vietnam. She looked at him as if seeing him for the very first time.

"How much of this is true?" she asked.

"Most of it," he said.

"I didn't know. Why didn't you say anything about this before? I knew you were there but you never told me any of this. I feel so sad for you," she said as she wiped tears from her eyes.

"That was a very long time ago. She's a pleasant memory now. She's one of the few woman I've known that I have nothing negative to say about," A. said as he sat beside her.

"Nothing at all?" R. asked.

"Not a single thing," he replied. "She had no ulterior motives. No guile. No secrets or baggage. She was exactly who she appeared to be. A sweet, gentle and trusting soul."

"What about me?" she asked.

"You actually reminded me of her when we first got married," he said.

"Not M.?" she asked.

"Her, too, to some extent," he admitted. "All in all, I'd say that I really lucked out big time when I married you."

She smiled and kissed him.

"I think now, I finally understand you. Forgive me," she said.

"There's nothing to apologize for, so there's nothing to forgive," he replied as he put his arm around her.

"Who else knew about her?" she asked.

"No one. I've never told a soul. I guess I was trying to bury it," he said. "I never should have. Now I know that. One day, I'd like to go back to that village."

"To see if her grave is still there?" R. asked.

He nodded.

"What if it isn't? she asked.

"I'll try and leave some sort of marker," he replied. "To let her know she's not forgotten."

R. leaned against his shoulder and cried.

M. woke and stretched. As she did, she noticed an aged sheet of folded paper on her pillow. She picked it up and opened it. As she did, her blood turned cold.

It was a poem.

And it was addressed to A.

She looked around nervously but saw no one. She got up and walked to her desk. She took out an envelope, placed the poem inside of it and sealed it. Then she placed it into the drawer.

She knew now.

Everything made sense now.

And the clearer things became, the more her hopes turned to ashes.

Hitoribotchi no yoru

When M. opened the door and saw him standing there, her heart just about leapt from her chest. She took his hand and led him inside, surprised that he had come.

They sat down in the living room. She beamed at him. It was a smile filled with love and expectations.

"I am delighted to see you again. It has been far too long. Why didn't you tell me that you were coming?" she said as she poured them each a cup of tea.

"I wanted to surprise you," he said.

"I am so happy that you are here. And I am so sorry to hear about your wife," she said as she tried to bring her heartbeat under control.

"Thank you. That was a difficult loss. I mourned for almost a year. I still cry at times. Arigato for helping me get through it," he said.

"I am here if you need me, A.-san. As you were for me," she said softly as they held hands across the table.

"You are a very dear and special lady. That's why I love you so much," he said. "I was very saddened to hear about K. He was a very good man."

"That was two years ago. The house still feels so empty to me. Is it the same for you?" she asked.

"Yes. It feels almost abandoned. It has no heartbeat now," he answered.

"I understand what you mean," she nodded.

"That's why I've come here. I want you to return to St. Louis with me and help me restore the heartbeat of my house. I want you to make it feel like a home again. Our home," he said.

She stared at him.

"Are you proposing to me?" she asked hopefully.

"Hai. Anata wa aishimasu, M.-san. Will you marry me?" he asked as he took both her hands.

She smiled.

"We are both growing older and I would be the happiest woman on Earth if we grow old together. Hai! I will marry you!" she almost shouted as they hugged and kissed.

M. immediately phoned her three children to tell them the wonderful news. None seemed surprised.

"I knew this would happen sooner or later," O. said. "It's karma."

The wedding was simple yet elegant. It took place in the Asakusa shrine on the other end of Tokyo and it was a traditional Buddhist ceremony. M. wore a bridal kimono of pure white with gold thread designs and he wore the traditional groom's kimono. M.'s family and a few close friends attended.

Everyone said they looked perfect together. M's children commented that they had never seen her look happier and everyone wished them along and happy and healthy marriage.

"Where are you going on your honeymoon?" asked Y.

M. looked into A.'s eyes. He smiled.

"Everywhere," he said.

M's granddaughter, R. took several photos.

"It's amazing. You both look so young! So full of life. This is so romantic!" she gushed as she hugged each of them.

He winked at M. and whispered.

"Actually, our honeymoon began that first afternoon in Tokyo."

"And I hope it never ends," she said with a huge smile.

She stood before him in her wedding kimono. He knelt in front of her and smiled as she gave him step-by-step instructions on the proper way to unwrap her. He did it one golden cord at a time and worked slowly. With each passing second, their anticipation grew and grew. Eventually, the obi came undone and she let it slide to the floor.

Then, ever so slowly, he unwrapped the kimono. The outer silken layer went first. Then the second. Then the next. Each time, she spun slowly around to tease him seductively. When she was completely nude, he swept her up in his arms and carried her to the bed...

For the next several years, they were inseparable. They traveled throughout Japan. They revisited places he'd been to in Vietnam. They traveled to India and Nepal, Europe and all over North and South America.

It was just as he'd promised.

Better than she ever imagined or hoped.

It was a never-ending honeymoon.

They loved deeply and often.

They laughed and joked and spoke their minds.

They sang and painted and wrote.

And they filled albums with memories.

They looked and acted eternally young. It was a new life for them both. A fairy tale life.

He was her samurai.

Her knight in shining armor.

And she was his lady. His one and only.

And nothing else in the entire universe mattered.

One warm August morning, A. woke with a start. Hi sudden stirrings woke M. who slept next to him. She stretched and looked at him. Then blanched when she saw the look in his eyes.

It was the moment she'd prayed would never come. The moment she'd always dreaded. It had finally arrived and there was no denying it.

He saw her expression and pulled her close. Their lips met as they had thousands of times before and he felt her tremble as he gently stroked her hair.

"It's alright," he whispered.

"No it's not," she said stoically. "No it's not."

"I have to go," he said as they lay back down.

"Can I come with you?" she asked as she choked back her tears.

"Not yet. The time isn't right for you. You can join me later—when you're ready. But for now, I must travel alone," he said.

"Are you certain?" she asked, hopefully.

"Yes. It's time," he said calmly.

"I don't want to lose you!" she sobbed as she held him tightly.

"You can't lose me. Not ever. I'll always be here for you," he assured her. "Let's make love one last time. Then I must go," he said as he stroked her thigh.

She sniffed her tears back and smiled…

As A. got out of the taxi, S. and his family greeted him with bows and warm handshakes. A small boy about six years old hurried over and bowed. A. bowed back and smiled.

"This is my grandson, H." S. introduced. "He is staying with us for the summer while K. is away in Germany for his work. I have told him all about you. He is excited to get a chance to meet you."

"I am delighted to meet you, H.," A. said. "Do you like yakyu?"

"Hai. I love to play!" H. beamed.

"Good. I have a gift for you then. In fact, I've brought gifts for all of you," A. said.

"Please dine with us tonight. It will be like old times," S. offered.

"I'd be honored to," A. said.

"I'll show you to your room!" H. exclaimed.

"I remember when you showed me to my room when I came here many years ago," A. smiled at S. "We had many nice, long talks. You asked me a lot of questions, too."

S. laughed.

"I am afraid that you will find H. equally inquisitive. I hope he doesn't make a pest of himself," he said.

"Like father like son like grandson," A. joked.

"I am afraid that it is a family trait," S. said. "How is your wife, M-san?"

"She is well, thank you," A. said. "Just last week, we celebrated our 20th anniversary. She looks every bit as lovely as she always has."

"Twenty years? How time flies," S. mused. "You look almost the same as you did on your last visit. You have aged very well. You still look very fit."

"You look the same, too," A. observed.

S. laughed.

"Why isn't your wife with you?" he asked.

"She will join me later—after I've done what I came here for," A. said as they walked to his suite.

He smiled.

It was the same room he'd used the last time. It hadn't changed much at all, either. The familiarity made him feel at home. Each of his stays at the ryokan had felt that way.

"I've brought a few mementos. I would like you to have them," A. said as he opened his suitcase.

He took out two 8x10 framed photos. Both were very old. The first was of an American baseball team. The small brass sign tacked to the frame read:

"New York Yankees 1969".

He presented it to H. The boy studied the photo and pointed to a players kneeling in the front row.

"Is this you?" he asked.

"That's me, alright," A. said. "I was just 18 then. "That was taken during spring training, right before the season started."

"Did you play in the majors?" H. asked.

"For a little while. Then I got injured and decided to try something else," A. explained.

Oh? What did you do?" asked H.

He showed him the second photo. It was of a group of young, battle-weary soldiers gathered around a Quonset hut. The metal tag read:

"Vietnam 1970-1971."

He gave it to S. He immediately recognized A. standing off to the left, cradling an M-16 in his hands. They all looked as if they'd been through Hell and back.

"That was taken just before I left Nam," A. explained. "We had just gone through a firefight the night before. I handed the captain my camera and asked if he'd take a picture of us. He took three. I'd like you to have this because you seemed to be really fascinated with my war stories."

"I am honored. Arigato gozaimasu. I will hang it in a prominent place," S. said with a smile. "You said he took three such photos?"

"Hai. I gave one to my son in the States and M. and I have the other on a wall in our house in Hachioji," A. said.

H. beamed at him.

"Were you a good player?" H. asked.

"I used to be," A. replied.

"Can you teach me to play baseball?" he asked.

"I'd be glad to. I even brought my glove," A. replied.

"Why did you bring your glove?" H. asked.

"I always bring my glove with me when I travel—just in case I meet someone like you," A. smiled.

"Many years ago, you showed me how to play baseball like they do in America. The last time you were here, you showed my son K. Now you will teach my grandson," S. said.

"It's en," A. said using the Japanese term for the wheel of fate.

"I believe it is. The wheel has made a full turn and brought you back here to repeat what you did before," S. agreed.

A pretty young woman entered the room. She bowed to A. He returned it.

"This is my daughter-in-law N.-san," S. said. "She is H.'s mother."

"I hope my son is not being a nuisance," she apologized.

"He's going to teach me to play baseball!" H. shouted as he showed her the photo.

"Arigato for being so kind to H. His father has no time to teach him as he is always traveling for his work," she said.

"I understand. It's the curse of modern Nihon. Lucky for me, I've never had to do that," A. said.

"Oh?" she queried.

"I've never had respect for money. I've never allowed it to rule my life," he said.

"That is a refreshing attitude. I wish my husband felt that way," N. said. "I hardly see him anymore. We miss him, too."

"How long will you be in Yufuin?" S. asked.

"About a month," A. said.

"Then I truly hope that my son doesn't become nuisance to you," N. said with a smile.

"I'm sure that H. and I will get along very well," A. said.

Koinu sat on a cushion with his back propped up against the wall. He was on his back porch, looking out at the Zen garden M. had so carefully arranged many years ago. She knelt beside and held his hand tightly. He smiled at her.

Her hair was snow white now—like his.

But her eyes still glimmered with love and her smile still brought joy to anyone she chose to share it with. She has always been his M. She always would be.

Seated around them were his children, grandchildren and even great grandchildren and several very close friends. He had outlived two daimyo and his two best friends. He had been to far too many funerals.

Now, it was time to attend his last one.

"I don't want to lose you," M. wept.

"You will never lose me. I'll wait for you. We'll be together again soon. Believe in that," he assured her. "Even if our souls become separated, I will find you. No matter how long it takes, I will find you."

"Anata wa aishimasu," she whispered as she hugged him.

"Anata wa aishimasu," he said as he held her close and closed his eyes...

He was 97.

S. watched as A. played catch with his grandson. He had shown the boy how to throw a rather nasty-looking curve ball and two other pitches. Now, H. was busy trying to master each of them. They had been at it since early morning. A few other boys had come to watch at first. He had graciously shown them a few things as well.

And it didn't matter that there was snow on the ground. None of them seemed to notice and they were too engrossed in what they were learning to worry about the chill in the air.

A. was in his element, S. thought.

Just as he'd been when he first came to the ryokan.

Watching him, he found it hard to believe that A. was over twice his age. He had so much energy. So much zest for life.

They kept at it until dinner time.

S. wife, O. came out and told them it was time to eat. A. caught the last throw from H. and smiled. Then they walked inside. Over dinner, he told them about Vietnam. It was the same he had told S. and K. many years ago. They ate and chatted for hours.

Early the next morning, A. went down to the front desk.

"I need to make a trip," he said.

K. looked at him.

"And where do you wish to go and when?" S. asked.

"There's a certain old house I'd like to see," A. said.

"Oh. I understand. I'll have a taxi here after breakfast," S. said.

"Does it still stand?" A. asked.

"Hai. It stands—mostly thanks to the repairs you made to it many years ago. For a little while, M.-san returned. She finished restoring it. Then she moved in. She stayed for several years. She came by here once in a while and we chatted. She asked about you many times. I told her what I knew, which was not very much. Only that you married again," S. said. "She was still very pretty. She was slender and kept her hair long and wavy. She always seemed so sad to me, too."

"Is she still there?" A. asked.

"If she is, she is there in spirit only. M.-san passed away five years ago in a hospital in Meguro. Her son had her buried at the same temple as her parents. He was heartbroken. So was her daughter in law and grandchildren. I didn't know where you were or I would have informed you," S. said sadly.

"I'm so sorry," A. said softly. "So very sorry."

"Do you still wish to see the house?" S. asked.

He nodded.

"I understand. I will call the taxi for you," S. assured him. "Before I forget, her son left this letter here. He said he had no idea who wrote it or how his mother came to possess it. But since your name was in it, he asked me to give it to you if I ever saw you again."

He went to his file cabinet, took out an envelope and handed it to A. He looked it over and took it up to his room. As he ate his breakfast, he opened the envelope. Inside was a very old piece of notebook paper. He unfolded it carefully and almost forgot how to breathe when he realized what it was.

As he read it, his hands trembled and tears flooded into his eyes and ran down his cheeks. It was a love poem.

He'd seen this before.

Long ago.

But how in God's name did M. happen to have it?

There was no doubting its authenticity. The handwriting was clear an unmistakable. Yet for M. to have come into possession of it and for him to be reading again now defied all possible logic, odds or explanations.

He folded the poem, slid it back into the envelope, and stuffed it onto his jacket pocket. He finished his breakfast and went down to the desk. S. noticed that he looked as pale as the snow on the ground.

"Was the letter bad news?" he queried.

"It was more like impossible," A. replied. "When will my taxi be here?"

"I called him ten minutes ago," S. said. "May I ask what was in the envelope?"

"It's a poem that someone wrote for me many years ago," A. said. "It's something I never expected to see again."

"Did M-san write it?" S. asked.

"No. It was written for me by someone else," A. said. "In another place."

S. looked at him.

His wife O. had heard them talking. She looked at A. and nodded. He nodded in return.

The taxi pulled up outside. A. saw it and they walked out to it. S. gave the driver the address. A. rolled down the window.

"I should be back in time for lunch," he said. "We'll talk more then."

S. and O. watched as the taxi drove off. S. turned to his wife and asked why she had nodded.

"When A.-san said it was a poem, I knew who wrote it. You should know that, too. Think about the stories he told us about Vietnam when he was here last and you will understand. What I don't understand is how M-san came by it," she said.

"You're crazy! "He smiled.

"If so, then how do you explain the poem?" she countered.

Two hours later, the taxi returned. To S. surprise, only the driver got out. He seemed agitated and confused as he ran up to the desk.

"Did the gaijin return to the ryokan?" he asked.

"No. How would he return without a car?" S. asked. "And where is A.-san? Did you leave him at that house?"

"That's just it. He's not at the house. I searched every inch of it for him. But he's gone/ Vanished into thin air. He didn't even leave footprints in the snow! It was like he was never there at all," the driver said in a shaky voice.

O. looked at him.

"Perhaps we should call the police?" she asked. "A.-san has to be out there somewhere!"

S. phoned the police.

They sent two men out to the house and found nothing. There was no trace of A. anywhere. In fact, they claimed that the house had not been disturbed for many years. They even accused the driver of making it up.

"But he was here! We ate with him and talked with him. H. even played catch with him!" O. said when he gave her the news. "You saw him. We all saw him."

S. looked up at the photos on the wall to remind himself that he hadn't imagined it. Just to be sure, he walked upstairs to the suite and looked inside. The suite was empty. In fact, it looked like it had never been occupied.

He shook his head and wondered what the Hell happened. He turned, and was about to leave, when he saw the old leather first baseman's mitt on the table near the window...

After looking around the house, A. sat down in the chair next to the desk to rest. He looked up and smiled at the drawing on the wall as he recalled the day he bought it for her. As he did, a sense of weariness came over him. Before he realized it, he'd fallen into a deep, peaceful sleep.

A pleasant kind of sleep.

He was awakened by the light touch of hand on his shoulder. He opened his eyes and looked back at the beautiful, young woman smiling at him.

"I knew you'd come here. That's why I waited," she signed.

Tears filled his eyes as he recognized her. Tears of joy mixed with sorrow mixed with regret and every other emotion one could feel.

"Is it really you?" he asked.

"Yes," she nodded as she held out her hand.

He took it.

As soon as he did, he felt the years fall away. His body renewed itself. He felt young again. Stronger.

"Anh yeu em," he said.

"I know. I've always known. Walk with me, A.," she signed.

He rose and they walked downstairs and out of the house through the back door.

"Where are we going?" he asked.

"Where we belong," she said. "Where we have always belonged."

He smiled and held her hand tighter as they walked across the sun drenched field and into the village...

M. smiled at the serene expression on his face. She leaned over and gave him one last kiss, then sat back and wiped the tears from her eyes.

"At least you were mine for a little while," she said sadly.

The samurai had gone home...

I look up as I walk
So the tears won't fall
Though my heart is filled with sorrow
For tonight I'm all alone.

---Kyo Sakamoto

Dedicated to Kwa Ma Li (1957-1972)